Praise for *You Can't Stop Me*

"Max Allan Collins delivers cutting-edge action and suspense!"
—**David Morrell**, *New York Times* bestselling author of *The Shimmer*

"Reality TV turns thriller! A killer yarn from a master of suspense."
—**James Rollins**, *New York Times* bestselling author of *The Doomsday Key*

"*You Can't Stop Me* is not only the title but also a mantra I said to myself whenever something threatened to interrupt my reading. I look forward to more stories with J.C. Harrow."
—*Crimespree*

"Engrossing."
—**Rod Lott**, *Bookgasm*

"An exhilarating ride . . . A fast-paced page-turner that moves like a semi down a mountain road with the brakes burned out."
—*Pulp Fiction Reviews*

"An all-out thriller with plenty of twists and turns. Maybe the title should have been *You Can't Stop Reading* because this one's hard to put down."
—*Bill Crider's Pop Culture Magazine*

MAX ALLAN COLLINS

and

MATTHEW CLEMENS

NO ONE WILL HEAR YOU

PINNACLE BOOKS
KENSINGTON PUBLISHING CORP.
www.kensingtonbooks.com

PINNACLE BOOKS are published by

Kensington Publishing Corp.
119 West 40th Street
New York, NY 10018

All Kensington titles, imprints, and distributed lines are available at special quantity discounts for bulk purchases for sales promotions, premiums, fund-raising, educational, or institutional use. Special book excerpts or customized printings can also be created to fit specific needs. For details, write or phone the office of the Kensington special sales manager: Kensington Publishing Corp., 119 West 40th Street, New York, NY 10018, attn: Special Sales Department; phone 1-800-221-2647.

ISBN-13: 978-0-7860-2135-2
ISBN-10: 0-7860-2135-7

First printing: March 2011

10 9 8 7 6 5 4 3 2 1

Printed in the United States of America

For Paul Bishop—
cop, writer, friend

Love means never having
to say you're sorry.

—Eric Segal

No doubt Jack the Ripper excused himself
on the grounds that it was human nature.

—A. A. Milne

Naked, shivering but not cold, Crystal Haggerty huddled behind bushes.

Sweat streamed through her long, blonde hair, and down her face, stinging her eyes. Her breath came in ragged gasps as she stared back through the darkness, toward the house.

Nothing.

Then she swiftly scanned the woods for any sign of her pursuer.

Nothing.

Shit, she thought, anger at herself spiking through the terror. That usually infallible bullshit detector of hers had failed her big-time, her hunger for a gig, any damn gig, sending her home with a charming indie movie producer . . .

. . . who behind closed doors had transformed into a raving psychopath with a butcher knife!

His silhouette appeared on a rise, in the distance, and the lovely blonde saw the outline of that weapon in his *right fist—the same blade she'd glimpsed him fondling thanks to the cracked bathroom door, a sight that had sent her on a headlong run through his kitchen, out the back door, and into a sticky California night and moonlit woods.*

When they met after that acting class, he'd told her he was a producer—Louis St. James. She did her research and his story rang true, so she accepted his request for dinner.

After that impressively expensive restaurant, she allowed him to drive her to his place on the pretense of looking at a script, not at all surprised when he began kissing her the instant they got inside. She was a big girl and he was a handsome enough guy. An actress and a producer—not exactly a new story.

When he led her into the bedroom, the roses on the nightstand struck her as a little over the top, but what the hell? She fawned over them for him, still hoping he'd haul out a script after she had, well, paid for dinner.

She was naked on the bed, and they were kissing, tangling tongues, before she got a hint of anything off-key. He still had on most of his clothes, but then . . . some guys were shy. They continued to make out, his hands finding her breasts. She didn't mind sharing them with him—she'd paid enough for them.

Then when his lips wandered farther south, Crystal decided he wasn't shy. . . .

"I want to get inside you," he murmured. "Deep inside you. . . ."

Just when she was ready to let him do that, he backed off—not something she was used to. Still clothed, he excused himself to use the bathroom, leaving her naked and confused.

Crystal never had a guy walk out on her that close to the moment of truth. Not ever. Guys were guys. He'd proved he wasn't shy, and he sure didn't seem nervous, so what was his problem? He'd hit the men's room back at the restaurant, hadn't he?

Discreetly, Crystal followed him. That was when the cracked door revealed her host standing at the mirror, holding that knife in a troublingly sexual way.

He wanted to get inside her, all right!

The crazy damn thing was: she had played this part before, running through the woods, naked, terrified. Mixed in with her hysteria was the ridiculousness of playing out this cliché, a cliché she had worked so hard to bring reality to as "Naked Female Victim Number Five" in that low-budget embarrassment, Slasher Camp 3: Body Check.

But an actress whose latest performances were chiefly at Hooters in Long Beach took what she could get . . . like dinner with a producer. . . .

She had almost outwitted the killer in that dumb flick. Hidden behind a tree and leapt out and clouted the clown with a rock. In the movie, though, a rock couldn't hurt the killer, who was a supernatural freak. St. James, though, was a flesh-and-blood freak.

So she had, in a bizarre B-movie way, lived this scene before . . . only this time she would survive.

When her pursuer's silhouette swung in her direction, Crystal ducked even lower behind the bushes. Finally, she peeked out to see him moving to his left, away from her. Then she was up and on the run again.

The hard ground and underbrush tore at her bare feet as she sprinted blindly between trees. In the movie, she had hard-sole slippers on, except in the long shots, and then they'd cleared the brush for her, but these woods were doing her no favors.

She didn't care.

The pain wasn't devastating, not at all, and it said she was alive, and that was how she wanted to stay.

Her goal was to get far enough away from the bastard that she could set her trap for him and be waiting when he lumbered past. He knew these woods and she didn't. But he would never expect her to go from hunted to hunter.

This, she felt, was her best chance.

Maybe her only chance.

Just past a huge-trunk tree, Crystal saw a low-slung overhang of brush she could hide under and, when her pursuer came past that tree, spring out. She scurried into the nest, brambles nicking her, but she didn't give a damn. Making sure she didn't make too much noise was a larger concern.

Beneath the overhang, nestled in night, Crystal crouched, animal-like. She could hear him moving through the brush, hear the twigs and leaves crunch—he still had ground to cover. Not close yet. Not yet.

She planned to tackle him, just take him down, maybe make him fall on that knife, or at least get on his back and work her long natural nails over his face and eyes.

Crunching twigs and leaves, louder.

Still not close.

Closer, but not close. . . .

Her mind, like her heart, raced. If she had a weapon, a branch that could be a club, a rock that could be a blunt instrument, like in Slasher Camp, *she might do better than just flinging her damn self at him.*

But the darkness hampered any search. Like a blind woman, she moved her hands across the ground around her, trying not to make a sound, or much of one.

Then fingers found it and her hand grasped it: an egg-shaped rock that fit her fist as if God had fashioned it for her.

From what she heard, she judged her attacker to be about fifteen yards away. Wouldn't be long now, and she would have him. Son of a bitch thought he could get her, but she would get him. *This time Naked Female Victim Number Five would* not *die. . . .*

She waited, the mushroom of brush protectively over her as she crouched. She held her breath—not a sound— and then St. James strode into view, his back to her.

Perfect!

Crystal leapt out and raised that rock high, and he spun and thrust the butcher knife deep into her abdomen.

The pain was immediate and as sharp as the blade it- self.

She heard herself gasp.

"I saw that movie," he said.

The rock dropped from her hand and thudded onto the ground.

He yanked the knife free and her body shuddered, and then she, too, thudded down.

He was hunkered over her now, the knife flailing into her chest, burning pain almost instantly replaced by numbing cold as the knife arced down again and again.

She felt the blows, but not any more pain. Breathing

came hard, yet she felt peaceful, drifting away as the blows came in a blur, as unreal as celluloid, until finally they were an abstraction and she lay cloaked in silent serenity.

The stars faded. The moon shut its big eye. She gave herself to the night.

Rage drove him.

He'd been cool before, but now anger had him, and he could not control it. *The stupid bitch!* She had ruined everything, and she was dead for it, he was sure of that, even as again and again he slammed the knife into her.

With each blow, his mind screamed, "*Cut! Cut! Cut!*"

She had left the bed—*no professional gets off his or her mark in the middle of a damn* scene!—and moved off set, out of camera range, and run the hell out here.

If the action had been captured, that would have been one thing.

But none of the climax was on camera! The whole evening, and all the planning that had gone into it, had been a waste.

The actress had ruined their one and only shot at it, their one and only take. You don't get a second, much less a *third* take, when an elaborate stunt is involved! What the hell kind of professional *was* she?

This was to have been his first episode, the introduction to a new breakthrough reality series.

And—thrust—*she*—thrust—*had*—thrust—
screwed—thrust—*it*—thrust—*up!*

He sagged, the bloody knife slipping from his hand, his face covered in sweat mixed with blood. Hers.

All the conventional methods of making it in this merciless business had been tried and tried again and, talent be damned, had led nowhere.

But now *Crime Seen* had come along—*thank you, God*—and a new opportunity presented itself. This was *his* time, *his* chance, at least till this stupid inexperienced damn *day-player* actress came along and padded her damn part.

Next time he would use a sedative, Rohypnol, to calm his costar's anxieties, and not just rely on his charm. He would make sure subsequent actresses would be more pliable.

All right—so this would not work as a first episode. But almost every series shot a pilot episode, right? Often never to be aired, merely to iron out the kinks and get the show up on its feet?

He got on his feet.

Calm now.

Reflective.

Sometimes a series needed to be recast and reshot. This wouldn't be the first time—hadn't Lisa Kudrow been fired from *Frasier* and replaced by Peri Gilpin? Even William Shatner hadn't been the first choice for captain of the Enterprise.

Of course, the lead in *this* show would not be recast. He would correct the small errors, bury the day player in the woods, and get himself another actress for the *real* first episode. Changes, tweaks, that was show biz. But the lead, at least, was perfect.

After all, he was the star.

He was Don Juan.

Chapter One

John Christian Harrow sent a narrow-eyed gaze from the Colorado woods toward the rambling, rustic, one-story house nestled on a bluff in a small clearing maybe twenty yards away. It might have been the idyllic home of a *Waltons*-esque happy family, and not a meth lab filled with dangerous felons.

A light was on in the living room at the front, another toward the back, either a bedroom or the kitchen. Harrow—J.C. to his friends (and the audience of UBC Network's top-rated reality television show, *Crime Seen*)—had no floor plan, so it was hard to know which.

Crime Seen's resident computer expert, petite blonde Jenny Blake, was ensconced in the show's mobile crime lab down the road, tracking the house's blueprints on the Internet. A tall order, but if anyone could make that happen, it was Jenny.

Right now, however, Harrow's earbud remained silent, and he wondered if for once Jenny might come up empty.

The night was surprisingly warm for early spring in the Rocky Mountains, the sky Coors-commercial clear, the quarter moon a sliver of silver, the stars as bright as they were countless. This felt akin to the Iowa night sky Harrow had grown up with, and far preferable to the smog-filled air over his adopted Los Angeles.

Beside Harrow stood Billy Choi of *Crime Seen*'s forensic all-star team. Son of an Asian father and Caucasian mother, Choi—with his long black hair, chiseled good looks, and taekwondo-sculpted body—was a tool marks expert, firearms examiner, and door-kicking-in ace. His eyes followed his boss's to the house.

Like Harrow, Choi wore a black *Crime Seen* Windbreaker (Kevlar beneath), camo-chinos, and boots. There was a Batman-and-Robin effect to the two men, as the brown-eyed, rugged, Apache-cheekboned Harrow—his brown hair gone fully white at the temples—towered at six foot two over Choi's five eight. If Harrow's eyes were any darker brown, they'd have been black (the network-mandated blue contacts, demanded for season one of the show, were a thing of the past).

Around them at the edge of the woods, seven or eight Denver County deputies were checking shotguns and other equipment, preparing for an assault.

At the rear, cameraman Maury Hathaway—his

heavyset frame covered, typically, by a Grateful Dead T-shirt and bandolier battery belt—waited with his Sony digicam at the ready, like the deputies with their shotguns.

Local sheriff Jens Watson, a flinty-looking string bean in jeans and a cowboy shirt embroidered with a Denver County star, was about Harrow's age—late forties—and seemed to be a good cop. But Watson had wanted nothing to do with having Harrow and Choi along on this raid.

Like Harrow (back when he'd been sheriff of Story County, Iowa), Watson had to run for reelection every four years. This meant making good decisions to keep the voters happy, like accepting twenty thousand dollars worth of new lab equipment from Dennis Byrnes, president of the United Broadcasting Company.

Now, out here in the dark, on the edge of the county, the unreal sense that time had stopped draped them all in frozen tension. The house sat half a mile from its nearest neighbor, surrounded for the most part by woods, except for the long, twisting drive up the hill and the scrubby clearing that formed a modest front yard.

The law enforcement team that Harrow and Choi accompanied had gone past the driveway to park around a bend, just off the road on a fire-break. The posse trudged up the hillside through thick trees and dense undergrowth to this vantage point above the house. They could see all of the front, one side, and into the backyard, though not much of the latter before its slope fell away down a mountainside.

The trek up the steep hill found Harrow sucking air like the two-pack-a-day smoker he'd once been. While he slipped off the wagon occasionally (now that his wife, Ellen, and son David were gone), he wasn't even half the smoker now.

He took only mild pleasure that the other flatlander, Choi—half Harrow's age, a nonsmoker in terrific shape—was sucking air himself.

For their part, the deputies, used to living in the troposphere, breathed as calmly as if the tromp through the woods were a leisurely stroll.

"Not much movin' down there," Sheriff Watson said.

Choi, in thermal-imaging goggles, said, "One for sure in the living room in the front."

"You can't see anyone else?" Watson asked.

Choi turned the goggles toward the back of the house. "Two heat signatures in that room. A person and something smaller."

"Smaller?" Watson asked. "What, a dog?"

"Hard to tell . . ."

"Kid, maybe?"

Harrow offered, "Could be they're cooking up their next batch."

Choi said, "It's a small heat source, but it's getting hotter fast. Think you're right, boss."

Watson turned to his deputies, raising his voice a hair. "Could be hot chemicals in there, fellas— let's stay alert."

The protocol probably dictated protective suits and the bomb squad and a hundred other things that Harrow knew Watson wasn't about to wait for.

Harrow, Choi, and the Denver County contingent were poised at woods' edge on this mountain tonight thanks to a *Crime Seen* viewer tip.

A comic book dealer, Michael Gold, had become suspicious when he suddenly found himself serving new customers who seemed to have neither knowledge of nor enthusiasm for the collectibles they were buying. They were simply interested in purchasing high-end comics.

When other dealers started showing up at comic conventions with those same books—sold to them at a loss by Gold's clients—the comics dealer grew suspicious. Who bought pricey comic books they weren't interested in, and then turned right around and sold them at a loss?

Only somebody very stupid . . .

. . . or somebody very smart.

Gold knew damn well he was dealing with smart criminals laundering money.

The team tracked Gold's *Crime Seen* line tip to this house, leading to this moment—a televised raid on a meth lab (albeit one taped and edited for next Friday's show).

Finally, in his earbud, came Jenny's small, almost timid voice: "Sorry to take so long, boss. There've been additions to the original home. Room you're talking about, behind the living room, is a bedroom. Kitchen is on the other side of the house."

"Thanks, Jenny," Harrow said into a lavalier mic, clipped to his shirt. A bedroom converted to a meth lab.

"You're welcome," came Jenny's voice, as if they'd just transacted a sale over a counter. "Uh, J.C.?"

"Yeah?"

"If they're using meth, not just making it? They may be excitable."

He smiled. "Thanks, Jen. Keep it in mind."

Unbidden, Warren Zevon's song "Excitable Boy" began to play in his mind.

Harrow passed the new information along to Sheriff Watson. "The comic book 'collectors' in there are frying up a new batch of crank."

Watson turned. "Jenkins—you, Siegel, and Hartley get around back, and be goddamn careful. We don't want to blow that house, and us, to hell and gone . . . and take Mr. Choi with you."

Choi looked at Harrow. "I should be out front."

"Neither one of you," Watson growled, "oughta be *anywhere* around here."

Calmly Harrow said, "A *Crime Seen* tip brought us here. It's our bust as much as yours."

"Don't see it that way," Watson said. "No chance either of you civilians goes in with my team."

Harrow knew when to back off. "No problem. You want Choi around back, that's where he's going—right, Billy?"

His voice friendly and his eyes cold, Choi said, "Right."

But before Choi could fall in with the three deputies, somebody saw headlights at the bottom of the hill.

"Truck," the deputy said.

They ducked when headlights swept the hill, then clicked off, as a white Cadillac Escalade crept up the drive and came to a smooth stop next to the house.

The driver climbed out—a good six feet, scruffy beard, jeans, and a black-and-red plaid flannel shirt. At the open rider's side window of his vehicle, he was handed a weapon—looked to Harrow like an AK-47.

"Oh shit," Sheriff Watson muttered.

No one disagreed with this sentiment.

Though the vehicle mostly blocked their view, Harrow could see both doors on the passenger side.

Two more men got out.

The doors of the SUV were closed carefully, quietly. The no-headlights approach confirmed something wasn't right here. . . .

Watson said, "Great—more guests at the party."

"Not welcome guests," Harrow said.

"Huh?"

"Those aren't reinforcements."

The three men eased away from the Escalade and moved silently toward the house. Each carried an automatic weapon.

Acid burned in Harrow's stomach—he knew what they were about to witness.

So did Choi: "It's a hit."

And took off through the woods in the direction of the house.

"It's a *what?*" Watson asked, not sure he'd heard Choi correctly.

"A hit," Harrow threw back, falling in behind Choi.

Too late for Harrow to advise Choi this wasn't their battle. Choi had a cop's instincts.

Loping down the hillside, Harrow could make

out the driver cutting around back while the other two crept up to the front door.

He glanced back at the sheriff and the deputies trailing them—confusion on their faces plain even in the dark.

Cameraman Hathaway was behind Denver County's finest, having the good sense to hang back.

Thrashing through the undergrowth behind Choi, Harrow was just waiting for the gunmen to turn those AK's in their direction and chop them down, unless an exposed root in this darkness beat them to it, to send Harrow tumbling, breaking his goddamn neck.

Neither Harrow nor Choi had a weapon, the older man wondering if that had even dawned on the younger one. Harrow wasn't sure which scared him more, being unarmed out here or Choi not caring as they charged unarmed toward three men with automatic weapons.

Choi circled the house, so that he—Harrow tailing him—could close the distance with the lone gunman, heading for the rear.

Glancing back, Harrow saw Watson and most of the deputies peel off to try to take the two out front. Up ahead Choi was keeping low, making rapid progress toward his target.

If our Escalade interloper will just stay focused on his own prey for another few seconds . . .

Gunfire erupted out front—the distinctive bark of an AK-47!

The interloper's head snapped around, and he caught movement in the brush nearby. His gun came up, and he dropped into a shooter's crouch and squeezed the trigger just as Choi broke through the undergrowth, kicking the barrel of the gun, sending its rounds flying harmlessly into the mountain air.

As the interloper brought the weapon around, Choi elbowed the guy in the chest, grabbed the gun by its barrel, and the two men tumbled to the ground, wrestling over the damn thing.

Harrow narrowed the distance quickly, ready to give Choi a hand . . .

. . . then the back door of the house slapped open and two T-shirted occupants came bursting out. The pair took off across the yard and, judging from the sounds of a firefight out front, Harrow had no choice.

He took off at a dead run after the meth cookers. The shorter, squatter one was catchable, even if his lankier partner wasn't.

In Harrow's earpiece, Jenny's small, breathless voice was saying, "Boss, we heard gunfire! Everything all right? Boss?"

"Get back to you," Harrow said breathlessly.

Sucking wind but closing fast, Harrow could hear his prey's heaving breath over his own. Just short of the woods, Harrow threw a flying tackle, driving the guy down.

The two rolled, meth cooker squealing like a pig, trying to kick free of Harrow's arms. As the kicks thumped painfully into his chest and arms, Harrow finally released his grip and bounced up, getting to his feet ahead of the meth cooker.

When the pudgy kid finally rose, Harrow was already in a combat stance.

"You're caught—give it up!"

The kid threw a wild, looping right, which Harrow sidestepped easily.

Harrow said, "Don't make me—"

The meth cooker interrupted with a lashing kick that Harrow easily avoided. The man's momentum took him up in the air and landed him on the lawn with a hard *whomp*, air gushing.

Kneeling and grabbing the kid by his T-shirt, Harrow advised, "Stay down, son—you're caught."

Blinking furiously, sweat pouring off him, the meth cooker looked up at his captor, with a goofy smile. "*Hey*—you're that guy on TV! J.C. Harrow!"

"Please—no autographs."

Harrow no longer heard gunfire from around the house. Choi ambled up, gunman in tow, hands behind his head, the firearms expert holding the AK nonchalantly in the bad guy's general direction.

"On your knees, dickweed," Choi said.

The gunman spat two angry words at Choi.

Who said, "Isn't one ass-kicking enough tonight?"

Though still glaring, the gunman relented and knelt next to Harrow's captive.

Choi looked around. "Where's the other meth cooker?"

"In the wind."

"You let him go?"

A gentle dig.

"Bird in the hand." Harrow grinned at his young colleague. "*My* guy recognized me. Did yours?"

Choi's hurt frown was answer enough.

In Harrow's ear, Jenny was saying, "Boss, what's happening? Please report!"

"Easy, Jen," Harrow said fondly. "We're okay."

Sheriff Watson and his deputies came through the backdoor of the house and approached the *Crime Seen* pair and their prisoners.

"You two okay?" Watson asked.

Choi's cocky grin was back. "Better than these buttwipes."

"Better than the two out front, too," Watson said, his voice a little shaky.

"Your men all right?" Harrow asked.

Watson pushed his hat back. "Sure as hell not what they're used to . . . but they did fine. One bad guy dead, other wounded. We'll get forensics support out here and I hope to send my men home to their families before too damn long."

"I hear that," Harrow said.

"Judging from what we found inside," Watson said, "your tipster hit it on the button. All the ingredients for meth, boxes of vintage comic books—*Superman*, *Batman*, *Captain America*—and a big old pile of cash money."

"Great."

"Look, uh, Mr. Harrow—we appreciate the backup. If I didn't make you feel welcome, I surely do apologize."

"I'm a former sheriff myself. I know what it's like to have your turf invaded."

The two men traded respectful nods.

As it turned out, Maury Hathaway had snagged great footage of both Choi and Harrow's takedowns, plus the sheriff's firefight with the would-be thieves.

Once the crime scene unit cleared it, Harrow did an on-camera wraparound from inside the house, showing off the comics, the drug paraphernalia, and, of course, the impressive stacks of money.

As they loaded out, Harrow could just hear network president Dennis Byrnes laughing like a gleeful kid. Taking down a meth lab, stopping four felons, pleasing UBC's president—all that should have given Harrow a nice Colorado high.

Instead, with the second season of his hit show winding down, Harrow felt tired beyond his years.

Not long ago, he and his team had tracked down the maniac who had slaughtered his family—which had been the sole motivation behind accepting the *Crime Seen* job, and allowing himself to become a public figure. A TV star, for Christ's sake.

But now he'd accomplished everything he set out to, and more. Standing here in the cool spring mountain air, watching bad guys get carted away, he felt no real satisfaction.

When one of the sheriff's vehicles had trouble gaining traction on the dirt road, he grinned without humor into the night.

Me, too, he thought. *Spinning my wheels . . .*

Chapter Two

Barely over the LAPD minimum height requirement of five feet, Lieutenant Anna Amari had to let her work as a lead investigator at the LAPD Sex Crimes Division walk tall for her.

She keep her makeup to a minimum and her dress low-key professional, like the dark gray blazer, light gray silk blouse, and darker gray slacks she wore on this cool May morning.

Still, she was a strikingly attractive woman of forty-two, with a naturally busty, narrow-waisted figure, deep olive complexion, and brown razor-cut hair brushing her shoulders. Brown almond-shaped eyes missed little, and—despite the bleak nature of her work—her smile came easily and often.

She and her latest partner—LeRon Polk, a somewhat inexperienced African-American detective—had been called to a murder scene at the Star Struck Hotel in West Hollywood.

Himself only a few inches taller than Amari, Polk seemed skinnier all over, from his black tie on white shirt under black suit, to the slash of mustache with his wispy goatee. He had a vintage detective look, close-cropped hair under a black-banded gray fedora.

As they left their Crown Vic to walk toward the uniformed officer at the hotel entrance, Amari said to Polk, "You *do* know nobody wears hats like that anymore."

"That's an inaccurate statement."

"Is it?"

"It is," Polk said, firm if good-natured. "Because *I* wear hats like this. Anyway, *all* the great ol' detectives wore this kinda hat."

"Shaft didn't."

Polk considered this as they moved into a high-ceilinged lobby whose carpet had such a busy pattern, it was hard to discern wear marks.

At the front desk, a uniformed sergeant was talking to a tall character in a well-cut charcoal suit, a clerk or more likely the manager. Couches and a few chairs were spread somewhat casually around the lobby. A few Grecian-style statues of nude men posed here and there.

Amari approached the uniformed sergeant, a lanky, white-haired white cop named Thompson.

"Bring me up to speed, Sarge," Amari said.

"Homicide upstairs," Thompson said. He might have been ordering coffee. "Room 425."

"ID the victim?"

"White male," Thompson said. "Room is registered to a Jeff Bailey."

Polk asked, "That our dead body?"

"Your guess is as good as mine. This is Mr. Far-quar, the manager."

Amari gave the manager a quick nod. Farquar's salt-and-pepper hair was slicked back; this, with his pointy face, gave him the look of a sleek gray otter.

"Did you see anything, Mr. Farquar?"

"No. I had no idea anything had happened until the guests started burning up the phones."

Thompson explained, "Maid found the body this morning, freaked out, started screaming."

"Angelina is one of our best employees," Farquar said, pointlessly.

Amari asked Thompson, "Did you talk to the maid?"

The sergeant nodded. "Nice lady. Scared out of her gourd. Probably never seen anything like that before."

Amari noted a slight inflection in Thompson's voice. Nothing rattled a twenty-year vet like the sarge, but this murder seemed to have gotten to him.

"Mr. Farquar," Amari said, "the crime scene team will need to take any surveillance video you have."

The manager blanched a little. "Um . . . that is . . . I mean to say, our clientele? It's somewhat special-ized. They come to the Star Struck expecting a cer-tain amount of . . . discretion."

The Star Struck wasn't a flophouse by any means, but this hotel, like West Hollywood in gen-eral, had a reputation for being a haven for the gay community, whether in or out of the closet. She understood and respected their need for privacy.

But now, such considerations were as dead as the victim upstairs. They needed that security video.

Amari gave the manager a hard look.

Wilting, Farquar said, "It will be ready when your people ask for it."

"Thank you. We appreciate your cooperation." To Thompson, she said, "We're going upstairs."

Soon, on the fourth floor, elevator doors whispered open and Amari and Polk stepped out. The corridor was empty save for a uniformed officer outside what Amari assumed was room 425.

"Crime scene team and the coroner," the young officer said, looking a trifle pale, "are already inside."

"Thanks," Amari said.

The door stood widely ajar.

Trailed by Polk, she went into a well-lit room with gaudy silver brocade wallpaper and white furnishings, including a bed where a sheet had been spread over a body. Two youngish crime-scene techs in blue disposable coveralls were at work—a male on the far side using an alternative light source to comb the floor for clues, a female dusting for prints in the bathroom.

Devin Talbot, a veteran assistant coroner, gave up a rumpled smile, seeing Amari. He was a compact, balding fortysomething man, with a halo of brown hair and sorrowful brown eyes.

"Anna, how the hell are you?"

"Doing fine, Dink," she said. "Back from vacation, I see." She didn't know the history of the nickname, but Talbot had been "Dink" for as long as Amari had known him.

"How do you like my tan?" he asked. He was just a little paler than a fish belly. Probably went all the way to his den to read.

She said, "Thought you were George Hamilton for a second there. Let's have a look at your customer."

Talbot looked past her at Polk. "Close the door, will you, son?"

The young detective did so.

Talbot lifted the sheet and pulled it back to the victim's waist.

Caucasian, probably early to mid-thirties, with short blonde hair and wide-set blue eyes staring at the ceiling. Red marks stood out on both wrists. The sheet beneath was soaked in blood, crisp and black from drying now, and Amari's eyes immediately were drawn to two gaping wounds in the man's chest.

"Knife?" she asked.

"Honking *big* knife," Polk interjected before Talbot could answer.

Talbot offered up the same condescending smile he would give a child who had spoken out of turn. "If our weapon *is* a knife."

Polk asked, "What makes you think it wouldn't be?"

The coroner pulled the sheet back farther.

The victim's genitals had been cut off.

"Not much bleeding," Amari said, matter of fact.

"Postmortem wound," Talbot said. "Our killer

wanted to keep the mess to a minimum—he waited for the blood to begin to settle before he took the genitals."

Polk asked, "Blood to settle?"

"You know this stuff, LeRon," Amari said, mildly impatient. "Heart stops beating, gravity takes over, blood starts seeking the lowest levels."

Polk nodded. "Yeah, I know, I knew. It was like . . . rhetorical."

Amari let her young partner get away with that as she studied the wound. "Were his genitals somewhere here in the room?"

"Gone," Talbot said with a shrug. "My guess is, the killer took everything with him."

"A trophy?" she said.

"Damn messy one," Polk said.

"*That* was rhetorical, LeRon."

"Oh. Right. Sure."

A killer specializing in emasculation of victims, combined with taking the genitals as trophies, had all the earmarks of someone who might strike again.

And again.

Polk was asking, "Who the hell does something like that to a guy?"

"Someone filled with rage," Talbot said. "The uniforms who were here, when we got the call? They already had a name for him."

Polk asked, "What?"

"Billy Shears," Talbot said.

"Great," Amari said. "I hope no media heard that."

"Billy Shears?" Polk asked.

Amari turned to him. "The Beatles? 'Sgt. Pepper's Lonely Hearts Club Band'?"

Polk shrugged. "Before my time."

"I thought you said you had Rock Band."

"Yeah, but not that ancient-ass crap."

Suddenly Amari felt very old.

Talbot said, "Anyway, the vic was stabbed twice in the chest . . . then the killer waited."

"How long?" Amari asked.

"Twenty minutes, maybe," Talbot said. "Doesn't take as long for the blood to settle as people think."

"There is *some* blood down south," Polk noted.

"Yes," Talbot said patiently, "but not nearly as much as if he'd been alive when this happened."

"Let's not go there," Polk said with a shiver. "What the hell was our killer doing with himself, while he waited for the blood to settle?"

Talbot shrugged.

The female crime-scene tech, hearing this conversation, emerged from the bathroom. Taller than Amari, with red hair pulled back in a ponytail, she was fair and freckled and wore no makeup. Her nameplate read RYAN.

"Judging from the odor," Ryan said, "the killer just sat back and had a cigarette. It's a nonsmoking room, but that didn't stop him."

"Butts?"

"Nope. Must've flushed 'em."

The blond male crime tech, McCaffrey, was (like his partner) a stranger to Amari.

"Nothing out here," he said. "No fingerprints, no footwear impressions in the carpeting, nothing."

"What," Polk said, "was he was freakin' *barefoot?*"

"No," Ryan said. "Probably wore shoe coverings, like ours."

She held up a foot to indicate the clear plastic booties.

"Ours say 'Police' on the soles," Ryan said, "so our prints don't get confused with the criminals. But even in the bathroom on the tile floor, the electrostatic print lifter couldn't find *any* footprint. This tells us something."

Amari asked, "Which is?"

"The perp is knowledgeable. And *way* careful."

Amari turned her attention to Talbot. "Dink, is this D.B. Jeff Bailey?"

"Why, is that the name on the register?"

"Yeah," Polk said.

McCaffrey called over an answer: "No ID! I bagged his clothes already."

Amari looked down at the body, the close-clipped blond hair, the blue eyes. A third of the men in California looked like this. Hell, McCaffrey looked like this. A glance to the vic's left hand revealed a wedding ring.

Somewhere, someone was missing this man. Probably a female who might or might not be surprised that her husband had died in a hotel like the Star Struck.

Amari said, "All right, he's a John Doe till further notice. When we get back to the office, we'll run his prints, check with Missing Persons, track Jeff Bailey. . . . LeRon, you know the drill."

Polk nodded.

"The killer wasn't nervous or ill at ease spending a bunch of time with a dead body." She shook her head. "Stabbed like that, and no noise? The neighbors didn't hear anything?"

Ryan said, "From what I got while the uniforms were clearing the rooms? Nobody heard a damn thing."

Talbot added, "No defensive wounds on his hands or arms, but the ligature marks on his wrists tell us he was tied up."

"Kinky sex?" Polk asked.

"Or a captive," Amari said.

"Is it possible," Polk said, "he was dead *before* he could scream?"

"Probable," the assistant coroner said. Talbot pointed to the lower of the two wounds. "This blow is almost certainly the first one—up and in, probably piercing the heart, the liver, and/or one of the lungs . . . and God only knows what else."

Polk asked, "And this other blow?"

"That one was anger. More show, less lethal."

"Adding insult to injury."

"That's right. Though what I take to be the second blow was delivered with enough force to crack the sternum and bleed like hell, it would not have been as immediately fatal, had it come first."

Amari said, "And if the chest blow came first, someone would've heard him scream?"

"Yes," Talbot said. "If our John Doe was healthy when that higher blow was struck, it would have hurt like hell, and he'd have let the world know."

"Our vic was surprised?"

"Or asleep. And in either case, he wouldn't have been able to put up much of a fight."

"Any idea about the weapon?"

Talbot shook his head. "Not until I get the body back to the lab, where I can get a closer look at the wounds and run some tests. Something with a big, long blade though."

The coroner's crew showed up with a gurney. Amari, Polk, and Ryan waited in the hall while Talbot and McCaffrey stayed in the room keeping watch on the evidence.

"I told the manager," Amari said to Ryan, "that you'd be by to pick up the security video."

Ryan nodded.

Polk said, "Lovers' quarrel?"

Amari shook her head. "Nobody's reported so much as a raised voice. I think this is something different."

"Robbery got out of hand?" Polk suggested. "Thief is boosting the room, guy in bed wakes up, and . . ."

"And the thief takes out a big pair of scissors and stabs the guy twice, then cuts off his fishing tackle for the hell of it?"

"Maybe not," Polk admitted.

"On the other hand," Ryan said, "his wallet is gone. Watch and cell phone, too."

"Any luggage missing?"

"We don't know if the John Doe *had* any luggage," Ryan said. "Plenty of people use this place just to hook up."

"Right," Amari said. "But why leave the wedding ring?"

The trio stood silent as a small honor guard of two from the coroner's office rolled through a gurney with a body bag filled with Jeff Bailey or John Doe or whoever the poor bastard was. As the men rolled their cargo down the hall, the only sound was the whisper of wheels on carpeting.

Amari had just heard the elevator doors close when Talbot stepped out into the hall.

"You better come back in," the assistant coroner said.

McCaffrey was on the far side of the bed, holding up a clear plastic evidence bag that appeared empty.

"Got something?" Polk asked.

"Red hair," McCaffrey said. "Long one. Female?"

Amari said, "Vic's hair was blonde, and short."

Polk asked, "Could the hair be from a previous guest?"

Ryan said, "Probably not. Bailey checked in early yesterday afternoon. That would mean clean sheets. My guess is that *this* . . ." He waved the bag around. ". . . belongs to the killer."

"A hair isn't much," Polk said.

"But it's something," Amari said with an enthusiasm she didn't really feel. "No sign of break-in— so can we assume this is an assignation gone very wrong? Victim willingly brought his killer into this room."

"Or *let* him in," Polk said.

"Right," Amari said. "And whatever weapon the killer used to make those huge wounds came *with* him."

Polk frowned. "But the killer couldn't have hauled a bulky murder weapon in with him, if he and the victim had hooked up somewhere, hotel bar or whatever. . . ."

Amari nodded, "And even if the victim was someone the killer *knew*, and it wasn't just a casual pickup, how do you bring along a weapon like that?"

Polk was caught up in the theorizing. "So maybe the killer left after the sex, came back, *with* his weapon this time. And the victim went to the door, and opened up for his lover. Who is holding the weapon behind his back or something."

"Reasonable scenario," Amari said. "Dink, can we establish that the victim had sex shortly before he died?"

Talbot laughed harshly. "With the genitals gone, and the bed covered in blood?"

Polk gave Amari a look. "Sounds like another one of those rhetorical questions."

Amari was thinking, prowling the small space. "This is cold, methodical, *planned*. Almost . . . ritualistic."

She stopped and turned to the longtime coroner's assistant.

"Dink—I know you don't traffic in opinions. But if I said I thought this death was more a beginning than an ending, would you disagree?"

"I wish I could," Talbot said.

Chapter Three

Something special was on the docket for the *Crime Seen* group that regularly went out for lunch on Monday—with the exception of co-host Carmen Garcia, these were the "superstar" forensics experts of the show's *Killer TV* segments.

Carmen had chosen Doreen's on Sunset, one of her favorites, for a couples' lunch where she would introduce her coworkers to Vince Clay, whom she'd been dating for several months now.

Jenny Blake would bring Chris Anderson (the computer geek-ess and the Mississippi scientist had their own kind of chemistry going now) and Laurene Chase would be there with audio tech Nancy Hughes (they had hooked up shortly after Kansas).

The other guys had their own lunch plans, Billy Choi and Michael Pall off somewhere eating meat, no doubt, while Harrow never intruded on his team's luncheons, though he'd have been welcome.

Not long ago Carmen had been a PA in T-shirt and jeans; now the slender young brunette, so loved by the camera, was an on-air personality and co-producer in a well-tailored blue business suit, running late.

She knew Vince would be understanding. They'd only been on half a dozen dates, but Vince was always thoughtful to a fault. When he didn't kiss her till after their third date, she'd asked if something was wrong, and he'd only said, "I just know what you've been through. I'm fine taking it slow."

The world, or anyway that part of it who watched *Crime Seen,* was well aware that Carmen Garcia had been held hostage at the climax of the team's first investigation—broadcast live. She appreciated Vince's consideration—particularly since he couldn't know that he was the first guy she'd gone out with, since that traumatic time.

Perhaps five years older than her, Vincent Clay had a small but thriving insurance agency in Westwood (a "boutique business," he called it, handling well-off clients personally). Laurene had given her a good amount of grief for dating somebody with such a boring job, until Carmen told her how many of Vince's clients were in the entertainment industry.

"*Everybody* in this town's in the entertainment industry," Laurene had said, but Carmen knew she was impressed.

The über-shy Jenny, on the other hand, did not

join in with the laughter, nor the ribbing, however good-natured.

Privately, Jenny had said, "Carmen, never mind them. Whatever makes you happy."

This two-sentence speech indicated just how much Jenny had come into her own lately, in part due to her TV exposure but mostly to the blossoming romance with Chris.

Vince was waiting out front, with the valet pre-tipped and ready. Insurance man or not, Vince might have been posing for an Armani ad in that cream-colored suit, light blue shirt and no tie.

A few inches taller than the in-heels Carmen, Vince had short brown hair, a hawkish nose, high cheekbones, and pale blues eyes that jumped out of his deep tan.

Carmen turned her Prius over to the valet, and Vince opened his arms for a quick hug. She gave him a peck on the cheek.

"I'm sorry I kept you waiting," she said. "Something came up at work. Should've called. . . ."

"It happens. You're worth waiting for."

"You're a figment of my imagination, aren't you?"

"You must have a good imagination, because this figment is famished."

They passed arm in arm through the open wrought-iron gate into the enclosed outdoor portion of the restaurant. The other women and Chris Anderson occupied four of six chairs around a circular wrought-iron table in a back corner near a brick wall.

Carmen found Doreen's unpretentiously classy—

linen tablecloths, bone china, polished silverware, elegant water glasses, a chichi ambience but with all-American comfort food. Huge umbrellas ran down through the center of the glass-topped tables nearer the sidewalk.

As usual, Laurene—a statuesque African American with gun-metal gray glasses matching her tailored gray suit—had managed to snag the chair with her back to the wall, so she could see the rest of the restaurant. Must have been a gunfighter thing—the criminalist *was* on loan from the Waco PD, after all. . . .

Harrow did that, too, Carmen knew from frequent meals with her boss. Pretty soon these ex-cops were going to run out of walls.

She squeezed Vincent's hand, not just to give him a shot of courage before meeting her friends, but also relishing having *somebody* in her life who would sit with his back to other diners.

As they approached, Laurene said, "So this is your new catch?" She wasn't known for subtlety.

Planting herself and her guy before them, Carmen said, "Vince Clay, meet Laurene Chase. Official *Crime Seen* welcoming committee."

"Seen you on the tube," he said, leaning in to shake hands with Laurene, smile very white against his dark tan. "Or anyway, on the plasma screen."

"You're almost cute enough," Laurene said to him, "to make me consider changing teams . . . *almost.*"

"Well, I guess that's a compliment." To the others, Vince said, "Of course, I also recognize Chris and Jenny from the show. Okay if we go right to first names?"

"You bet," Chris said, rising to shake Vince's hand. "You may've gathered from Laurene, here, that we don't exactly stand on ceremony."

Chris wore a blue button-down shirt, his bright brown eyes and wide white grin making him probably the most telegenic of the team.

Jenny said, "Hi," and they shook hands, too, though she remained seated. In typical fashion, Jenny was in jeans and a brown T-shirt bearing the logo of the University of Wyoming Cowboys.

Laurene said, "This is Nancy Hughes. She's a sound designer on the show."

Nancy, in a *Killer TV* tee and jeans, said with a smile, "That's a fancy way to say I'm an audio guy. Mostly I run boom mic."

"That takes muscle, I understand," Vince said with a smile that mirrored Nancy's.

"It's not for sissies," she allowed.

Two side-by-side chairs were waiting. Vince held Carmen's for her; then they both sat. Conversation was interrupted as they considered menus briefly, ordered, then made small talk waiting for their food.

"Let's get something established right now," Vince said. "I don't expect anybody here to pretend the insurance business makes an interesting topic of discussion. And even if it did, I could hardly compete with *Crime Seen*. So no polite questions are required."

This put everybody at ease, but Carmen knew she wasn't home free, not yet. The grilling for this lunch would not be limited to the kitchen, and it started—predictably—with Laurene.

"So, Vince," Laurene said, bringing a chatty tone to her interrogation. "Lived here all your life?"

Under the table, Carmen squeezed Vince's hand again. She had warned him that this luncheon might be akin to a job interview.

"Moved out here a few years ago."

"By yourself?" Laurene asked.

"With my sister. Jana."

"What does Jana do?"

"Well, she has something in common with you folks. She's in the entertainment field. Actually, she was on one of your reality shows."

"You mean on UBC?"

"I'm, uh . . . embarrassed I don't know the answer to that. Not sure what network it's on. She's a good actress, and I find it vaguely embarrassing she had to stoop to reality TV—uh, no offense meant."

Laurene shrugged. "None taken. What show?"

"*Speed Date*? Familiar with that?"

"No," Laurene said. "I mean, I've heard of speed dating, of course. Never subjected myself to it."

Carmen said, "Everybody knows *Speed Date*, Laurene, and it's not on UBC. I'm sure Dennis Byrnes wishes it were."

Laurene shrugged. "I don't watch TV."

Vince seemed intrigued. "Not even your own program?"

"*Especially* our own program. I don't even have one of those . . . what they are called, Nancy?"

"TiVos," Nancy said. "And her TV is a nineteen-inch tube number. She's hopeless."

"Anyway," Vince said with an embarrassed half smile, "my sister was on this *Speed Date* thing for . . . two weeks, I guess."

"Two weeks doesn't sound very speedy," Jenny said.

"Even Jana would be first to tell you it's a dopey idea. Camera focuses on several couples speed dating, then the audience votes on who should go out together."

"Why America eats that junk up," Laurene said, "is a mystery to me."

"You should call the *Crime Seen* tip line," Vince said good-naturedly. "I hear those people solve mysteries."

Jenny smiled. "Nice one."

Boy, Carmen thought, *she is coming out of her shell. . . .*

When their food arrived, the little group ate in relative silence, occasionally commenting on how tasty the fare was. The *Crime Seen* coworkers tended to lapse into silence over meals, since the shop talk that might accompany most business lunches was liable to be less than appetizing.

As their plates were cleared, Nancy asked, "How did you two meet?"

Carmen and Vince exchanged a look.

"You're the communicator," Vince said to her.

Grinning, Carmen said, "But *you're* the salesman. . . ."

Leaning in, Laurene said, "Look, I like 'meeting cute' as much as the next guy, but I just ate. Somebody tell the story. I promise to be nice."

Carmen knew Laurene was just screwing with them. She glanced at Vince.

"It was a couple months ago," he said.

"Wow," Laurene said to Carmen. "You've *really* been keeping this one under wraps. . . ."

Carmen said nothing, but her smile turned a little brittle.

Vince was saying, "I was on my way into a restaurant in Burbank—JB's Brewhouse?—and I noticed Carmen in the parking lot."

Laurene gave him a look. "This isn't one of those 'love at first sight' stories, is it?"

"Flat-tire-at-first-sight story," Vince said, drawing a mild laugh from the group. "I heard her say some words that I don't think you can use on TV."

"Not on network, anyway," Carmen admitted.

"So," Vince said, "I changed her tire. She wanted to know how she could repay me, and we worked something out."

Nancy said, "This sounds interesting. . . ."

"I said yes to a date," Carmen said.

"I may be sick at that," Laurene said.

But Laurene was smiling, and Carmen could tell they all liked Vince. This was almost as good as getting the stamp of approval of her parents.

With everything going so well, naturally her cell phone vibrated in her purse. She got it out and saw HARROW on the caller ID. But she still had enough Midwestern upbringing not to answer the phone at the table.

"Excuse me, everybody. . . . I've got to take this. J.C."

"Christ himself?" Vince asked impishly.

"Close. Very close. . . ."

After a brief conversation with her boss, she returned and made her apologies to the group, and told Vince, "Sorry, babe, I've gotta go. They've moved up some promos I need to shoot."

"See you tonight?"

She shrugged. "Could be running late. Call you when I can."

He pecked her cheek. "Do that."

She would call him even if just to apologize again for bolting from lunch.

"Anyway," Vince said, walking her out, "I need to get back to the office myself."

Carmen did not notice Michael Pall, the team's resident DNA expert and profiler, approaching the restaurant as she got into her Prius. He slipped inside and joined the now-smaller group.

"I saw Carmen heading out," he said, sitting.

Body-building enthusiast Pall wore wire-frame glasses and a mild manner that belied the Superman he was, physically and mentally. He was in a navy polo with a *Crime Seen* logo stitched over the breast.

Laurene said, "Maybe for the best."

"That was her guy, huh?"

"Yes," Laurene said crisply, "but you missed that part. Look, we have to get back ourselves, so let's get on with it."

Chris frowned. "We're doing this without Carmen?"

"She's management."

Jenny said, "Billy isn't management."

"No," Laurene said, "but we know where he stands, don't we? So . . . everybody up for this?"

Jenny shivered. "J.C. doesn't like ultimatums."

"Who does?" Laurene said. "But sometimes that's what it takes."

And for half an hour, they intently talked.

Chapter Four

Ten days ago Lt. Anna Amari had stood in a West Hollywood hotel room with a dead body that might or might not belong to one "Jeff Bailey." And all she had to show for it was a severe tension headache.

Her partner, Detective LeRon Polk, had gone through the security video from the Star Struck Hotel.

Even though the video quality was (as Polk put it) "medium shitty," Amari could clearly see that the man who'd registered was not their corpse. Their as-yet-unidentified vic had died in that bed, but the room had not been his.

This man was slighter, had dark hair, and was obviously shorter than Bailey.

They had two males tied to this room, one via the front desk, the other by a blood-soaked bed. And either male—or *neither*—might be named Jeff Bailey.

Also, the hotel thoughtfully honored their guests' privacy by positioning security cameras only in the lobby.

Consequently, Amari had no footage of the victim anywhere else in the hotel, nor of the man who'd registered as Jeff Bailey. And zero footage of the two together—anywhere.

Even the assumption that only "Bailey" and the victim had been in the room was unsupportable— "Bailey" might be the killer, or an accomplice, or none of the above. A third party might have been there. A fourth. A fifth . . .

The bull pen of the Sex Crimes Division was set up in an old-fashioned way for such a cutting-edge facility—the Police Administration Building at 100 West First Street across from City Hall was new enough you could almost smell the fresh paint. Sex Crimes needed a constant interchange of ideas, so cubicles or separate offices (except for the captain's) were out.

Seated at her desk with a morning cup of black coffee, Amari raised a hand to her temple and rubbed, making small concentric circles with three fingers.

Both her desk and Polk's nearby were relatively free of clutter. Polk's was particularly spare, because he was compulsively neat; Amari's side, however, came a close second, because other than evidence, she kept most things in her head.

Beyond her phone and desk lamp, the clutter was pretty much limited to one Dodgers coffee cup and three Dodgers bobble heads: Jackie Robinson, Sandy Koufax, and a very dreadlocked

Manny Ramirez. No one in the division dared touch them—they were her holy trinity.

The joys of Anna Amari's life were her work and a passion for the Los Angeles Dodgers. The latter had been passed down to her by her late father.

Polk said, "Rubbin' your head like Aladdin's lamp again, huh? Think a genie'll pop out? You do know it's only Monday, right?"

"Weekend was too short," she said.

"That's 'cause you had me workin' both days."

She shot him a murderous look, but he survived it somehow.

After a frantic weekend in the Southland, the bull pen seemed a haunted house this morning, only a few other detectives scattered here and there. All the sex crimes detectives had heavy caseloads. Hell, all the detectives anywhere in the department had heavy caseloads, from Central Division to Hollenbeck, from Mission Division to Pacific and all points between.

The city was averaging around two homicides a day. Crime was up, good publicity down. That the cops had dubbed the killer "Billy Shears"—essentially giving that gift to the media—had pissed off everybody from the captain on up, until the shit, as was shit's wont, started rolling back down hill.

Amari was at the bottom of that hill.

Well, actually, Polk was; but she didn't have the energy or the ill will to do any more than just share the misery with him.

On the other hand, it wasn't every day she got a call from the chief himself, and on her cell phone on the way to work, at that.

"Would you like to explain, Lieutenant Amari, how it is that Fox News knows that this department has come up with a comical name for a killer but not a name for the victim?"

"I take responsibility for the case, sir, but not for the uniformed officers out of Hollywood Division. As for not identifying the victim, we've exhausted every traditional avenue—AFIS and CODIS come up empty. He's not the room's registrant. Fingerprints, DNA gave us nothing, so far. We *are* still waiting on some lab results."

"What about dental?"

"Sir, we can't do dental without knowing the dentist."

This had made the chief look stupid, which was really a smooth move on her part, she at once knew.

"Well, I would like a progress report, Lieutenant, *if* you ever *do* make any progress."

And he hung up on her. Imagine that.

She told Polk about the call from the chief, and for once her partner was speechless. On the other hand, his expression was eloquent; it said, *How the hell much trouble are we in?*

She ignored the unspoken question, asking him, "Any word from the lab yet?"

"There's a backlog. You know what it's been like the last couple weeks."

"So the chief is calling personally to say hustle it up, and the lab crew are sunning themselves. Well, at least local news ran the drawing."

"Yeah," Polk sighed, "pretty much every broadcast since Saturday night. And the newspapers ran it yesterday. So that's good."

"It is if we got some hits out of it."

"We *did* get hits."

"Could you be more specific, LeRon?"

"You talking legit leads, or total calls?"

She didn't like the sound of that. "Legit leads, LeRon."

"Uh . . . that'd be zero."

"Not a one?"

"Not a one, Lieutenant."

"Out of *how* many calls?"

"Four."

"Four? A city this size, and we're on every newscast, and every paper, and we get four freaking calls?"

Polk nodded. "There were half a dozen obvious cranks. Four were what you might call . . . sincere. But none amounted to anything. I even checked the FBI Kidnapping and Missing Persons web page. If you were wondering how desperate I got."

Without realizing it, she began rubbing her right temple again. "Who the hell *is* this guy, anyway? If he wants his murder solved, why can't he cooperate, goddamn it?"

"Thoughtless prick."

"He's from out of town," she said grimly. "Gotta be. Let's e-mail a link of the drawing that's up on our website to the Doe Network, and the Forgotten Network, too."

These were websites dedicated to finding the identifies of missing people.

"Somebody *somewhere* has to know this guy," Polk said.

They had gone back to the hotel repeatedly to interview staff and guests—nothing. Various routes had been used to try to identify the victim—nothing. With the crime lab in slow motion, this case was already starting to feel like an unsolved murder.

"Okay," Amari said, realizing she was rubbing her temple, and stopped. "We're not having any luck with IDing the vic—what about the killer?"

Polk gave her a look that said, *What* about *him?*

She answered the unasked question sternly: "This guy's definitely going to kill again."

"With us gettin' no help from the crime lab, he will," Polk said, shaking his head. "We haven't got jack. Maybe I should check that FBI Missing Persons web page again and see if our lab rats turn up *there.*"

"What about video from other buildings, LeRon? Traffic lights?"

"I've been taking DVDs home at night like a coach studying game films. There's nothing there, Lieutenant. The only shot where I saw the guy who rented the room comes from a traffic cam, and he ducks his damn head. Like he *knew* it was there, and avoided the sucker."

"He was in his car?"

"Yeah."

"So this is where you turn the whole case around, right, LeRon? And surprise me with his license number?"

"Wrong. Mud smeared on the plate. Kinda artfully smeared, but smeared."

"And the car?"

"Silver Honda Accord."

Amari snorted derisively. "And how many of *those* in California?"

"Lieutenant . . . there's no chance of tracking that car, with no more than we have."

She rubbed concentric circles on her clean desktop with the same three fingers that had massaged her temple. Maybe the desk had a headache, too. "What have we *missed?*"

Polk considered that briefly. "Something, probably. This was a brutal, bloody kill. There should be plenty of forensic shit to help us along."

The lab again.

Amari's mouth tightened to a slash. "Then . . . god-*damn*-it . . . there's probably only *one* way we're going to catch this son of a bitch. . . ."

Polk's face was solemn as he nodded. "Catch him when he screws up on the next one."

Her sigh started at her toes and seemed to make its way through her psyche before emerging from her mouth.

"Okay," she said. "Let's back up a step. Our victim was not the guy who registered at the front desk."

"Check."

"So . . . if we assume for the sake of argument that 'Bailey' is the killer, we have him registering on the day of the murder, well *before* the murder. Plenty of time for him to take his weapon up to that room and stow it somewhere . . . somewhere convenient for his purpose . . . ready and waiting for when the vic showed up."

"Yeah," Polk said. "Maybe what we have is a homophobic killer—he picks up a gay guy, lures him to a hotel room, and then butchers the poor bastard. Because he sees gays as evil or something, and oughta be killed."

"Don't get ahead of yourself, LeRon. Same scenario works for a closeted gay man who lures a pickup to that room to have sex with him, and then murders his sex partner out of shame and guilt."

"Killing himself, in a way."

"Either of those scenarios makes sense of a sort. But there are others that work just as well. Let's focus on what we *do* know."

"Okay, Lieutenant."

"The vic is from out of town." Amari rose. She thought better on her feet, and pacing alongside their nearly abutted desks was a common practice of hers. "That's not a fact, but is it an assumption we can buy?"

"*I* buy that," Polk agreed. "Nobody in Southern Cal seems to've ever seen the dude before."

"So . . . how does a guy from Bum Fart, Utah, end up at the Star Struck in West Hollywood?"

Polk shrugged. "If he's a gay man, a closeted one from out of town here to play . . . or work with a little play on the side . . . he might well know all *about* the Star Struck."

"Granted," she said. "But remember—he wasn't booked to stay there. He's *not* Jeff Bailey. Or anyway he's not the guy who checked in calling himself Jeff Bailey."

Polk frowned at her.

"What, LeRon?"

"We don't believe he was a guest in room four twenty-five," Polk said tentatively. "But could he have been a guest in some other room? Who got picked up in the hotel bar by the guy in four twenty-five?"

"That means he hasn't been around to check out in the last ten days."

"Not when he's cooling his jets in the morgue, he hasn't."

"Right. Check with the Star Struck and see if there were any deadbeats—any guests there who skipped without paying in the last week and a half."

"Damn good thinkin', Lieutenant!"

"If that's the case, and he *was* a guest, his stuff would still be there. It's worth a try, LeRon—call the hotel."

Polk did so, and he was still holding the receiver in his hand when his expression turned disappointed and he shook his head at Amari.

As he hung up, she said, "Well, the basic idea is a good one. See if you can get a couple of the Explorers to call around to all the hotels in town, starting with West Hollywood and the surrounding area, and see who's skipped out on their room in the last ten days, leaving their stuff behind."

The Explorer program allowed interested high school–age kids to learn about law enforcement by helping out doing menial office activities, freeing up officers to get out on the street.

Amari's cell chirped. She plucked it from her jacket pocket. Caller ID: WOMACK.

The head of the Sex Crimes Division, Captain Charles Womack, owner of the immediately recognizable gruff tenor in her ear.

"You and Polk need to get your butts out to Griffith Park."

"Care to be more specific, Cap?" Amari asked, not unpleasantly. "Last time I looked, Griffith Park is forty-two hundred acres."

"Mount Lee. The Hollywood sign."

"Not *really. . . .*"

"Really. Dead nude girl."

It would be.

"Better haul ass," Womack said. "Sounds like we've got a real sicko this time."

Womack clicked off; then so did she, feeling a tug in her gut.

Turning to Polk, she said, "We've gotta shake it."

"What is it?"

"Murder scene."

"Billy Shears again?" Polk asked.

He almost seemed eager—another Shears murder would mean a chance at fresh clues. A twisted way to think, but every cop who worked on serial murders wound up doing it.

And Billy Shears had all the earmarks of a serial.

Amari shook her head. "Don't think so. Female victim. Womack said this killer's a real 'sicko.' "

"And Billy Shears *isn't?*"

Her sentiment exactly.

Chapter Five

Monday was casual day around the *Crime Seen* offices, and Harrow took advantage, button-down blue chambray work shirt, faded jeans, and his customary Rockys, the preferred footwear of police everywhere.

His cell phone rode on his right hip like his pistol back in his sheriff days in Story County, Iowa. After he'd stepped down from the sheriff's post, to please his late wife Ellen, he'd signed on as a field agent for the Iowa Department of Criminal Investigation—his job at the time of his wife and son's murders.

He had lunch with cameraman Maury Hathaway at a deli two blocks from the UBC complex, in plenty of time for the regular start-of-the-week production meeting.

But when he entered the eighth-floor conference room, sunlight filtering in through the tinted windows, everybody else had beat him there. A first.

The long oval table was surrounded by a dozen chairs, five filled with the people Harrow had recruited to help him hunt his family's killer in the on-air investigation that had made *Crime Seen* a national obsession. No Carmen Garcia, though—she was tied up shooting promos.

Harrow's chief lieutenant, Laurene Chase, occupied her usual seat to the right of Harrow at the head of the table.

To Chase's right sat Clark Kent clone and DNA expert Michael Pall. Having retired from the Oklahoma state crime lab to join Harrow's team, Pall had made an excellent addition as much for his profiling skills as his original discipline.

Beyond Pall, Billy Choi seemed the DNA scientist's polar opposite, dark longish hair disheveled, his *Crime Seen* T-shirt no more wrinkled than your average Shar Pei.

Opposite were the other two team members, who'd begun tentatively dating, although the tabloid media assumed theirs was a love of the ages, nicknaming them "ChrisJen." Individually, they were computer expert Jenny Blake and chemist Chris Anderson, the latter on loan from Shaw Services, a private-sector crime lab out of Meridian, Mississippi.

Taking his seat, Harrow said, "So . . . am I late for my own meeting?"

"This isn't exactly your meeting," Chase said. "We wanted to talk before any weekly grind stuff. Okay?"

Harrow wasn't loving the sound of that. "Normally I wouldn't say this to a roomful of ex-cops, but . . . shoot."

"End of the season is coming," Chase said.

"Yes it is."

"We signed on for just this second season," she said. "We weren't even around for season one. So naturally, we're all wondering what's going to happen now."

"I don't see why we don't just keep going," Choi said. There was something stubborn, even sullen, in his tone. "We're in a position of strength to ask for new contracts and raises. People, we're a *hit*, for crissakes."

The DNA expert, Pall, shot him a look. "You were unemployed when J.C. recruited us. And the job he recruited us for wasn't *really* to play TV star."

Choi frowned. "Is that a crack?"

Pall shrugged his considerable shoulders. "I was about to retire, Billy. I was headed for a nice white beach. I can see where, from your perspective, you're better off now."

"And you're not?"

"Attention and money don't mean jack to me. No judgment to anyone who feels different is meant or even implied."

"Compared to the crime labs we all came out of," Choi insisted, "this is *like* retirement . . . with pay. And it's at least as sunny out here as on that white beach of yours, Michael."

"Billy," Anderson said, "the rest of us have day jobs to get back to." His southern drawl had faded slightly with his time on the coast.

"And *lives* to get back to," Chase added. "J.C., we didn't quit our jobs, we took leaves of absence. You know that."

Choi was about to say something, when Harrow raised a hand.

"Before this goes any further," he said, "you should know I might not be coming back, myself."

A net of surprised silence dropped over the room.

"Not coming back?" Choi asked, as if the words were foreign and untranslatable. "We've got a hit *show*, J.C.! Am I the only one that sees that? People would kill to be in our position!"

"People kill for a lot of reasons," Harrow said. "As we know all too well. And we all know that our show's a hit. That the hard work we did tracking down my family's murderer is *how* it became a hit. But nobody in this room went into law enforcement to be a TV star."

"Jesus!" Choi blurted. "The six of us do more good with our big budget and high profile than any sixty other cops in America! We are paid well, and we have state-of-the-art lab equipment. Why the hell are you all so eager to leave it behind?"

Jenny Blake sat forward a little. "You like this life, don't you, Billy?"

"What's not to like?"

"What's not to like is not being able to go out to eat or to the grocery store or to a movie or *anywhere* without someone taking your picture."

Choi smirked. "Well, I think that's pretty cool."

"Nobody else here does," Chase said flatly.

Choi's eyes went from face to face and his features fell. Nothing cocky remained in Choi's voice as he asked, "You're on the same page as everybody but me, J.C.?"

"Afraid I am, Billy," Harrow said. "For several years, I had to put up with this TV nonsense, because that was what it took for me to accomplish my goal. Justice for my family. I admit we do some good with *Crime Seen*—and that a case can be made for staying on."

Choi frowned in obvious frustration. "Then why are you on *their* page and not mine?"

"Because life in a goldfish bowl was not the point of the exercise. Take Chris and Jenny, here—they sure as hell didn't sign up for a tabloid relationship."

Anderson and Jenny traded a look.

"Honest to God," Anderson said to Choi, not unkindly, "I never once thought about all this fame stuff. I just signed on to help out Mr. Harrow, and maybe get some experience outside my home state."

Harrow turned his gaze on Choi. "Let's face it, Billy, except for you and me? Everybody else gave something up to be here. To come and help me."

"All right," Choi said softly. "But then why are *you* leaving, J.C.? I don't mean to be tactless or anything . . . but what do you have to go back to?"

A sharp intake of air came from Chase, and everyone sensed the immediate discomfort. Choi saying he didn't mean to be tactless made it no less a breach to trivialize the loss of their leader's family.

"I didn't say I was leaving."

Choi frowned again. "J.C., are you trying to drive me frickin' nuts?"

Harrow smiled just a little, still playing his cards close. "Billy, I said, 'I *might* not be coming back.' "

"Okay," Choi said. "So you're on the fence. *Why* are you?"

"I would stay, Billy, and I would try to convince our friends and colleagues here to stay, if I could answer just one question to my . . . to *all* of our . . . satisfaction. Namely—what's left to do here?"

Nobody, not even Choi, seemed to have a ready answer for that.

Harrow sighed, smiled wearily, and said, "Tell you what, Billy. If I do go, I'll put in a good word with Dennis Byrnes for you to take my place."

Choi was smiling in a shell-shocked sort of way. "You'd do that for me, J.C.?"

"When I recruited you for this, Billy, I asked only that you learn to play well with others. You've held up your end. I'll hold up mine."

"I . . . I don't know what to say, J.C.," Choi said.

Chase said, dryly, "Try 'thanks.' "

Choi admitted to Harrow, "Laurene's right, J.C. Thanks. You gave me a second chance when nobody else on the planet would have."

"You're welcome, Billy."

"Look, Billy," Chase said, no sarcasm now, "none of us're trying to burst your bubble. It's just that I'm a crime-scene investigator, it's what I've always been. Feels like maybe it's time I got back to it."

Turning to the shy couple, Choi asked, "We know where Michael stands. Where does that leave 'ChrisJen'?"

Anderson said, "I've got a job waitin' back in Mississippi."

"Me in Wyoming," Jenny muttered.

Or maybe Mississippi, Harrow thought.

Harrow's cell phone thrummed in his pocket. A text from his assistant, Vicki: D.B. WANTS YOU NOW.

In cop parlance, "D.B." was dead body. But this D.B. was the living breathing president of UBC, Dennis Byrnes.

Harrow told his team that they would have to adjourn the meeting for the present, but he'd get back to them as soon as he could.

But he didn't share what he might tell Byrnes.

I quit.

Chapter Six

After the captain's call dispatching her and Polk to the Hollywood sign, Amari had gone to the locker room to exchange her suit and silk blouse for jeans, blue Dodgers T-shirt, navy blazer, and New Balance running shoes.

In the driver's seat next to her, however, Polk maintained his usual "Superfly meets Ralph Lauren" look, gray suit, lavender tie, purple shirt, and Bruno Magli loafers.

"Looking sharp," she said, over the siren.

"Dress for success, my old man taught me."

She smiled, weaving in and around traffic. "Like me, you mean?"

"Lieutenant, you know I respect you. We only been partners, what, a month? But I already known you're a hell of a cop."

"Thank you, LeRon."

"Only . . ."

"Only?"

"You look like you're going to the division softball game."

"Ever been to the Hollywood sign before, LeRon?"

"Seen it all the time. I can see it right now."

Heading north on Gower, Amari took a second to glance up at the Hollywood sign in the distance. Facing south, near the top of Mount Lee in Griffith Park, the huge white letters were as iconic of Hollywood as Bogie, Marilyn, or James Dean.

"Yeah," she said, "but you ever been *up* there?"

Polk shook his head. "Why?"

"No reason."

Amari navigated the twisting streets and their slower traffic until she got into the park and eventually wound her way around to Mount Lee Drive. She shut off the siren and removed the roof bubble.

To one side of the normally locked gate sat a patrol car; the officer within waved their unmarked car through. Only the security company that kept an eye on the sign had the right to use the road, except in the case of emergency. Murder qualified.

They followed the curving road to the top of the seventeen-hundred-foot rock. At the summit, Amari added her unmarked vehicle to the three patrol cars and the coroner's wagon already crammed in the scant space just in front of the jungle of radio antennas.

One officer stood near the edge of the parking lot above the sign, and the coroner's assistant and his helpers were near their vehicle. The other five patrolmen who went with the three patrol cars, as well as the security guard who'd called in the body, were not in sight.

Still in their car, Polk frowned and asked, "Where's everybody at?"

"Down at the sign," Amari said.

"Which way are the stairs?"

"Stairs?"

"I mean, this is a famous place—it's all fenced off and maintained and shit, right? Like a park?"

"Well, it's fenced off. But otherwise . . . no."

He gave her a sick look. "Which is why you wore jeans and sneakers."

She shrugged, threw open the door, and got out, knowing her young partner had no alternative but to follow.

Which he did. Amari was already out front a little. "Careful, LeRon—rattlesnakes up here."

"Now you're just screwin' with my head, Lieutenant."

"Am I?"

From up here, Los Angeles went on forever. At a distance, she could even feel a fondness for the badly misnamed City of Angels. Sure there was smog, and crime, and traffic, and a hundred other bad things. But you couldn't tell from this sunny view. On the other hand, a nude murdered woman awaited them not far down the hill.

A lone officer met them at the top of the slope. Clancy Jackson was a heavyset light-skinned African-American cop.

"Anna Amari," Jackson said, and exchanged quick nods with Polk. "Been some time. How is it you still look twenty-five?"

"Morning, Clancy," Amari said. "Does that ass-kissy bullshit work on your wife?"

A big white smile blossomed. "Now and forever. And I'm in full-gear now—six months till retirement, and Betty'll have me underfoot 24/7. Got to keep on her good side."

"She'll cut you plenty of slack. She can finally stop worrying for a living."

"You got that right, Anna." He nodded down the hillside. "Weird one."

"Yeah?"

She could see the seven-foot cyclone fence surrounding the massive assembly of letters—forty-five feet high, two hundred feet long. A narrow dirt road cut down to a gate, unlocked and open, a red car from A2Z Security parked just outside.

Next to the gate, perhaps a foot off the ground, partially hidden in some scrub brush, a squat gray box was attached to a low pole.

Inside the gate, down the far side of HOLLY-WOOD's first O, stood five uniformed cops and a scrawny guy in the drab gray uniform of A2Z Security. Just barely visible beyond the O's nearest edge were a pair of bare white feet.

"What's the story, Clancy?"

"Dead nude woman, mid to late twenties."

Not the first dead nude woman under the sign. In 1932 actress Peg Entwistle had famously jumped to her death from the top of the letter H. For a sign that represented the glamour of Hollywood, to cops it meant suicides and vandalism.

Amari said, "Chief indicated this was murder, not suicide. How'd she die, Clancy?"

"Stabbed and . . . well . . ." The veteran cop seemed uncomfortable, a warning sign to Amari. "Anna, better get down there and see for yourself."

How did the killer get in that fenced-off area? Was the woman already dead and carried in? Was she a willing participant on a daring expedition to the famous sign? Either way, there were locks, cameras, motion detectors to get past. . . .

"Better take the road down," Jackson advised. "Not much better than a trail, and steep as hell, but it's something."

Amari trotted down the dirt hill, Polk barely keeping up as he watched out for his shoes. And snakes.

Stopping short of the gate, Amari went over to the gray electrical box that contained the controls for the cameras and motion detectors. Careful to avoid adding to a group of preexisting footprints, Amari squatted to one side.

A gray metal box maybe twelve inches wide and eighteen inches tall. With a clasped padlock.

Judging from the footprints, someone—either the guard who discovered the body, the killer, or both—had been near this box.

Yet it was locked.

She hoped that the guard had not closed the lock after finding it open—she'd find out. In the meantime, she studied the ground around the box, seeing nothing other than footprints . . . and when she got a closer look at those, they didn't seem that promising. Not a clean print in sight.

"Anything?" Polk asked, still standing on the dirt path.

Amari shook her head. Then she spotted something. Or was the sunlight playing tricks?

"Whatcha got, Lieutenant?"

"Not sure."

She took a couple of steps back up the hill, then stopped, withdrew a latex glove from a jacket pocket, and snapped it on. Squatting, Amari picked up a small red tube no longer than a quarter of an inch, and dropped it into a cellophane evidence bag.

She held it up to the sun, studied it, then returned to Polk and handed him the bag.

"Some kind of casing?"

"I think it's the sheathing from one of the wires in that control box."

"It's padlocked."

"*Now* it is. Does that look fresh to you?"

Polk nodded. "Still a bright red. Hasn't been in the weather long."

"That's what I was thinking too. File that in your pocket and let's go see our body."

Polk obeyed.

They passed through the gate, carefully stepping down between the giant letters to where the group of six uniforms, four patrolmen, a patrolwoman, and the security guard stood in a semicircle around the body.

A young uniformed cop, unknown to Amari, joined them. His nameplate read KAYLAN, and he had curly dark hair and glasses. He looked just a little older and more with it than a kid dressed as a policeman at Halloween. The other patrol officers, who seemed to be holding an impromptu memorial service over there, looked equally young.

So many babies on the force now, she thought.

After making introductions, Amari said, "Forensics team been here, Kaylan?"

"Not yet," he said.

"So, are you fellas finished trampling the crime scene? Or do you need a little more time?"

Kaylan froze, agape.

Polk, perhaps happy to find someone below him in the pecking order, said, "Were you absent that day?"

"Uh . . . what day?"

"The day they did footprints at the Academy?"

"We . . . uh . . . we . . ."

"Round up your friends," Amari said quietly, not wanting to start a stampede, "and get up the hill. Send the crime-scene unit down when they get here."

"Yes, ma'am," the officer said.

"Nobody leave. CSU will want your shoes."

"Shoes?"

Polk asked, "First crime scene?"

The young officer nodded.

Amari told him, "Now that you've all walked through an active crime scene, and had a good long look at a nude dead woman, CSU will need your shoes . . . so they can separate your footprints from those of the killer."

"Yes, Lieutenant," the rookie said.

"Don't cry. Just get up the hill and keep an eye on that security guard—we'll want to talk to him after we've had a look at the body."

"Will do."

"Don't yell over to them! Go over and quietly round them up and tell them to watch where they step."

Kaylan nodded, went over, and passed along Amari's orders to the others, who looked back at her in various ways (alarm, resentment, fear, confusion), then led the parade back up the hill.

"Damn rookies," Polk said.

Amari felt it was to her credit that she didn't smile.

Thing of it was, civilians weren't the only ones who gawked at a crime scene. Often, it was cops, too. Not just young ones—you could be a cop for a long time in a city this big and never encounter a murder scene . . . particularly one with a nude woman as its HOLLYWOOD star.

Chapter Seven

Last night

Appraising herself in the restroom mirror in Kyuui—LA's trendiest new sushi bar—twenty-five-year-old Wendi Erskine felt nervous, excited, and fortunate all at once.

The diminutive blonde—born in Hermon, Maine, near Bangor—had gotten out of the snow belt and come to Hollywood only two weeks after high school graduation.

Now, seven (often frustrating) years later, she was at a chic LA eatery with a movie producer (slash prospective boyfriend) waiting for her in a dining room far swankier than those at the half dozen restaurants where she'd been a waitress in this very tough town.

She granted herself a final look in the mirror. Her hair just right, eye makeup fine, lip gloss emphasizing the natural fullness of her mouth. And the little black dress showed off her shapely, slender figure to fine advantage without making her look slutty. She wanted to look desirable to Louis, but not available.

Anyway, not *readily* available. . . .

When he had ordered a second round of drinks before dinner, she'd excused herself to the ladies' room. This was a date, definitely, but there would be business talk as well, and she wanted to stay sharp.

She hoped when she returned to the table, their dinner would beat her there, and she could nurse the second cosmopolitan through the meal. Of course these fancy-schmancy restaurants took their time serving up meals. *Come on*, she thought, *how long does it take to prepare raw fish, anyway?*

The way his smile blossomed, seeing her return, was really cute. But "cute" didn't quite cut it for the suave filmmaker. Lacking this town's usual tan, Louis had longish black hair, a nicely trimmed matching goatee, alert brown eyes, and dimples when he showed off those blindingly white teeth.

Probably caps, but who cared? She had implants, didn't she? Hollywood was *always* part illusion.

Her date's natural good looks were amplified by his well-tailored charcoal pinstripe suit, off-white shirt, and geometrically patterned black-and-gray tie.

Louis St. James had approached Wendi after seeing her in a showcase production of *Bus Stop* at a little theater in Santa Monica where she had played Cherie, the Marilyn Monroe part (actually,

Kim Stanley part). After the show, he'd come back-stage, introduced himself, and told her he thought she had a big future.

Instead of hitting on her, he had given her a business card.

"There are a lot of lovely girls in this town," he'd said. "But only a handful have your sensitivity. And if the camera can capture the charisma that comes across on stage . . . do give us a call."

Seemed sincere, but a lot of creeps in LA were capable of smooth lines like that—town was full of actors, after all—and back when she'd first got off the bus, Wendi might well have fallen for it.

But not now.

She checked out Louis St. James on the Internet Movie Database, where he looked legit, and a link was provided to his website. He had plenty of pro-ducing credits and several projects "in develop-ment" and a several more "in pre-production."

Admittedly, most of his credits were lower-budget indies she'd never heard of; but then the two movies she'd been in would fall into that same category.

And a faker would have made himself look like a bigger shot than this. His credentials seemed legit enough.

He'd turned out to be articulate, and sophisti-cated, with a genuine interest in her, and not just her body. Mostly he wanted to know about roles she'd played, on stage and the handful in movies and TV. Even the infomercials that had been her steadiest gig, outside of waitressing.

"I have the perfect role for you," he'd said several times, once calling it "the role of a lifetime."

When she reached the table, he rose, held her chair for her, and only returned to his own place when she was seated. Wow—a gentleman. In Los Angeles, California, yet.

"You look especially beautiful tonight," he said, with a gentle smile. "You have a glow."

"Stop it," she said, returning the smile.

He gestured toward her cosmo, which had come while she was gone. She took a tentative sip.

"I thought our food would be here by now," she said. "I don't like to drink on an empty stomach."

"Shouldn't be long. You know these places—they put ambience ahead of appetite."

She laughed lightly and took another sip.

"You know," he said, "you did a fine job in that infomercial. It's a thankless task, but you really came across well."

"*Which* infomercial?" she asked. She was grateful he didn't look down on her for doing them; infomercials paid well, and gave her the opportunity to act, sort of.

"The tortilla press," he said.

"The Sancho!" she said. "Whenever did you see that?"

"Oh, at three a.m. a couple nights ago, when I was fighting insomnia."

"That's prime time," she said with a half smile, "in the infomercial biz."

"Well, I've seen a lot of your work, thanks to

sleepless nights—Snuggie, ShamWow. . . . You *rocked* the Flowbee."

"Now you're teasing," she said.

"No. You did a good job with what was not exactly Shakespeare. Not even Mamet. Anyway, I'm a professional, and I admire professionalism. Here's to you, Wendi."

He raised his glass and she did hers, and they both drank.

Finally dinner arrived. They made small talk through the meal. Wendi finished her second drink and allowed herself a third, though Louis was still nursing number two. She was not a heavy drinker and wasn't surprised when, as they left the restaurant, she felt a little tipsy.

Still, she hadn't had *that* much, and Wendi wondered if maybe the sushi was bad. She knew all about restaurants selling fish that was off.

"I hope we know each other well enough," Louis said, "that I can suggest we go back to my place, and look at that script."

"Actually," she said, "I'm not feeling so great. . . . Not opposed to stopping over, but . . ."

"I understand. Could be the drinks—they don't skimp on the alcoholic content at Kyuui. That's why I held it to two."

"I was stupid to have so much to drink. I'm really sorry, Louis. I don't think I could give you much of a reading tonight. . . ."

He helped her to his Eclipse in the parking lot.

"Maybe you'll feel better after a little drive. It's a delightful evening. We can put the top down and let the warm breeze roll through."

"I don't know," she said.

"Give it a try. If you feel better, we'll have a run at that script."

"Maybe you could just take me . . . take me home. . . ."

He started the car and they were moving. She tried to focus on where they were going, but the more she tried to settle her eyes on something as they sped past, the worse she felt.

Finally, she just gave up and shut her eyes.

When she finally opened them again, the car had stopped and Louis had the rider's side door open to help her. He'd already removed her seat belt and was half lifting, half dragging her out of his car.

"Where . . . where are we?" Her voice sounded strange and faraway in her own ears, her tongue dry and thick.

"My place," he said, getting her on her feet and putting an arm around her as he helped her walk from the driveway to the house.

Her vision was blurry, like a soapy film was over her eyes. Just a bungalow. Nice lawn. She could smell fresh, clean air. Were they in the country?

"Your place?" she asked.

Her legs felt weighted down and her brain felt fuzzy.

"You said take you home," he said. "This is my home. You wanted to go over that script, remember?"

"Did I say that?"

"If you meant I should take you back to *your*

apartment, I can do that. You fell asleep. Are you feeling better?"

His arms felt so good, supporting her, holding her up. Some citrus-scented masculine cologne. Nice. He was warm, gentle.

Next thing she knew, they were in the house. The lights were out and she'd never been here before, so she just went with it as Louis guided her.

"I think you need to lie down for a little while," he suggested.

"Yeah, rest a little while," she managed. "So sorry about this. So sorry."

He guided her to the bedroom, her feet dragging more with each step, and she still couldn't figure out why she was so darn drowsy. Oddly, though, a mild euphoria had come upon her. And she felt safe with Louis. Secure. He had been such a perfect gentleman. . . .

He sat her on the bed and, when he suggested that she remove "her lovely dress so it doesn't get wrinkled," she had no argument.

The euphoria shorted in and out with another feeling, the sense that she was sitting on the edge of a black abyss and the more she tried to rear back, the more the abyss beckoned.

When she finally forced her eyes open again, she realized she was naked, Louis next to her, kissing her breasts in a sweet, loving way, and the lights were on in the bedroom, not bright, fairly dim, but on . . . and despite a sense that she really should protest, it felt nice. . . .

She didn't dispense sex like so many actresses,

and she was never a one-night-stand kind of girl. She'd had regular boyfriends though, even lived with a few, so sex was nothing unnatural to her.

But she had never been casual about it. . . . Was this a shameful slip? Was she trying to buy a role from a film producer? Was he just another asshole who had gotten her tipsy and was taking advantage?

None of that seemed to matter, because his kisses soothed her, and when his lips moved down her belly, she didn't resist. She felt something within her heating up, though drowsiness still flirted with her. . . .

Then he was crouching between her open legs, his tongue finding its way inside her, the portal of her thighs widening.

Gently, he rolled her over onto her stomach, slipping a pillow under tummy, the satin sheets smooth against her erect nipples, the bed warm against her stomach. She was afraid for a moment that he would take her in her private place, but then he was inside her right where she wanted him, gently at first, filling her as no one had in a very long time, then with more force, but not rough. Not rough. Her hips rose to meet him, of their own accord.

His driving became more insistent, and she did her best to stay with him. She moaned, the feeling of him making love to her spreading through every nerve ending. He was good. Very good. . . .

She was almost there, as he thrust ever faster; then suddenly the wave crashed over her and she involuntarily moaned and filled her fists with the sheets as she shudderingly came.

He held her as the waves of passion ebbed away; then she felt him withdraw. She purred with contentment and managed to turn onto her back and willed her eyes to open. The room was dark, and all she could make out beyond the bed was his silhouette and the outline of a vase of flowers on the night stand next to her.

Roses?

She wanted to kiss him desperately, and she tried to rise, but couldn't seem to navigate the task. She slumped back to the bed. She tried again with even less success and simply surrendered to the afterglow.

He leaned over and brushed blonde hair from her eyes.

"I'll be right back, sweetheart," he said softly, and was gone.

She wanted to drift to sleep, but she also wanted to hold him first, and for him to hold her. When she opened her eyes, a figure hovered over her. . . . Louis? Just a pale shadow really, in the dimly lit room. She looked up to see something metallic flash in the moonlight, filtering in through the curtains.

Something burned on the flesh of her throat and a quick, unbidden gurgling gasp escaped from her. She felt liquid spurting, then falling, like warm dark spattering rain, onto her face, shoulders, and breasts. There was a vague pain in her neck and she struggled to get her hand up to try and wipe it away, but her fingers only got wet, too.

She fought to breathe, worked to stay awake, not awake, *conscious*, struggling against an eddy of darkness pulling her down.

When the blade flashed again and again, sinking into her body as if it were mud, she felt nothing, her performance already ended.

Chapter Eight

The dead woman had long blonde hair, neatly brushed—remarkably pristine, as if she had been carried down from the top of the hill. A pretty face, eyes closed, Sleeping Beauty effect. Lipstick looked fresh, as if it had been applied *after* she got here.

Her carotid artery had been severed.

Seven jagged stab wounds in her chest and abdomen—the blood had been cleaned away, though; no sign of blood anywhere.

Amari frowned in thought. *So she had been carried in and left here. Otherwise the ground would have been soaked with blood, and—unless the killer had washed the blood from her at the scene—she would be covered in it.*

And she wasn't.

Neatly draped over one arm, almost as if she were carrying them, were a dozen red roses—an actress at encore presented with a bouquet. A note protruded from the top of the gathered, still fresh-looking blooms.

That was one good thing about cop gawkers as opposed to the civilian variety—none of the children in blue had taken the note as a souvenir.

The dead woman's body was white, lividity having taken the blood to the lowest parts of her body. Amari touched a finger to flesh—rigor mortis had set in.

"Probably sometime last night," Amari said. "Coroner's assistant can give us a better idea, when he gets liver temperature."

They had a look at the surrounding footprints, but the police parade had turned the place into a mess, doubtful they would get anything worthwhile. She wanted to see, to *read*, the card on the bouquet, but had better sense. The crime-scene unit would have it bagged and tagged soon enough.

Murders were often described as having been committed "in cold blood"; but Amari knew that most were in the heat of rage. "In cold blood" better described her own rage, a detached but no less intense desire to remove from society the twisted individual who had stolen this young woman's life.

Actually, not so young—this girl was dead, wasn't she? And you didn't get any older than that. Years, probably many, many years, had been stolen from her. That the killer had left her remains here, under the Hollywood sign, indicated a desire for the whole world to see the result.

Well, Amari had seen the result, all right, and she would do something about it.

As they headed up the hill, she and Polk passed

the crime-scene team, coming down. Polk gave them the plastic bag with the wire casing. Amari indicated where they found it, and filled them in on the state of the crime scene. Then she and Polk continued on up.

Two patrol cars had pulled out. Remaining were the veteran Jackson and the rookie Kaylan, the coroner's team, and the security guard, who leaned against the cop car.

Skinny, with military-short dark hair and wire-framed glasses, the security guard gave off the vibe of somebody who'd taken this job hoping he'd be issued a gun someday. His nameplate read WYLER.

Even so, the first question Amari had to ask was, "Name?"

"Jason Wyler," the guard said, extending his hand.

Amari shook it, introducing herself and Polk, who (she told Wyler) would be recording their conversation.

"Cool with me," the guard said. "Anything to help move the investigation along."

"You discovered the body, Mr. Wyler?"

Almost whispering, as if this were a secret to be shared only between professionals, he said, "Yeah, I was the one. That was me."

Patiently, Amari said, "Tell us about it."

"Well," he said, a little too eagerly, "it was between five and five-thirty this morning—I was on my regular rounds. I have regular rounds I make."

Polk asked, "See any cars, coming in or out?"

"I didn't see nobody. And I'm always looking.

That's part of my job. I've been working security for three years now."

Amari said, "So you came up here like usual—what was different from any other time?"

"Nothing. It's always kind of dead up here."

He didn't seem to realize what he'd said.

Amari said, "Think, Mr. Wyler. You're a pro. There *had* to be something—do you always drive down there to check the sign on your rounds? Every single trip?"

"Well, no."

"Then why did you *this* time?"

"I guess it was the tire tracks."

Polk blurted, "*What* tire tracks?"

Wyler pointed toward the dirt road that wound down to the sign. "Over there. Those tire tracks."

"Show us *where* exactly," Amari said, already walking that way. Polk and Wyler trailed.

Catching up to fall in beside Amari, Wyler said, "Right at the top of the road, Lieutenant! I thought I saw tracks in the dust. I hadn't seen them on any of my other rounds tonight. So, of course, I got suspicious."

Looking at the blacktop lot, where the dirt road met the blacktop, Amari could see several tire tracks. "Did you, uh, drive through the tracks? To get down the hill, and check things out?"

"Yeah, well, sure I did," Wyler said, confused. "That's where the *road* is."

Amari knew that showing this fool her temper would not help matters. So she calmly asked, "What did you find when you got down to the gate?"

"Everything looked pretty normal," the security guard said. "At first, anyway."

Polk asked, "Looked no different than usual?"

Wyler nodded. "Same-o, same-o."

Amari asked, "How about the gate? Was it locked or ajar?"

"Yeah, it was shut, it was locked—that's why I thought everything was okay, tire tracks or no tire tracks."

With you on the job, Amari thought, *it's no tire tracks. . . .*

Polk asked, "Then why did you go have a look?"

"Just my . . . you know, *cop* instincts. Even though everything seemed okay, I still had that feeling."

"That feeling?"

"That something wasn't right, y'know? You musta had that feeling lots of times."

"Oh yeah," Polk said, with an encouraging nod.

"So, I started by using the spotlight. . . ." Wyler pointed down at his car with its door-mounted spot similar to those on patrol cars. "I swept the scene, starting down at the *D*, then moving toward the *H*. That . . . that's when I saw the woman's feet sticking out. By the *O*."

Wyler appeared nervous now. He'd turned a sick shade of white.

Amari said, "You're doing fine, Mr. Wyler."

"You know, just 'cause I'm a pro, that doesn't mean I'm not human. I don't mind telling you, I about pissed myself right then and there. All these years on the job, and I never was around a real live dead body before."

"Did you check the control box?"

"With the spotlight, yeah, but it was locked."

She nodded. "What did you do next?"

"Called 911."

"You unlocked the gate?"

"Yeah, when the first squad car got here. They wanted to make sure she was dead."

"So, the gate was locked, when you got there."

"Yeah."

"And right now, all the electronics are working, the camera and the motion detectors?"

Wyler nodded vigorously. "I even called in to the security center after I called 911. They said everything was working fine and they didn't see anything."

Polk was shaking his head. "Smart mother. Hacked the system somehow."

Amari asked, "And the control box was definitely locked?"

"Oh yeah," Wyler said, nodding vigorously. "It was locked. Definitely locked. I didn't—"

Wyler was cut off by the approach of a tech from the crime scene. Marty Rue—mid-forties, dark hair, black glasses—approached Amari. They had worked on several cases together over the years.

"Morning, Anna," he said.

"Marty, any jewels among those squashed acorns?"

"Footprints around the body are a mess, as you promised. You folks got the USC marching band working your crime scenes for you now?"

If Wyler understood he was part of that insult, it didn't register. He had the happy look of an amateur suddenly accepted by a group of professionals.

"Marty," she said, "what about those roses?"

"I'll know more when I get them back to the lab, but I bet you'd like a look at that card."

"Oh yeah."

"You're gonna love this." He held out a cellophane bag.

Amari took it and read the card within: *With Love, Don Juan.*

She heaved a long sigh and passed the bag to Polk.

Polk read it and said, "I mean, I know these sick killers leave a signature—but an *actual* signature?"

"He's got an ego," she said. "We're gonna see more of him."

Polk frowned. "Lieutenant, could this be the same killer as West Hollywood? I realize that was a male victim, but they both were stabbed, they're both dead, they're both naked. Maybe killed after sex?"

"That's good thinking, LeRon. Really is. But the signatures are different . . . including this very specific signature of roses *and* a hand-signed note. Eyeballing it, I'd say different weapons. For this to be the same killer, particularly if your scenario were to hold, we'd have something very unusual— a bisexual serial killer."

She asked Wyler, "Do you have a key for the control box?"

"Yeah," he said, unconsciously jingling the ring attached to his belt. "Why?"

She asked Rue, "You lifted footprints from in front of the control box yet?"

"Nope."

"Well, do that, then let's have a look at that box. My guess is our killer got into it somehow. He had to defeat the camera and the motion detector."

Rue nodded, and was gone.

Amari said, "All right, Mr. Wyler, spell out a typical night for me."

Wyler smiled at the thought of helping his fellow pros. "I come on at eleven. I'm here by eleven thirty, then pretty much every hour and a half or so after that. Usually, around one, two-thirty, four, five-thirty, then one last pass on my way back to the barn at seven."

"Earlier, you told us you were here between five and five-thirty."

"Yeah, yeah, that's right. Maybe twenty after or so. I was a little early, but not much."

"You noticed the tire tracks on your *five-thirty* trip," Amari said. "Is it possible you missed them earlier?"

Wyler considered that. "No, I don't think so, really don't. Tracks in the dust on the blacktop? That's something I look for every time I'm up top. I would have seen 'em if they were here before that."

"That means the killer was here between four and five-thirty."

"Had to be," Wyler said, nodding.

To Polk, Amari said, "Which tells us she was dead before that—bled out, cleaned up, ready for display. Killer drove her here in his car."

"Risky," Polk said.

"But if the killer knew he had ninety minutes and had cased the area, he could minimize the risk."

From the control box, Rue gave them a wave.

"All right," Amari said. "Which key is it?"

Wyler took the ring off his belt and handed it to her by the box key.

As they walked back down the path to the box, Polk said, "Killer opened it, did whatever he did, then locked it up again."

"Yeah," Amari said, "and we want to see *what* he did."

Polk put a hand on her forearm and stopped her. "What if he booby-trapped the frickin' thing?"

She thought about that.

"Why lock it back up," Polk insisted, "if it's *not* booby-trapped?"

"To slow us down?"

"Right. And what would slow us down more than it blowing up in our damn faces?"

"Shit," she said.

Polk was right.

They conferred with Marty Rue and, in the end, did the smart thing.

Called the bomb squad.

Chapter Nine

The network president wore his dark hair clipped close, his lightweight gray suit no more expensive than Harrow's first car. He was smiling, but the gray-green eyes were cold stones in the well-tanned, conventionally handsome face.

Dennis Byrnes said, "Let's get right to it, shall we, J.C.? With the ratings *Crime Seen*'s enjoyed, you are right to expect certain rewards. Including a raise."

Seated opposite the network president, Harrow said, "I've had another offer."

Byrnes raised a hand. "I'm sure you have, J.C. You were bound to. Assembling your forensics team, taking them on the road, that was smart showmanship. Plus you got lucky, and some great television happened. The kind that will be written about and studied for years. So I don't play down your contribution."

"Dennis . . ."

"Now, J.C., I'm being straight up with you. But despite all this success, you *know* what kind of economy we're facing, and your road trip was extremely expensive. So I don't want you to be offended if the increase seems unduly modest, and—"

"I said, I've had another offer."

"J.C., don't be ridiculous. You know your contract includes an iron-clad non-compete clause."

"Not quite iron-clad, Dennis."

". . . Explain."

"The non-compete clause applies only to other offers in broadcasting."

"Actually, J.C., it's more than just broadcasting—you *do* know it includes cable."

"All of television, sure."

"And radio, and really anything in media. Throughout the universe, if I remember the language."

"It's not a job on Mars, Dennis, that I promise you."

"Where then?"

"Iowa."

Byrnes frowned, as if Harrow *had* said Mars. "That's where you used to work."

"Right. In law enforcement."

Byrnes had a flummoxed look. "Well, J.C., regional, local broadcasting, that's covered by non-compete, too."

"I'm aware."

"Who's made you an offer, anyway?"

"You don't know them."

"And it's *not* television?"

Harrow gave him a single head shake.

"How much is the offer, then?"

"Twenty-seven five."

Byrnes erupted in something that was vaguely a laugh. "You're making *seventy-five thousand* per show, J.C. And I'm about to offer you one hundred."

"Not talking about weekly salary."

"What . . . what *are* you talking about?"

"The offer is per year."

Byrnes frowned in incredulity. "Twenty-seven thousand five-hundred a *year?*"

"Plus certain perks. Three weeks' paid vacation. Medical and dental."

"That doesn't sound like work. That sounds like welfare. What the hell kind of job pays twenty-seven thousand a year?"

"Twenty-seven-thousand five. Police chief of Walcott, Iowa."

"There's no such place!" Byrnes grinned in desperation. "You're punking me, right? Is that brat Ashton Kutcher in the hall?"

"No, but he's from Iowa, too. He'd know Walcott's a real place. If I stay five years, I climb to thirty-three thousand and change."

Byrnes was a man trying to awaken from a bad dream. "Small-town police chief. You want to trade it all for small-town police chief. Who the hell quits a hit show without something better already lined up?"

"This *is* better, Dennis. Better for me. Look, I know we're a success. I know we've done a good job. But surely this can't be *that* big a surprise."

"*Really?*"

"Dennis, when I took this gig, I told you it wasn't about the money."

"You also wouldn't have called it a 'gig'! J.C., you're a show-biz guy now, like it or not. You really think it will be so goddamn easy going back?"

Harrow shrugged. "Whether there's a life back there for me, after what I lost, I don't honestly know . . . but I need to find out."

Byrnes's eyebrows lifted. "Find out *after* doing a third season for us. I *know* you took satisfaction, during season one, helping bring all those bad guys to justice."

"I know we did some good. . . ."

"You did a *lot* of good, J.C. *We* did a lot of good. You can contribute more here than being a Podunk lawman, no offense. You want to go back to Iowa? Why not spend another year here first, socking big dough away for your golden years—you're no spring chicken, after all . . . particularly for a TV star."

That actually made Harrow smile.

"J.C., give me one more year, and I'll have time to properly replace you for season four . . . unless you change your mind and want to stay on."

Harrow shook his head. "Dennis, it's not just me—my *Killer TV* team is ready to get back to *their* lives, too."

"Unacceptable," Byrnes said, with what a stranger might have mistaken for a smile.

Harrow knew better. "Pardon?"

"The network holds an option on all your contracts for next season. We intend to pick up those options."

"Suppose we went public with our unhappiness," Harrow said. "Suppose *I* went on strike."

"I don't think you will, J.C."

"And why not, Dennis?"

"Because you owe me."

And Harrow did.

When Harrow had gone off script, on live TV, pledging *Crime Seen* resources to track down his family's killers, Byrnes could have fired him. Could have sued him, and hung him out to dry.

Instead, Byrnes had backed his play.

Ellen and David Harrow's murders would have almost certainly gone unavenged without Dennis Byrnes.

". . . Okay, Dennis. You're right. I do owe you."

Byrnes did not allow anything gloating to come in his smile.

"I owe you and I'll stay, for *one more season . . .* but my people? They're free to go."

The executive shrugged elaborately. "I will exercise my right to try to convince them with pay raises, J.C., but they will not be held to the options in their contracts. I promise you that."

"Okay."

Harrow's phone vibrated—caller ID: CARMEN.

Harrow didn't leave his seat—there was nothing Carmen Garcia might call about that Byrnes couldn't hear.

Without preamble, Carmen said, "She won't let me in."

"She who?"

"Byrnes's secretary."

"*Kate*," the secretary said loud enough to carry over the phone. "My name is *Kate*." The last part Harrow and Byrnes both heard through the door.

Pushing a button, Byrnes said, "Kate, what is going *on* out there?"

The answer came by way of the door flying open and Carmen Garcia bursting in, dark hair bouncing off her shoulders, open laptop computer in her arms, the unhappy blonde secretary in her wake.

Carmen was holding up the computer as she strode straight to Harrow. "You *need* to see this. *Now*."

"We're in the middle of a meeting here," Byrnes protested irritably.

"This is more important," Carmen said, fearless in the face of the network president. "You might explain to your secretary that news has a shelf life."

While Byrnes and Kate looked on in offended surprise, Carmen set the computer on the executive's desk but facing Harrow, who quickly found himself watching a video stream. Though the image was surprisingly high quality, it seemed to be nothing more than amateur porn.

And the absurdity of that made Harrow wonder if Carmen had lost her mind. News? What made homegrown smut *news*?

On-screen, a long-haired blonde lay stomach-down on a bed, obviously having rear-entry sex, face turned toward camera, her lover almost entirely off camera, his back to the viewer, but not blocking the blonde much from this angle, as she writhed, her moans of pleasure loud and long, distorted through the computer's small speakers.

"Carmen," Harrow demanded, patience frayed, "what the hell is this?"

"Not what you think it is—keep watching."

The blonde on screen was clearly enjoying the vigorous lovemaking, but the longer Harrow watched, the more he realized that something was slightly off-kilter.

Maybe the woman was drunk or high, but something, *something*, seemed amiss. When the man finished, the blonde turned over on her back, her eyes open but half-lidded and unfocused. She was very pretty.

Harrow threw Carmen a look, but she pointed to the screen. "Keep watching."

As the man disappeared completely off camera, the woman tried to get up and slowly slumped back to the bed.

Byrnes and Kate had moved around to where they could see the screen better.

"What's wrong with her?" Byrnes asked.

"High," Kate and Carmen said in unison. They exchanged an awkward pause, adversaries suddenly teammates.

Shaking his head, Byrnes asked, "Why get so high you can't even enjoy . . ."

"You assume," Kate said, cutting him off, "it was her choice. Ever hear of roofies, Dennis?"

Even as the pair traded a frowning glance, Carmen shushed them.

On-screen, the woman was on her back on the bed, head lolling slightly. She had given up trying to rise.

A metallic voice came through the speakers. *"Beautiful, isn't she?"*

"Voice filter," Harrow said.

A hand came into view, stroked the woman's hair, getting it out of her face, improving the view of her blurry-eyed beauty.

"You may call me Don Juan," the voice said. *"This is my audition tape—I intend to become your next star . . . the new star attraction of* Crime Seen"

All eyes went to Carmen for some sort of explanation.

"Watch," she said, grimacing. An order, but an apologetic one.

A knife flashed through the frame and slashed into the woman's throat, severing the carotid artery. Blood spurted and a weak gurgling scream reminded Harrow of a rabbit's cry when a hawk swooped in and carried it off. Then the scream dissipated amid more gurgling and the struggle for air as a victim drowned on her own blood. . . .

Kate recoiled from the computer, and Byrnes had to catch her.

Harrow, though, remained glued to the screen, watching this beautiful young woman grasp feebly at her neck, trying to hold in the spurting blood, turning her fingers runny, smudgy scarlet. She only grew weaker, her attempts more feeble. . . .

Then she was gone.

"Don Juan again. When I love a woman, she has been loved so completely, so well, that she has no more reason

to live. Nothing else to look forward to, since I never re-peat myself—no woman is worthy of receiving my love twice."

"Sick," Kate said, looking like she would be.

"I do apologize for making demands—I know produc-ers do not like to be bossed around by talent."

Harrow and Byrnes shared an awkward glance.

"You will cast me as your new star on Crime Seen, *or I'm afraid, face the consequences. Give me my rightful glory, my proper respect . . . and air time . . . and I will keep my fatal seductions down to one a week."*

Harrow frowned.

"But if you do not accede to my demands . . . let's call them 'requests,' we are all friends here, collaborators . . . I will have to accelerate the frequency. Now, you may be asking yourself if you have just witnessed a master of spe-cial effects . . . no. This is real. This is realism. By way of proof, you will find the body of my latest lover within twenty-four hours. She will serve as proof that I am sin-cere."

Harrow said, "My God—he's not kidding. It *is* a goddamn audition tape. . . ."

"I will expect your answer on this Friday's show, or next week you will meet two *of my satisfied lovers. The week after,* three *lovely women will die on camera . . . and I have the stamina and will power and seductive skills to expand to daily conquests if need be. So it's up to you, UBC. And to the star of the show—J.C. Harrow? I have this personal message."*

"Bastard," Harrow said.

"Don't be envious. My popularity will soar—it will exceed your own. But jealousy is beneath real artists like ourselves, Mr. Harrow. You know . . . and I know . . .

that a true hero is only as strong as his adversary. And now you have a worthy one."

Carmen's laptop went blank, and the audio ended.

Feeling like he'd been poleaxed, Harrow said, "Where in the hell did this come from?"

"Cyber tip line," Carmen said. "Came in as an attached file."

"Is it real?" Byrnes asked.

Verging on hysteria, Kate said, "It *looks* real! It looks *terribly* real!"

Carmen said, "Effects on screen—like the *Saw* movies, and those Rob Zombie ones—*they* look real, too."

"I missed those," Harrow said dryly. "But like Don Juan himself said—those aren't special effects. Not in my opinion, anyway."

Kate leaned into Byrnes, who put an arm around her, a protective father standing there, just shaking his head.

"Get Jenny on it," Harrow said to Carmen.

Byrnes finally found his voice. The tanned exec was now blister pale. "My God . . . we created a serial killer."

"No, Dennis," Harrow said. "We didn't."

The network president stared at him blankly, his mind obviously awhirl.

"Dennis, a killer like this? He'd be at it whether we had a show or not. In his twisted mind, *Crime Seen* provides a rationalization—it tells him that his actions are somehow acceptable."

Byrnes pointed to Carmen's computer, the way

the Ghost of Christmas Future pointed at Scrooge's headstone.

"You meet the parents of that young woman," he said, "you think they'll give a damn about semantics? 'Don Juan' said he wanted to star on *Crime Seen,* and that's all people will hear."

Well, Harrow thought, at least Byrnes hadn't reacted by saying they had a new ratings sensation on their hands. But it would have been more encouraging had the exec acknowledged that they just watched a young woman die. On screen.

Byrnes was saying, "Kate, get legal on the phone and get them the hell up here."

Steady in the storm, Harrow said, "Dennis— there's something far more important to do first."

"What could *possibly* be more important than protecting the network's ass?"

Harrow held Byrnes's gaze. "Assuming that film is real? We need to call the LAPD, and help them get this madman off the street."

Chapter Ten

Nursing an abiding anxiety neither would have admitted to the other, Lieutenant Anna Amari and Detective LeRon Polk stood in the parking lot above the Hollywood sign, at the edge of the hill, looking down. Next to them loomed the black truck of the LAPD bomb squad.

The vehicle looked like a fire engine, but rather than hoses and axes, its cabinets were filled with the tools of the bomb-disposal craft, the robot with the tank treads used for observation and disposal, and the suits of the technicians who actually disarmed the bombs.

Sergeant Platt of the bomb squad had provided Amari with a headset, so he could communicate with her while he worked on the suspicious control box just outside the Hollywood sign's fenced-in area.

Below, Platt knelt before the metal box as if in prayer (Amari wondered if prayer was constant in that phase of the process). But his hands weren't in prayer mode—they held a ten-inch vitamin-pill-shaped XR-150 portable X-ray machine.

Polk said, "What's he doing? Should this be *takin'* this long?"

She covered her headset's mic. "He's x-raying the S.O.B. And, yes, he should take as long as he feels necessary. Would you rather he rush?"

"He can take all day," Polk said, backtracking. "We safe up here?"

"Hide behind the truck if you like."

Polk's expression said, *That's not fair*, and it wasn't, but she saw him glance at the truck, as if considering the offer.

Down the hill, Platt rose in slow motion and stepped back the same way.

In her headset, Amari heard, *"We'll develop the picture, then we'll know if we have a problem or not."*

"That a lengthy process?" Amari asked.

She didn't run into bomb-squad situations much on the sex crimes beat. Actually, this was a first.

"*Not long*," Platt said, and he turned and climbed up toward them.

Platt might have been an astronaut in his olive drab spaceman-style suit. When he finally reached the top, he handed off the XR150 to a colleague, not so attired, and pulled off the hooded helmet with its clear plastic visor. He stood before them dripping sweat and grinning, a guy with a military-short blond crew cut and friendly, regular features.

"I'm pretty sure there's something in there," he said. "We'll know in a few minutes."

Amari nodded.

"Probably a good call," he told her, "bringing us in."

Perhaps feeling bad for being short with her partner, she told the bomb squad guy, "It was Detective Polk's idea. I'd've got us both blown to hell."

Platt nodded to Polk. "Better to have a good head on your shoulders, son, than to get it blown off."

She could see Polk was trying not to show he was proud of himself. She'd had worse partners.

Platt's buddy handed the spaceman a Diet Coke and a towel and they waited. Amari thought, *If I was risking my life on a daily basis, I'd drink a regular Coke—hell with calories.*

When the X-ray had been developed, Platt showed Amari the device they'd discovered inside the control box.

"Pretty straightforward," Platt said, studying the picture. He showed it to the detectives. "This wire that's shadowed? That might be something."

Polk frowned. "Might?"

"I'll know better when I get the box open . . ." Platt shrugged. ". . . but it looks pretty simple."

"You sure?" she asked.

"No," Platt admitted. He slipped the helmet back over his head and lumbered back down to the control box.

They watched as he again approached the metal altar, knelt before it, and used bolt cutters to take the lock off.

"*Here we go,*" he said into Amari's ear.

Superficially, Platt seemed calm. But she could hear the anxiety.

Platt popped the door . . .

. . . *and a ball of fire erupted.*

"Shit!" Polk said, jumping back.

"*Shit,*" Platt said in Amari's hear, so close to simultaneously that it might have been comic in other circumstances.

She had jumped, too, and now watched in horror as gray-black smoke consumed the area where Platt had stood. Before the smoke had utterly blotted the lower hillside out, she thought she'd seen Platt blown backward.

Then she was running, Polk's footfalls echoing just behind her, crunching dry grass.

They got to Platt in just seconds, the plume of smoke already thinning, rising into nothing, and they only coughed a few times as they found him sitting on the ground with his legs out, like a picnicker waiting for a basket. He was pulling off the helmet.

"Are you all right?" she asked, sliding to a stop next to him.

"Yeah, yeah," he said, irritably. He lumbered to his feet, Polk helping him. "Small explosive, nothing really—smoke and sparks. Just enough to burn up any evidence . . . and put a scare into us."

"Worked," Polk said.

"It did," Platt admitted. "I damn near pissed myself, which is no fun in this suit, let me tell you."

Amari said, "So it was more a 'screw you' than anything?"

"Yeah."

Platt trudged up the hill, to get out of his space-man suit and snag another Diet Coke and towel.

The smoke was gone, just an acrid memory, by the time the crime-scene techs moved in, and when they were done with the scorched box, all Marty Rue had to show Amari was several plastic bags filled mostly with burned wiring from where the killer had spliced into the camera feed.

"That's the whole shootin' match?" Amari asked.

"From an evidentiary standpoint," Rue said, "yes indeed."

"Well," Polk said, "what is there *not* from an evidentiary standpoint?"

Rue pulled off his glasses, wiped the sweat from his face with a hand, then put the glasses back on. "Most of it was burnt to a crisp, but I *did* see enough to know how the bastard did it."

"That's something, anyway," Amari said. "How?"

"Spliced into the webcam and fed in a loop of a normal night—something he had recorded in the last few days, probably."

"What about the motion detectors?"

"That's the cool part," Rue said.

"Cool?" Polk asked skeptically.

Rue shrugged. "From the killer's standpoint, cool. From a security standpoint, stupid. Y'see, when he got into the box, and spliced into the camera feed? He just turned off the motion detectors."

"No," Amari said, wide-eyed. "Flipped the switch?"

Rue nodded, half smiling. "It's still in the off position. But I checked to make sure. No evidence the motion detectors had been tampered with or that there were any extra wires in there. He knew his stuff, Anna."

Amari said, "Some serious planning."

"Oh yeah," Rue said. "Guy either picked the lock or had a key. He sure as hell didn't hurt it." Rue held up a bag that contained two pieces of lock, the hasp still neatly clasped.

"Thoughts, Marty?"

"This is an organized killer," he said. "And my guess is he's one smart bastard. You better find a way to stop him fast, Anna, or this 'Don Juan' of yours will be collecting more lovers."

Amari smirked. "You *do* know we already have a psycho in West Hollywood to catch?"

"I heard. You know what the song says, Anna."

"I do?"

"Never rains in California. It just pours. Just pours."

While Amari and Polk walked back to their car, the coroner's team was bringing the body up the hill to their wagon. Up top, she watched the sad procession, Polk at her side.

When the body bag had gone into the back of the vehicle, she said to Polk, "That girl was alive and well yesterday, LeRon."

"Yes she was."

"Let's do our best not to have to stand and pay these kind of respects to any more victims. Okay?"

"I hear you, Lieutenant."

As the coroner's van pulled away, Amari called her boss to deliver a preliminary report on what they knew so far.

When Captain Womack answered, the first words

out of his mouth were, "Just getting ready to call *you*."

"Yeah, sorry," Amari said. "Took longer than we thought." She filled him in on the booby-trapped control box, then gave him the details about the crime scene.

Womack asked, "You say he signed the note Don Juan?"

Her boss's voice had a funny edge.

"Yeah," Amari said, brow furrowing. "Why, does that mean something to you?"

"Hell, Anna, that's the reason I was getting ready to call you."

"What is?"

"Don Juan."

"Really."

"Really. Anna—before you come in, stop by UBC."

"What, the TV network?"

"Yeah. They received some sort of video communication from somebody calling himself 'Don Juan' just this morning."

"Hell. Okay. Who do I ask for?"

"J.C. Harrow."

"Aw shit," she said, rolling her eyes. "Frickin' *Crime Seen*'s got this? So we can't even grab a breath before this goes straight to media circus?"

Womack paused, then: "You don't know Harrow, do you, Anna?"

"No, but I saw the show once," she said, not wanting to confess she watched it every Friday night.

"Well, I've met the guy," Womack said. "He's former law enforcement, as you must know. A straight shooter, Anna. He'll work with us. I think you can probably trust him."

There was a ringing endorsement.

"All right, Cap," she said with a sigh.

She rang off and told Polk about the call.

"J.C. Harrow's a damn *TV* star," Polk said. "What makes the cap think he's going to play ball?"

Amari shrugged and put the car in gear. "Ours is not to reason why, LeRon. Ours is but to—"

"I know the rest of it," Polk said.

Chapter Eleven

Laurene Chase and the rest of the *Killer TV* team group took the chairs provided in a loose semicircle around Byrnes's desk, where the network president already sat. Harrow and a massive, bald, well-dressed African American were at Byrnes's shoulders, like bodyguards.

To nobody's surprise, Harrow took charge.

"Meet Lucian Richards Jr.," he said, "from UBC legal."

"Sorry to take you away from your lunch break," Richards said, in a God Almighty voice. "You'll soon understand why."

The team traded wary looks.

The attorney's navy-blue three-piece suit draped smartly, for so large a man, and Chase figured his gold Vacheron Constantin Patrimony watch retailed in the neighborhood of twenty grand.

Harrow swung the laptop on Byrnes's desk toward the group, merely saying what they were about to see had come in on the tip line.

Chase watched until it turned gruesome, then turned her attention to the team. She saw them all, from stoic Harrow to boisterous Choi, set their jaws firmly when Don Juan's metallic voice cut through the speakers.

Carmen was looking away—she had seen it enough times already.

When the homicidal home movie ended, Michael Pall spoke. "Lot of fake snuff flicks out there. This one looks real."

His voice uncharacteristically soft, Choi said, "Those weren't special effects."

Jenny, with no more expression than a bisque baby, said, "Nothing digital there."

Someday, kiddo, Chase thought, *all of that stuff you push down is going to come roiling up.*

Carmen said, "I was going through the overnight stuff and ran across the damn thing."

Harrow said, "We'll get Jenny right on tracing it, after this meeting."

"Done deal," Jenny said.

With a nod toward the laptop, Harrow said, "Does anyone doubt we've witnessed the birth of a serial killer?"

Pall, the profiling expert, said, "Not necessarily his debut. More a coming-out party."

"A serial killer *we* spawned," Byrnes said, face as gray as clay.

A rich baritone rumbled in like thunder.

"There are those," the attorney said, "who may

think the network itself is behind this, to boost ratings and ad revenue."

"Ratings?" Anderson said. "*Revenue?* Why would anyone think that? You've already heard us say this is no fake."

Richards said, "How many shoulders would you have to tap, down on the street, before you found somebody who thinks the moon landings were staged? And somebody else who thinks the president was born in Kenya?"

Harrow said, "All due respect, Mr. Richards, I don't think our audience is that cynical. They know we're sincere about what we do on *Crime Seen.*"

"J.C.'s right," Carmen said. "No significant number of viewers will think that we elaborately faked this video, much less set a serial killer loose to goose ratings."

"Wouldn't be the first time a show created 'killer' ratings," Richards said. "A Brazilian TV host, one Wallace Souza, was indicted for hiring hit men to provide him material to cover on his reality show."

"No," Choi said, eyes wide.

"Yes," Richards said, calm as a funeral director.

Chase, anger spiking her voice, said, "Are you suggesting we copied this Brazilian dipstick's MO? What sort of absurd—"

"I'm not suggesting anything, Ms. Chase," Richards cut in. "I am here to advise Mr. Byrnes, and yourselves, of the legal ramifications of this unfortunate situation. And to provide you with some . . . call it, informed kibitzing."

Choi said to the attorney, "If we *do* come under fire, or suspicion, or whatever . . . are you going to represent us?"

But Carmen answered for him, "No. His job is to protect UBC."

"And how do you propose to do that?" Choi asked Richards.

This time Pall answered for the attorney: "Yank our show off the air and sweep that video under the rug. Out of sight, out of mind."

"No, they won't do that," Choi said, cockiness returning. "We make them too much money."

Carmen said, "We could also *cost* them a lot of money."

"I agree," Pall said. "We have apparently inspired one of our viewers to 'try out' to be our next 'guest' villain. Even if legal payback proves impractical for the parents of the victim, the attacks on us and UBC from the media would be as merciless as what that maniac did to that poor girl."

They all pondered that.

Chase sighed, shook her head. "J.C.—what do you think? Should this tape, with the killer's request for attention, be buried?"

Harrow didn't hesitate: "No."

"You'd give *in* to him?" Jenny said, the disappointment in her voice palpable.

"I didn't say that."

Anderson, similarly disappointed, asked, "You'd *air* that foul thing?"

"I didn't say that either." Harrow moved up alongside the seated Byrnes. "We *don't* air it . . . but neither do we bury it. We can't shrug it off and pretend we thought it was a hoax."

"What's left?" Carmen asked.

Chase said, "Call the police, like good citizens."

Harrow nodded. "We're just TV performers, after all. This is a matter for the authorities."

Richards said, "I speak for network legal when I say I agree with you, J.C.—I must insist upon you calling the police. And do *not* air this video."

Pall said, "Stop and consider, Mr. Richards— everyone. I understand that if we were to give in, and air this thing, a maniac owns us. But remember, he does not ask us to keep the police out—in fact, he *wants* to go public . . . *TV* public."

"Agreed," Harrow said.

Pall went on: "But if we *don't* air the video—if we fail to give him what he wants—we risk two women dying at this madmen's hands next week."

Looking sick, Byrnes said, "If word gets out that two women died because we didn't air a video . . . then what becomes of *Crime Seen,* and UBC?"

"You might add the two *women* to that list," Carmen said sharply.

Good for you, Chase thought.

Then Chase said, "J.C., the cops are understaffed and overworked right now. Even if they decide Don Juan presents a genuine threat, there isn't a hell of a lot they can do about it."

Pall said, "I hear the crime lab is backed way the hell up."

"Meanwhile," Choi said, "we sit on our hands? *Really?*"

Clearly Harrow had been mulling all this.

He said, "*Crime Seen* has the best team of forensic scientists anywhere, and thanks to Dennis here,
some of the most cutting-edge lab equipment on
the planet. Maybe we could . . . lend a hand."

Byrnes's eyes flashed. "Well . . . if you *do* . . . it's
as part of the show. Cameras come along."

Harrow shrugged. "You and UBC are paying the
freight, aren't you? Sure, the cameras come along."

Anderson was shaking that surfer-boy blond
head of his, saying, "The LAPD is *not* about to let
us in on this investigation."

Chase said, "Why, were we planning on asking
permission?"

That got some smiles, but Anderson pressed:
"Those small-town sheriff and police departments
we ran into on the Kansas case, they were under-
manned. They were happy for the help, and glad
to rub shoulders with TV personalities."

Choi said, "Is that what we are?"

Chase said, "You wish."

But Anderson kept going: "LAPD are pros
among pros, they're good, and they live in, you
know . . . Tinsel Town. They are *not* impressed by
faces a heck of a lot more famous than ours. We
step on the toes of the LAPD and there will be hell
to pay."

At least he said "hell," Chase thought, *not "heck."*

Jenny said, "So we go sub rosa."

Everybody looked at her, surprised.

"Hey," she said, with a shrug and a girlish smile.
"You know what the bad guys say? It only counts
when they catch you."

Smiles blossomed on the *Killer TV* faces, even

the skeptical Anderson's; but Byrnes and the attorney remained somber.

The latter looked at his expensive watch, cleared his throat for effect, then said, "I, uh, just remembered I have another meeting. Anything you've said so far is strictly hypothetical, understood? Why don't you people discuss the situation, while Dennis and I step out of the office."

"No," Byrnes snapped, "I want to *hear* this."

"Actually," Richards said, with a meaningful glance, "you don't."

Not used to being ordered around, the executive seemed about to protest when Richards held up two fingers, as if he were making the peace sign.

In his deepest, richest baritone, the attorney said, "Two words, Dennis—plausible deniability."

Byrnes rose. "Funny thing is, I have an appointment, too."

They left.

"Alone at last," Choi said.

Taking the president's desk chair, Harrow said, "Look, if the cops find out we're working on this, the shit will be about chin high. Anybody got a problem with that? You might not get a job in *real* law enforcement again."

Nobody said a word.

"Okay. Jenny, start tracing the sender of that foul thing. You *can* do that?"

"Depends on how smart he is," Jenny said.

"We'll assume extremely. Carmen, you start working on identifying the victim. Get a good screen capture of her face and discreetly distribute it. Rest of you, go through this video frame by damn frame. We need *something* and we've only got five days till air. After that, we're going to have him on the prowl again."

Chase asked, "What about the LAPD?"

"We cooperate. We do whatever they ask, short of staying out of the investigation. We don't advertise that we're conducting, as Jenny put it, our own sub rosa inquiry."

"With cameras on us," Chase said.

"Yes. Dennis gets his due. And what we're up to eventually will come out—within five days, likely." Harrow sent his eyes from face to face. "Everything comes to me first, then straight to the LAPD."

Carmen said, "We'll need an LAPD officer to be our liaison. I can look into that."

"Do it." Harrow rose, and so did everybody else.

Jenny collected the laptop from the desk.

Quietly, Harrow said to her, "I don't want this video sent around by e-mail. Strictly DVD copies to our key team members."

"Sure. I'll get on that right now."

"Then how soon do I call the police?"

"Fifteen minutes."

He nodded.

Then to the team: "Let's go, people. Clock is running and, the opinion of the Rolling Stones notwithstanding, time is definitely *not* on our side."

Each team member had his or her own office—glorified closets, admittedly, but home when they weren't on the road. The furniture was strictly functional, gray metal office gear, although some had brought in their own stuff, to lend the cubicles a personal touch.

Chase's furniture was strictly what UBC had provided. Her only homey touches were a framed desk picture of Patty, her life partner who'd succumbed to cervical cancer two years ago now, and another of current squeeze, Nancy Hughes.

Also a philodendron that she had brought from Waco. The plant hadn't taken over the office yet, but the threat was there. *Feed me.* . . .

Choi somehow finagled a slightly larger space and seemed to have moved in, lugging in a dilapidated couch Chase refused to touch, let alone sit on (she had the feeling it had been lifted from a particularly nasty crime scene).

Before long, Jenny brought around a DVD for her, and Chase settled in with a bottle of vending-machine iced tea and prepared for a terrible afternoon at the movies.

She watched the disturbing images straight through, once. She had no doubt she was watching a genuine snuff film—a real murder captured on film. Or anyway, video.

Second time through, she turned her head away from the screen, not out of disgust (though she had plenty), but to take in only the sound, searching for any background noise that might provide a clue.

Chase was well aware that Jenny and her computer could do this better than such old-school methods, but she listened hard anyway. And anyway there was still plenty her human brain could process that an electronic one couldn't. She got nothing out of it, though. She repeated the process and again zippo.

Turning the sound down this time, she started working through the video a frame at a time.

The video was high-def. At least that small detail told her something—this killer either had some money or was a thief. Home-video high-def camcorders had come down in price, but were not cheap.

No sign that the woman, during the sex act, sensed anything wrong until the last second. Nor any indication the victim knew she was being recorded.

Still, this was *the* acting town, so who could say? The camera stayed in a fixed position, hidden, possibly behind two-way glass.

Next time through, Chase studied the room itself. Walls were dark, furniture limited to the brass bed and a barely visible nightstand, covered with some sort of filmy fabric, atop which sat what appeared to be a simple glass vase filled with roses.

She focused on the flowers. Aside from that philodendron, she knew squat about plants. Roses came in colors and there were scads of varieties, but that was the extent of her expertise.

Bed against a wall. Not a hotel room—Don Juan had a place of his own, she figured. She looked for shadows that might give away the position of a window or the sun or any damn thing . . .

. . . but there was nothing.

This bastard would kill again if they didn't stop

him; he would accelerate, as promised, if they didn't get him before he knew Harrow had not acceded to his demands.

There had to be *something* in this video, but Chase was damned if she could find it. Sitting back and sighing and shaking her head, she hoped the rest of the team was having better luck.

Then she started again.

Chapter Twelve

Amari felt something twist inside her as she watched this morning's corpse return to life. Not quite vibrant life, because the blonde seemed druggy to Amari. Still, the woman appeared to be enjoying the sex she shared with her barely glimpsed lover.

She made a mental note to make a priority of checking the victim's tox screen. She already suspected that Don Juan had dosed his victim with flunitrazepam, better known by the trade name Rohypnol, more commonly called roofies.

When the video ended, Harrow closed the lid of the laptop with a somber finality.

Polk sat with a wide-eyed, bloodless expression, still trying to process what he'd just seen.

They were in Harrow's office at UBC. Harrow was behind his desk, and network president Dennis Byrnes and attorney, Lucian Richards, Jr., bookended Amari and Polk, in visitor's chairs.

Amari said to Harrow, "When exactly did you receive this, Mr. Harrow?"

"One of our writer-producers, Carmen Garcia, showed it to me early this afternoon She interrupted a meeting I was having with Dennis."

Amari nodded. "But you didn't call the police until *when?*"

"I'm sure you *know* when the call came in."

Byrnes said, "We wanted to get an educated opinion on what this thing is, before calling you."

"Well, it's somebody cutting a woman's throat, Mr. Byrnes, and then stabbing her repeatedly."

"Lieutenant Amari, we get a lot of prank and crank tips at *Crime Seen.* We needed to try to ascertain if this was genuine or staged, before possibly wasting your time."

"Just what scientific standards did you use to deduce whether or not this is footage of a real murder?"

Harrow said, "You probably know we have a top forensics team, culled from law enforcement all around the country. We got their read on it. Subjective but informed."

The lawyer, Richards, said, "Mr. Byrnes also called me in for an opinion. I'm no forensics expert, but if this is genuinely someone committing murder to try to blackmail his way onto one of the network's shows, getting a legal read on the situation was prudent."

Amari's half smile joined an arched eyebrow. "Obstructing justice is *prudent* in your view, Counselor?"

"Obstruction of justice was hardly our intention. We called you, and you're sitting here now, and we're cooperating. Why are we splitting hairs over a few minutes?"

"Your intention here is pretty clear, Counselor. Mr. Byrnes was trying to figure a way not to get burned by this thing . . . and *you* made *him* call *us*."

"Actually," Byrnes said, raising a forefinger in a point of clarification manner, "I didn't make the call. . . ."

She frowned at the exec.

Harrow leaned nearer her. "*I* did."

"Why you?" Amari asked.

"Because I'm at the top of the *Crime Seen* food chain."

"Not over the network president, you aren't. What made any of you decide to call at all? You could've buried this thing. Deleted it, and if somehow you got called on it, dismissed your actions by saying you thought it was a hoax."

He nodded toward the laptop. "I think a young woman is dead, and somewhere a family is wondering why they haven't heard from their little girl."

Amari said nothing, just cast a glance toward Polk, who was watching the exchange intently, but staying out of it.

Harrow caught the look.

"You already knew," he said.

Byrnes said, "Already knew what?"

Both Amari and Harrow ignored that.

"I already knew," she admitted with a nod.

Byrnes insisted: "Knew *what?*"

The lawyer answered in his sonorous rumble: "That the woman was dead."

Harrow said, "You found her. Where?"

Amari's smile was gentle despite the tension. "Do you really expect me to answer that?"

Harrow smiled back. "Sometimes I forget I'm the media now. I was a cop for a long, long time."

"I could tell you off the record."

Polk said, "Lieutenant, I don't think—"

She raised a hand to silence her partner.

"Off the record," Harrow said quietly. "Have you identified her?"

Amari gave him the broad outline—the body at the Hollywood sign, the roses, the note, the booby-trapped control box.

"I appreciate this," Harrow said.

"Don't be too grateful. That's no more than'll be on the LAPD press release. You're just getting it a few hours early." She nodded toward the laptop. "Obviously we need that video."

He shrugged. "My computer expert, Jenny Blake, will arrange to give your techs access to everything you'll need. In the meantime, we can give you a DVD."

"Appreciate that. And we'll want to talk to Ms. Garcia. But there's one more thing. Something you won't like, Mr. Harrow."

"Try me."

"You and your people—your so-called *Killer TV* forensics superstars? You need to stay away from this investigation."

Byrnes sat exclamation-mark straight. "Lieutenant, *Crime Seen* is, in its way, a news show. We reserve our constitutional right to cover a news story . . . and this is most definitely a news story."

Amari glared at the exec. "First of all, *Crime Seen* is not a news show. It's reality TV. Don't piss in my ear, Mr. Byrnes, because I know rain when I hear it."

Byrnes shifted in his chair.

"Second, if you interfere with this investigation in any way, you will soon learn how serious a charge obstruction of justice can be. And all of you connected to that video, and the decision on how and when to bring the LAPD into it, will quickly find out just how much fun it is cooling your heels as material witnesses in lockup."

The attorney spoke gentle thunder: "Lieutenant Amari, UBC will do whatever you ask, whatever you say."

"Good," Amari said. "Because I say butt out of this investigation. And I'm *not* asking."

"Done," Richards said.

"And you are not to air *any* portion of that video. Not *one second.*"

"Agreed."

Her eyes swung to Byrnes and gave him a laser look. "Mr. Richards, I want to hear *him* say it."

The attorney nodded to his client.

"We won't air it," Byrnes said unenthusiastically.

She turned to Harrow. "You're quiet."

"I could be saying something about First Amendment rights right now."

"You could be."

"But I won't."

"Really?"

"Really. I wouldn't have run that vile thing even if Dennis had fired me over it."

She wanted to believe him. But this was a man who had once shot a perp dead on live TV. How much farther over the line could you go than that?

She sneaked a look at Byrnes. The executive appeared glumly exasperated. Evidently, *he* believed Harrow.

"Why *not* run it?" she asked, as if casually exploring the hypothetical. "Just pixilate the areas of nudity and gore, and you've got a real ratings winner."

"Ratings aren't my job," Harrow said. "We try to do the right thing at *Crime Seen*, and if the public doesn't like what's on offer, I'll find something else to do."

Polk chuckled. "Are you kiddin', man?"

Byrnes muttered, "I wish he were."

"Okay, Mr. Harrow," Amari said. "I'm gonna choose to believe you. But if you're playing me, you'll pay for it."

He grinned at her. The first full-on grin she'd got from him. "I can tell you this much, Lieutenant—I believe *you*."

With a smile, Amari rose, nodded to the exec and the lawyer; then Polk trailed her to the door.

Falling in just behind, Harrow said, "To whatever extent you might want or need it, Lieutenant, know that you'll have the complete cooperation of *Crime Seen*."

"Thanks," Amari said, if somewhat warily.

"I'll walk you out," he said.

They were in the hallway, Byrnes and Richards behind a closed door now, where Amari began, "Look, Mr. Harrow . . ."

"Make it 'J.C.,' would you?"

"J.C. I'm sorry if I seemed to come down hard-ass on you in there."

"Hey, Lieutenant, I've—"

"Make it 'Anna.' "

"Anna, I spent plenty of time on your side of the fence—sheriff, DCI investigator . . . that's Iowa's criminal investigation department. I know what it's like to have pressure from above to close cases, and I sure as hell know it's easier to do that if the media isn't breathing down your neck."

"That was a nice speech, J.C."

"Thanks. And I didn't even use a teleprompter."

That made her laugh. Suddenly Polk was tagging behind as the trio headed back toward the elevator.

As they were standing there waiting for a down arrow, Amari suddenly realized she had the host of *Crime Seen* as an audience. How surreal.

In a what-the-hell moment, she said, "Say, J.C.—there *is* another case we're working on I wouldn't mind some help with."

She caught Polk cocking his head, frowning slightly.

"What can I do?" Harrow asked.

The elevators doors opened and they got aboard, Polk hitting the button for the lobby, keeping an eye on the other two, like they were kids up to no good.

Amari said to Harrow, "We're on another murder, too, a brutal thing—took place about ten days ago."

"You do work sex crimes, right? Not homicide?"

"Right. But this is like Don Juan—it falls on our side of the line."

"However we can help," Harrow was saying, "we will."

"Okay," she said. "A week ago Friday we caught a homicide at the Star Struck Hotel. Very nasty. Male victim, emasculated and stabbed to death."

Harrow just listened.

"That's in West Hollywood," Polk put in.

Amari said, "Room registered to Jeff Bailey. Body we found does not match the security video of the guy who checked in as Bailey the day before."

The doors opened and they walked in lockstep into the lobby, footsteps making little gunshot echoes.

"And you have a dead body with no ID," Harrow said, "and I'm guessing no clues as to the identity of the killer, *or* the man who checked into the hotel in the first place."

"Sums it up," she said.

"Well," Harrow said with an easygoing shrug, "we could broadcast pictures of your vic and the man who checked into the room."

"That might *really* help," Amari said. "A forensic artist has done a drawing of the victim—it'd be better that than a photo of the corpse."

"Agreed."

"Just so you know, we already ran it on the local news and got bupkes."

"I did see that," Harrow said. "You didn't let the papers know about the emasculation aspect."

"Right." She'd actually slipped, revealing that; but she found herself feeling cop-to-cop with Harrow. "And that's off the record."

"No problem."

A petite ponytailed blonde in a T-shirt and jeans materialized.

Harrow said, "Lieutenant Anna Amari, this is Jenny Blake, our resident computer guru."

Amari smiled and extended her hand. "I recognize Ms. Blake from your show, of course."

Handshakes and introductions over, Jenny and Polk went off to work out the LAPD getting the Don Juan video and access to UBC computers.

Meanwhile, Amari and Harrow stood near the glass doors onto the street.

"I'll get you a copy of the artist's drawing and the pertinent hotel security video," Amari told him. "How soon can you get them on the air?"

"Friday night," Harrow said. "I'll showcase it right at the top. We have a hell of a lot bigger audience than local news."

She smiled. "Well, thank you."

"Not a problem. Always ready to look after a fellow officer's interests."

"Only you're not a fellow officer anymore."

"Really, I am. Better you get to know me, more you'll see that."

"This assumes I get to know you better."

"Call it wishful thinking."

"You're not trying to soften me up, are you?"

"*Moi?*"

That coming from this craggy ex-cop made her laugh; it echoed a little in the lobby. Then she turned solemn.

"J.C., you're not going to stay out of this Don Juan thing."

"Was that a question?"

"Not really. I was paying attention when that sleazeball boss of yours and his pet lawyer were making all those promises . . . and you? J.C., you weren't saying shit."

Harrow didn't say shit in response, either.

"I know you're pissed this Don Juan prick has singled you and your show out. I get that. This guy is trying to blackmail you. He's taking the good things you've done on *Crime Seen* and twisting them into something ugly, something dark. But surely you can't imagine that, in some weird way, you're to *blame* for what he's done."

"I don't," Harrow said simply.

". . . Really? Not playing with me, J.C.?"

"No.

I don't blame myself for the actions of this evil son of a bitch. Anna, you and I are both cop enough to know this one would be killing whether or not *Crime Seen* even existed."

She only nodded.

Then she said, "Okay, here's the deal. You get in my way, I mow you down—got it?"

"Sounds fair."

"You air anything you find without bringing it to me first, I'll run your ass in for obstruction."

"Promise?"

"Are you flirting with me, J.C.?"

"Maybe. But there's one thing we can agree on."

"What's that?"

"Don Juan has to go down—soon. He has all the earmarks of somebody who will kill and kill and kill again."

"No argument."

He extended his hand.

They shook. His hand felt warm, not at all moist, strong, reassuring.

"Go get him," Harrow said.

Chapter Thirteen

At six-foot-three, weighing in at around one-eighty, Danny Terrant sometimes felt that in his Santa Monica police uniform he resembled nothing so much as a sandy-topped, navy-blue number-two pencil.

This morning, he and his partner Bobby Nucci had caught a domestic disturbance call at an apartment on Euclid—their first of the day, but one of countless in their experience.

Short, plump, black-haired Bobby was Oliver Hardy to Danny's Stan Laurel. The pair had buddied up at the academy and, not long ago—after stints for both with older, more seasoned partners—had found themselves back together.

When they got to the Gruner residence, the wife met them at the door, one hundred pounds of frazzled punching bag for the angry three hundred pounds of husband looming behind her. Patsy was a thirtyish bottle blonde and husband

Lloyd was a helmet-haired behemoth in a XX-L Knicks T-shirt.

Nobody was screaming, which was good, but Danny could sense the Gruners were merely resting between rounds. As Danny took Patsy's statement, Nucci led the husband to a neutral corner in the cracker-box apartment. This was not far enough away to prevent Lloyd from hearing his beloved refer to him disparagingly—i.e., "That fat-ass son of a bitch hits me *all* the goddamn time and I'm *sick* and goddamn *tired* of it."

And the bell rang and the battle was on again.

Burly Lloyd, his lank brown hair running down over his shoulders, made like a bull and charged past Nucci, heading for the kitchen table where Danny and Patsy sat.

Nucci got knocked out of the way by the husband and could do nothing to halt the giant except grab a handful of hair and another of Knicks tee and hang on, getting dragged like Randolph Scott behind an Indian's horse.

Rising from the table, right hand going for his hip holster, Danny just managed to get between husband and wife as Gruner barreled into him, cabbage-sized punches coming from every angle as the giant and Danny crashed into Patsy and sent furniture and bodies careening to the floor in a cracking crunch that the lanky cop hoped was wood and not bones.

Although Patsy managed to roll clear, Terrant hit the tile floor hard, Gruner landing on him, still punching, Nucci jumping on top of Gruner and trying to restrain him. Danny felt like he'd been working under a Buick and somebody kicked the jack out.

For a moment the skinny cop thought he might die, the air driven from his body by the weight of the pair wrestling on top of him, a big fat man and a small fat man. It probably looked way more comical than it felt. . . .

Danny struggled to get out from under, grappling with the pepper spray at his belt, while Patsy was getting to her feet. Hoping she might supply some sort of help, Danny was dismayed when her contribution turned out to be leaping atop Nucci, pulling the policeman's hair, and yelling shrilly to "leave my poor husband alone!"

This change of heart on Patsy's part put three people on top of skinny Danny Terrant, and he could feel himself growing lightheaded from the lack of oxygen. *I'll be the only underweight person*, he thought, *ever to die from not shedding enough fat.* . . .

But then the pepper spray found his hand and he was spritzing it everywhere he could. If his partner caught some, well, that was tuff-ski shit-ski. . . .

As if by magic, the bodies atop him tumbled away in various directions. Nucci and the Gruners were yelling and flailing and rubbing their eyes as they rolled around on the tile.

After sucking down two deep breaths, blessed oxygen once again coursing through his lungs, a triumphant Terrant rose, his Glock drawn.

Amid the screaming, Lloyd blindly lumbered toward Danny, yelling, "You mother fuh—"

That was as far as the big man got before Danny sidestepped him and brought the pistol down on the back of a neck rolling with fat. Despite the padding, Lloyd sagged to his knees, paused in what appeared to be buggy-eyed prayer, then flopped to the floor, unconscious. With some difficulty, Danny managed to handcuff the man, wrists behind him.

Nearby her tubby hubby, Patsy writhed, feverishly rubbing her eyes and screaming incoherently.

"Stop rubbing," Danny advised the woman. "You're only making things worse."

"Go screw yourself!" she shouted, still rubbing away.

Ah, he thought. *To serve and protect. . . .*

"You got it, Mrs. Gruner," he said.

"You *sprayed* me," Nucci moaned, as his partner helped him up. "I can't believe you sprayed me."

"I didn't spray you. I just sprayed. I was getting my ass crushed."

Nucci had nothing more to say, too busy trying to keep from rubbing his own peppered eyes. Danny knew what kind of agony Nucci was in—their training included getting similarly sprayed—and felt bad for his partner. But he would have done it again.

With the cuffs from Nucci's belt, Danny returned to Patsy and restrained her, as well, while she shrieked about "suing you *and* your goddamn department."

This and other obscene threats were hurled by the woman who had summoned them via 911 as Danny helped navigate the tap at a sink full of dirty dishes so his partner could flush his eyes.

They got the Gruners off to jail without further incident. The unhappy couple would face an impressive list of complaints, but other than a possible court appearance, Danny figured that was the end of it.

Not hardly.

Once the story got around the station, embellished vigorously by the red-eyed Nucci, Danny took a merciless ribbing from fellow officers the rest of the day. *Danny pepper-sprayed his own partner, high-lar-ious!* This, even though everybody agreed he'd done the right thing, even Nucci himself, when his eyes gradually cleared.

In fact, Bobby had said in the locker room, "You know, Danny boy, you probably saved *both* our asses. Those two mighta killed each other and made collateral damage out of us along the way."

Bobby was a good guy, but Danny didn't hang out with him off-duty much. Single, living in a low-rent apartment on Twenty-eighth Street, Danny Terrant didn't often socialize with his brother officers. Most were family men, and the few single guys hung out at meat-market-type clubs, trying to look as cool as the drug dealers they busted.

Danny Terrant wanted none of it. Just wasn't his style. Instead, he would go to Reseda, by himself, at least once every couple of weeks, to the Prairie Lights Bar. There, he could be somebody else, not an off-duty cop, just a nice single guy with an interest in something that was really fun, *real* fun . . . but something his coworkers would likely have made a laughingstock out of him over, had they known.

Line dancing.

Yes, Danny Terrant was into line dancing, into it all the way, and he didn't care to expose himself and his wholesome hobby to the ridicule of his "cool" brother cops.

That evening, having grabbed a fast-food supper on the way home, Danny outfitted himself in black western shirt (snaps not buttons), black chinos, his favorite cowboy boots, and a black cowboy hat. Finishing touch was the black belt with audaciously large silver belt buckle he'd won a couple of years ago in a mechanical bull riding contest.

In apparel like this, his lanky frame looked good. Looked *real* good. Checking out the effect in the mirror, he pronounced himself ready for fun, and hit the trail. Driving his new Mustang, he took off north from Santa Monica on the 405 headed for Reseda, listening to a Clint Black CD.

Before long, within the barn-wood walls of Prairie Lights, dancing to the blasting of Brooks & Dunn's "Boot Scootin' Boogie," Danny saw his day change from crapola into possibly the best night *ever*. . . .

She was a tall drink of water with curly red hair that framed green eyes, high cheekbones, and lush, red-glossed lips. Though she was slender, she had curves complemented by her tight jeans and a spaghetti-strap green top that contrasted nicely with the creamy white of her shoulders and glimpse of bosom. All this was set off by hand-tooled leather green-and-brown cowboy boots that must have cost a small fortune.

She sidled up next to Danny and gave him an

easy smile, which he was happy to return. They danced next to each other through another fast song, then another, and another. Finally, when a ballad began, they left the dance floor together, old friends.

At the bar, Danny introduced himself and asked if he could buy the lady a drink.

She nodded, but the blaring music, ballad or not, made it tough to be heard without shouting.

When bottles of beer arrived, she took hers, smiled, and leaning close said, "Gail Preston!"

"Nice to meet you, Gail!" he said, and they clinked bottles together in a tentative toast.

Funny thing was, she wasn't his type. She was tall and slender and so was he, and he preferred short, shapely little things who frankly made him feel big.

But something about her, something magnetic, even charismatic, drew him to her. And it wasn't like she was skinny—she had a nice full rack, and that bottom was sweet. Hell, Gail was a babe, a four-alarm fox.

Small talk at the bar was followed by what qualified as a quiet corner in Prairie Lights, where they ordered another round. Never a heavy drinker, Danny might have three or four beers over the course of an evening here. That might add up to a beer an hour, and he felt he danced 'em off.

Still, trips to the john at the Prairie Lights were hardly a rarity for him. He was a little surprised, however, to find his sea legs wobbly on his third trip or so.

When he got back to the tiny table, he found another bottle waiting for him. He *knew* he had to slow down. But he hoisted the beer and said, "Thanks."

She smiled and took a swig from her latest bottle.

"You know," Danny said, "most women don't come here alone. It's not a rough bar or anything, but . . . people tend to show up in groups."

Her smile was playful. "*You're* not a group."

"No. *We* could be a group. Our *own* group."

"There's an idea."

They clinked bottles again, not so tentatively.

"Achy Breaky Heart" was playing. Such an old corny song, and playing so *loud*. But it lent itself to line dancing, and the bunch out there was having a great time.

He thought about taking Gail back out onto the floor, but he didn't quite feel up to it. Anyway, he liked this quiet time with her.

As the world continued to wobble on its axis, Danny wondered if he was drunk not on beer but on this pretty woman, and the silly, giddy sense he was falling in love. He hadn't felt this way about a girl since high school. They just seemed to *connect*.

"Good thing you're in my group," he said.

"Is it?"

"Dangerous for a girl to come to a bar alone."

"Really?"

"There's a lot of date rape, and worse." He couldn't believe he'd said that. Not exactly romantic. . . .

"You said you were a cop. You must deal with some bad people."

He'd told her he was a cop in Santa Monica; she'd told him she worked for a Chicago company and made regular California visits.

"Bad people? Sometimes I do, yeah."

He told her about this morning. It had suddenly become an hilarious anecdote, and she laughed often and in a sweet, fetching way.

"Now I *know* I'm safe," she said, and she looped her arm in his. "With you."

"I don't know. I know some pretty rough characters on the PD."

"Then am *I* in danger?"

"From me? No way."

"Not even . . . date rape?"

She said that with a smile. A suggestive one. His head was doing a dipsy doodle.

Suddenly his voice sounded defensive to him. "I wouldn't . . . force a woman. I would never take advantage."

"I was just teasing. . . . Look, it's getting a little loud in here. Crowded, too. Maybe we should find someplace quieter. Where we can really . . . talk."

The noise was getting to Danny, too, contributing to his wooziness. Leaving the bar seemed like a good idea. He tried to think of some quiet place in Reseda, maybe a restaurant, when she made a much better suggestion.

"My motel's not far from here," Gail said, her smile just a glimmer at the corner of her mouth. Her expression held promise but also excitement, and a certain nervous edge.

"Uh, sure. Sounds good."

"I don't *ever* do this."

"What?"

"I don't pick up men. You need to know that. It's just . . . Danny, you're different. I feel like I've known you forever. So please . . . don't think badly of me."

"I don't! I'm not!" This was the soberest he'd felt in about an hour.

They rose, Danny hoping he could hold it together—his legs unsteady, his stomach, too. He was feeling like he might be getting the damn flu or something.

Following the lovely redhead toward the exit, he had the fleeting thought he should maybe beg off, collect her contact info, and just head for home. He could just see himself folding her into his arms and moving in for the kill and . . . throwing up in her lap.

But her swaying hips, in those tight blue jeans, were like the swing of a watch in a practiced hypnotist's hands.

Outside, with the sun down, a cool breeze swept in off the ocean, providing the fresh air Danny needed to feel a little better.

A concerned Gail took his arm. "You look a little green around the gills, honey. You okay?"

"I'm fine . . . never better."

Screw it.

He drew her close and kissed that lovely moist mouth, and she kissed back, her tongue darting into his mouth, like a teasing snake's. They kissed again, and again, then broke the clinch to come up for air.

"You're fine, all right," she said, her smile taking on a wry tilt. "You up to driving?"

No.

"Sure," he said.

She studied him. "Honey, you had twice as many beers as I did. . . ."

"Did I?"

"Why don't you just ride with me, and we'll bring you back here when you're feeling better?"

This was a decent enough neighborhood and his off-duty piece was safely hidden away in the spare tire compartment and locked inside the trunk.

"Good idea," he said. "You drive."

She led him to a white Kia Sorento. And then they were inside the vehicle, kissing in the darkness behind tinted windows. When he started nuzzling her shoulder and trying to get a hand under her top, she said, "Whoa there, big fella—don't leave it all in the gym. Save a little for the big game."

He grinned at her goofily. "Is there gonna be one?"

"I've got a nice big king-size bed in my motel room where we can discuss that."

"Okay," he said, with an even goofier smile.

As she pulled out of the parking lot, he asked, "What kind of work you do?"

"I'm a headhunter," she said.

"That sounds scary."

"Not for the one doing the hunting."

". . . If I wanted a better job in police work, could you help?"

"Sure."

Gail made a right onto Roscoe and he settled back into the seat and enjoyed the ride with the window down, the fresh air gliding over him. By the time they got to the motel, he was feeling better and—given this company—he figured he wasn't likely to pass out or fall asleep on Gail.

Tomorrow, he would have something to talk about with Nucci that wasn't the goddamn Gruners. In fact, when he got to Gail's room at a former Ramada Inn, and they were safely inside, her arms wrapped around him tight, his ribs—where Lloyd Gruner had piled on him—didn't even hurt anymore.

They kissed standing up for a while; then Gail fanned herself, let out some air, rolled her eyes, said, "Wow," and took a short breather. She built them each a mixed drink from some bottles of liquor and soda on the dresser; these they downed quickly, both eager to finish what they'd started.

Soon she was wrapping herself around him as they stood by the bed, kissing him hard, tongue darting in and out of his mouth, his hand on her blouse cupping a full, firm braless breast, its tip diamond hard.

The lightheaded feeling was coming back, but Danny didn't think that was the drink—he was drunk on Gail, and anyway there wasn't any blood in his head, not the *big* head, anyway. . . .

She unsnapped his shirt, quick but methodical; then her mouth moved down his neck onto his smooth, nearly hairless chest, even as her hands started fiddling with his belt and that giant, prize-winner's buckle.

Her kisses reached his stomach as she pushed him backward onto the bed, where he sat, legs dangling off its edge. She peppered his stomach with kisses as she unbuttoned his jeans, then tugged them to his ankles.

Danny fumbled with her top, but wasn't having much luck. For some reason, his hands seemed to be about half a minute behind his brain.

She stuck a thumb inside the waistband of his shorts, tugged them down, too, as his erection sprang up and had a look around, as if seeing what it had missed. The throb of his member was a pleasant ache, oddly the only feeling that seemed to dent the haze.

Then everything turned soft and warm as she slipped him into her mouth, suckled, then moved up and down the shaft as hypnotically as her sway-ing hips when they had lured him to this room.

She must have sensed how close he was and let him ease away. Rising, she said, "I have to slip some-thing in me, lover, before you can slip inside *me*. . . ."

"Mmmmmm," he said.

"Only be gone a minute. Get those damn boots off and be buck nekkid when I get back. I'll show you the kind of dancing you don't do in a line. . . ."

She smiled mischievously, and moved away.

Groggily, Danny sat up and tried to focus on her fine, sweet shape as she headed toward the bath-room. She was still dressed, but there was no mys-tery about the heart-shaped bottom awaiting under those tight jeans. Slowly, she pulled the spaghetti-strapped top over her head and showed him the ivory skin of her lovely back.

With a smile, before ducking into the bathroom, Gail turned off the room light, scant illumination filtering in through sheer curtains on this second-floor window. For a moment she was caught in a shaft of light from the bathroom, a topless beauty with a wicked smile.

Then she shut herself within.

He bent down and started tugging at a boot. Then another boot. Finally he sprawled out on the bed. He was there a while. Long enough for his erection to lose interest.

When the bathroom door did open, the light wasn't on. Danny had no idea how long she had been gone. Had he drifted off awhile? Might have been ten seconds or ten minutes. In the darkness, all he could make out was curly hair, the ivory skin of one shoulder, and the fact that she was holding something.

In this light it was impossible to tell what. If he didn't know better, he would have said she was hauling over a pair of those big garden shears, like the ones back in his folks' garage. The ones the old man to this day used to trim the hedges. No Mexican gardener for *his* old man. . . .

But in this pitch-black room, he'd seen very little, really, and the thought that had registered seemed absurd. *Garden shears—really.* . . .

She was coming to him now, cooing . . . or was it more like . . . purring, even . . . growling? He tried to reach out for her, but his arms felt leaden and he wondered if he could even lift them.

The wooziness seemed worse now; then the figure was towering over him, only he could no longer focus, his eyelids heavy, so very heavy. *He would swear she was holding garden shears.* He tried to focus on the point of the object, but it dropped out of sight.

There was a quick, terrible, sharp, excruciating pain at his gut, forcing horrible momentary clarity upon him, followed by warmth, all-encompassing liquid warmth, spreading over his stomach, dripping onto his legs.

That feeling was followed by overwhelming cold in his upper body, as if all his body heat were being siphoned off. He worked hard at keeping his eyes open, but could not. Thoughts flitted through his brain, butterflies on a sunny day, but he couldn't catch them, not any of them; then the butterflies were gone and so was the sun and any other light.

As the coldness seeped through him, Danny Terrant thought, *I think those* were *garden shears.*

Then the world turned black.

Chapter Fourteen

Harrow's take on Lieutenant Anna Amari was this: she was efficient and smart and tough; and she smelled really good for a cop.

Tuesday, she'd brought over the sketch of the John Doe victim and a copy of the security video from the Star Struck. Apparently not content to leave them with Harrow's assistant, Amari had handed them over personally.

They had discussed the drawing briefly, then took a pass through the grainy footage. She was a knowledgeable cop and provided some insights.

"Real planning went into this," she said, as they sat together at Harrow's desk before his computer screen. "Killer did his homework. Knew where the cameras were, not just in the hotel, but along his route."

"You've checked the traffic cams, then."

"Yes, and every convenience store and other

business that might have a view on the streets approaching the Star Struck."

"Were you able to tie him to a car?"

"No." Abruptly she rose. "Okay, gotta get back at it."

And she was gone.

On Wednesday, she called. She grilled him pretty hard about his team and their capabilities. Not nosy, exactly, but clearly up to something. He had no idea what.

Now here it was Thursday, and Vicki had just buzzed him to say that Lieutenant Amari was on line two. If she was stalking him, he didn't think he minded.

"Harrow," he said.

"What's your opinion of the Dodgers?"

He smiled. "I never thought about it, Lieutenant Amari. Are they suspects in the Star Struck investigation?"

"What kind of straight male has never thought about the Dodgers?"

"We can talk later about how you made that deduction. I'm an Iowa boy. We don't have any big-time professional teams. I always kind of dug the Yankees, though."

"That's just sad."

"What is? That Iowa doesn't have a big-time baseball franchise, or that I've watched a Yankee game in my time?"

"Yankees. Just so obvious. You need retraining. I'll pick you up at your office."

"Okay. When?"

"Six-thirty. Dodgers and Cards tonight. That's the Cardinals?"

"Yeah, I know that much."

"Prepare to be reborn, J.C."

"Sounds messy."

"Just be out front at six-thirty."

"Okay—dinner after?"

"Dinner *during*. Dodger Dogs."

"What's a Dodger Dog?"

"Jesus, J.C., you really *were* born in a barn."

She hung up.

He smiled. He hadn't been bossed around by a woman like that since . . . his smiled faded a little. Since Ellen.

Funny thing, he caught himself checking his watch as the afternoon rolled by. Did he actually have a date? Beyond his life at *Crime Seen*, and the colleagues who'd become his surrogate family, he had no real friends in California. He knew people out here, of course, had neighbors he spoke to, retail businesses where he was friendly with staff, but that wasn't much of a social life. . . .

Back in Iowa, he had work friends extending from the sheriff's department to the DCI, and through his wife and son, other friendships had been forged. None had lasted beyond the Christmas-card level, after he moved out here. He'd heard that when couples divorced, friendships with other couples fell away; but he'd never have guessed the same was true when a spouse *died*.

So he found himself oddly excited by the prospect of an evening out with Anna Amari. But was it because she smelled good (for a cop)? Or because he was hoping to get an update on Don Juan? Probably both, as he really did have that madman on his brain.

Since the snuff video on Monday, they had received no further communication from Don Juan; and the *Killer TV* team's discreet efforts to track him down were getting nowhere.

Other than the video, the police had a lock on all the evidence, so there just weren't that many directions to go. If the LAPD had made a victim ID, they hadn't shared it with the media. And *Crime Seen*, like the rest of the press, had acquiesced to the chief's request to keep the details of the murder to themselves. For now.

On her Tuesday visit, Anna had responded to Harrow's seemingly casual inquiry about Don Juan with a single piece of information: "The dead woman's fingerprints aren't on file anywhere."

Which meant not in any applicable database— law enforcement, local licensing, federal government, you name it.

As the afternoon wound down, Harrow stopped by Jenny Blake's office and found the small, tidy space empty.

Jenny had reduced the standard desk, filing cabinet, and trio of chairs to just desk and chair. If not for the open laptop on her desk, Harrow might have thought the office vacant.

The laptop, however, meant she was still at work—it was an appendage of hers, and you don't leave an arm or leg behind.

So he was not surprised when the petite blonde

appeared in the doorway, popping the top of a diet soda.

"What's up, boss?" she asked.

"The Hollywood sign victim—still unidentified?"

Jenny, with her hacking skills, was always the first to know.

"Yep," Jenny said. She passed Harrow, moved behind her desk, and sat. "Why?"

He stood opposite her, folded his arms. "How good is our facial recognition software? By 'our,' I mean yours."

The laptop was to Jenny what the utility belt was to Batman—whatever she needed was in there.

She raised an eyebrow and her expression indicated she was a trifle insulted by the question.

He asked, "Can you hack DMV records and match a frame from that video to a driver's license photo?"

"But that's illegal," she said, with a lyrical lilt.

"I didn't ask if it was legal."

"Take some time," she said, with a shrug. "Have to try to isolate a frame where she's not screaming . . . and preferably has her eyes open. But you know what the little train said."

"I think I can?"

She nodded and smiled.

Wow, he thought, *she's come a long way. . . .*

He glanced at his watch. "I have a, uh, an appointment this evening. But call me when you've got something."

She was already at it.

He would wait for another time to suggest she add a visitor's chair to her office ensemble.

In the corridor, his phone vibrated.

"It's six-thirty-five," she said. "You're late. I'm in a yellow zone. Shake it."

Anna clicked off.

He did, too, getting into the elevator. He liked this woman. She didn't take any crap nor was she afraid to dish some out, and there was a nice spiky sense of humor underneath.

When he stepped into the late afternoon sun, Harrow found Anna in a silver Mazda Miata, top down—the car's, not hers, unfortunately. . . .

She bestowed him a faintly mocking smile as he approached. "I said shake it, big shot. Don't make me give myself a ticket."

He was chuckling as he climbed in.

Anna wore a home Dodgers jersey, the white shirt's blue lettering a striking contrast with her dark hair, olive complexion, and red-glossed lips. Blue shorts showed off perfect tanned legs. Oh my.

Harrow had the sudden realization that he wasn't going to a ball game with a fellow officer, but a beautiful woman. And a second realization, dawning slowly not suddenly, said: *You haven't had a date since . . . since you were a goddamn* kid *going out on dates. . . .*

As she goosed the gas and the car leapt away from the curb, Harrow tried to think of something to say. He had the awful feeling that he would never again think of· *anything* to say. . . .

"I was a little early," she admitted, "and almost came up to your office. But in this wardrobe, maybe your team would get the wrong idea."

He glanced at her legs, then looked at the sky, where the sun was making its escape.

She threw a look at him, amused, stopped at a light. "Are *you* getting an idea?"

"I might be."

"Well, there's no crime in that. Ideas aren't illegal."

"Some should be."

She smiled, studied his face even as she drove. "You look uncomfortable."

"You don't. You look real comfortable. Very comfortable. Look, I haven't been on a date for a while. You're gonna have to forgive my awkwardness."

"I'm not going to forgive it. I'm going to exploit it. I'm going to give you a very hard time."

He was already having a hard time.

She hung a left onto Sixth Street, headed for the 110 and the short-distance, time-consuming ride to Dodger Stadium.

Anna laughed, her dark hair streaming in the breeze that the Miata was kicking up. "I wish you could see your face."

"That right?"

"You look like you can't decide whether to shit or go blind."

He broke out laughing. "I never heard a woman say that before."

"Get used to it." She smiled. "I was *hoping* you'd have a sense of humor."

"Heaven help the cop who doesn't."

The car was going too fast as she swept up the

ramp onto the 110, and Harrow felt like he was racing to try to catch up.

He asked, "What made you think I might not have a sense of humor?"

"Because you are *sooooo* serious on that show of yours."

The wind was really flapping her hair now as she sped up to, and caught, the rush-hour traffic. But within seconds, as so often happened in Los Angeles, they were sitting at a dead stop.

"So you're a fan," he said. Teasing now.

"A Dodgers fan? Sure."

"I mean a *Crime Seen* fan. You obviously watch the show."

"I've seen it."

Kidding on the square now, he said, "Just because I'm not cracking jokes on *Crime Seen* doesn't mean I'm some kind of humorless—"

"You're serious right now, aren't you?"

He stuck his tongue out at her.

She laughed. "Why don't you do that on your show? You're always Mr. Stone Face."

"Oh, right—coming up next, the story of a man who butchered his coworkers when his boss failed to give him a raise, and then somebody gets hit with a pie?"

"Might boost ratings."

He smiled. Just a little. "Can I be serious now?"

"Can I stop you?"

"It's the work at *Crime Seen* that's no nonsense. If you do watch, you know that. But that doesn't mean I have a stick up my butt in my personal life."

"Do you have one?"

"A stick up my butt?"

"A personal life?"

"Yes, actually."

"Tell me about it."

"There's this woman in my life."

"Really? Tell me about her."

"Well, she's very serious about her work, but she has a fun, silly side. She's probably pushing forty, but her body didn't get the memo. Looks maybe . . . twenty-five."

"I hate this woman."

"Then don't look in the mirror."

She didn't. She looked at him. She leaned over and gave him a kiss. It was just threatening to last awhile when a horn honked behind them as traffic finally started to move.

"I *am* basically a serious type," she admitted, looking at the road, not Harrow. "But you *have* to laugh. All cops know that, otherwise they go nuts or eat their piece."

"No argument."

"Like those numb-nut uniforms who came up with 'Billy Shears' as a nickname. I *get* it. You can't be in a job that makes you look at death on a regular basis and *not* develop a sense of humor."

"Working sex crimes must be tough."

She nodded. "You run into just about every nasty kink in the human psyche that you ever heard of. And then you run into some more. It's when kids are involved that I have to self-medicate."

"How do you do that?"

"White zin, mostly."

"And beer over a Dodger Dog?"

"And beer over a Dodger Dog."

Traffic crept forward.

"I don't do sick humor," he said. He sounded almost ashamed of himself.

Her eyes narrowed. "You never went to an electrocution and came out saying, 'That came as a shock to the bastard'?"

"Nope."

"Never caught an asphyxiation vic and told your partner, 'Takes my breath away'?"

He shook his head.

"Bullshit, J.C."

He held up three fingers. "Scout's honor."

"Never? *Never* never?"

Sheepishly, he said, "I got called to a crime scene once—when I was with DCI? A dead accountant. He had screwed up a guy's taxes and the client got so pissed, he stabbed the CPA with a letter opener. Twelve times."

"Damn."

"Yeah," Harrow said. "I said to the detective, 'Bet he never figured on this.' "

"I *knew* you were as sick as the rest of us!"

"Actually, I wasn't. I just said it and accidentally made a stupid joke. Hey, I'm not funny. But I have a sense of humor. A sense of humor doesn't mean you're funny, it means you *understand* funny."

"Wow."

"What?"

"You're boring."

He laughed out loud at that, and so did she.

They were pulling into the stadium lot. Anna

paid the cashier, then found a place to park. As they meandered toward the stadium, the sun setting, the warm breeze from the south, Harrow said, "Another case, a pissed-off wife shot her cheating husband—a dentist?"

"You *didn't.*"

"And I said he got—"

"Drilled?"

"No. I said this time *he* got a new cavity."

"Okay, J.C.—now you're just screwing with me."

"Just screwing with you, Anna? Isn't that what they call a straight line? The funny people, I mean?"

She gave him a friendly elbow, then slipped an arm through his.

Inside, good as her word, Anna sprang for dinner, Dodger Dogs and beers. They took their time eating, and as they watched the game, Anna occasionally made a comment about a player or a bad (or good) call, but didn't overdo the play-by-play. Harrow was enjoying the anonymity of the crowd as they sat up high, behind the plate.

"You know," he said, "I could have gotten UBC to get us better seats. Box seats, even."

"There *are* no better seats. These are season tickets. The Amari family's been in these babies since Dodger Stadium opened."

He lobbed it out. "Ever come here with a husband?"

"Just my own. Don't worry—it didn't take. Amari's my family name—I never *did* use his."

"Sorry."

"Don't be. He had a great sense of humor, by the way. But I lost mine when he ran around."

She said that with her usual flippancy, but he caught the hurt.

"He was a fool," he said.

She shrugged. "I don't know. Not easy being married to a cop. . . . Oh, J.C., I'm sorry."

Apparently she realized she'd accidentally invoked his late wife.

"You have mustard on your mouth," he said.

He gave her a quick kiss and removed it.

She studied him, between innings. "Are we moving a little fast?"

"Maybe. Considering this is my first date in five years."

"You're sweet." She squeezed his arm and then left her hand there.

The warmth of this woman's flesh on his gave him a sudden rush of guilt.

He was, after all, a healthy male who had been married for over twenty years but had, after his wife's death, made zero effort to find new female companionship. He had his doubts about the existence of God—he'd seen too much horror on the job not to—but he allowed himself a vague sense that someday he and Ellen would be reunited.

Anna's husband had cheated on her.

Was he cheating on Ellen?

In the meantime, he was having trouble concentrating on the game and Anna's hand seemed in no real hurry to leave his arm.

His cell phone vibrated.

A few fans glared at him as he answered, softly, "Harrow."

"Don Juan's date?"

It was Jenny.

"Yes?" he prompted.

"I know who she is."

Next to him, Anna's phone chirped. She turned away slightly and answered it. Everyone in their section hated them now.

"Wendi Erskine," Jenny said.

"Good. Anything else?"

"Nope—facial recognition software just pulled that."

"Keep digging."

No good-byes—they both hung up.

Anna was saying into her cell, "Where is it?"

Harrow watched, making no pretense of not eavesdropping.

"All right," she said. "Okay. Gotta change first, then I'll be there."

She clicked off and rose. "Sorry. Got something."

Then he was following her up the aisle steps, the crack of bat meeting ball not even getting her to pause for a glance.

Harrow asked her back, "Another body?"

They were starting down the tunnel before she answered. "You know I can't tell you."

"Can't blame a guy for trying."

"Sure I can. Look, it sucks, but I can't give you a ride back to your office. Heading the other way."

"The network will get me a cab."

"But you aren't working."

"Sure I am. I'm on seduction duty to make an LAPD detective tell me everything she knows."

She was smiling. "Maybe you *are* funny."

He smiled back, sighed. ". . . I *was* having fun."

"Me, too."

They were walking down the ramp toward the ground level.

"One more thing," he said, stopping her.

"What?"

"Your Hollywood sign vic—her name is Wendi Erskine."

She frowned. "Where did you get that?"

"Did you have it already? Had you ID'ed her?"

"No! Where did you get it, J.C.?"

He shrugged. "Not important."

An edge crept in as she said, "At least respect me enough to tell me how you got the information."

He told her that Jenny had made the ID using facial recognition software.

"That's fricking *illegal*!"

"You want to bust us, Anna, or take the info and use it? That assumes you're telling me the truth and you didn't already know the victim's name."

"I don't lie to you, J.C., but you've been lying to me. You said you'd stay out of this investigation."

"No. You told me to stay out of the investigation. I said I'd do my best to stay out of your way. Two different things."

"Are you out of your mind? You're not a cop anymore!"

"I never stopped being a cop. Anna, this son of a bitch is trying to use my show to make himself famous. You can bet your very sweet ass that I am going to do everything I can to stop him."

"Like broadcast that dead girl's name?"

"No. You have my word—I won't share that

woman's identity with anyone outside my staff, not till you announce it. If it gets out, it wasn't us, that I promise you. I'm not looking for a scoop or ratings—I want this evil prick stopped."

Her lids were at half-mast, but her eyes were sharp. "So you're going to keep digging."

"Yes."

She was frowning, though he did not sense she was angry. Suddenly she touched his arm again, generating that now-familiar warmth. . . .

"Look, I've got to go . . . but we need to talk about this."

"How about after my show tomorrow night?"

"Okay." She turned, took several quick steps, then looked back at him. "I forgot something. . . ."

She went to him.

Kissed him on the cheek.

Just on the cheek, but kissed him.

They exchanged small, meaningful smiles, and when she was gone, Harrow got out his cell. He didn't call a taxi, just Billy Choi.

"It'll take a while in this traffic."

"Fine, Billy. I'll be waiting."

He had time to kill, but Harrow had no real interest in the ball game. He did have enough appetite for another Dodger Dog.

Chapter Fifteen

Amari kept a change of clothes in her trunk. You could never know when a night out might be interrupted by a work call, so with the Dodgers on their way to an easy win—and J.C. Harrow maybe on the verge of scoring himself—she found herself leaving the stadium behind and pulling into the nearest gas station.

When she returned from the ladies' room to the convertible—now in cotton shirt, jeans, sneakers, and LAPD Windbreaker—she opened the rider's side door, unlocked the glove compartment, removed her holstered Glock, and clipped it to her belt.

She had only asked Harrow how he came up with the name Wendi Erskine to cover her bases (well, and her ass). She never expected a straight answer, and—while the way he'd come upon the info was infuriating—his frankness had floored her. Such honesty was a pleasant change from men she'd dated in recent years.

On the other hand, she'd never considered telling him that Captain Womack had called to say a second Billy Shears victim was waiting on a bed of blood in a motel in Reseda.

She took the 101, the Hollywood sign zipping by on her right, just before she turned onto the Ventura Freeway to get to the 405 for the drive to Reseda. Driving fast to get to a crime scene was a favorite perk. She flew through the cool evening, no siren but the red light on the dash flashing a path . . . some traffic even moved to the right, out of her way, like they were supposed to.

When she got off the 405, she turned west on Sepulveda and sped past the Van Nuys Airport. Before long the motel popped up on the left, its parking lot arrayed with emergency vehicles flashing blue and red.

She parked two spaces down from Polk, who was just getting out of the Crown Vic. They fell in step together as they crossed the lot.

Her young partner looked typically sharp in a black pinstripe suit with an Oxford shirt and red-and-gray striped tie. A gray fedora topped the outfit and gave him a Capone mob aspect. Should she break it to him that Big Al and the boys were stone-cold racists? Naw.

"What got ruined for *you* tonight, Lieutenant?"

"Dodgers–Cardinals game. Up six to one. You?"

"Dinner with a very fine lady."

"Same fine lady as last week?"

"One I met *this* week."

Amari glanced from the dapper-dressed Polk to their nondescript unmarked.

"How fine can she be," she asked with good-natured skepticism, "if you took her to dinner in *our* wheels?"

"Told her my Benz is in the shop."

"What Benz?"

He flashed a grin. "Exactly."

This was a mom-and-pop inn that had once been part of the Ramada chain, and she and Polk might have been walking into 1993.

The lobby furniture was decent, if threadbare and/or scuffed. A couple of couches shared space with a coffee table (strewn with complimentary newspapers and things-to-do pamphlets) and a corner credenza with a coffee machine. The carpeting was worn but clean. Near the front desk, a wall-mounted tube TV showed CNN, volume off.

In this exhibit at the Hall of Ancient Accommodations, Amari was pleased to note two video cameras aimed at the front door and the desk.

A uniformed officer, name tag: LEE, met them as they came in.

"Brutal one," the Asian American cop said, after the introductions.

"So I hear," Amari said.

"Looks like our boy Billy Shears again. Killer collected the victim's package."

Shuddering, Polk said, "You know, I *wanted* to be a fireman."

"You're young," Amari said. "Never too late for a career change."

They followed Lee through the lobby and up the stairs to the second floor and down a hallway, stopping at the top of its T, where cameras pointed in either direction.

Good, she thought.

"Room's on the right," Lee said, "all the way to the end."

Amari asked, "Who found the body?"

"One of the owners—Mrs. Olmstad."

Polk said, "Don't tell us Mrs. Olmstad changes all the sheets herself."

"It's not *that* small an operation, but it's on the cheesy side, all right." Lee shrugged. "Clock radio went off full blast tonight, at seven, and just kept blaring. Guest next door phoned the desk to complain. Mrs. Olmstad came down to check and, when she got no answer, used her key to get in and, surprise—dead frickin' guest."

They took the right and started down the corridor, Lee out front.

"Anybody see or hear anything," Amari asked, "besides that alarm going off?"

Lee shook his head. "A couple of my guys did a prelim canvas of the few guests who are in. Of course, some have checked out recently and, as you'll see, *this* guy checked out a while ago. Plus, this joint's got more vacancies than a Clippers game."

"The current guests have anything for us?"

"Nobody heard anything, nobody saw anything, nobody wants to get involved."

"Who's the room registered to?"

"Al Roberts. Of Chicago, Illinois. No street address."

"Is Roberts our victim?"

They were at the room now; a uniformed officer stepped aside so they could enter.

"No ID," Lee said, letting the two detectives go in first. "Everything's gone—clothes, wallet. No car in the parking lot that's unaccounted for, either by a guest or the staff. You're the lucky winners of a John Doe."

This room, fairly good-sized, was more generic than the one at the Star Struck—no San Francisco whorehouse touches. The major similarity was the nude male corpse sprawled dead-center on the bed, a sheet draped from the waist down, a large black-bloody hole, mid-torso.

A crime-scene tech in the bathroom was working with an electrostatic footprint lifter, while balding assistant coroner Devin Talbot sat at the shabby little writing desk on the far side of the room.

"Working nights, Dink?" Amari asked cheerfully. "Who did *you* piss off?"

"Nobody, if you can believe that." He shrugged. "Couple people on vacation—we're stretched thin."

"So I noticed. Got anything that might make my life easier?"

"Not really," Talbot said, rising to move to the bed. "Fewer wounds this time, but the first one is deeper, certainly fatal. This perp is strong."

"So," Polk said, "he was less angry this time?"

"Maybe," Talbot granted. "More likely, he's just

getting better at it. Looks to me like he's more confident than last time."

Amari asked, "What makes you say that?"

"Last time there were secondary wounds we attributed to extreme rage."

"Yeah?"

Bending over the body, Talbot said, "Maybe we were wrong. Maybe on that first one? He wasn't sure he'd gotten the job done with that first blow, and kept at it. This time, well, his first try was the kill shot."

"If it's not about anger," Polk asked, "what *is* it about?"

"Not saying anger doesn't enter in," Talbot said. "But this kill is also about control . . . control and *power*—over both the victims and himself."

"Control," Polk said, like he was tasting the word.

"Over life and death," Talbot said. "Whether the victim lives is the killer's choice. But this is also about . . . shall we call him Billy Shears?"

Amari sighed. "Why not? Everybody else is."

"Well, this is about Billy Shears and how he sees himself. This time, when he took his trophy of the victim's genitalia, the cut was more assured, more controlled."

Having a peek under the sheet, a grimacing Polk said, softly, "It *was* more jagged last time."

"Right," the coroner's man said. "Billy hesitated a couple of times. Not *this* time—we're talking one smooth stroke. Like a tree surgeon cutting off a leafy branch."

Polk shuddered again and let the sheet down.

Talbot was saying: "Billy waited longer this time, too, before trophy time. Less blood. Your boy's getting better at his job."

"A fast learner," Amari said with quiet disgust. She sniffed, turning her head as she did so. "Smells like smoke again, too."

The crime-scene tech emerged from the bathroom—Glenn Madlin, an old vet Amari knew well, tall, thin, silver-haired, nearing retirement.

"Smells like more than one cigarette," Madlin said in his unemotional tenor, "judging from the bathroom."

"Hi, Glenn," Amari said. "He flush them?"

"Hi, Anna. Seems to be the case. No fingerprints on anything, and the only footprints are from shoe-covered booties."

"So," Polk said, with an awful sigh and a worse smile, "we got nothin' again?"

"Nothing on my end," Madlin admitted.

Amari asked, "What say you, Dink?"

"Nothing yet," Talbot said. "Maybe another hair'll turn up. When I get back, I'll run the prints and do a tox screen. My guess is Mr. Shears roofied this one, too. Who knows, maybe we can at least ID the poor bastard."

"Shit," Polk said. "*Nothing?*"

He was asking the coroner's man, but Amari answered.

"*Something,*" she said. "We have at least four video cameras. One had to catch something—I don't care how careful Billy Boy was."

Lee had been lurking around the doorway. Now

he stepped in deeper . . . and he looked sick. "Umm, guys—there isn't any video."

Amari blurted an f-bomb, then calmed herself. "Sergeant, how is that possible? I saw *four* cameras."

"Seven," Lee said with a shrug, "if you count the ones outside—it's just . . . the system was installed when the hotel was still part of the Ramada chain. When the main tape deck . . . it's tape, not DVD . . . busted, about six months ago? The Olmstads didn't spend the money to fix it."

Amari glared at the sergeant. "And you saved this sweet tidbit for me till now *why*?"

"It slipped my mind. You didn't ask and . . . sorry, Lieutenant."

She raised a hand to silence any further apology.

"They're waiting in the office, just off the front desk."

To the coroner's assistant, Amari said, "Call me when you've got something, Dink."

"Will do."

In the corridor, Amari accessed the geography—the victim's room was near the end of the hall. A doorway to the stairs down to the parking lot was nearby. She stuck her head back in the room.

Madlin and Talbot both looked up.

Amari said, "Glenn, make sure you dust this exit door, will you? My guess is the killer used it."

"You got it, Anna."

Madlin was not one of those techs who got irritated when you told them how to do their jobs.

Not that either Amari or Madlin expected Billy Shears to leave his prints behind. . . .

"These cameras being defunct," she said, pointing at one, as they headed back down the corridor, Sergeant Lee bringing up the rear. "That might tell us something."

Polk smirked. "That we are unlucky as hell?"

"No. That Billy Shears does his homework. . . ."

Soon Amari and Polk—leaving Lee behind—joined the motel owners in the small, cluttered office off the desk.

Mr. Olmstad was paunchy but in decent enough shape for his age, his hair barely graying. He must have been working the desk, because he was in a navy blazer with what Amari guessed was a yellow turtleneck dickey.

In a yellow blouse and navy slacks, Mrs. Olmstad was thin, her shortish hair bottle blonde, bifocals on a black cord around her neck. She was dabbing at red eyes with a tissue, sitting at the metal desk in the small space, her husband towering behind her.

"I know this was very unpleasant for you," Amari said.

Mrs. Olmstad nodded. "We've had deaths here before. All hotels do. But this . . . *this.* . . ."

"The guest who was killed—was it Al Roberts?"

"Who?" Mr. Olmstad asked.

"Al Roberts is the name on your guest register. Of the man who checked in."

Olmstad gave a facial shrug, but his wife said, "No, that was not Mr. Roberts. Mr. Roberts I checked in on Wednesday afternoon. His room is paid for through tomorrow morning."

Amari nodded. "How did he pay?"

"Cash," Mrs. Olmstad said.

"No credit card for incidentals?"

"No. He paid for two nights."

"Don't you usually insist on a credit card for incidentals?"

"We don't have room service."

"Couldn't you get nicked on long-distance calls?"

"Yes, but, uh . . ."

"But what, Mrs. Olmstad?"

"He gave me one hundred dollars on deposit. Said he wasn't planning on making any long-distance calls, and I could keep the deposit, either way."

Polk asked, "What did he look like?"

"Not too tall. Kind of heavyset, and you might call him handsome, only he had a scar on his left cheek. Ugly one, too. First thing you saw about him."

Amari asked, "Could you describe the scar?"

"Long . . . jagged. Ran clear from his eyebrow almost all the way to his chin."

"Eye color?"

"Brown, I believe." She closed her eyes momentarily. "Yes, brown."

"Hair?"

"Brown. Kinda on the long side, but well groomed."

This sounded nothing like guy who'd checked into the Star Struck.

"Do you think you could describe the man who checked in to one of our forensic artists?"

"Certainly."

"Now, about the security cameras . . ."

Mr. Olmstad jumped in. "I am *so* sorry about that. We never thought we'd need them here. We just never have any problems."

Amari couldn't help herself—she gave the man an arched eyebrow.

And he said, "Well . . . till *this* awful thing happened. We're the kind of place you go when you forgot to make a reservation, or your hotel loses your reservation, or . . . frankly . . . if you meet somebody you want to spend a few hours with."

"The cameras been down for six months?"

"Yes, ma'am, more or less."

"Who might know they were broken?"

"Chiefly, just the staff. That's me, the wife, and three part-time desk clerks and four maids."

"We'll need their names and contact information."

"Oh my," Mrs. Olmstad said, fingertips touching her thin lips. "I can't think *any* of our *help* would be involved with *anything* like this. . . . They're all so *reliable*. A few may not have their green cards. Will that be a problem?"

Polk said, "We're not Immigration."

Amari said, "Mr. Olmstad, could you tell me one thing—and I promise it won't get you in trouble. You admitted this is the kind of hotel where couples can go to spend a few hours together."

He shrugged uncomfortably.

"Did you ever have a guest ask about the cameras? Whether they worked? Maybe how long the tapes were kept before they were disposed of, or reused?"

"Well . . . sometimes guests say something in a kind of joking way. Guy checking in with a girl . . . or even a guy checking in with . . . a guy. Might kid me, and say something like, 'I don't have to worry about these cameras, do I?' "

"Oh-kay," Amari said. "And what might *you* say?"

"I might . . . I guess I maybe might kid 'em back."

"Yeah?"

"Yeah, I might say . . . don't worry about *those* cameras. They been busted a long time."

Amari and Polk traded tortured glances.

"But," Amari said to Olmstad, "you wouldn't know who any of those guests would be?"

"Sorry. No. Well, there's probably some named 'John Smith,' that kind of thing. But as far as our staff, I've got a list out front that we can photocopy for you."

"Oh," Polk said innocently, "your *photocopy* machine works?"

"Oh yes."

"That's nice."

Amari gave her partner a look, but she could hardly blame him for the dig, not that either of the Olmstads picked up on it.

"That staff list will be helpful," Amari told the couple pleasantly. "We need to rule them out as suspects and see if any might've mentioned the broken cameras to anybody who innocently passed that information along."

Soon Olmstad was handing Amari a photocopy of the single-page list, which she folded and slipped into a pocket of her Windbreaker.

"Thank you," Amari said. Then to both: "Can

you think of anybody *not* staff who might know the cameras were out of commission?"

"We don't advertise that they're not functioning," Mr. Olmstad said, as if joking with guests about it didn't qualify. "We figured if no one knew they were busted, the things'd still work as a, you know, deterrent."

"All due respect, sir? You might want to reconsider that policy."

Chapter Sixteen

With her pale complexion and skinny frame, Jenny Blake might be taken for an anemic. But there was nothing anemic about her—as a teen, she'd engaged child molesters online. Then when they showed up at her foster parents' house, she would call the cops. She'd done this on her own, and after a few times, law enforcement had stopped scolding her and hired her.

So Harrow telling her to keep digging into the background of Wendi Erskine had been entirely unnecessary; she figured he probably knew as much, but bosses liked to give orders to make them feel they were in charge.

Since facial recognition software had matched the victim's face to DMV records, Jenny started there.

Twenty-five-year-old Wendi Erskine had blonde hair, blue eyes, weighed one hundred eighteen pounds and owned a silver 2007 Honda CRX. She had a couple of parking tickets (paid), but no moving violations. Her address was in Pomona. She was an organ donor.

There had been only one red flag, but it was very, very red. . . .

Harrow came through her open door. "Tell me what you've found."

She liked that, him assuming she'd found something. She gave him the DMV info.

"Any employment?"

Nodding, Jenny said, "Actress—a few indies, a little TV, quite a few infomercials."

"You don't go to Julliard hoping to work in infomercials."

"I don't have anything saying she went to Julliard—"

"I just meant—little girls don't dream of growing up and starring in a Juice Master spot."

"Probably not," she admitted, "but Wendi was making better money at it than you'd think."

"Why, is that significant?"

She hesitated.

The straight line of his mouth curved faintly into a smile. "Okay, Jen—who'd you hack?"

"Her money was in a small savings and loan in Pomona. Their security isn't exactly . . . secure."

"So?"

"So Wendi had a checking account with a little over two hundred dollars, a savings account with just under twelve thousand, and a Roth IRA she started last summer. Less than three thousand in that."

Looking thoughtful, Harrow leaned a palm on

her desktop. "Wendi wasn't rich, but she was doing pretty well for a kid only twenty-five."

"Yeah," Jenny said with a few nods. "Plus, she'd been doing infomercials since she was eighteen, and the TV and independent film stuff I mentioned. And she didn't spend much."

"Okay. What *aren't* you telling me?"

"The Roth is fine, but the other two accounts aren't."

"What's wrong with them?"

"They're empty."

"As in . . . somebody emptied them?"

"Yup."

Harrow's eyes narrowed. "Somebody was stealing from our victim. But was that part of *why* she was killed?"

"Yes."

"You sound confident."

"She was murdered over the weekend and the accounts weren't emptied until Monday morning."

Harrow's eyes widened. "Holy . . . you're saying *Don Juan* did it? *He* wiped her out?"

"We have no evidence that says that," she admitted. "Everything else does, though."

He half sat on the edge of her desk. "Okay, Jen. Now you're going to tell me *how* he did it."

She was loving this. "Sure. Easy. He went online as Wendi, then just wire-transferred it all to an offshore account. He had her passwords and everything."

"How the hell did he get her passwords?"

"There are a couple of ways," she said. "First, he

could have sent her a Trojan horse e-mail that allowed him to capture her log-ons, keystrokes, basically everything that she did with her computer."

"Well, that's scary. And second?"

"He found a way to get her to give them up while he held her."

"That's scarier." Harrow thought for a few moments. "Of course, there were no *signs* of torture. . . ."

She said nothing. Harrow had emphasized the word "signs," she knew, because there were lots of ways to inflict pain and instill fear that didn't show.

Harrow asked, "Can you trace the computer activity?"

"This guy knows his stuff, boss. I followed the video he sent us through seventeen countries and fifty-two remailers, then the trail died. I'll try. Gonna be tough, savvy as Don Juan seems."

"You're saying you can't do it?"

She cocked her head and gave him a look. "You're just trying to push my buttons now, aren't you?"

"Maybe. Let me know when you have something more. Get some sleep, though—tomorrow is show day, remember."

"Watch me sparkle," she said deadpan.

They both knew she'd likely work most of the night.

From the doorway, he said, "One other thing?"

"Yeah?"

"Would you *please* get a visitor's chair? Guy my age likes to take a load off, now and then."

"We'll see."

Jenny got back to it. Hacking the credit union had been hard, even for someone with her skills. The off-shore account in the Caymans was maybe a hundred times worse, and after two more hours, she was barely any closer to her goal.

A knock at the door frame made her jump, and she looked up to see Chris Anderson standing there in a pale yellow polo and chinos.

"Sorry, Jen—didn't mean to startle you."

"That's okay. Kinda woke me up." She rubbed her eyes, then stretched in her chair as he strolled in.

"Gonna be much longer?"

The bottom right of her computer screen told her it was just shy of midnight. Suddenly she realized her back ached, her eyes were sore, a dull headache was going, and here stood her cute chemist, in whose arms she could curl up . . .

. . . when she got her work done.

"A while," she said at last. "You shouldn't wait."

He came around the desk, gave her a quick, awkward hug, then a little kiss.

"Get a room," said a voice from the doorway.

Anderson jerked away and Jenny backed up in her chair.

Carmen Garcia came in, laughing gently, looking typically professional in a silk pale blue blouse and navy skirt.

"Good Lord," she said, "but are you two jumpy."

An embarrassed Anderson was heading for the door. "Night, Carmen. Jenny. See y'all in the morning."

The California sun had baked most of Anderson's southern drawl out, but it still turned up now and then. Usually that made Jenny smile. Right now she was giving Carmen a dirty look.

Carmen caught it, and called after Chris, "Hey! Don't go away mad! Chris. . . ."

From the hall, he gave them both his shy grin. "No, really, girls, I should go. Jenny here's got work to do."

And he was vapor.

Carmen made an "jeesh" face and said to Jen, "I'm sorry, honey. Spoiled things, huh? Boy, is he touchy."

"It's the paparazzi thing," Jenny said. "They've made us both gun-shy."

"I've been pretty lucky, I suppose," Carmen said.

Jenny's guest sat on the edge of the desk, crossing and exposing her enviably shapely legs. Jenny decided maybe she did need a visitor's chair at that.

Carmen was saying, "I was getting some of that tabloid attention, right after we got back from Kansas."

Jenny had noticed that any reference Carmen made to a madman holding her hostage was always simply coded "Kansas." After the hell Carmen had gone through, Jenny wondered, could the woman *really* be as together as she seemed?

"Something I can do for you?" Jenny asked.

That came out colder than she meant it to.

"I was stopping by to say hi. Nothing about work. There is something I want to . . . but if you're busy, it can wait. . . ."

Jenny glanced at the dead trail on her monitor and decided it could keep. "Actually, a break from this would be nice. What's up?"

Desk-perched Carmen leaned in confidentially. "This is kinda personal, and hardly worth chasing that cute boyfriend of yours away, but . . ."

"But?"

"But I just wanted to know . . . how did you know Chris was . . . the one?"

"The one what?"

"The *one!* Prince Charming, Mr. Right . . . don't pretend you don't get what I'm talking about."

"Well . . . I don't know that Chris is 'Mr. Right.' If there is such a thing."

"So then, what? He's Mr. Right Now?"

"No. I just really like him."

"He's cute. He's shy. Nice buns. I get all that. But what else attracted you?"

"Chemistry."

"That—special connection, you mean?"

"No. Chemistry. He's a chemist. I like people who have a scientific bent."

Carmen just looked at her.

"Why are you asking me this, Carmen? I mean, you know this is the last thing I'm an expert on."

"I just frankly . . . *envy* what you and Chris have. And, with Vince, I mean I *like* Vince. . . ."

Jenny said, "I like Vince too. He seemed really nice at lunch."

"He's very nice," Carmen said. "It's just . . . it's been so long since I've been in a relationship. Anyway, a relationship that worked. . . ."

"Relationships are hard," Jenny said.

She didn't mean her and Chris, really. More, her and every other human in the world.

Carmen was studying her, as if Jenny were an interesting but bewildering lab specimen. "Even hounded by the media, you and Chris seem to do fine. How do you pull that off?"

"Well, he makes me feel . . . comfortable."

"That's the way I feel with Vince," Carmen said, looking off wistfully. "Comfortable. But I don't know if there's the right . . . chemistry. And I don't mean in the test-tube way."

How, Jenny wondered, had this confident career woman managed to reduce herself to a teenage girl with boy trouble?

"What is this *really* about, Carmen?"

Carmen drew in a breath, let it out, then leaned close again and whispered: "Did you two start doing it, you know, right away?"

"It?" Jenny asked.

"Stop! *Sex*, you high-IQ airhead. How long before you two jumped into bed?"

Jenny laughed. "Oh, we haven't had *sex*."

Carmen's eyes popped. "But . . . but you guys have been together for like . . . what . . . six months?"

"Eight."

"And you haven't . . . done the deed?"

"If by deed, you mean had sexual intercourse, that would be no."

"Well . . . why not?"

"We aren't rushing it."

"Eight months. Not rushing it."

"Yes. What about you and Vince?"

Carmen didn't answer. Her face took on a melancholy cast.

"You okay?" Jenny asked.

"Well, I *was* kind of worried," Carmen said, and laughed just a little, "but now that I hear you and *Chris* haven't been intimate. . . . You see, I guess because of Kansas, well, Vince has been very . . . gentlemanly."

"That's good, right? He respects you?"

"It's sweet. It's just that sometimes I feel like he's afraid to touch me. Like I might . . . break."

"You went through a lot, Carmen. Everybody knows that."

She rolled her eyes. "Tell me about it. It was on *TV*."

Jenny had to smile. Shake her head. "So of all the people in the world, how was it you came to choose *me* for relationship advice?"

That made Carmen smile, too. Even laugh.

"Shows you how messed up *I* am," she said.

Carmen reached over, squeezed Jenny's hand, climbed off the desk, and went out.

Jenny thought about switching off her computer.

Then got back to work.

Maybe Don Juan could afford to rest, but she couldn't.

Chapter Seventeen

The PA whispered, "Five, four, three . . ." and, at ". . . one," touched Harrow's sleeve and the host stepped past the edge of the curtain.

Bright lights burned as he strode out into the studio, the applause like friendly fire as he approached his mark.

He couldn't see the audience well. Just movement, colors, faces lost in the blur. These occasional live broadcasts were perhaps the most surreal aspect of the *Crime Seen* experience.

"For there to be a war on crime," Harrow said, beginning with his famous catchphrase, "we must *all* be warriors . . . Ladies and gentlemen, good evening."

Another round of applause preceded Harrow's seemingly off-the-cuff but wholly scripted preamble.

"This is another of our rare live broadcasts," Harrow said. A typical sweeps week stunt, actually.

"You may be surprised that UBC would allow me on the air *live* again, after *last* year. . . ."

A knowing laugh rippled across the audience. And even Harrow had a wry smile. But the subtext was not at all comical: that memorable moment in broadcasting history when J.C. Harrow went on the air live to call out the killer of his family.

How he wished tonight he could do the same thing with Don Juan—the maniac who had targeted *Crime Seen* itself to fuel his own sick fame-seeking.

But Harrow had promised Anna Amari otherwise.

And what he did instead—as the teleprompters instructed—was start the show with a piece on Billy Shears, including the video footage from the Star Struck and the forensic artist's victim sketch.

As he glanced at the stage-right monitor, he could see that drawing with the show's eight hundred number and website on the Chyron below.

After the segment, Harrow introduced Carlos Moreno, former White House correspondent, reporting on gang violence in Taos, New Mexico, and how *Crime Seen* was aiding local law enforcement in their efforts.

Throughout the hour broadcast, Harrow would periodically return to introduce segments, none involving the *Killer TV* team. Dennis would be unhappy about that, but the team was focusing on Don Juan, including the very popular Carmen Garcia, probably the most conspicuous in her absence.

As the final segment—a report on bankers using

government bailout funds to invest in white slavery—played on an offstage monitor, Harrow wondered if his Billy Spears segment had served to get the phones ringing. The crime-scene photos showed the victim wearing a wedding ring. Somewhere in America, someone would be missing this man.

As the segment wound down, Harrow's assistant Vicki approached him to whisper: "Both the tip line and the website are going crazy."

"Good. Spread the word—we work late tonight."

"Yes, J.C."

"Oh, and call Lieutenant Amari at the LAPD."

"She's already here. I'll have her meet you at your office."

She disappeared and the PA materialized, mouthing, "Thirty seconds."

Thirty seconds suddenly seemed an eternity.

He could still go out there and call out Don Juan, just as he had the killer of his family. Tell this bastard that J.C. Harrow was coming and bringing his superstar CSIs with him. In seconds, he would be live, on air, and he could let fly, like Gary Cooper opening a six-shooter on a brace of bad guys.

But he wasn't Gary Cooper. He was a broadcaster and the team leader of professionals who trusted him, and betraying Anna Amari was just not possible. Not professionally. Not personally.

Still, it galled him knowing that Don Juan would undoubtedly be in their viewing audience. Watching. Waiting to see what J.C. Harrow would do about him. . . .

Then he had a jarring, even frightening thought: *What if Don Juan was in tonight's studio audience?* Harrow would have the *Killer TV* profiler, Michael Pall, go over the studio's security video.

Thirty seconds were up.

And Harrow went on without mentioning Don Juan, reading the scripted tease for next week's show, repeating his "war on crime" catchphrase. Then the LIVE sign switched off and he all but ran from the set, filled with the frustration of not using tonight's bloody video pulpit in the way he would have liked.

In seconds he was out a rear door onto the loading-dock area, and let out the f-bomb he had been holding in, bathed in the sickly amber security lighting of the parking lot with the twinkling darkness of the Los Angeles night hovering like storm clouds threatening lightning.

He took two quick steps to a Dumpster and delivered it a swift kick; it didn't seem to mind, though his foot protested a little.

A female voice behind him said: "Feel better?"

Embarrassed, he turned and saw Lt. Anna Amari.

"Busted," he said.

She wore a dark sleeveless silk top with just a hint of cleavage. Tight jeans and sneakers. An unlikely cop with dark hair framing a lovely face, lush lips lightly touched with lip gloss.

She smiled, ambling toward him, offering a pack of cigarettes—his brand.

"You a smoker, too?" he asked.

"Yeah. But ex. Been years since I kicked."

"I've cut way back, but sometimes . . ."

"Your girl Vicki said you come out and have a smoke when you're stressed. I was watching the show backstage on a monitor—I saw that vertical line between your eyebrows."

"And figured that was stress. You're a detective."

"You were dying to tell Don Juan to go screw himself, weren't you? Right there on live TV."

"Maybe."

"Like Wyatt Earp telling the Clantons, 'Hell is coming.' "

"Could be."

"Why didn't you?"

"I promised somebody I wouldn't."

"Me?"

"You."

"Thanks."

"Don't mention it."

Harrow plucked a cigarette out of the deck, which he started to hand back to her, but she shook her head. He pocketed the pack, lighted up; he stood there sharing the smoke with his lungs and the night awhile. She fell in beside him.

"Sorry," he said. "It's just . . . I feel like the son of a bitch outsmarted me."

"Don Juan?"

"Yeah."

"And you hate that."

"Don't you?"

"Not really. Just because he made the first move doesn't mean he wins."

"He killed a woman."

"Yeah, he was going to do that even if there was

no *Crime Seen* and no J.C. Harrow to challenge. Somebody told me that once."

He laughed, dropped the cigarette to the asphalt, and heeled it out. "All right, I get it. Maybe living in LA has made me self-centered like the rest of the citizens."

"From where I stand, you're doing all right. Hey, I've lived here my whole life, J.C. I've seen self-centered, and trust me, you don't qualify."

Her smile was teasing. He had to kiss her. He *had* to kiss her right now. He leaned in. . . .

That floral-scented perfume, not heavy, just tickling his nostrils. . . .

His hand on her shoulder, he asked, "Anna— what is that scent? Don't mean to be personal."

"Oh, it's a local fragrance. Little boutique I go to. Lily of the Valley, stuff's called."

No wonder the aroma was familiar. Lilies. Like the ones on Ellen's coffin.

Vicki leaned out the door and called, "Boss, you're going to want to get back in here!"

"A moment!"

Vicki was gone, and Anna—still close enough to kiss—asked, "Is something wrong?"

"No. Not at all. We just better get to work. I bet something good's come in on the tip line. . . ."

So the moment was over. He didn't know whether to feel disappointed or relieved. He just knew he couldn't tell this woman that he hadn't kissed her because she'd suddenly reminded him of his wife's funeral. . . .

Just inside, backstage, Anna caught up to Vicki and asked, "Have you got something?"

But Vicki didn't answer, glancing back at Harrow to say, "Everybody's in the conference room, boss. . . ."

When he and Anna entered the conference room, Jenny Blake, Laurene Chase, Michael Pall, Billy Choi, Chris Anderson, and Carmen Garcia were all seated around the big table.

Anna paused and said, under her breath but knowing Harrow could hear, "The *Killer TV* elite. Impressive."

Harrow quickly made introductions, then took the "daddy" chair, which had been left waiting for him. He nodded to a seat for Anna, nearby but not at the table proper. She sat.

Chase launched into a summation of what had transpired during air time.

"As soon as that drawing went on the air," she said, "calls started pouring in."

"Hundreds," Jenny said.

Choi added, "Damn near crashed the switchboard."

"Same with the website," Jenny said. "The hits just keep coming."

Harrow asked, "Any helpful ones?"

Chase nodded. "Greatest number from Ohio."

"Huber Heights, Ohio," Jenny added. "Suburb of Dayton, largest community of brick homes in the United States."

Nobody reacted—such trivia came with the Jenny Blake territory.

Harrow asked, "We learn anything germane to Lieutenant Amari's case?"

"I'm pretty sure," Pall said, "one of the calls we recorded is the victim's wife."

From the sidelines, Anna popped in: "Why are you 'pretty sure,' Mr. Pall?"

"Have a listen," Chase said, nodding toward Jenny.

Who tapped a key on her laptop, and they all sat in uncomfortable silence as a weeping woman said, "*Please, please,* please *help me.*"

"*How can we help?*" The *Crime Seen* operator was female and professional yet sympathetic. "*And could you give us your name, please?*"

"*Vicker. Becky Vicker. The drawing . . . on your show . . . I just know it's my husband. Brent.*"

"*You feel you recognize the drawing as a likeness of your husband?*"

"*Yes. Yes. I know my own husband when I see him.*"

"*Mrs. Vicker, I must ask your patience. Our lines are inundated with calls, from individuals claiming to recognize that likeness.*"

"*But I'm his* wife.*"

"*You are not the first call to make that assertion, Mrs. Vicker. That's why need to gather certain information to narrow down the possibilities.*"

"*Yes, yes, anything.*"

"*When did you last see or hear from your husband?*"

There was a long pause.

"*We . . . we're separated, Brent and I. We have been for almost two months. I spoke to him last week. He said he was going to California on a business trip.*"

"*Who does he work for?*"

"*Springfield Pump Corporation. Here in Huber*

Heights. They have a subsidiary office in Van Nuys. When we spoke . . . Brent said he'd like to come back home, after the California trip. He said he was willing to go to a marriage counselor. He's always refused in the past. We don't have any children, you know, so sometimes I think it's just not worth it to. . . ."

"He didn't call from California?'

"No."

"Do you think he may have changed his mind about—"

"No! He was adamant *about giving us a second chance. But there won't be a second chance, will there? There won't be. . . ."*

The woman broke down again.

The conversation resumed for another several minutes, but no new information came from it.

When Jenny had switched off the recording, Anna said, "I wonder if she's really our victim's wife?"

"I would say so," Pall said.

Anna frowned at the short, muscular man. "You're a DNA expert, right, Mr. Pall? That's your field?"

Harrow said, "Michael's also been through extensive profiling training at Quantico."

Pall continued: "Her grief seems genuine, and the details Mrs. Vicker discussed closely follow what we know of this case."

Jenny said, "Several calls came in from employees of Springfield Pump, all remarking on the resemblance of the drawing to Brent Vicker—who had not checked in with his company in several days."

"That," Choi said, arching an eyebrow, "is not exactly a surprise."

Chase slapped the tabletop. "It's our best lead—no contest."

Anna rose, stood next to Harrow. "Okay," she said. "First thing in the morning, I'll get my boss to get the locals out to talk to her."

Harrow glanced a question at Chase, who nodded.

In the pre-show meeting, they had discussed what to do if this particular scenario played out. Harrow didn't want to overstep with the LAPD, but they were the ones who had come to *Crime Seen* for help with this murder.

That meant Byrnes and the network were involved and the president would insist—not without justification—that the show get something out of the deal. And what Harrow had in mind could serve the purposes of both UBC and the LAPD.

"I can do you one better," Harrow said.

Anna's expression was openly wary. "Is that right?"

"Laurene is a seasoned police interviewer. She and our top reporter, Carmen Garcia, can be on the network's corporate jet tonight, flying to Ohio."

Anna frowned, but Harrow raised a hand.

"We're willing to have you join our two team members. That is, unless the LAPD has unlimited funds for flying investigators around the country to chase down leads?"

"You know it doesn't," she said flatly.

"You can even lead the interview. Obviously, we

want a story, but the most important thing for us is that you solve your homicides."

The detective considered this.

Chase said, "Wouldn't your boss rather *you* did the interview than some unknown Ohio cop?"

Anna said, "Let me make a call."

Cell in hand, she stepped into the hall, closing the door behind her.

Harrow asked, "Any other prospects? They were identifying a drawing, not a photograph, remember."

Pall shook his head. "This is the guy—I'd bet a month's salary . . . *mine*, boss, not yours."

"All right," Harrow said, nodding. "We've helped the LAPD with their John Doe, now let's have a quick update on Don Juan."

Jenny said, "You already know I couldn't track the e-mail he sent to us—trail went cold in Siberia."

Choi said, "Everything's cold in Siberia."

Jenny was saying, "Money he emptied from Wendi Erskine's accounts is gone from the Caymans, too. That trail's gone cold, too."

"Despite the beaches," Choi said.

Harrow said, "Have we passed that info on to the police yet?"

Jenny nodded. "I called Detective Polk earlier with an update."

"Good. Anything else?"

"Just that I'll try to be ready if Don Juan contacts us again—maybe we can get lucky."

"We'd sure be better off," Anderson said, "if we could get a look at the evidence."

Harrow shrugged. "I doubt that Lieutenant

Amari will go for it, but I'll give it a shot. If we can get her to go along with the Ohio excursion, and she sees how helpful we can be, things will go smoother, after."

Anna came back in. "You fly me out," she said, "I'll interview Mrs. Vicker."

"And then?" Laurene asked.

"Then it's your turn. Talk to her in front of cameras, if she'll let you. We don't care."

"Good," Harrow said. "You need to go home and get a bag or anything?"

"We'll be back tomorrow?" Anna asked.

"ASAP," Carmen piped in. "I've got a date."

"I'll alert the media," Choi said.

"Then I'm cool," Anna said. "Consider me packed."

Chapter Eighteen

Don Juan screamed.

Or more accurately, the actor who *played* Don Juan screamed.

The low animal howl built to a shrill crescendo as he rose from his seat before the massive flat-screen TV and hurled the remote at the wall. The shattering crack of plastic as it spilled its batteries and tiny shards put a pathetic period at the end of the cry of anger.

J.C. Harrow . . . *all* the bastards at *Crime Seen* . . . they'd ignored his warning. Ignored *him*. *Why hadn't the video been shown?* What kind of heartless monsters *were* they? Hadn't the horror of his example been enough to show them he meant business?

Moving through the sparsely furnished living room, he knocked a glass coffee table over and it cracked in ice-floe-like chunks on the hard-tile floor. He marched down the hall past the bathroom and his home office, stopping at the darkened bedroom at the end of the corridor.

Walls painted out black awaited him, with black metal blinds covering the two corner windows, the only lamp a tiny nightstand gooseneck he rarely used. Black sheets, pillowcases, and comforter covered the single bed. Even the carpeting was ebony. Less a room, more a womb.

He shut himself within, flopped onto the bed and lay in the dark, regaining control, listening to his own harsh, ragged breathing. Gradually his rage subsided.

You made a move, he told himself, *they made a move. Yes, they did make a move. Their non-response was itself a response.*

He beat back the urge to go down to the UBC Broadcast Center and find J.C. Harrow and choke the goddamn life out of him. Rage was not what was called for, rather cool detachment. . . .

After all, that *Crime Seen* might dismiss him out of hand had always been a possibility. How many cranks did they hear from in any given week? They might mistake him for a loony tunes. They might mistake his reality video for a skillful fraud.

If they hadn't believed the video, then his promise to increase the frequency of his conquests would've been written off as an empty threat.

He would need to prove himself.

To show *Crime Seen* his value as on-air talent. He must not take the rejection personally—all actors knew as much. Auditions were, after all, inherently brutal.

Peace settled over him, in the inky blackness, as it always did. As serenity soothed him, his mind coolly examined his plan, piece by piece, like a Legoland castle.

His next conquest would convince them.

And what a lovely costar he had nurtured for himself. Enveloped in his blanket of sweet silence and darkness, he felt himself getting aroused just thinking about her. Strange—outside of his role as Don Juan, he felt an almost asexual indifference to even the most attractive females.

But in assuming the Don Juan role—his *signature* role—arousal *would* come, particularly in the darkness of room. When he was alone, and contemplating what this next conquest would mean for his career, for his *art* . . . that was *certainly* arousing. . . .

This next conquest—like the previous one—was a lovely blonde with lush legs and ripe breasts. All that blonde hair ran halfway down her back, like a lion's mane (not a lioness—in the jungle, the king of the beasts was the real beauty).

Perhaps Harrow will make a brilliant deduction on air, he thought, smiling, *and declare that blondes are part of Don Juan's M.O. Then I can make him look stupid when my next conquest is a redhead or brunette. . . .*

That she was a blonde was happenstance. What was significant about this particular conquest was her bank balance. An influx of cash right now would help Don Juan achieve his true goal—stardom. The important half of show business was, after all, business.

You have to spend money to make money.

And he would spend his victims' money. . . .

Without even touching himself, his arousal grew more intense. Partly it was the beauty of his next conquest—Don Juan loved beautiful women. Part of it was her money—the actor playing Don Juan loved money.

He smiled in the dark, imagining the dismayed look on Harrow's face when the great "warrior" against crime viewed Don Juan's *next* production. The blonde, the money, a humiliated Harrow—it all came together and his hand found himself and soon there the shudder of blessed relief. . . .

Don Juan had arranged to meet Gina Hannan at a bar in the Valley. She was (*of course*) an aspiring actress (*these poor talentless, deluded kids—they don't have a chance in this tough town!*).

He had chosen this older, quieter hideaway for its seclusion and lack of security cameras—just the sort of anonymous spot where a Hollywood producer might arrange to meet an aspiring actress.

Tonight mirrored the previous conquest, and others he had lined up for the future.

He would arrange to "run into" a likely, pre-selected target, introduce himself as Louis St. James, independent film producer, with a website and IMDb listing by way of bona fides. This would be enough to fool them, whether bright bulbs or dim, blinded as they were by the lure of "making it."

And he knew how hard it was out here. He was

talented, wasn't he? Gifted beyond reason? And wasn't he having to take his career in his own hands?

The couple was sitting in a back booth. Her lips made a kiss as they plucked her appletini's maraschino cherry from its stem. Then she chewed, swallowed, and leaned forward, saying, "You *really* think I'm right for this part?"

An old-fashioned air conditioner was chugging over the bar's front door and a ball game was on behind the counter; but otherwise the place was quiet, the bartender and handful of customers keeping their own counsel. Chirpy blonde Gina in her low-cut, silky orange blouse and tight jeans, was the loudest person here.

"Certainly you're right for it," he said. "It's a small but showy part."

"But a *kindergarten* teacher . . ."

"My screenwriter has researched this, and says most kindergarten teachers are under thirty. *You're* under thirty. . . ."

"*Way* under thirty," she said with a laugh that seemed a little brittle to his ears.

". . . and we'll just have to . . . play down your glamour some. That's the only drawback—you're so . . . lovely."

She lowered her head and blushed.

Blushed? Really? Or is she actually that good an actress?

Then her dark blue eyes focused on him like lasers. "I *loved* what I saw of the script."

"I wish I'd thought to bring it," he said. "I haven't even printed out the current draft yet—

screenwriter just e-mailed it to me. I . . . well, after our first interview? I asked him to beef up the schoolteacher part a little."

"You *did*?"

"When we get a chance, I'll give you the new sides and you can read for me again. . . . Would you like another drink?"

"I shouldn't. We haven't even had dinner yet. I don't want to overdo, in case we end up going back to your place. For me to read those new pages for you?"

"Sure. But I think I *will* have another, if you don't mind. I'll hold it to three, since I'm driving . . . but we're kind of celebrating, aren't we?"

"Are we?"

"You're about to get a part in a movie, aren't you?"

She beamed. "I guess one more appletini won't kill me."

Don Juan glanced toward the bar. "Bartender's wrapped up in the game. I'll get this. . . ."

He collected his tumbler and her martini glass and left the booth.

On the way back, he slipped a few drops of a liquid from a tiny vial into Gina's drink.

Then he set the doctored appletini before her and resumed his seat, taking a nice long pull from what his date had been told was a vodka tonic but was club soda.

As they finished their drinks, he asked, "Are you ready to go get some dinner?"

Gina smiled. "What did you have in mind?"

"Well, I know a nice little Italian restaurant near

where I live. I was thinking . . . and please don't get the wrong idea . . . actually it's an idea *you* gave *me* . . ."

"What is?"

"We could stop by my place, I could run off a copy of the new draft of the screenplay, and pull your pages. We could talk about the part a little. You could read for me. Then we could have a lovely late dinner. Have you home before either one of us turns into a pumpkin."

"I'd love to! But what about my car?"

"I'll drive you back here to pick it up."

"Okay . . . I don't think I should be driving right now, anyway. . . . Have to be honest . . . think I shouldn't have had that third appletini. A little woozy."

"Nap in the car on our way to my place."

She smiled brightly. "Okay. Why not?"

They rose and he left a twenty as a tip, giving Gina a glance at the wad in his money clip. He wanted her confident in his affluence. He was already confident in hers.

Gina wasn't your typical starving actress who worked waitress jobs to survive. Don Juan vetted all of his lovers carefully and Gina had passed with flying colors—one of those colors being a nice money green. . . .

This attractive young woman worked as a dental assistant in Burbank for twenty-five dollars an hour. She lived in a modest apartment with several roommates as a way of saving money, banking the bulk of what she made.

Apparently she knew the road to stardom was a tough one (*tell me about it!*) and was preparing for the day when she started getting roles and could phase out of her day job.

Don Juan had worked day jobs, too, in addition to training to become an accomplished actor. His area of expertise was computers, which had proved very, very helpful of late.

After he'd first met Gina, at one of her acting classes, he sent her an e-mail with a Trojan horse. With her computer infiltrated, he could take control. He could even watch her through her own camera, unaware.

He followed her keystrokes and learned the passwords for her every registered site, including of course her bank.

All that frugal living and savings-account hoarding had added up, which made Gina a perfect candidate for conquest. After the loving, he would sweep in, electronically transfer her nest egg to an off-shore account, where he would finally put her cash to good use.

And Gina would not be the first to be so unknowingly generous.

The trick was to find women who were well-endowed in several senses—money *and* beauty. Despite his tepid personal interest in the female sex, he knew that as Don Juan his standards must be high. In Hollywood, image was everything.

She leaned against him as they made their way out of the bar and into the cool night air. The parking lot was unlit, but a three-quarter moon provided an ivory glow. Gina was a lovely girl, curvy and with all that blonde hair . . . though her wobbliness detracted, some.

He helped her over to his little red Mitsubishi Eclipse—sporty but not over-the-top expensive, just right for a successful indie producer. He lifted her into the passenger side, and by the time he settled in behind the wheel, she looked like a junkie on the nod—heavy eyelids, chin sinking.

She slept through the drive toward Chatsworth where Louis St. James kept a bungalow near the almost-empty reservoir. The actor playing both St. James and Don Juan did not live at this address.

Finding a place to perform as St. James—actually, perform as *Don Juan* playing St. James, a tricky, layered reading—had not been tough. Housing-crunch foreclosures had provided any number of out-of-the-way bungalows to choose from, for an indie producer wanting to live away from the Hollywood rat race.

He pulled in under the darkness of the carport, where its one solid wall protected him from view by his only neighbor, fifty yards away.

Gina had faded into a malleable heap that he half carried, half dragged through the side door into the house.

She woke, groaning. "Oh . . . I . . . I . . . don't *feel* too good. . . ."

"Well, you look lovely," he said. "You just need to lie down awhile. You'll feel better. Trust me."

"Okay," she managed.

They moved through the small kitchen, the

neat, barely used living room, then down a hall to the bedroom, already arranged for tonight's tryst.

A rather plain wooden double bed, with a spread of pink satin, elegant in its simplicity. Bouquet of roses in the nightstand vase. A wall mirror with a gold-gilt frame.

You would never guess an HD camera was behind the reflective glass, ready to document tonight's lovemaking. And postcoital surprise. . . .

As he swept Gina past the mirror, she noticed the flowers and wobbled toward them.

"Roses," she said, blinking as if trying to see underwater. "So pretty. They smell so good."

"They're for you," he whispered into her ear.

He kissed her neck. Softly.

Then she turned, a languid turn but a turn, and gave her lips to him, her arms going around him, her tongue as quick and darting as her movements were otherwise slow.

The pair tumbled onto the bed and, stoned or not, she became a passionate thing. She didn't bother to get under the covers, just stripped out of her clothes, watching him hungrily as he undressed, and her mouth was on him, swallowing him, and he liked it, he did like it. . . .

Then he was on her, his mouth moving quickly from one breast to the other, licking and nibbling at the hard pink tips, so caught up in the role of Don Juan he could not get enough (*he* was *Method*).

Her hands went to the back of his head, guiding him, as his kisses moved down her tummy. Her legs parted as he moved even lower, knowing the camera was capturing every erotic moment he lavished upon this beautiful woman.

His tongue explored her center, her thighs tightening around his head, her moans growing deeper, more passionate with each second.

"Now," she whispered. "Put it in me *now!*"

But he wasn't ready yet.

He had been ignored by Harrow and his team of superstar losers. Well, soon they would see that Don Juan was the greatest of all lovers, he would take his time satisfying his conquest, and when the moment came for the *real* climax, he would show Harrow, show all of them, that *Crime Seen* was wasting precious air time on nothings like scam artists and gangbangers and white-collar crooks, when they *could* be covering a star.

A real star!

Even if he did have to keep his back to the camera.

Chapter Nineteen

Amari felt a hand gently shake her shoulder and opened her eyes to the glow of sunshine around the edges of the drawn shade of the airplane window.

Laurene Chase said, "Welcome to Dayton, Ohio, where the time is ten-thirty a.m. Be on the ground in about an hour, Lieutenant."

Then Chase was gone, and Amari was sitting up, stretching, yawning. She had the first-class-style seat to herself in the small, cream-colored cabin of the Cessna Citation XL, UBC's small corporate jet. The only other passengers were Chase and Carmen Garcia, up in their own single-seat rows. No camera crew.

Carmen had explained that despite the success of the "Kansas thing," network budget cuts meant the Dayton UBC affiliate would supply camera and sound.

Amari squeezed into the tiny bathroom and gazed

into the tiny mirror. She cleaned up as best she could. She put a breath strip on her tongue, applied some fresh lip gloss, then pronounced herself human. Before boarding, she'd changed into a black suit with white blouse from the trunk of her Mazda.

Forward in the cabin was a conference area and this is where she found the other two women, having coffee. Garcia was in a gray designer suit and Chase in a lavender silk blouse and dark slacks; they looked professional, rested, ready.

Amari joined them and poured herself a cup, black.

"It might help," Chase said, "if you brought us up to speed on Billy Shears."

Amari hesitated only momentarily.

"We've found a number of people who vacated their hotel rooms," she began, "leaving behind some or all of their luggage."

Carmen frowned. "Is that typical?"

"Surprised me, too. Particularly since skipping out on a hotel bill is next to impossible these days, with credit card check-in."

She filled them in on the second murder and its as-yet-unidentified victim.

"Staff at the former Ramada in Reseda checks out clean. Nobody remembers mentioning the busted security system to anyone, or anyway admitted as much. They all have more or less decent alibis for what appears to be a second Billy Shears killing."

Carmen's frown was both thoughtful and troubled. "Billy Shears. Don Juan. Two gaudy serial killers appearing at the same time. Anybody think this might be one case?"

Chase shook her head. "Signature's too different."

"Dead sex partners? Stab wounds?"

"No sexual mutilation on the female victim. And we'd have to have a bisexual killer."

"Is that impossible?"

"No, but it's rare. What do you think, Lieutenant?"

"Two killers," Amari said, as if that were the final word, which she thought it was. "No prints on the exit nearest the motel room, but our crime-scene tech thinks Shears must have used that door, since it appeared wiped clean of prints. And that, I am sad to say, is that."

"Thanks for filling us in," Carmen said.

"Least I can do. This Ohio trip may jump-start a stalled investigation. First real break was identifying Victim Number One—that was your doing."

Chase said, "Care to fill us in on the Don Juan investigation now?"

Amari finished her coffee, smiled, said, "No," and returned to her seat.

She also didn't tell her new colleagues from *Crime Seen* that Captain Womack seemed a heartbeat away from taking both cases away from her. And that the chief would likely appoint a task force combining the cases, and call in the FBI, if for no other reason than to cover his ass.

On the ground, they found a cool overcast spring day waiting, and a driver with car on the tarmac. Amari got out her cell, checked her messages—nothing from Harrow but one from Polk, wishing her luck.

Today Polk would be working with the bank where Don Juan had somehow gotten to Wendi Erskine's money, chasing down the security breach.

She clicked off to join the other two women in the late-model Lincoln. So much for budget cuts. Since Carmen and Chase had taken the backseat, Amari slid in front.

The driver, an older guy with wire-frame glasses, short gray hair, and an extra thirty pounds, screamed ex-cop. His black suit fit him pretty well, considering his girth.

"Anna Amari, LAPD." She offered him a hand to shake and he did. "How long were you on the job?"

The hint of a smile appeared. "Twenty-seven years, Dayton PD. Gus Lewin."

"Mr. Lewin, how did we happen to get you for a driver?"

"Don't miss much do you, Detective Amari?"

"It's Lieutenant, Gus, but you can call me Anna. I try not to miss anything. Somebody think I need a bodyguard?"

They glided off the tarmac, and through a gate, before he said, "Your Mr. Harrow thought I might be able to smooth the way some, need be."

Chase in back sat forward. "You know the family, Gus? I'm Laurene, by the way."

To Amari, Lewin said, "This one doesn't miss much either."

"Waco PD," Amari told him. "How do you know the family?"

"Rebecca's my goddaughter. Becky's dad, Ben Cummings and me, we were pals."

"Ben also a cop?"

A nod. "In Huber Heights. Dropped dead of a heart attack, year from retirement. I tell everybody, take that Social Security soon as you can. You never know."

They were on the interstate now, I-70, heading east. After one exit, Lewin pulled off.

Amari asked, "You know Brent?"

"Kind of a screwup, but a nice kid."

"Screwup how?"

"Nothing major. Some guys just don't know how good they got it, is all."

She withdrew a photo of the deceased John Doe from her pocket, passed it to the driver.

"Shit," Lewin said, handing it back. Suddenly he was concentrating very hard on his driving.

Amari glanced in back where Chase and Carmen were both nodding. They would take this reaction as a positive ID.

"Sorry for your loss, Gus."

"I said he was a screwup."

"You okay?" She could see his eyes were tearing up, but the emotional rain wasn't quite falling.

"I feel bad for Becky. She loved the idiot. Gonna break what's left of her heart. You know, they was talking about getting back together."

"Okay, Gus. One more question. Something I'd rather not ask Mrs. Vicker cold."

"You mean, was Brent doing drugs?"

"Why would you say that?"

"Twenty-seven years as a cop. When you're worried how a survivor's gonna take it, it's usually either drugs or . . ."

He didn't seem able to complete the sentence.

Amari, in a way, did it for him: "Brent died in bed at a hotel that caters to a gay male clientele."

Lewin frowned. "Did he like boys? I can't say it's impossible. I know he ran around on Becky, some. I never heard *that* about him, or saw any signs."

From the backseat, Chase said, "Closeted gays can be very discreet, Mr. Lewin."

"Well, I don't buy it."

Amari said, "I need to ask Mrs. Vicker that question. How is she likely to react?"

"I have no idea," Lewin admitted.

"Okay. I assume you still have Huber Heights PD contacts."

"Sure."

"Let's get some locals out here. You've made the guy in the photo as Vicker, so they'll want to talk to Mrs. Vicker. And they can leave somebody with her."

He made the call.

That was all the talk before Lewin pulled up at a squat brick ranch-style like every other house in Huber Heights, Ohio. The driver got out to get the door for his two backseat passengers while Amari climbed out on her own.

A van from the local UBC affiliate pulled in behind them.

The camera crew piled out—a skinny guy about thirty in a Bengals sweatshirt and jeans, lugging the Sony cam, and a heavier, older dude in jeans and a Reds away jersey, hauling the boom.

Amari let Carmen take the lead as the three women approached the two men. Introductions were made.

Carmen said, "Lieutenant Amari does her interview first. Don't even turn the camera on till we say it's kosher—got it?"

Both men nodded.

A Crown Vic pulled up and parked across the street. *Unmarked car,* Amari thought. Two guys got out, jeans, button-down shirts, ties, cheap sport coats. *Detectives.*

She approached them, displaying her ID. "Lieutenant Anna Amari, LAPD."

"Hamilton," a middle-aged, dark-haired detective said, shaking her hand, not bothering with ID.

His young blond partner introduced himself as "Deeter," and he and Amari merely exchanged nods.

The blond cop was looking at Carmen and Chase, who were discussing logistics with the camera crew on the lawn.

"That's Carmen Garcia," he said, wide-eyed. "And Laurene Chase!"

Amari gave him a look. "Oh, then you *do* get the tee vee out here in Ohio."

The young cop gave her a puzzled look, and the older one an embarrassed one.

Soon the small army trooped up to the front door, Amari and the *Crime Seen* duo trailed by the cops and techs, and driver Lewin, too.

The LAPD detective had barely knocked when the door was opened by a thirtysomething blonde woman in a black blouse and black slacks. Had Becky Vicker consciously chosen widow's weeds?

The three women stepped inside, and introductions were made, the men remaining grouped on the porch. The woman was holding it together, but when she glimpsed Lewin, that triggered tears. For a moment, Amari thought the woman might collapse.

She and the ex-cop must have had the same thought, because Lewin slipped inside and both he and Amari grabbed an arm and swept Becky Vicker into her living room, depositing her on a sofa.

Lewin produced a handkerchief and gave it to his weeping friend, he and Amari bookending the woman. Finally the two detectives filed in, camera crew still on the porch.

Chase and Carmen took chairs opposite the sofa in the modest living room with its contemporary furnishings. An end table bore a photo of Brent and Becky Vicker taken perhaps five years ago.

When Mrs. Vicker stopped crying, Lewin introduced the two Huber Heights detectives, who stood in the nearby entryway.

Hamilton asked, "Is there someone you would like us to call, Mrs. Vicker?"

Her eyes were a lovely pale blue, the white filigreed red. "My mother. Melinda Cummings."

The woman gave Hamilton the number and he excused himself.

Amari said, "Ms. Chase and Ms. Garcia have a

camera crew outside. After we finish, they'd like to interview you on camera."

"Can I . . . can I think about that?"

"Certainly," Carmen said, jumping in. "We can step outside while you and Lieutenant Amari talk, if you like . . . ?"

Mrs. Vicker's eyes questioned Amari.

"I don't mind them staying," she told the woman. "I'm only here because of what their television program was able to do. We frankly hadn't been able to identify your husband."

"You sound . . . sound *certain*. . . ."

"Mrs. Vicker, I'm sorry to have to tell you this. The man in that photo with you . . ." She indicated the end-table portrait. ". . . is our murder victim."

That brought on a brief relapse of tears.

Then Amari said, "We do need to ask if you have something we can use to match DNA. Toothbrush, comb. . . ."

The woman's eyes flickered with hope, but Amari had to say, "It's just a formality, really."

Hope died.

In that all too familiar shell-shocked way, the victim's wife said, "We were separated. For several months. I don't think you'll find any personal items like that here, though maybe you could."

"Where was he staying locally?"

"A motel. I'll give you that address. He was at a motel in Los Angeles, too, but it wasn't . . . what was the name of that hotel mentioned on TV?"

"Star Struck. In West Hollywood."

"He wasn't staying there. Brent's motel was in Van Nuys. That's where SP's subsidiary is."

"SP?"

"Springfield Pump. Subsidiary is overstating it, really—just one IT guy, that was Brent's field, information technologies. You know, he said he wanted to come back home and try again. He said he missed me, missed *living* with me. . . ."

Two Billy Shears victims, each with a connection to Van Nuys, one staying there, one found nearby.

Amari asked, "What motel in Van Nuys?"

"It's a chain Brent liked. . . . Sleep and Stay? One of those long-term places that caters to business travelers. He was at a Sleep and Stay here too, out by the airport."

"Mrs. Vicker, your husband's body wasn't discovered at a Sleep and Stay."

"I know. . . . You said that. . . ."

"This is difficult, but there's something unpleasant we have to deal with."

The woman drew a deep if shaky breath; let it out. Her response was mildly defensive: "Lieutenant, my husband was murdered. How much more unpleasant could it be?"

Quite a bit more, actually.

Amari said, "The Star Struck in West Hollywood caters to a specific clientele—a mostly gay clientele."

". . . What? Are you asking me if my husband was a *homosexual?*"

"Could Brent have been gay, or possibly bisexual?"

"No! Absolutely not." She laughed. It was shrill, unpleasant. "If you knew Brent, you'd know how foolish that notion is. His problem was *women*, Lieutenant, not men."

"We're merely trying to understand why he was found at this particular hotel."

"Do you have to be gay to stay there? Do they ask for your gay membership card at the desk?"

This was getting uncomfortable, and it was getting out of hand. But Amari bet the *Crime Seen* gals wished their camera was rolling. . . .

"I hate to upset you further, Mrs. Vicker," Amari said. "But if I can find out *why* Brent was at the Star Struck, perhaps it will lead us to his killer."

"I . . . I do understand," Mrs. Vicker said, much more calm now. "But Brent was, if anything, a little . . . what's the term? *Anti-*gay?"

Chase put in: "Homophobic."

This was a slight breach of etiquette, as the *Crime Seen* pair wasn't to participate in this initial interview. But Amari understood, and even appreciated, Chase's point of view on this subject, and flashed her a look to give momentary approval.

Chase seized this permission and said, "Some gay men who are passing as straight will say hateful things about homosexuals. It's part of trying to pass."

But Mrs. Vicker began to shake her head halfway through that.

"No," she said. "My husband . . . I won't say this on camera, understand, but I *will* tell you right now—he was a *letch.*"

An awkward silence followed.

Amari glanced out the picture window at their

backs. That cop Hamilton was meeting a car that was hurriedly pulling up. A woman in her sixties hopped out, in sneakers, jeans, and a kitty T-shirt.

Amari said, "Mrs. Vicker, I may have a few further questions, but I think perhaps you should go ahead with the *Crime Seen* interview, if you're willing."

She was.

The techs came in and Carmen and Laurene began the process. Amari felt confident Carmen, after that traumatic Kansas episode, would handle the woman considerately.

Outside, Hamilton introduced Amari to Mrs. Cummings, then left them alone in the front yard.

The LAPD detective expressed her condolences, then asked Mrs. Cummings a few preliminary questions before getting to the same explosive subject that had so upset her daughter.

Mrs. Cummings coughed out a cigarette laugh even as she was lighting up a Camel. "Brent *gay*? I didn't think I could *ever* laugh on this sorry day, lady, so thanks for the tickle."

"I take it that's a 'no.' "

"That's a *hell* no. That man was a certifiable poon hound. He'd screw mud."

"But not other men?"

"Make it female mud. Dumb-ass even hit on *me* once. I mean, I was foxy in my day, but that day passed about twenty years back, being generous."

"Did you tell Becky?"

"That he hit on me? No. That he was no good? Yes. But what can you do? She was in love. And if I may be crude?"

Hadn't she been?

"Certainly," Amari said.

"There were *always* females after that man. Word got around—my son-in-law's hung like a horse."

Not anymore.

Mrs. Cummings went inside to console her daughter, probably not to include a discussion of her late husband's sex habits.

When Carmen and Chase emerged from the brick bungalow, they had the names of a couple of Brent's coworkers. Lewin drove them around to interview them, and both *Crime Seen* reporters agreed that Brent Vickers was a lot of things, but gay or bi-curious weren't likely among them.

At the airport Sleep and Stay, Hamilton and Deeter collected from Vicker's room a comb and a toothbrush for Amari, no court order required.

As ex-cop Lewin drove the three women back to the airport, night coming on fast, they were whipped. Return trip, Chase sat up front, Carmen and Amari in back texting.

Carmen tucked her cell away and said across the aisle, "I've got a sweet one."

"Sweet what?"

"Guy. Cancelled a date with him for about five minutes from now. Meeting him for breakfast to-morrow instead."

"This is all the notice you give him, and he's not cranky?"

"Naw. Vince is special. Who were you texting?"

"My partner. He's a young black kid."

"Cute?"

"Very."

"Interested in you?"

"Naw. I'm way too old, plus there's already some-body in his life."

"Who?"

"Himself. . . . Speak of the devil . . ."

Return message from Polk.

Checking Wendi Erskine's savings and loan seemed a dead end, so far. No other accounts had been touched and the bank couldn't track who'd made the wire transfer.

Maybe Harrow's girl Jenny Blake will do better, Amari thought.

She returned to Polk's text.

Billy Shears's second victim, in the mom-and-pop motel in Reseda, had been made by finger-prints.

Daniel H. Terrant.

An off-duty Santa Monica *police officer.*

Amari's return text was simply . . . WTF?

Chapter Twenty

Sunday nights were hard for Harrow.

Back in Iowa, Sunday evening had been a family time for Ellen and David and him (they all led busy lives)—a quiet evening of TV, sitting around an electronic hearth.

This Sunday evening was worse than usual. He was on a second tumbler of Scotch, feeling guilty about allowing Anna into his life; and feeling guilty about not calling Anna or even texting her since the Ohio trip, instead getting the skinny from Laurene Chase.

He looked at the forty-inch flat screen, some talking head on an evening news magazine, yapping in silence. He'd put the mute on for the commercials, but the self-important commentator seemed worthy of it, too. Harrow wondered how many people muted *him.* That, at least, provided a momentary smile.

He thought about Ellen and David every day because it kept them alive. Yet he knew they would both want him to go on with his life. He just didn't know if he could do that without a sense of betrayal.

He was half awake in his recliner, an expensive well-padded brown leather number, looking like a freeloading relative in sweatshirt, jeans, and sneakers.

Channel surfing landed him on the ESPN Sunday baseball game. He turned on the sound and the announcer said, *"That's out number three. No runs, hits, or errors. At the end of eight, the score remains Cardinals 2, Dodgers 1."*

As a commercial took over and he muted it again, Harrow shook his head.

Would be the damn Dodgers. . . .

On the table next to him, his landline rang and he hoped it would be Anna and feared it would be Anna. . . .

No—caller ID announced Carmen.

"What's up?"

"I . . . I need to see you," she said.

Her voice sounded . . . *off*, somehow.

"Can't wait till work tomorrow?"

"No. Now."

"What?"

"Tell you when I see you."

"Where are you?"

"Your driveway."

He half rose and glanced out the window: Carmen's Prius out there, all right.

"Come," he said.

His people rarely dropped in on him, so this

must be important. And he kept himself accessible to them. No gated community or tall walls with wrought-iron gates for Harrow. His Nichols Canyon address was just a nice ranch-style on a street of million-dollar homes worth a hundred grand back in the Heartland.

By the time he got to the door, she was standing there, hair tucked under a baseball cap, *Survivor* T-shirt, jeans, sneakers, laptop under her arm— the professional woman of the workplace suddenly a college student.

But what looked most different was her face, her bloodless complexion, eyes wide and . . . terrified?

He ushered her in, closed the door behind her. "What's the matter, Carmen? You all right?"

"Not really," she said with a weak smile.

She didn't wait for any further invitation, just strode into the living room, Harrow trailing her. She settled on the edge of the couch and rested the laptop on the coffee table.

Her dark eyes were unblinking. "It's him again."

He sat next to her. ". . . Don Juan?"

She said nothing. Didn't even nod.

When the computer was up, she found the right screen and clicked PLAY.

A lovely nude blonde woman (*another blonde?*) on the same bed as before, a bouquet of roses in their familiar vase on the nearby nightstand. Love-making already under way, the passionate but obviously drugged or drunk woman apparently enjoying the attention of her barely glimpsed male partner.

She was loud, screaming her delight, and as she reached her climax, she distorted the laptop's speakers, as if Don Juan were killing her already. . . .

As her passion subsided, and she lay back in a postcoital haze, the lover (back to the camera) moved off-screen, and they heard mechanical-sounding voiceover.

"*I warned you this would happen,*" Don Juan said. "*You did not meet my request, Mr. Harrow, and now the responsibility is yours. Are you enjoying the show? Why not call this segment 'Don Juan's Lover of the Week'? But* next *week there will be a double feature, if you do not commit to airing what you're viewing now.*"

The blonde woman sat up, blinking drowsily, smiling dreamily; then her expression changed, as if a switch had been thrown, sending her into abject terror. Her eyes managed to grow huge, her mouth agape, as her attention was drawn toward the camera.

This time her scream was not of passion.

This was fright, in its purest form, a shrill cry for help that no one could hear but the off-camera killer and the helpless viewing audience of two at the laptop.

Then something blurred across the screen, in a metallic winking flash, something vaguely an arm, a hand, a blade, and the scream was cut off, literally, as blood burst from the woman's throat, a scarlet flood, her hands going to the slice-wound, desperately trying to hold her literal life's blood in as it sprayed through her fingers and finally dripped down to coat the camera lens.

Through the ghastly red filter, her body could

be seen slumping onto the bed, in a terrible backward bow, her performance over.

The metallic voiceover returned: "*Quite the little scream queen, don't you think? Share her—and my art—with the world, Mr. Harrow, or I will be forced to share my love with* another *costar . . . and another . . . and another . . . and another. . . .*"

Don Juan faded out, and the awful red screen went thankfully black.

Carmen had shrunk into a corner of the sofa, face averted from the computer.

"Sorry you had to see that," he said. "Cyber tip line? Does the LAPD know?"

She shook her head. "This came to my e-mail. *Just* came in. . . ."

"Damnit, that's the problem with these network e-mail accounts—"

"No, J.C.—this came to *my* e-mail. *My* account. One only my closest friends and family have. You're not even on the list."

He stared at her. "How in hell?"

She sighed heavily. "Guess you'd have to ask Jenny."

"Exactly what I intend to do," he said, getting out his cell.

In seconds he was telling Jenny Blake to meet him at the office, and to round up Chris Anderson, too.

Jenny didn't hesitate—that it was mid Sunday evening was irrelevant.

She asked, "You want me to make the other calls, too? Everybody on the team?"

"Please. I have Carmen with me, and I need to call Lieutenant Amari."

"Another body?"

"Another Don Juan video."

"Which will mean another body. Okay."

She clicked off.

My God, that kid is a cool customer, he thought.

Amari picked up after the first ring. Her voice sounded sleepy. "I was starting to wonder if you'd ever call. . . ."

"Not social," he said. "Don Juan sent us another video."

"Where are you now?"

"Home, but heading to the office. This didn't come in on our tip line—Carmen's personal e-mail account."

"Shit! I'll collect Polk and meet you at UBC. Listen, there's something else. . . ."

"There's plenty to talk about," he said self-consciously. "Uh, Carmen's here with me."

"I'm not talking about personal matters, you big dope. Strictly business. . . . We've confirmed the Reseda motel kill as the second Billy Shears, and identified the victim. Fill you in later."

"See you at UBC," he said and clicked off. He turned to Carmen. "Okay if I ride with you?"

"Sure."

"You okay driving?"

"No problem."

As they went out the door and he set the alarm, he noticed Carmen giving him an odd look.

"What?" he asked.

"Had you talked to Anna since she got back from Ohio?"

"Not a subject for discussion," he said.

And that ended it.

He looked at Carmen at the wheel in the darkened car as they hit the freeway, the lights on the ramp illuminating her for a moment. A beautiful young woman, in every way. If he and Ellen had ever had a daughter. . . .

She glanced at him. "I know why I'm driving."

"Why?"

"That was Scotch in that glass, wasn't it?"

"We'll make a detective out of you yet."

His cell vibrated.

Caller ID: DENNIS BYRNES.

How the hell had Byrnes heard about the Don Juan video already?

"Harrow."

"Goddamn son of a bitch!"

"Whoa, Dennis, I was going to call *you* next—"

"Call *me?* What the hell are you *talking* about?"

"Uh . . . after you."

"Do you have any idea what that son of a bitch Don Juan has pulled this time?"

"Actually, I—"

"Goddamn maniac made a deposit! Left one right at our goddamn front *door!*"

"One what?"

"A girl! A woman! A victim! What the *shit* do you *think* I'm talking about?"

Harrow knew at once.

The body of the woman in the latest video had been dumped somewhere at UBC.

224 *Max Allan Collins and Matthew Clemens*

"We just got another video, Dennis. Came in on Carmen's home e-mail. She and I and the team are all heading for UBC right now. Your 'deposit' must be the woman in this new video."

"Bad enough he kills and dumps her on our doorstep! Bastard goes and calls every TV station, every other network in LA, to announce what he's done. Of course, he doesn't give *us* the courtesy of a call!"

"Settle down, Dennis. This isn't *about* UBC—"

"What the hell *is* it about, then?"

"It's about young women being slaughtered. Get a damn grip, man. This is a police matter."

"You're telling me. There are cops all over the place. But not that Amari woman."

"She's on her way. I called her about the video."

"You called *her*, but not *me*? First her, then your boss?"

"Settle the hell down. Yes, I call the police about murder evidence before I call a network executive. Learn to live with it. Listen—do you mean *literal* front doorstep?"

"Yes! Right in front—the lobby doorway. Know how we found out about a story every other network and news service already had? One of our security guards noticed CNN shooting out there! Thank Christ the cops have cordoned off the place and pushed these vultures back."

There was an easy irony there that Harrow was in no mood to pursue.

"Dennis, make sure the police know to allow me and my team in."

"Okay. All right. Will do."

Harrow clicked off.

Carmen had gathered most of it from Harrow's half of the conversation, but he filled her in on the rest.

"Is this what they mean," she asked, "when they say this shit is getting deep?"

"It's exactly what they mean," he said.

They were almost there now, and blocks ahead, Harrow could see the flashing lights of the police and, on either side of the UBC building, the raised antennas of a dozen news vans.

"Damn it," Harrow said, sitting forward, red and blue blushing his face.

"What?"

"A young woman's murder is going into homes all over America—very possibly the home of family members."

"It sucks."

"Yeah. And we're vultures, too."

"Huh?"

"Nothing. They won't let this vehicle in—park around the corner, Carmen. We'll walk."

Chapter Twenty-one

Los Angeles averaged about five hundred murders a year, roughly twice the number of the state of Mississippi, which was where Chris Anderson would have long since returned, if it weren't for Jenny Blake.

Shaw and Associates back home was the largest private-sector crime lab in the United States, so Chris already knew people might kill each other at the slightest provocation. He just hadn't had to live in the thick of it until now.

A lab rat by nature, he found TV stardom nerve-racking, especially having his budding relationship with Jenny splashed across the media. His mother had practically had a conniption fit when a supermarket tabloid ran a story alleging her baby boy was cheating on Jenny with Jessica Simpson.

First of all, was it cheating if you hadn't ever slept with the girl you were going with? Second of all, he'd never met Jessica Simpson.

Still, the *Crime Seen* money was good (but the cost of living in LA high) and his house in Glendale was nice (if a nasty commute to the office).

Having Jenny make him her first call tonight was a help. He'd thrown on a *Killer TV* polo, khakis, and running shoes, and soon was heading for UBC in his brand-new Dodge Ram. Made good time only to find the whole blessed block closed off, with a mess of news crews massed on the periphery.

Driving a pickup didn't make parking downtown easy, even on a Sunday night, and with the UBC ramp inside the cordons, he parked three blocks away on a side street. Hoofing it really wasn't bad, though, not on this breezy spring evening, under a clear sky and a scattering of stars.

Then rounding a corner, he ran smack into a local news crew—an affiliate of a rival network.

Like an escaping prisoner, he got hit with flood lights, and the red eye of a camera tracked him like a sniper scope.

A striking, well-dressed, dark-haired woman blocked his path. She spoke to another camera that had positioned itself just behind him.

"This is Renee Oxley reporting live for KDLA News outside UBC Broadcast Center. Chris Anderson from *Crime Seen* is here with us. Mr. Anderson, what can you tell about the dead woman found outside the UBC lobby?"

What *dead woman outside the UBC lobby?*

"Excuse me," he said, a hand over his face in murder-suspect fashion, and brushed past the reporter.

He damn near jogged, the news team trying to keep up. If he stopped, he'd be the limping zebra when a pride of lions was chasing the herd. First sign of weakness and they would eat him alive.

"Can't you give us *some* comment, Mr. Anderson?"

Having no idea what the woman was talking about, he stayed tight-lipped and kept going, but even with their cameras and microphones, they were keeping up.

He patted his pocket for his cell phone—the reporter wasn't asking about the new Don Juan tape. This was something else, and Harrow or Jenny would surely have called. . . . Finally he realized he'd forgotten to grab the thing on his way out the door.

"*Mr. Anderson, please!*"

Then he was up against a barrier of yellow crime-scene tape behind which a bored-looking cop stood watch, and the attractive reporter was on him, thrusting the mic at him, demanding just *one* comment. . . .

"I'm sorry. I have no information you don't already have."

In fact, he had less. . . .

The reporter turned to her cameraman and said, "It seems even UBC's own highly touted *Crime Seen* forensics team remains clueless about this bizarre tragedy."

Ignoring this distortion, Chris stood at the barrier and sent his eyes on a desperate search for a friendly face. He spotted Lt. Amari, in a gray blouse and dark slacks with her badge necklaced, and called out.

She came right over. When only the yellow-and-black barrier separated them, she smiled and said, "Mr. Anderson, good evening."

"Am I glad to see *you*, ma'am."

The "ma'am" seemed to amuse her. "All you had to do, son, was tell the officer who you were, show some ID, and step on over. We have clearance for your entire *Killer TV* team."

"No kidding?"

He glanced behind him, hoping that darn TV crew was catching this, but they had moved on.

Chris ducked under the tape, asking Amari, "What's this about a body dumped at UBC?"

"Don Juan. He left a victim here. Follow me."

He did, saying, "We just got a tape from that creep. That's why Mr. Harrow called us in, but nobody said anything about *this*."

"Don't you have cell phones in Georgia?"

"It's Mississippi, and of course we have cell phones."

"Well, where's yours? I know your boss tried to call you with the update."

"Uh, it's back at the house."

"You see, you need to take these newfangled gadgets along *with* you, Mr. Anderson."

"You having a little fun with me, Lieutenant?"

"Just a little. It's a night that could stand some levity."

She led him over to the front of the building, where walls of canvas, held in place by steel poles, gave the police and coroner's people a place to work in privacy.

"Can't let you in there," Amari said. "I know you're an expert, but you're not LAPD, and that's an active crime scene."

"Understood."

But he could see inside, the work lights giving plenty of illumination to the corpse as various techs moved around in there.

He'd been to his share of crime scenes and seen hundreds of photos of others, but the tableau on the sidewalk outside his workplace made his gut tighten.

Not that it was gory—barely any blood. The shapely naked blonde on the sidewalk looked impossibly white against concrete gray and the red of the bouquet of roses arranged beside her. Her face was turned away, but Chris just knew she'd be pretty, like the last victim.

Don Juan had made sure he could no longer be ignored, leaving this one on their doorstep and alerting the media.

Amari asked, "You okay, son?"

"Yeah. It's just so sad. Feel kind of . . . embarrassed for her."

"She's past that. Past any suffering, too, remember. Nothing left to do for her but solve this."

"I hear that, Lieutenant."

He followed Amari inside, the quiet of the lobby a welcome sanctuary from the bustling surrealistic scene behind the tinted glass.

At the elevator, Amari said, "Rest of your team is already here, except for you and Jenny."

Chris stopped cold. Jenny might need help getting through that zoo out there.

"Can I use your cell, Lieutenant?"

"Sure. . . ."

Soon Jenny was in his ear, saying, "Lieutenant Amari, I just got here. . . ."

"It's not the lieutenant," he said. "I'm using her cell. Left mine at home."

"Ah."

This single word meant she had tried to call him perhaps a dozen times.

"Just got here myself," he said.

"You made good time," she said, but not on the phone. Right behind him.

He whirled and there she was, laptop in a bag slung over her shoulder.

In short order, they were upstairs, joining the rest of the team at the conference room table.

Jenny was in her usual jeans and T-shirt, everybody else casually attired, dragged away from their Sunday evening. Only the normally extra-casual Choi seemed overdressed, in a black sport coat and dress shirt, new-looking jeans, and Italian loafers (no socks).

Choi noticed Chris staring, and said with a glower, "Don Juan ruined a perfectly good date. This time it's personal."

Chris took the chair next to Jenny while Amari took a waiting seat next to Harrow at the head of the table. Choi, Pall, and Chase were opposite Jenny and Chris. Carmen had taken a seat at the far end, off by herself.

When Harrow explained that the Don Juan

video had come in over Carmen's e-mail, Chris understood why the young woman looked so shell-shocked and pale.

As Harrow was addressing the group, network president Dennis Byrnes—in a dark brown suit, looking sharp as to attire but otherwise ragged—slipped in a door toward the back and, leaving a seat between them, deposited himself near Carmen.

Harrow said, "Thanks for joining us, Dennis."

The executive nodded, but said nothing.

"I'll get the lights," Harrow said.

He did.

Carmen averted her eyes as Harrow showed the video of the second Don Juan murder, uncomfortably large on the wall screen behind him and Amari.

The rest watched with cold, clinical eyes, and if any emotions showed among these seasoned investigators, shock or horror weren't among them—only controlled anger and resolute purpose.

Lights up again, Harrow said, "Lieutenant Amari understands that this crime has come to our doorstep. Literally and figuratively. She is willing to work with us."

Quiet expressions of thanks all around the table were accepted by Amari with a single nod.

Chase said, "So we get to work?"

"We get to work," Harrow said. "Billy, go down to security. You'll find Detective Polk waiting there for you. Get all the security footage. No way this maniac got *this* close carting a dead body and those roses without getting snagged on video."

Choi nodded and went.

Harrow said, "Michael, you're our profiler. What's your read?"

"He's going to kill again," Pall said with a matter-of-fact shrug.

"Anything else?"

"Yeah. It'll be soon."

Chase said, "Then we need to find something fast. This guy has us chasing shadows and smoke. Maybe at least this grandstand stunt will give us some real clues to work with."

Harrow asked, "What about Wendi Erskine's finances?"

Jenny said, "Money's gone. Not in the Caymans anymore either. And the trail is cold."

"Do we have *anything*?"

Nobody offered a response.

"Do we think there's a connection between Don Juan and Billy Shears?"

Chase shook her head, but nobody else responded.

Then Pall said, "I grant you there are similarities—the sexual aspect, chiefly. But remember Don Juan was self-named and the cops came up with Billy Shears. Two serial killers of this stripe turning up simultaneously strains credulity, I admit, but the signatures are decidedly, distinctly different."

"First thing tomorrow," Amari said, "we'll be looking into the second Shears victim, the off-duty Santa Monica officer, Danny Terrant."

Chase said, "You'll have to talk to his cop buddies. That'll be touchy. They may have payback on the brain."

"*We* could interview them," Carmen said, way down the table. "Might take the edge off any cop-to-cop strain."

"No, Detective Polk and I will handle that," Amari said. "You'd just be media to them."

Carmen raised her eyebrows and nodded.

Byrnes was just sitting there, taking it all in.

Harrow said, "I understand Vicker's family and friends insist he was straight."

"Supposedly a regular . . . Casanova," Chase said.

Chris wondered if she'd almost said *Don Juan*.

Harrow asked, "Do we know Officer Terrant's sexual proclivities?"

"Haven't got that far," Amari admitted.

"Okay," Harrow said, took in air, let it out. "Let's look hard at Officer Terrant. . . . You don't mind, Lieutenant Amari?"

Amari answered by asking a question—of Chris. "Do you guys have a mass spectrometer?"

"Yeah, we got a mass spec," Chris said. "Mr. Harrow got us all kinds of toys last year, and it wasn't even Christmas. Whatever lab equipment you need, we should have."

"So . . . if I were to bring you, say, a hair from a crime scene . . . ?"

Chris frowned at her. "But wouldn't bringing us evidence from a homicide break your chain of custody?"

She smiled at Chris in a tight, businesslike fashion. "The chief himself has given us permission to utilize whatever resources your show can provide."

Jenny said, "Cool."

Still not wholly on board, Chris said, "Ma'am, that doesn't answer my question about chain of custody."

Amari arched an eyebrow. "Aren't you, technically at least, still on leave from Shaw and Associates?"

"Yes, ma'am."

"Well, handing evidence to an employee of a certified lab wouldn't be breaking chain of custody, would it?"

"No. No, it wouldn't."

Harrow assigned several other duties to various team members, then said to the group, "We have two homicidal maniacs preying on innocent citizens of this city. Let's nail these bastards before either of them kills again."

They were about to break up when Byrnes cleared his throat and all eyes went to him; a few people who were getting up sat back down.

"I'm pleased to see *Crime Seen* and the LAPD working together," the network president said. His voice had an unsettling surface calm. "But we need to discuss the network's response—and your *show's* response."

Harrow said, "The priority here is stopping these—"

"Fine! Yes, of course. But we have a madman who has dumped his grotesque handiwork, as has been noted, on our very doorstep. So I want you, J.C., to record a video that can go out immediately to every national news outlet, network and cable, stating simply that all the resources of *Crime Seen's* superstar forensics team will be brought to bear upon the serial killer calling himself Don Juan."

Raising a finger, Chris said, "Uh, sir—the FBI won't consider Don Juan a serial killer until he has accumulated three victims, and—"

"Mr. Anderson," Byrnes said acidly, "I don't believe semantics is our concern right now. And this is not a request or a suggestion. J.C.—I don't often say this, but this is an *order.*"

All eyes went to Harrow.

"Fine," Harrow said.

All eyes went to Byrnes.

"What?" Byrnes said.

All eyes went to Harrow.

"You're right, Dennis. Give him a little attention, and maybe we can save a life, or at least slow him down a little."

Amari said firmly, "You're *not* broadcasting any Don Juan videos."

Harrow said, "Not suggesting that. If we appear to be conceding, he might demand even more."

"Such as?" Byrnes asked.

"He wants to be a regular segment on our show, doesn't he, Dennis? And what does *Crime Seen* do, during a sweeps week? To generate our top ratings? Our biggest audience?"

"Oh Christ," Byrnes said.

"Right," Harrow said. "Show that video, and we're on the path to Don Juan demanding we broadcast his next kill *live.*"

Chapter Twenty-two

Amari hated interviewing other cops. First, they were a tight-mouthed group when it came to talking about their own. Second, they spent so much time with lying lowlifes, they became masters of the craft themselves.

Chief Scovill at the Santa Monica Police Department, however, was friendly and cooperative, providing a look into Danny Terrant's file, which included neither commendations nor complaints. The chief also gave them the officer's cell phone number, so Amari could run the phone records.

In the hallway outside Scovill's office, Polk said, "I don't think that guy ever *met* Danny Terrant."

"No argument," Amari said.

Next up was Terrant's partner, Bobby Nucci. They caught up with the youngish, dark-haired uniformed officer in Chess Park, just south of famed Muscle Beach. As they walked, a radio blared hip-hop, cars rolled by on Ocean Avenue, and chess players hunkered in silence under a warm sun in a gentle breeze.

"Danny was kind of a loner," Nucci said. "Don't get me wrong—we always got along fine, and he was aces as a partner. . . . But he never let anybody get close."

She asked, "Not even his own partner?"

"I knew him going back to the academy, and he kept to himself back then. Nice, friendly, but on his own. We partnered up, what, two years ago? And I still don't know shit about his personal life."

Amari was wondering if she should just come right out with it when Polk blurted: "So was he gay?"

Nucci shot him a look. "I didn't *say* that."

Polk said, "We're not attacking him, Officer Nucci. It's a murder investigation. Somebody killed your partner, and you want the bastard caught and we want the bastard caught."

"Of *course* we all want that. But truth is . . . I just don't *know* if Danny was gay. I don't *think* he was, but . . . I don't really know."

Amari said, "Partners two years, and you can't hazard an informed guess about whether or not the guy was straight?"

"If he had a girlfriend, I never saw her. If he had a *boyfriend* I never saw him."

Polk said, "Did he seem to like the ladies?"

Nucci shrugged. "If I'd say, 'Wow, nice rack' . . . sorry, Lieutenant, just making a point . . . he'd say, 'Yeah, sure is' or some such. But he was never the one pointing *out* the nice rack, if you know what I mean."

She knew. "I take it you two didn't socialize away from the job."

"Not hardly at all. Like I said, Danny was private, and me, I got a wife and two baby girls—twins."

Polk said, "Got your hands full."

"Do we ever. Anyway, I'll say this for Danny. He saw I was worn down by a busy home life—midnight feedings, you know? And I always knew he had my back. Just because we didn't hang out off the job, that don't mean I didn't value the guy."

Amari asked, "You have no idea why he kept so much to himself?"

"Only thing I can think of—he was a tall, skinny dude, and he got some ribbing over it. Some guys, when they get a hard time like that, on the job? They give it right back. Other guys, they kind of pull in. Danny pulled in."

Polk pressed. "But you wouldn't be surprised to find out he was—"

"*Look*, man—if he was gay or bisexual or a goddamn Ken doll down below, what the hell's it to me? He was my *partner*—dude probably saved my life very day he got killed."

"Yeah?"

Nucci told them the story of the domestic call that had turned dangerously violent.

"Sounds like a stand-up guy," Amari said. "I know you want to protect him, but he's past that now. If you know something about his private life, hiding it from—"

"You think if I had the faintest idea how this could have happened to Danny I wouldn't tell you? I loved him as a partner. As a brother. You two don't look like you hang out together, off the job—but I'd bet my next paycheck you watch each other's backs."

There was nothing to say to that.

They collected a few names of other officers with whom Terrant had been friendly (a short list); then Amari handed the cop her card.

She and Polk were heading back to the car when Nucci called after them.

They met each other halfway.

Nucci waved Amari's card at her. "This reminded me—while back, we got business cards from this robbery victim. She runs a western store on the Third Street Promenade."

Polk said, "This sticks out in your memory why?"

"We responded to the alarm, Danny and me. Caught the guy, woman got her money back."

"Okay," Amari said patiently.

"Gal was so happy, she gave us each a business card and said she would make us a 'real deal' on some 'fine-ass' boots. I threw my card in a receptacle on the street, but when I climbed behind the wheel, in the squad? Danny climbed in, tucked that stupid card away in his wallet, like it was . . . I dunno, a goddamn prize or something."

Amari smiled at the officer. "Bobby, you wanna come along with us and talk to the boots lady?"

"Try to stop me."

Third Street Promenade was a three-block-long, tree-lined shopping area—over sixty stores and twenty-five restaurants, popular with tourists and locals alike.

Bart's Bunkhouse was midway in the promenade. As they entered, with Nucci in the lead, Amari was pleasantly assaulted by the smell of leather. The store was rife with western apparel— shirts, jeans, hats—and leather items—jackets, purses, belts, boots. Lots and lots of boots.

Several sales people were on hand, and perhaps half a dozen shoppers, but they were immediately approached by an attractive, slender, fortyish woman with dark, blonde-highlighted hair. She rushed over to give Nucci a big, sad hug.

"So sorry about Danny," she said. She wore skin-tight jeans, a huge silver belt buckle, and a red T-shirt inscribed in white: SAVE A HORSE, RIDE A COWBOY. "Oh, Bobby, I'm so sorry. . . ."

As the hug broke, Nucci seemed a shade embarrassed as he said, "That's why we're here, Megan."

Nucci made the introductions. Megan Fields was the owner.

"Ms. Fields," Amari said, "we'd like to talk to you about Officer Terrant."

"Poor Danny. Hell of damn thing. He was *so* sweet. . . . Come on, let's sit."

An area for trying on boots wasn't currently populated, and they sat, the owner next to Amari with Polk and Nucci just across the way.

"You offered a discount on boots to Danny Terrant," Amari said. "Did he take you up on that?"

"Sure did. He knew just what he wanted."

Nucci was frowning in confusion.

Amari prompted her. "He did?"

"Oh, yeah. He was a dyed-in-the-wool line dancer, you know."

Nucci's eyes popped. "I *didn't* know."

"Well, he probably thought you'd give him a hard time. People are either into things, or they aren't, right?"

"Right," Amari said, not really sure she followed that.

"See, I could tell he knew his stuff, because of the questions he was asking me, and how he knew the different styles and brands. So I said, 'You're into *line* dancing, aren't you? How cool!' And he said, 'I surely am.' "

"Did he order the boots? Did he pick them up?"

"Oh yes. I can show you the boots he chose. Real beauties."

"Please."

She had a pair in stock, smaller than the ones Terrant bought: dark red with white and green highlights forming white lilies.

Polk, at Amari's shoulder, whispered, "This is *gay*, right?"

"Not necessarily," Amari whispered back.

After the western store, Nucci headed back to work and the two detectives continued their interviews.

Other officers echoed Terrant's partner—Danny was a good cop, nobody knew him off the job. If he was gay, he didn't advertise it. Two openly gay officers said they had only known Terrant to say hello.

And when asked, "Did you know Officer Terrant was into line dancing?" the answer was uniformly the same: "*What the eff?*"

Amari had a search warrant for Terrant's apartment, since he might not live alone (the officer's SMPD file listed no next of kin, and no family member had stepped forward to claim the body). The manager at the small complex on Twenty-eighth Street seemed to barely know his tenant.

Terrant paid his rent. It was nice having a cop in the building. Terrant didn't entertain much if at all.

"Saw him on his way out," the white-haired, pot-bellied manager said, "dressed like a cowboy every now and then. But to each his own. . . . Just pull that door shut when you're done. It'll lock automatically."

Terrant's apartment had the sort of anonymity that might belong to a closeted gay afraid that some work friend or other acquaintance might drop by. Small, neat living room with an entertainment center—no magazines, a few books on a shelf (paperback westerns), no stacked-up mail, no photos.

Kitchen counter was bare save for a coffeemaker, the only personal touch a magnet on the refrigerator for a Reseda bar called Prairie Lights. Fussily neat bathroom. Two bedrooms, one a home office with a laptop computer that they would bag and tag—maybe to turn over to Jenny Blake rather than the backlogged LAPD crime lab.

Other bedroom was neat (big surprise), the closet orderly, two extra uniforms, an array of cowboy shirts, jeans, and even T-shirts on hangers. A safe in the closet probably held his service weapon; crime-scene unit would find out.

One empty hanger among the cowboy shirts, another among the jeans. An empty spot among the shoes and boots.

"This place," Polk said, "reads gay to me."

"No. Just secretive. What's missing here?"

"Well, I don't see his off-duty piece, and it sure as hell wasn't in that Reseda motel room."

"Right. Did the killer get it?"

"Could be. What's the other missing thing?"

"Where are those custom cowboy boots from Bart's Bunkhouse?"

"Not here."

"What do we know, LeRon?"

"Dude played his cards close to the vest."

"Agreed. See anything personal at all in this pad?"

He thought. "No."

"How about that refrigerator magnet?"

"What refrigerator magnet?"

"Come with me," she said. He did, and she showed him.

"So," Polk said, eyes bright, "he has a favorite place to do this line-dancing shit."

"Would appear so."

"And he left here wearing some of his cowboy duds."

"Seems like."

"So he was going line dancing?"

"Yup. A man has to do what a man has to do, you know."

"And he had to go to Reseda to line dance."

"And what else did he do in Reseda?"

"Got his ass killed?"

"Got his ass killed."

There were two good things about heading to Reseda in the late afternoon. One, Prairie Lights would be open, which meant there would be people to talk to, and two, the parking lot was still pretty empty, meaning it didn't take long for Amari to find what she was looking for.

"New Mustang," she said as she pulled in next to it. "What kind of car did Terrant have?"

"New Mustang," Polk said. He was already running the plates. "It's his. You're good, Lieutenant."

"*We're* good."

Soon Amari was using a slim jim to open the door. She unlatched the trunk from inside the driver's compartment.

She told her partner, "Check the glove box—I got the trunk."

Terrant's off-duty piece, a snub-nose .38, lay holstered in the spare-tire compartment of an otherwise empty trunk.

"Got it," she called, relieved.

Polk came around with the car's registration and Terrant's insurance card—both laminated.

"This guy may not've been gay," Polk said, "but he sure was a neat freak. I mean, who the hell gets *this* shit laminated?"

"A very careful man," Amari said.

"Not *that* careful," Polk said. "He's dead."

"Yeah, and doesn't it bother you?"

"Cop getting killed bothers hell out of me."

"Right, but you're not seeing it. I don't think the killer *knew* Terrant was on the job."

Polk studied her.

Amari said, "He's very careful, our Terrant."

"Okay. . . ."

"Trained observer, a cop, anal-*retentive* careful."

"Right."

"So what does Billy Shears, possibly unaware he's zeroed in on an off-duty cop, have to do to penetrate that much defense?"

"Be one sneaky mother," Polk said. "Smart, too."

Amari said, "I'll say. . . . Let's go in and see if we can be smart, too. And maybe even sneaky. . . ."

The interior was dark barn wood, cowboy paraphernalia, and a hardwood dance floor; a mechanical bull lurked in one corner, a seventies artifact on display. Customers were scant, with a female bartender on hand, as well as the owner, a tall woman, six-two easy in her cowboy boots, towering over Amari.

Her name was Julia Stowe and her jeans were tight, her tank top emblazoned with the bar's logo. She and Amari spoke in a corner booth while Polk talked to the bartender and handful of patrons.

Once they were seated, Amari felt a little less like one of the munchkins interviewing Dorothy.

Hard but attractive, the owner asked, "So is this about that murder over at the old Ramada Inn?"

"Yes, Ms. Stowe. This is the victim."

Julia looked at the photo. "Christ, it's Danny. . . ."

"Friend, or just a regular customer?"

"Both. He came in to dance damn near every week. Good guy. Cute-ass scarecrow, our Danny."

The woman wasn't tearing up, but her sadness didn't seem faked.

"Was he here last Wednesday?"

"Think so."

"Think or know?"

"Know."

"His car was in your parking lot."

"That Mustang?"

"Yeah."

"Peggy, she's the bartender talking to your partner?"

"Yes?"

"She mentioned the Mustang on Friday, said it'd been here a couple days."

"Why didn't you have it towed?"

"Well . . . I knew it was Danny's."

"And you didn't call him, or do anything else about it?"

"I did call. Left messages on his cell Friday, Saturday, too—fact, I just called about an hour ago and said if he didn't get it out of here tonight, I *would* have to have the damn thing towed."

"You have the cell numbers of a lot of your customers?"

"No. Danny and me were . . . friendly. No wonder it went straight to voice mail. . . ."

"You see him Wednesday night?"

"Yeah, sure. I said I did."

"Talk to him?"

"Just said hi. Not a real conversation."

"See him *with* anybody?"

"Well, he was dancing. That's why he came here. Saw him with a few different girls. He didn't have a regular partner, if you know what I mean."

"I don't know what you mean."

"He wasn't a . . . one-girl guy."

Amari nodded. "You ever . . . dance with him?"

"A few times."

"So then he wasn't gay?"

The owner grinned. "Danny Terrant? Boy, are

you confused. Danny had plenty of notches on his belt. And they *weren't* guys."

"Could he have batted for both teams?"

"No. Trust me, honey. He liked girls."

What the hell was going on?

The family of their other Billy Shears victim insisted their man was straight; now someone who knew Terrant—probably had slept with him—was telling her their second victim was straight, too.

Had the West Hollywood hotel been strictly to throw them off the track? Smart. Sneaky.

But who . . . *what* . . . was Billy? A cross-dressing man who could conceivably be perceived by his victims as a woman?

Or was Billy Shears really . . . *Billie* Shears?

Amari said, "Tell me about your security cameras."

"One by the bar, one by the door, another on the parking lot."

"Do we need a warrant?"

"No need. I liked Danny. Just Wednesday's DVDs?"

"For now," Amari said.

"Be right back," the woman said, climbing out.

Polk came over, jerked a thumb toward the bar. "Danny hooked up with that cute bartender."

"He also nailed the owner."

"For a shy beanpole, boy got around. Probably not gay."

"Probably not."

"You think our killer's maybe a transvestite?"

"Maybe. Or a woman."

". . . A *woman*?"

"Yeah. A woman. A female. The fairer sex?"

Polk sat down. "This is some screwed-up shit, Lieutenant."

"You think?"

Chapter Twenty-three

Show day again—not another live show, strictly speaking, but because of Don Juan, Harrow would be doing live wraparounds. Decisions had yet to be made about just what he would say about—and *to*—Don Juan.

No studio audience, thank God. Harrow was in his office going over material for tonight, feeling the strain of a fast-moving, brutal week.

The team had been working very long hours since that body had been left as a grisly message on their doorstep. LAPD had quickly identified the victim, a dental assistant named Gina Hannan, by her fingerprints. Turned out in college Gina had been booked for disturbing the peace when she had been arrested at . . . a peace rally.

But Don Juan had already emptied Gina's bank account into a Caymans one, and by the time Jenny tracked it down, the funds in the Islands had disappeared.

The video from the network's security cameras revealed very little—a shoulder here, a blur of rear view there, killer walking away. He wore a baseball cap, jeans jacket, gloves, jeans, and work boots, and Jenny figured him at medium height. Dark shaggy hair.

Don Juan had cased the building well. He knew the holes in the cameras' coverage and exploited them.

Though the delivery of the corpse was not caught on camera, there was footage enough to pinpoint the time—9:28 P.M. Downtown Los Angeles, around the UBC complex, was a ghost town Sunday evening.

Jenny hacked traffic cams for blocks without spotting Don Juan returning to his car. Security footage from UBC and its neighbors offered no indication the killer had parked out front when he dumped the body.

Pall and Choi helped Jenny check security footage of the parking garages within three blocks of UBC. Carting the body more than a relatively short distance seemed unlikely, and a parking garage would provide some shelter for whatever preparations were needed to transfer the corpse (*wrapped in some fashion?*) from a trunk or backseat.

Each tech took a garage and, finally, Jenny spotted something: a Ford Focus pulling out of a parking ramp nine minutes after the body had been dropped.

"Gotcha," she said, blowing up a still frame to where she could make out the license number.

Frowning, Pall asked, "Who waits almost ten minutes before he leaves a crime scene?"

Choi put in: "And what the hell was he doing for ten minutes?"

"Nine," Jenny said. "Calling the media?"

Her associates paused; then both nodded.

Soon she'd hacked the DMV to learn the plates on the Ford Focus were registered to a rental company's silver Nissan.

Another dead end.

Like the card stuck in the flowers—a run-of-the-mill greeting, available in a hundred flower shops around the Southland.

The roses, on the other hand, were rare. Michael Pall was able to identify them as Black Pearls, an uncommon variety.

Utilizing interns and production assistants, Harrow's team contacted the over seventeen hundred retail and wholesale florists in the greater Los Angeles area. None had received orders for that particular type of rose.

"He's got to be getting them somewhere," Harrow said to Pall and Jenny. "Either he has a rose garden, a greenhouse, or works at one. Find out who sells Black Pearl roses and start digging from that direction."

Meanwhile, Amari was keeping Harrow posted on what was now being called the *Billie* Shears case—the gay angle of the first killing apparently a red herring courtesy of a killer, who was likely female.

Internet searches for Jeff Baileys generated just under one hundred thousand hits. The computer search for Al Roberts—the guest in whose room Danny Terrant died—yielded another forty-three thousand hits. A mountain of information to scale.

As he sat at his desk, morning of show day, Harrow didn't have anything resembling a workable plan. Too much information was almost as bad as no information.

His cell vibrated—Amari.

"We have another apparent Don Juan victim."

The bastard had finally made good on his promise. Double-feature indeed. . . .

Harrow felt sick. "Where?"

"7008 Hollywood Boulevard. In front of a coffee shop. Body's sprawled across several Walk of Fame stars—including Errol Flynn's."

"Cute," Harrow said bitterly. "Errol Flynn played—"

"Don Juan, yeah. Plus, she's diagonally across the street from Grauman's Chinese Theater. Our guy's a showman, if nothing else."

For this early in the day, he felt awfully weary. "Nude? Bouquet of roses? Same as before?"

"Almost. Brunette. And that damn card again."

"And no one saw anything." Not a question.

"Not that we know of," Amari said. "I'm getting video from the traffic cams."

"I can think of another difference—besides the hair color."

"Which is?"

"*Crime Seen* didn't get a video before the body was found."

"Maybe he sent it to somebody else."

"Or is he accelerating and getting hurried, even sloppy?"

"That sounds like wishful thinking."

He sighed. "You want me down there, Anna?"

"No. No, there'll be media, and while the chief likes us cooperating with you, discreetly, he doesn't want the public to think the LAPD is leaning on a TV show."

"That sounds like a paraphrase."

"Yeah. I skipped the colorful qualifiers. You're a Midwest boy. Tender sensibilities. . . . Keep you posted."

"Please."

He had barely clicked off when Dennis Byrnes stormed in, unannounced.

"Morning, Dennis."

Byrnes arranged himself in the visitor's chair opposite Harrow, sitting straight, trying to assume his natural superiority despite being stuck on the wrong side of the desk.

"I need your word," he said.

"About?"

"You have to stay on script tonight."

"Where Don Juan is concerned, yes, understood. But we haven't finalized it yet."

"I expect you and the writers to have something to me by two o'clock. Lucian Richards at legal needs to clear it, and he says that will take time."

"Two o'clock might not be practical."

"Why is that?"

"There's been another Don Juan murder."

"Christ!"

Harrow filled the exec in.

"So you want to cut it closer to the wire," Byrnes said, thinking, "since this is breaking news. . . . Okay, I'll talk to Richards. Everyone is agreed that no portion of any of these videos can be shown on the air—third one hasn't shown up yet?"

"No."

"For once I wouldn't mind if the competition had it instead of us. This is dangerous, J.C. Delicate. The network's financial life could be at stake."

"So are the lives of innocent women—three have died so far."

"Don't go self-righteous on me. I'm a husband and a father, not a monster. A lot of people depend on this network for their living, I'll have you—"

Harrow stopped him with a raised palm. "Understood."

Byrnes nodded crisply, rose, then stopped at the door. "Listen, J.C. I want your word—don't go ad-libbing us into another crusade."

"Last time I did that, your precious network made a fortune."

"Just don't. We'll behave responsibly, we'll behave professionally . . . and if you and your people, working with the LAPD, can bring this bastard in, I'll revel in it. I'll see to it you a get nice fat bonus, just . . . tonight? Stay on script."

"Sure. Soon as we have one."

Byrnes closed his eyes, nodded. "When we have one."

He was gone.

Show day was a pain for Harrow—as star and executive producer of *Crime Seen*, he had to view and approve edits of segments, a process that took many hours, often right up to air time. With live segments on tap, he also suffered through script read-throughs and (eventually) hair and makeup.

Today, after lunch, he sequestered himself back in his office for a session of answering fan mail.

Usually, he wouldn't mess with this on show day, but he needed a distraction. Though most of his business and personal correspondence was e-mail now, fan mail remained the old-fashioned, snail-mail variety—fifty or so letters a week still came his way, sometimes more.

He escaped into the task, finding it oddly relaxing, reading half a dozen letters, mostly requests for autographed photos; just one marriage proposal this week.

The next letter had his name and the network's address computer-printed on the envelope with no return address. Within was a single sheet of white bond with a short message, probably off the same laser printer.

JC

You are some straight Harrow. Ha! Ha!

When the lab geeks test this, they will see it's really me.

I just wanted to drop you a line to say I'm a fan of the show and to thank you for the coverage.

Like the old story goes, it doesn't matter what they're saying as long as they're talking about you.

One more thing, you know the trophy I take.

I want to add yours to the collection, that would be juicy. But you will have to wait your turn.

BS

He wished he hadn't touched it, but he had.

The "trophy"-taking aspect of Billy Shears (as the media was still spelling it) had been withheld; the letter writer apparently knew what he—or she—was talking about.

Setting the thing back on his desk, cognizant of where he had touched the paper, his first call was to Laurene Chase, their in-house crime scene investigator. She could bag it and tag it.

"I want everybody else on this," he told her on the phone. "I know it's show night, but I'm the only one going on live. I want every kind of test on the letter, plus let's invent some new ones."

"You don't think there's any way this could be a hoax?"

"No, I don't. And after you read it, you won't, either."

His next call was to Amari.

"Nothing for you yet," she said. "Spent most of the day at Errol Flynn's star."

"I just got a fan letter."

"So you're popular."

"From Billie Shears."

"Hell you say! . . . And you didn't know what it was, so you got fingerprints all over it."

"Not all over it. On it."

"I'll grab Polk and be right over there."

"Good," he said. "Laurene's coming up to bag it."

"Twenty minutes," she said and clicked off.

Eighteen minutes later, the two detectives entered his office.

They both read the letter in its new cellophane home. They also studied the envelope.

Polk said, "He's a little vague about the trophy."

"Seems pretty suggestive to me," Harrow said.

"If we send it to the lab," Amari said, "we won't know whether it's authentic for weeks—even if I put a rush on it."

Harrow shrugged. "I know where there's a pretty good crime lab."

"Is that right?"

"And you'll go right to the front of the queue."

Polk was frowning, but Amari wasn't.

She said, "I have the go-ahead from the chief himself to work hand in hand with you and your team."

"So the answer is yes?"

"Answer is yes. Use that kid Anderson as our conduit, to protect the chain of evidence, but the answer is *hell* yes."

"Good."

She frowned at him, not angry, just serious. "Listen, J.C.—Chief Daniels phoned Captain Womack personally today. Now that Don Juan appears to have killed three times—prerequisite for bringing in the FBI—the chief had to call in the Behavioral Science Unit. They'll have agents here tomorrow."

"Just for Don Juan, or Billie Shears, too?"

"That I can't tell you. I *can* say—as you see by my

eager willingness to get help from your TV show lab—I am feeling flexible. Normally the FBI is about my favorite thing next to stomach influenza. But right now anything that helps get these two evil assholes off the street is fine by me."

"Agreed."

She arched an eyebrow. "In the meantime, what does Don Juan want?"

"Attention," Harrow said without hesitation. He didn't need Michael Pall to feed him that.

"Okay," she said calmly. "If Don Juan wants attention . . . why not give it to him?"

"How exactly?"

"On tonight's show, announce that the FBI is coming in to lead the Don Juan investigation. Turn the heat up a little."

"Last time we turned up the heat, a dead body wound up on my doorstep."

"*Last* time you turned up the heat by *ignoring* him. This time, let him have all kinds of attention from J.C. Harrow and *Crime Seen*. Maybe he'll get cocky and make a mistake."

Harrow frowned. "Well, we'd *love* him to make a mistake, but we don't want another innocent woman paying for it."

Amari was shaking her head. "What I mean is . . . tell Don Juan he needs to communicate with you *now,* so you can help him tell his story. That the FBI will insist on taking *Crime Seen* out of the equation."

Harrow called in Michael Pall for his opinion.

"We have precious little forensic evidence," Pall said. "I'm starting to think the only way we'll catch this guy is to smoke him out. You don't need to be a profiler to know this one's a narcissist of the first order. He thinks he's the world's greatest lover—what more do you need?"

When Harrow ran it past Byrnes, the executive's only complaint was that he hadn't gotten the word soon enough to plug it on the UBC nightly news.

Everyone was in agreement—the show would deal with Don Juan by announcing that the FBI would soon join the investigation. Amari (and Polk) went happily off to arrange for that *Killer TV* crime lab work.

Harrow retired to his office. He read the latest drafts of his script, okayed them, sent them along to Byrnes. With still an hour till air, just killing time, he returned to his interrupted fan mail. After that, he decided to at least check his e-mail account.

Very few people had this address and fewer still used it, since everybody knew Harrow rarely checked it. Mostly what he got was jokes from his Iowa buddies.

One name and subject line did catch his attention: a message from Carmen, the subject line reading *Re: Don Juan*, with an attached file.

Carmen was high on the list of those who knew how rarely Harrow checked his e-mailbox.

He phoned her.

"I didn't send you an e-mail," she said. "You'd never read it."

"That's what I thought—thanks."

He ended the call before she could question him.

Then he phoned Jenny Blake. "Can you come to my office?"

"Shouldn't you be in hair and makeup?"

"I think I have an e-mail from Don Juan."

Her response was the click of a hang-up.

He tracked down Amari and Polk. Soon they and the rest of the team, including Carmen, were in his office. Bad news traveled fast.

Half were seated across from Harrow's desk, the rest standing. Harrow was on his feet, Jenny in his chair at the desk with the laptop before her.

Polk said, "So you really think it's from him?"

Whether he was asking Harrow or Jenny wasn't clear.

Jenny said, "Date is today, but the time is one forty-seven a.m."

"I was in bed then," Carmen said. "I did *not* send that."

No one had accused her of it, but she seemed a little rattled. After all, the last Don Juan video had come in via *her* e-mail.

Jenny downloaded the file, then played it.

Like the others, it showed a beautiful drugged woman being made love to.

When Amari saw the woman's face, she said, "That's her—Hollywood Boulevard victim."

She was a brunette, her hair longer than Ellen's, but with the same type body as Harrow's deceased wife. Another woman he couldn't save.

When she screamed, Harrow made himself watch.

Then when the blade flashed into the screen, there was a millisecond of red (*not blood—cloth?*), and the blade came in from a different angle. Though the woman was still centered in frame, the camera was more to her right now.

As usual, the metallic voice of the killer came on. "*A promise is a promise, Mr. Harrow. Next week, would you like to try for four?*"

"Something's different," Pall said.

"Very different," Harrow said.

"*What?*" Laurene asked.

"That camera moved. Don Juan has an accomplice."

Chapter Twenty-four

They were all idiots.

All of those TV stars and "forensics superstars" and Emmy-winning reporters—fools.

Billie Shears laughed and the sound was brittle and echoey in the bathroom of the nonsmoking motel room. The morons still seemed think she was a "he," unless they were withholding that theory for their own sneaky purposes.

Naked, she sat on the lidded john, listening to the muffled blather of commercials on the TV as she smoked her third filter-tip Kool. Exhaust-fan hum made it a little tough to tell when the show came back. She let smoke curl out her nose. What was the old axiom, never commit a misdemeanor while committing a felony?

Like she gave a crap!

She took another deep drag, held it in, blew it out. When she heard the *Crime Seen* theme music, she stood, lifted the toilet lid, pitched the butt in, let the lid slam back in place, and went out to where she could sit on the bed, next to her victim.

He was already dead, of course, dark, slender, handsome, in his mid-thirties, the blood pooling in the lowest places where his body touched the mattress.

Tonight's *Crime Seen* had given a good share of its attention to Don Juan. Had to hand it to ol' Don Juan—placing that nude slaughtered bimbo outside UBC's front door was real showmanship. She almost wished she could match him.

But Don Juan was less an artist and more an egotist. The kind of grandstander who thrived on the attention that such public displays brought.

Billie was more private. She was no exhibitionist, no sexual show-off—to her, each assignation was intimate. Lying back on the bed, she touched the corpse's cool shoulder.

This man, for example, was special to her. They all were, of course, but this one possibly more so. Until now, her victims had been straight men, seduced by a woman, though she had shrewdly led the police to misinterpret her work as gay-themed homicides.

Now she would throw the authorities this curved ball (*these curved balls?*): the late gentleman lying next to her really *was* gay—openly so (as their investigations would soon determine).

And this sweet gay man had fallen for her ruse as hook, line, and sinker as the police had. Could even Meryl Streep have delivered a performance so multilayered? An actress playing a transvestite male?

But Billie had pulled it off.

That was how her date had wound up on this bed next to her, slowly assuming room temperature.

She gazed over at him with clinical affection, the gaping wound in his abdomen, in and up, tearing through lung, liver, stomach, and heart. Swift, even merciful—he had been dead before he could know what was happening.

So stoned, he hadn't even managed a gasp. He had just issued a confused, loopy grin, seeing the hedge trimmers. . . . Then he was gone, head lolling to one side like a man who'd just reached a dreamy orgasm.

The blood around the edges of the wound was already starting to darken as it dried from exposure to the air.

Good, she thought. *I don't have all night. . . .*

Billie pushed up on a palm and gazed into his eyes, glassy now, a vibrant green when he was drawing breath. These eyes stared blankly at the ceiling as she rolled toward him, her lovely, lithe body as nude as her victim's. She leaned her face in only inches from the open wound, like a dog sniffing a hydrant, so she could *feel* the last vestiges of warmth seeping from his body. . . .

Since childhood, she'd been unable to comprehend why God took the lives of people who did others little if any harm, while leaving behind evil bastards who hurt anyone who crossed their path. Even members of their own family.

He worked in mysterious ways, all right.

She did, however, understand the Godlike feeling that came with choosing who lived or died. *The power of life and death . . . what greater aphrodisiac could there be?* A shivery little thrill ran through her.

On the small flat screen, Harrow was going on and on about Don Juan: *"This is footage of the live studio audience from our show last week, when Don Juan expected us to focus our attention on him."*

"I wonder what kind of lover J.C. Harrow would make?" she said softly.

The body on the bed next to her appeared to have no opinion.

"None of the studio audience members fit the profile of the killer we're helping the LAPD track down."

Profile! What a joke. The profile for *her* would say she was male. After all, worldwide, ninety percent of serial killers *were* male. Eighty-six percent were heterosexual, so if she was a male killing males, as the cops thought, she would be flying in the face of that particular statistic.

Eighty-nine percent of victims were white, and serial killers usually murdered within their race. The poor gent on the bed next to her backed up those numbers. She smiled at him. Billie was so much *more* than the sum of a bunch of statistics . . .

. . . and before this was over, the LAPD and Harrow's *Crime Seen* team would both learn that.

"Despite our best efforts," Harrow was saying, *"as well as those of the Los Angeles Police Department's Sex Crimes Division, Don Juan remains at large . . . though we are growing closer to apprehending this monster with every passing minute."*

She giggled, giving her victim a gentle elbow in

the ribs, forgetting for a moment that he couldn't share in her amusement at Harrow's silly melodramatics.

"What's he going to say next?" she asked her silent lover. " 'We don't want you good folks out there in TV Land to worry any, just 'cause two clever serial killers, who are way smarter than us, are at large terrorizing our fair city. My team of superstar blah blah blah will protect you from blah blah blah.' "

The victim made no comment.

She sat up and leaned over to press the pad of his big toe.

The indentation remained. Blood was gone from there, having seeped to the lowest spot, the heel.

Time to get back to work.

She loved her role. Few people in this life had as much fun at their craft, their art, as she did.

"You're going to spend over sixty thousand hours of your life working," she good-naturedly informed the corpse. "Well, not *you*, lover, you got *early* retirement. . . . But you might as well choose a profession you enjoy. That gives you job satisfaction *and* a real sense of accomplishment. And what a happier place this world would be."

No disagreement from the corpse.

"What's the old saying?" she asked. "Do something you love, and you'll never waste a day in your life. That's certainly the way *I* feel. . . ."

Glassy eyes studied the ceiling.

"Did *you* feel that way? When you were alive? I

hope so. Though I guess if you were living one of those quiet lives of desperation, maybe I did you a favor tonight."

Whistling a happy tune, she picked up the hedge trimmers and carefully positioned them across the victim's thighs. It would be a shame to nick his nice slender but muscular legs when she took her trophy. He was special—he deserved the care she was taking. . . .

On the flat screen, J.C. Harrow was closing the show.

"We have one final piece of business before we wish you good night. . . ."

She looked up toward the TV, hands leaving the handles of the shears.

"The Los Angeles Police Department has asked us to make an announcement on their behalf."

Interest bubbled within her. So few things in this world could actually perk her interest, and here she was getting that rush for a second time in one evening.

"Beginning tomorrow, the FBI will be taking over the investigation into the killings attributed to Don Juan and Billy Shears."

A lovely spasm coursed through her, a kind of mini-orgasm—Harrow had reported on the latest "Billy Shears" killing at the top of the show, but the emphasis tonight had been on Don Juan.

Now, as the program came to its conclusion, here she was getting a real primetime mention— *and equal footing with Don Juan!*

Since childhood she'd dreamed of it—being famous, becoming a star, a movie star perhaps, a TV star certainly, but a *star*.

FBI attention to Don Juan meant FBI attention to Billie Shears! So happy was she with her increased importance, she bent over the corpse as the titles ran on the show, and planted a tender kiss on lips dead a good hour by now. Cool, soft, pliant lips. . . .

"I know you're watching, Don Juan, so pay special attention now—once the FBI is here, you and I will no longer be able to communicate. These coming hours represent the last chance you have to talk directly to me."

She returned the already-positioned hedge clippers, opened the blades, and lifted his scrotum and penis over the bottom blade, letting them rest there. Tensing her arm muscles, she took one last look at her lover's face, then slammed the handles, the blades snipping off the trophy as neatly as if it were the small branch of a sapling.

When she had the trophy bagged, she wiped off the blades of her trimmers with toilet paper and flushed it.

She was tuckered.

Sitting on the lidded stool again, she lit up another Kool and let the thoughts drift in.

The LAPD bringing in the FBI, she liked that. Showing up the likes of the cops had been almost too easy. The so-called "all-star" forensics team of J.C. Harrow had presented no real challenge, either. So far, at least.

She blew smoke toward the exhaust fan.

Raising the stakes like that, they were doing her

a favor—she could accelerate the scenario. She had been waiting a long, long time to achieve fame—no reason not to get on the fast track now. Head for the ol' fast lane. She grinned, standing to drop the cigarette into the toilet.

Though the blood had mostly settled when she took her trophy, plenty of red had still got on the sheets, her tool, and herself.

Soon she was stepping under the shower's near-scalding spray. Felt wonderful, luxurious. Soaped herself slowly, enjoying the spray on her body, getting lost in a steamy cloud.

No need to shampoo. The alopecia universalis had taken care of that. She had not found any doctor who could figure out how to regrow the hair that had fallen out back when she had turned eighteen; they all said it was an "autoimmune disorder."

Her body hair had deserted her, just like her mother. Scalp, eyebrows, eyelashes, pussy, it was all gone, leaving her hairless as a baby—hairless-*er* actually, and never coming back.

What had been a crisis for a young woman had become the perfect gift from God. Being hairless was one of the reasons she could share a bed with her victims. If a crime-scene investigator found a hair, it would be her latest victim's, or from her latest wig.

Billie smooshed at the fogged-up mirror with a towel, then admired her hairless body in the glass. She was twenty-eight but still looked eighteen, a nice slender shape, like a model's, if bustier. She liked the way she looked without hair. She wore the fake eyelashes and thin fake eyebrows just so she would blend in with the outside world. At home, she didn't bother.

She put on the short, coal-black wig, tugging it into perfect place. It was modeled after one she had seen Kate Bosworth wear in a movie. The actress was beautiful, but Billie Shears looked even better in it.

Dressed again, her tools and trophy packed up, she took one last lap around the room. Her ensemble included plastic booties over her shoes—she had rubbed out her bare footprints in the carpeting and used a damp towel to wipe up any footprints on the bathroom's tile floor.

Her towel, from after the shower, hung from the rod. Knowing she wasn't in CODIS, the cops' DNA database, was a plus. That meant she could leave DNA behind and it would only further confound the police—and now the FBI.

What was a naked woman doing in a motel room with a naked gay man? they would wonder.

As she exited, she smiled. The cops, the FBI, J.C. Harrow himself, could ask question after question; but she would still have her secrets.

Chapter Twenty-five

When the call came in early Saturday morning, and Harrow saw AMARI in the caller ID window, he hoped it was personal.

It wasn't.

He threw on chinos, a tan polo, and a brown sports coat, climbed in his black Equinox, and drove quickly to the address in West Covina, a nondescript non-chain motel, two stories with a courtyard parking area.

Anna was waiting just outside the lobby. She was in dark slacks and a gray silk blouse, big black purse on a strap over her shoulder, her stylish dark hair nicely tousled by the balmy breeze of this overcast morning. He wished he could check in at this motel with her and spend a pleasant day getting to know each other in the Biblical sense. That wasn't going to happen.

"Billie Shears is pissed at you," she said, meeting him as he climbed out of the Chevy.

"Is she now?"

"Oh yeah. Appears you spent too much time on Don Juan last night."

He fell in alongside her as she headed inside a turquoise-and-gold lobby where it was still 1977.

"She left a note for you at the front desk," she said, "and a body in a room upstairs."

"Lucky me."

"Oh, there's more. Somebody's stopped by who wants to meet you."

He closed his eyes. "FBI?"

"Lucky you is right. He's waiting upstairs."

Evidence techs behind the front desk were gathering security video. The desk clerk, a young black woman in a light blue blazer, was trying to hold her emotions in check.

As they ascended an open stairway around which the airy lobby was designed, Anna handed Harrow a plastic bag inside of which he could see the note.

JC,

I said I would take your tackle—but now you have to wait your turn.

I will line my trophy case with prize after prize till you can't ignore me anymore.

Next week you make ME the star of CRIME SEED and maybe I will take a week off. But if you even MENTION Dong Wadd I will step up the fun! Maybe one a day—how would you like that?

It's what you get for ignoring me last night for that hack Dud Wand—get it? Hack! Ha! ha!

You will just have to wait your turn. But I'm coming and when I take yours, it will be nice and slow. Yumm.

Maybe I could shear you right on your show? Best ratings ever!

BS

"I wish this *were* B.S.," Harrow said. "But I don't think he . . . she . . . is kidding."

"Sick shit," Anna said.

He handed her back the baggie. "No argument."

They stopped at the top.

She tucked the note in her purse. "What do you make of this rivalry?"

"Dueling serial killers? Vying for attention on my show? What more could any TV star hope for?"

"Blaming yourself doesn't get us anywhere. But I bet that network stooge will love it."

"Dennis? I don't think so. He'll love the ratings, but he'll hate the legal exposure."

Polk was coming down the hall to meet them. He removed his fedora, ran a hand over his forehead. He looked vaguely ill.

Harrow said, "That bad?"

"Castrated murder victim," Polk said, "first thing Saturday morning? Not my favorite."

"Not a great way to start a day," Harrow admitted. "Any ID on the victim?"

"No wallet or anything."

Anna was in the lead, Polk and Harrow falling in side by side.

Polk said, "Name on the register is Eric Stanton, but the victim's name is Kyle Gerut."

Harrow asked, "How'd we get that?"

"FBI guy has a cool new toy that lets him take a vic's fingerprints and send them to the National Fingerprint Center. Half an hour later, the guy is made."

"So Gerut had a record?"

"Yeah—gay dude, got busted during some GLAAD rally a few years back."

"So is Eric Stanton a phony name just for check-in? Or is he the murderer?"

"The FBI doesn't seem to have a gizmo that can tell us *that.*"

They had made it to the uniformed officer at the door. Anna went in first, Harrow following, Polk lingering in the hall.

The cop on the door warned, "Crowded in there."

Immediately Harrow saw what the guy meant: a crime-scene tech was busy in the bathroom, collecting and bagging towels; another tech pored over the bed; and two coroner's office EMT types were struggling to load the sheet-covered body from the bed onto a gurney.

Years ago, college kids used to stuff themselves into phone booths—Harrow felt like that one last frat boy going for the record.

Across the compact room, a tall brown-haired guy in a crisp navy blue suit and a red tie was taking it all in—the FBI guy, obviously.

Harrow managed to edge beside Anna and whispered, "Collect the Fibbie and let's talk."

She nodded, and Harrow retreated to the corridor, where soon Anna returned with the FBI agent in tow. They moved a few doors down, away from the uniform on guard, and Anna made introductions.

The FBI guy was Mark Rousch.

As they shook hands, Rousch told Harrow he appreciated *Crime Seen*'s cooperation on the two serial killer cases. "A pleasure to shake the hand of a man who saved the life of the President of the United States."

Harrow had long since given up on saying anything modest or self-deprecating in response to statements like that. He just took the compliment with a smile and a nod.

"You know, J.C.—all right if I call you J.C.?"

"Sure, Mark."

"J.C., normally any special agent would tell you to butt the hell out of a federal investigation."

"Understood."

"And if you even tried to insert yourself into the investigation, like you did with the LAPD, you'd get your ass run in for obstruction."

The man's tone remained pleasant, chipper even.

But the second comment had been a step too far, and Harrow suddenly did not like this smiling son of a bitch . . . but did his best not to show it.

"However," Rousch said, "this is a rather exceptional situation. Plus, like the LAPD, the FBI needs all the good press we can get."

Harrow's voice was gentle as he rubbed it in: "Waco, Ruby Ridge . . . I get it."

Rousch's smile curdled a little. "What I'm saying

is, far as I'm concerned? You're still part of this investigation . . . in a supportive capacity."

Harrow said, "Happy to help."

"Glad to hear that," Rousch said cheerfully. "We would ask one favor. . . ."

"Shoot."

"Take a break."

"A break? What kind of break?"

"Take your show off the air till we catch these crazies."

"Are you kidding?"

"We have two homicidal nutjobs who are competing for air time on your program. Let's remove the program . . . for now. That may remove part of the problem."

Harrow let out a bunch of air he'd been holding in. "First of all, Mark, I don't have the authority to pull the show. Second, there's a scrap of paper with something called the First Amendment on it you may wish to refer to."

Rousch raised a palm as if he were swearing in in court. "This comes from higher up. Don't kill the messenger."

Anna closed her eyes, understanding the awkwardness of that remark, since it invoked the murderer of Harrow's family. And Harrow *had* in fact killed him. . . .

"You're former law enforcement, J.C. You're well aware the First Amendment doesn't cover yelling 'Fire' in a crowded building."

"It does if there's a fire."

"You can make the case to your network president—what's his name, Burnside? Who better to make an eloquent, reasoned argument for putting *Crime Seen* on temporary hiatus?"

Harrow's laugh was abrupt. "You can't really think either of these madmen will stop just because the show isn't on?"

"The brain trust at the BSU thinks *Crime Seen* is inflaming the killers."

"Want to see them inflamed? Take their platform away."

The agent frowned. "Then you won't talk to Mr. Burnside for us?"

"His name is Byrnes, and with all due respect, Agent Rousch, make the case yourself."

"J.C.," Anna began.

But Harrow had already taken off down the corridor. When he got to the stairs, he went down, listening for anyone following—no one was.

In the parking lot, he got Jenny on the cell. He filled her in on the new Billie Shears kill.

Then she asked, "We have anything beside the name Kyle Gerut?"

"He's dead and he was gay."

"Hate crime?"

"Billie Shears seems to be an equal-opportunity hater."

"Probably hates himself most."

"Pretty sure it's *herself*, Jen."

"Thought you said Gerut was gay."

"Yeah, but I think we have a real cute killer here. Playing us for chumps."

"We aren't chumps."

"That's good to hear. Listen, run Eric Stanton,

too." He spelled it. "That's the name used at check-in."

"Okay, boss. We have security video?"

"Maybe not. The LAPD is working with the FBI now. They're talking like we're still on the team, but I have reason to doubt it."

"Okay," she said, not asking why, and they signed off.

He turned and found Anna there.

"And just the other day," she said, "I was telling somebody how diplomatic you could be."

"He pissed me off."

She shrugged. "The Fibbies wrote the book on patronizing pricks. Listen . . . I didn't know Rousch would pull that. I didn't walk you into an ambush. Anyway, I didn't mean to."

"I know. And maybe I'd feel the same as Rousch in his place."

"No you wouldn't. Don Juan and Billie Shears are just looking for an excuse to escalate, and the show going dark would only hand it to them."

His cell phone throbbed and Harrow checked caller ID—ANDERSON.

The youthful Southern-tinged voice said, "So Billie Shears struck again, I hear?"

"He, she, or it did," Harrow said. He filled Anderson in, leaving out his confrontation with the FBI agent.

"Man, is this a grim one," Anderson said.

"And not in the fairy-tale way."

"Don't know if it'll help, boss—but I ran that hair that Lieutenant Amari gave us from the first Billy Shears crime scene?"

"And?"

"It's human, all right, but I couldn't get DNA."

"How's that possible?"

"The follicle is missing. Michael Pall took a swing at it, too, came up the same."

"So what's the explanation?"

"From a wig."

"A wig! How can you tell?"

"Sucker's soaked in acetic acid."

"*Vinegar?*"

"Bingo, boss. Human hair used for wigs is sometimes soaked in an acetic acid solution—to remove nits before the hair is woven into a wig? I thought Lieutenant Amari would want to know, soon as possible."

"Good work, Chris—she's right here. I'll tell her. Keep digging."

"Yes, sir."

Harrow clicked off and turned to Anna. "The hair found at the first Billie Shears crime scene—"

"Came from a wig."

". . . Yeah. How d'you know?"

She smiled. "Figured it out from your end of the conversation. I know some about wigs. My mother died of cancer."

"Sorry to hear."

"Long time ago. But when she was going through chemo, we got to know all about wigs."

Once the crime scene was wrapped, Anna, Polk, and Rousch followed Harrow back to UBC. They met up with the *Killer TV* team in the conference room, the three officers on their feet while Harrow took his seat at the table's head.

He introduced Rousch, then—to help get him caught up—had Jenny show the latest Don Juan video on the big screen.

As they got near the first blow from the knife, Choi said, "Here comes the *new* part—"

The camera moved ever so slightly, a flash of blade and another of red cloth, and the woman's neck erupted with blood.

Choi said, "The camera moved."

Rousch frowned. "You mean somebody bumped into it?"

"No," Choi said. "It *moved*."

"As in someone moved it," Anna said, getting it.

Choi turned to Jenny, "Run the last part again."

This time, Rousch saw it.

"Camera definitely moved," Anna said.

The FBI agent remained confused. "So it moved—what does that mean?"

Harrow said, "It means Don Juan has somebody running camera for him."

Choi said, "We figure it's a hidden camera, behind a two-way mirror or a peephole. We doubt these victims were participating in some kind of porno session, with a cameraman out in the open."

Chase said, "But it's possible."

Choi said, "Possible but not probable."

"And that means," Harrow said, "Don Juan has an accomplice."

"Holy shit," Rousch said. "*Two* are in on this?"

Harrow nodded.

"That could change *everything*. . . ."

"It does change everything," Harrow said, and leaned forward, eyes traveling from face to face.

"We thought we were looking for a single serial killer. This new perspective gives us a fresh start."

Choi said, "If Don Juan's had help through all of this, maybe we missed something—something that could lead us to the accomplice, if not Don Juan himself."

Rousch, impressed, said, "It's a breakthrough."

Harrow said, "You're welcome. . . . Laurene, where are we with the roses?"

Chase said, "They're rare, but not impossible to find—we're still running down the leads."

"Keep at it," Harrow said.

Anna asked, "Any luck on the computer front? Tracking the cyber theft side?"

Jenny shook her head. "Guy could give me lessons."

Everybody on the team gave her an astonished look—that was quite an admission.

Harrow said, "Might be we're looking at this bass-ackwards. He's choosing single, at least semi-successful women—what do they have in common?"

Jenny said, "They all were, or wanted to be, actresses."

"So Don Juan likely got to them by saying he was in show business, too—right?"

"Swell," Anna said, standing with arms crossed. "We've just narrowed our suspect pool to every breathing male in Los Angeles who ever hit on a pretty girl."

That earned some weary smiles.

Pall, not smiling, said, "But our man had to *stalk* them—he's cleaning out their bank accounts, so he's only going after women he already knows have money. *How* does know?"

Jenny said, "From their accounts."

"But how did he get in there in the first place?"

"By sending in the Trojan horse and getting their keystrokes and passwords—we've already got that."

"You're not seeing it," Pall said. "Don Juan isn't randomly e-mailing women, who turn out to have money. *Nobody's* that lucky. So he's starting somewhere."

"With actresses," Jenny said.

"Yes. And not every would-be actress has money—most are fairly broke, right?"

"Right," Harrow said, beginning to get it.

Pall said, "If he's going in the show-business door, maybe he's an agent, or an acting teacher, or producer. . . ."

"Or posing as one," Chase said.

"So," Pall said, "he must go through a number of women who don't meet his financial standards. But how many does he have to go through to get to the ones with money?"

Anna said, "And who are they, and how were they contacted?"

Choi said, "If you can't track the killer . . ."

". . . track the victims," Harrow said.

Chapter Twenty-six

The late-night visits from the old man started not long after their mother abandoned them. His sister—only twelve at the time—had been the first made to pleasure the old man.

A year or so later, the boy also would receive the occasional nocturnal visit—the old man stuffing that thing into this place and that. If the boy gagged or protested, beatings followed. For several years, sister and brother took turns keeping the old man happy.

Finally a new awful ritual began—their father using one of them for his pleasure while the other one was made to watch. 'Cause if you didn't watch, somebody got slapped. Maybe the watcher, maybe the watched, which somehow was even worse than getting slapped yourself.

This had all happened a long time ago . . .

. . . *but tonight he was back there again, back in that tiny, musty attic bedroom of his sister's. He had long since learned a price was paid when he turned his head, so he watched intently in the darkened room, or anyway his eyes went in that direction though privately, secretly, he was making them blur, as the old man towered over his now sixteen-year-old sister.*

That one time, she'd had the temerity to appear without panties, ready for him, having been completely cowed by the old man. That had been a mistake. Turned out, the panties were part of the ritual.

That night the old man had beaten her, severely, not to mention shouting at her that she was a slut and a common whore.

Ever since, they both made sure to play the game by the old man's rules. That way it would be over sooner and with less pain, if no less shame.

So, while the boy sat in a straight-back wooden chair, his eyes blurred on the action, the old man forced his daughter to stand there facing her brother as father stood sideways and unbuttoned daughter's blouse and moved in close to stroke her smooth, alabaster skin, nearly luminous with only the moonlight filtering through the flimsy curtains lighting their sins.

That was the only bad thing about the boy blurring his vision—it gave the acts a dreamy look, a kind of gauzy prettiness that wasn't right.

Dreamy look, but nightmare sounds, smells. Even sitting across the room, the boy could smell that fetid breath—liquor, cigarettes, the very odor of the old man's hollow existence . . . must be how Hell smelled. The boy's sister knew not to protest and had learned to make her whimpers and ouches sound like she liked it though her eyes screamed otherwise.

Briefly, the boy thought about having another go at

the old man, but fear overwhelmed him. Every time he had tried to stop their father, the boy ended up on his ass, blood running from his mouth or nose. Once, the old man had kicked him so hard in the ribs, the boy puked blood, continued coughing it up for days.

The old man was solid as a house and had a good fifty pounds on his son's narrow ass. Knowing he couldn't win the fight, the boy sat on the chair, willing himself not to cry, to try to show strength for his sister, his fists balled if impotent at his sides.

"Pretty," the old man said in his scratchy voice.

Even in the moonlit room, the boy could see the old man's paw tremble as he slowly pulled the girl's panties down her long, white legs. Then the old man helped her out of them, before he sat her on the edge of the bed.

The old man just stood there, towering over her, not quite blocking her from the boy's view. When she unzipped the fly, the scratchy sound of metal was like an echo of the old man's terrible voice.

The boy, biting his lip so hard he tasted blood, watched as his sister did what she had to, as he himself had done so many times. He blurred his eyes more, more, more, till he was almost blind, but when he heard the bedsprings and then his sister's sharp intake of breath, he could see it anyway, in his mind's eye. He couldn't blur that. *He couldn't make* that *go blind.*

Looking down, the boy saw the cord for the cheap plastic lamp that was the only light the old man allowed in here.

"What you doin' there, sonny? Eyes front!"

The boy's eyes snapped back to his father hunkered over the girl, but as soon as the old man's attention was back on what he was doing, the boy's eyes returned to the cord. Just pull the plug and run over there and get the cord around the old man's neck and then squeeze like a son of a bitch till the old man was dead. . . .

"Boy! You ain't watchin', boy!"

"Sorry, sir," the boy said. "I will, sir."

When the old man returned to his business, the boy did not hesitate.

He swooped down, grabbed the cord and lamp in his hands and jerked them free from the wall. The old man had just started to back away from his victim, hearing something, when the boy looped the cord around his father's neck and jumped on his back, pulling the cord taut.

The old man tumbled off the bed, taking his son with him, knocking the wind from the boy, who reflexively loosened his grip on the cord.

Like a wounded animal, the bare-assed old man rolled over, snatched up the cord and wrapped it around his son's neck, yanking the ends tight, like the old bastard was tying his boots. The boy choked but made no sound.

The naked girl flew at her father, but he backhanded her and she smacked against the door frame with a sick squish and slid to the floor in a human puddle.

The boy tried to scream, but still no sound came out, precious air harder and harder to come by. His mouth just kept working, though nothing happened, no air able to enter, no sound able to emerge. He could feel his eyes bugging and as he clawed at the cord, he could feel himself scratching wounds in his own throat, trying to get one finger under the killing cord.

Sweat streamed down his forehead, into his eyes, burning them. Still, he could see the wild eyes of his killer, his *own father, the perverted old bastard pressing down on him as he pulled like a madman on the ends of the cord.*

The boy couldn't inhale, yet still he could smell the old man's foul breath welcoming him to Hell.

When blackness enveloped him, it would have been a relief if he weren't also falling, endlessly falling, arms windmilling as he dropped into a bottomless pit. . . .

A man now, he woke up, coughing, choking for breath.

The sweat that had been part of the dream was with him still, as he sat up in his bed—not in the black painted womb of Louis St. James, but his real bedroom, in his own home, where he lived under his real name.

He looked at the clock, cursed the hour, then flopped back down. The perspiration-soaked pillow did not encourage a return to sleep. Maybe that was just as well, since sleep might bring that nightmare back with it. Even in his goddamn *dreams*, the old man kicked his ass!

As a child, he'd hated his parents. As an adult, he despised them even more—his mother for abandoning them, the old man for every disgusting, obscene damn thing he'd ever done to brother and sister.

Giving up, he clicked on the nightstand lamp and swung his legs over the edge of the bed. Sat there. In only his shorts, he reached for the folded towel he kept at his bedside just for nights like this.

After drying off, he sat for perhaps five minutes more, trying to drive away the images in his head. Some dreams disappeared on waking, others seemed to dissolve away, detail at a time.

This dream lingered.

No, more than lingered—persisted, its terrible images lodged in his brain like inoperable tumors.

Despite the hour, he grabbed his cell. Just before it kicked over to voice mail, his sister (thank God!) answered.

"The nightmare?" she asked, sleepy but forcing herself alert.

"Sorry," he said.

"You *know* it's not real."

"I know. *Feels* real."

"Think pleasant thoughts."

"That never occurred to me."

"Sarcasm?"

"Sorry."

"You should be happy. The FBI! That's the *real* prime time."

"I know."

"Concentrate on that. We have to be on top of our game."

"I know."

"The FBI, they're not stupid."

"Neither are we."

Her voice was almost a purr. "I know, dear. I'm just saying . . . we're getting close now, to what we want to achieve."

"What we *need* to achieve."

"Right. We can't get caught too *soon*, dear. We need to be careful."

"We're always careful."

"You know what I mean."

"I would *so* like to make the FBI look like fools."

Her voice had a smile in it. "Do you have something in mind?"

". . . There's a young woman I've had my eye on."

"Acting-class candidate?"

"No. But she's right for the part, anyway."

"That's good! This'll take your mind off all the ancient bullshit."

". . . Tell me we'll be famous."

"We already are. But right now all we have is our fifteen minutes. We want to live forever."

"We're *going* to live forever."

"Live forever, and do things the old man never thought we could!"

Their father's abuse had spoken volumes about how little he regarded them. Never once had he given them credit for being anything more than receptacles.

"We'll show the old bastard!" he said. "We'll show him! We'll show *all* of them!"

"Tell me about the new candidate."

"I've been watching her for a few weeks. She's a teller in a small bank in Newport Beach."

"Not an actress?"

"No."

"But will she bite for Louis St. James?"

"Oh yeah."

They always referred to Louis St. James in the third person. Although Louis was a role he played (like Don Juan), he and his sister referred to St. James as another full-fledged member of the team. Or rather . . . the cast.

"She's already met Louis," he said. "She was attracted to him, obviously."

"But a bank teller? That's a lowly profession."

"She dresses well. Designer clothes. I suspected hidden depths."

"So you e-mailed her."

"I did. And found hidden depths, all right. Hidden *riches*."

"You are *so* smart, dear."

"When Louis suggested that she'd make a better actress than most of the so-called actresses he had to contend with, she got very excited."

"Typical."

"Turns out she acted in high school, but never considered acting a practical goal. She's certainly pretty enough. But she comes from a conservative family, you know—business types."

"How you're raised *can* set you on a path, they say."

He laughed. "Imagine, finding a woman in Los Angeles who *isn't* an actress wannabe."

"It's like finding a unicorn."

"Well, *this* unicorn has money."

"How much?"

"Those conservative parents I mentioned? They died and left her a small bundle. Accounts I've accessed so far? Add up to just shy of a hundred thousand."

"*Oooooh*—that would keep us going for a while."

"She looks at me and sees a bright future. I look at her and see my own personal ATM."

"You are a *riot!* . . . When are we going to bring her into the production?"

"I'll call her in the morning. See if she'd like to have dinner with Louis. You all right with that? Not too soon, is it?"

"Not at all," she said. "We *should* step it up. J.C. Harrow's all in a tizzy about getting preempted by the FBI. I *love* it! . . . What preparations do we need to make?"

"Usual."

"I'll get the flowers after lunch."

"Cool. I'll prep the room. Get the camera loaded."

Her voice took on an ethereal quality. "You know—if we can keep this going, to where we want it to? We'll be Manson famous."

"*Son of Sam* famous."

"*Night Stalker* famous."

"*Bundy* famous."

"*Gacy* famous."

"*Dahmer* famous."

"*Jack the Ripper* famous."

"All stars, in their own right," he admitted. "But we're taking it to the *next* level. Something our role models never dreamed of."

"*Hollywood* famous," she said.

They bid each other good night.

His pillow was dry now.

He could try to sleep again.

Before he drifted off, he felt confident the nightmare would not return tonight. He *knew* the old man couldn't hurt him anymore.

Still, there was the lingering, bittersweet disappointment that came knowing hard living had killed the old man before son and daughter got the chance.

Chapter Twenty-seven

Billy Choi, in T-shirt and jeans, sleepwalked into the conference room with the LAPD Don Juan files under an arm and a mug of coffee in one hand. He flopped into his usual chair.

Eight o'clock a.m. Sunday—usually a day off—but at least cameras had been banished by boss man Harrow, who came in behind Billy followed by Pall, Chase, and Anderson.

Choi felt like he had been on a two-day bender—burning eyes, cotton mouth, and a stomach subsisting on vending machine food.

Chase, in gray sweats, looking awake but barely, squinted at Choi over her own personalized *Killer TV* mug. "Where's Jenny? She's usually first in."

Anderson answered, way too chipper: "On her way."

The cornpone chemist was in a striped blue and yellow polo and new jeans, as if he had fallen out of an old Beach Boys video.

The kid said, "Thinks she may be on to somethin'."

The boss had on black jeans and a white shirt with sleeves rolled up, looking like an old waiter.

Harrow said, "Till Jenny saves the day, what else has anybody got?"

Choi said, "Your cute sex crimes lieutenant called to say the Hollywood Boulevard vic has a name."

"Billy," Harrow said, narrow-eyed. "Respect is a two-way street."

"Yeah, I know. But you can still get run down. ID came from an ex-husband hoping there might be a reward."

Pall, in a brown suit (*a friggin'* suit) but no tie (*going wild!*) said, "How'd she ever let a catch like that get away?"

"Guess she didn't know what she had," Choi said dryly. "Anyway, her name was Megan Chavez."

Harrow asked, "What do we know about her?"

"Born Megan Kowalski, in Arizona, died twenty-six, in LA. At eighteen, she married a local bricklayer named Ramon Chavez, moved out here. Marriage went south. Ditched everything from her former life except the last name. Became a hairdresser, never owned her own shop, but worked on a few indie flicks and a couple cable TV shows. She was union."

Harrow said, "Show-business connection."

"Right. And like the other Don Juan victims, she had a tidy nest egg in her bank account. But by the time Jenny tracked that down, Don Juan had trans-

ferred her loot to an off-shore account, then removed it from there as well."

Chase said, "Love them and leave them . . .
broke."

Choi said, "As for the roses next to her body,
Black Pearls again. And that's all we have so far."

Harrow nodded. "Decent start. Michael, anything on the second Billie Shears note?"

"It's legit," Pall said.

Chase asked, "How do we know?"

"DNA from the envelope."

Choi said, "Licked it shut?"

Pall nodded.

Harrow said, "Matching the DNA to what?"

Pall said, "I got the DNA report from the towel
the cops took from the third Shears victim, Kyle
Gerut. Gerut was gay, remember, but the DNA on
the letter, and the towel? Belongs to a woman."

Harrow said, "So if we had any doubt, cross it
out—this is definitely B-i-l-l-i-e Shears."

No argument.

Chase cocked her head. "But this is a smart
killer—cleaning up after herself to near perfec-
tion. About all she's ever left behind is a hair from
a wig."

"Speaking of which," Anderson said, "the hair
from Gerut's bed—the black one? It'd been
soaked in acetic acid . . . vinegar . . . just like the
other."

Harrow narrowed his eyes. "So it's from a wig
too?"

"Yes, sir."

"Almost as if she's parceling out clues to us."

Pall said, "Maybe not 'almost.' "

Choi held up his hand with the force of a dumb kid in class finally coming up with a question. "I thought a *man* checked into the rooms every time."

"From the Star Struck on," Chase confirmed.

Anderson, grappling with it, said, "Maybe she's one of those . . . cross-dressers."

Pall shrugged. "We don't have any *really* decent video of the 'guy' checking in. Not impossible."

Choi said, "Or maybe Billie Shears has an accomplice, too—a male one."

Harrow blurted, "Son of a bitch!"

All eyes were on him.

"*Listen* to yourselves," he said. "It's right there in front of us."

Chase was the first to get it. "Oh hell . . ."

Then Choi got onboard and said, "Well, goddamn—Don Juan and Billie Shears . . . they're not *dueling*. They're together! They're *playing* us!"

Harrow was chuckling, in a dark sort of way. "Nobody in this room is old enough to remember, but years ago? Two very famous radio comedians, Jack Benny and Fred Allen, pretended to have a feud. Really they were close friends. But the ratings? Went through the roof for both their shows."

Pall said, "In non-broadcasting terms?

"We've been looking at these as unrelated investigations, chasing two separate killers in two separate cases."

Harrow was smiling, but his eyes were hard. "The evidence seems to be telling us that Don

Juan has a female accomplice, and that Billie Shears has a male accomplice—that there are two people involved in each set of cases."

Nods around the table.

"What are the odds of that, even in a city the size of Los Angeles? *Two* male/female serial-killing teams? When did that ever happen? Logically, we have one serial killing team, trading off victims."

"And," Choi said, "playing us for chumps."

Only Pall seemed at all skeptical. "Is there any way we can test this theory? Remember, we may have been stalled this long because we tried to fit the facts into a preconceived theory."

"Good point," Harrow said. "But there's one thing all the victims in both cases have in common."

Jenny, coming in at the rear of the room, answered him: "They were all drugged."

"With the *same* drug," Anderson said, as she nestled next to him. "Flunitrazepam. A.k.a Rohypnol."

Roofies.

Harrow asked, "Anything we can track?"

"As if," Choi said.

Anderson shook his head.

"All right," Harrow said, and sighed. "What about the *levels* of the drug in their systems?"

The chemist checked his notes. "More in the men than in the women, but roughly the same by gender."

"How much?"

"Pardon?"

"We know the dosages weren't lethal, right?"

"Ah, I see where you're goin', boss—they each, male *and* female, had enough of the drug in their systems to make them . . . well, *pliable,* but not knock them out."

"So whoever gave them the drug had some working knowledge of the stuff, including the correct dosage, right?"

"Yes, sir."

Pall asked, "Someone in the medical community?"

"Or a pharmacist," Chase said without enthusiasm.

"Yeah, I know, it's weak," Harrow said. "Let's go back to the victims. FBI Rousch said we should re-examine the victimology."

"Yeah," Choi said, "we should take advice from *that* stooge."

"Billy . . ." Harrow began.

Choi held up his hands in surrender.

"Well," Jenny said, "I *may* have something—the men who checked into those three motel rooms . . . Jeff Bailey, Al Roberts, Eric Stanton?"

All eyes were on her.

Harrow said, "What about them?"

"Really common names, but . . . they're also all characters from movies. Crime movies. Film *noir?*"

"Go on," Harrow said.

"Jeff Bailey was a character played by Robert Mitchum in *Out of the Past.* Al Roberts was from a movie called *Detour.* Played by Tom Neal, and Dana Andrews, that actor in *Laura?* He played Eric Stanton in *Fallen Angel.*"

Harrow said, "*Out of the Past, Detour, Fallen Angel.* Anyone think those are randomly chosen?"

No one spoke up.

Turning to their resident profiler, Harrow asked, "Any ideas, Michael?"

"Not yet. I'll need to think on it."

"Fair enough. Let's get started looking into the possibilities. Laurene, call Amari, Polk, and Rousch and share our theory with them, and this new information. Tell them I'd like to meet straightaway."

Chase nodded, and headed into the hall, cell phone in hand.

Harrow said, "Suddenly there's a movie theme running through the Billie Shears case."

Choi said, "But Billie Shears is a music reference."

"Doesn't matter. The cops dubbed her that. But Don Juan gave *himself* that name. We get the great lover significance—what about *movie* resonance?"

"Hollywood Boulevard body turned up near the Chinese Theater," Choi said, "on Errol Flynn's star, Don Juan himself. Wendi Erskine was an actress, infomercials mostly. Gina Hannan a dental assistant. Megan Chavez a movie hairdresser. . . ."

"Those last two may be day jobs," Harrow said, "for wannabe actresses. Let's find out."

Jenny said, "I'd like access to the e-mail accounts of the victims."

"I think," Harrow said, "we can arrange that."

Chapter Twenty-eight

Midmorning, Harrow met briefly in his office with Amari, Polk, and the FBI agent Rousch. Everybody quickly got on board the theory that Don Juan and Billie Shears were a single serial-killer team.

Anna looked casually great in an LAPD T-shirt and jeans. Polk was casual, too, or anyway his idea of it, black cargo pants and a black T-shirt. The FBI guy wore a suit.

"I'm fine with giving Jenny Blake access to the appropriate e-mail records," Anna said. "Anything else?"

Harrow leaned back in his swivel desk chair. "We *know* they're using roofies, right?"

"Right."

"Any chance you could track where they're getting the stuff?"

"No shortage of street sources," Polk said. "We can start there."

"One trackable source of Rohypnol," Anna said, sitting forward, "is veterinarians' offices. We'll check for any reported thefts."

"I can put some people on it," Rousch said, nodding at these good ideas. "We can check over a larger area."

"Great," Harrow said. "That kind of thing is beyond my team's resources."

Rousch offered up a lopsided smile. "Your people have done outstanding work. I apologize for suggesting you'd do better on the sidelines, the other day."

"No problem. Uh, Mark—are you still thinking you'd like to see *Crime Seen* go on hiatus till this thing is over?"

"I am."

"Well, now's your chance to make your pitch. When I knew you were heading over, I called the network president. He's in his office right now. Want to meet with him?"

"Burnside himself?"

"Dennis Byrnes himself."

"Well, uh . . . please."

Anna and Polk slipped out to work with the *Killer TV* team, and within five minutes Byrnes had joined Harrow and the FBI agent, taking the seat Anna had vacated.

The exec was in a pink polo shirt and black shorts, sockless in white deck shoes. He did not look his most intimidating.

On the other hand, another guest—unexpected by Harrow much less Rousch—seemed plenty intimidating.

Bald, black Lucian Richards entered and positioned himself in his folded-arms, living-statue, harem-guard way just beside the seated Harrow.

The attorney must have come directly from church or anyway had taken time to change—his sharply tailored, plum-colored suit sent two messages: *I am* not *here to screw around*; *and I am* on *the clock*. . . .

Harrow made the introductions. The handshakes between the FBI man and the network prez were perfunctory, and all Rousch got from Richards was a grave nod.

Rousch said, "Obviously, Mr. Byrnes, J.C. has informed you of what we would like done."

"Yes."

"Our top profilers are of the opinion that these perpetrators may back off, without the promise of celebrity that *Crime Seen* affords them."

Byrnes's shrug indicated an easygoing attitude that his unblinking gaze didn't back up. "We discussed temporarily pulling the show, after receiving the first Don Juan video."

"Yes, J.C. said as much."

"And we have never caved to this madman's demands that we air his sick handiwork."

"I know. And the Bureau appreciates that."

"But early on, Special Agent Rousch, we at UBC came to the decision that we cannot hide from our responsibility as communicators."

"Meaning . . . ?"

"Meaning the show will stay on the air."

Rousch's throat was reddening. "You would risk *more* lives? For what, more *money?*"

Harrow expected Richards to wade in, but the attorney remained a big, looming, silent presence. For now.

Byrnes said, "Can you guarantee that no one else will die if we yank the show?"

"Of course I can't!"

"Of course you can't. We have a top profiler, too, Special Agent Rousch. . . . J.C., what does Mr. Pall say?"

Harrow kept his voice soft, even. "His opinion—and mine—is that pulling the show plays into the hands of these egotistical maniacs. Makes them bigger, more powerful celebrities. And may well incite them to kill more, perhaps at an accelerated rate."

"The profiler you have on staff," Rousch said rather acidly, "took a handful of classes under *our* profilers, at the Behavioral Science Unit at Quantico . . . where profiling was invented? And they don't agree with him."

"Nonetheless," Richards said, his basso profundo rumbling the room as he suddenly entered the debate, "UBC has decided to keep *Crime Seen* on the air."

"Mr. Richards—"

"Unless you're ready to meet us in court, and try to shut the show down on legal grounds—and I can't imagine *what* those grounds might be—this meeting is over."

The red had risen from Rousch's throat to his face now. "A *judge* might put the public welfare over UBC's need to 'communicate' or make money, whichever is the real motivation. And have any of you people even *heard* of the FCC?"

Harrow raised a hand. "Special Agent Rousch, this argument becomes moot if we catch the killers before next Friday. Maybe we should concentrate on that."

Rousch, outnumbered and facing home-court advantage, let out the heaviest of sighs . . . then nodded.

Richards stepped forward and held out his hand; the FBI agent shook it without thinking.

"Whatever our differences, Special Agent Rousch," Richards said, "please know that UBC and *Crime Seen* want these killers off the streets every bit as much as the FBI. We'll do whatever can to help . . . short of taking the show off the air."

Rousch managed, "Thank you for that much."

Richards nodded to Byrnes, and then the white guy in shorts and the black guy from a *GQ* ad were gone.

The FBI man stared across the desk at Harrow. "What just hit me?"

"You've heard of good cop, bad cop?"

"I've lived it."

"Well, you just met Lucian Richards's good-cop side. You don't ever want to meet the bad-cop side."

"No. I don't."

"Well, *that's* out of the way." Harrow smiled at his guest. "Shall we go figure out how to catch two killers, keep my show on the air, and get you back to Quantico?"

Rousch's eyebrows went up, came down. He sighed again, but nothing earth-shattering.

"Sounds good," he said.

Chapter Twenty-nine

The lovemaking was over.

This woman, Erica Thornton, the teller from Newport Beach with ambitions to act, had been an enthusiastic sex partner—very giving, as well as voracious (despite the drugs), and if he had been the sort of man who was really *into* sex, he might have been devastated knowing she would have to die.

Instead, those first postcoital moments were merely bittersweet.

The *character* Don Juan loved sex, but once the mechanics of the act were over, he—the actor—ceased being that character, the performance over. Much as his costar's life would be.

Costar wasn't right, though was it? She was more a day player, in movie parlance. His *real* costar was working behind the scenes, handling the stagecraft, though her time to come *on* stage drew near.

Funny, while he was playing Don Juan, he liked

the sex, liked it well enough anyway, while the man behind the performance really only cared about the end result—how this video would further the plan and his career. *Their* career, his real costar and he. . . .

In what some called the afterglow, the brunette lay limp on the bed, naked, satiated, almost as if she were already deceased, but for the gentle rising and lowering of the generous breasts.

His time on stage, on camera, was over.

He arose and left the room to take his place *behind* the camera. There would be no elaborate camera moves; this was strictly D.W. Griffith–level cinema, because the camera behind the two-way mirror needed to appear to have remained stationary.

All he had to do now was look through the viewfinder at the action—his voiceover would be dropped in, in post-production.

The most important part of shooting the video was to make sure he didn't catch his sister when she came on stage, as his "stuntman" (*stuntwoman? stuntperson?*).

Off-camera, his sister entered with her usual swift grace, as nude as their day player but even more beautiful, supple, sleek, exquisite in her hairless beauty. She moved past her hidden cameraman, knife in hand held behind her back.

Camera trained on the brunette, his sister's white skin soon entered frame, luminous in the soft light of the room, her pink nipples hard and erect as she moved toward the bed.

(His sister's approach was Method, too—she lived her role, sense memory her thing.)

The day player's mouth opened, but she did not show the shock of the others at this other naked (bald all over) woman entering the room. This one licked her bottom lip.

"Kinky," she managed. "I'm . . . I'm *liking* this. . . ."

She soon wouldn't.

When his sister neared the bed and revealed and raised the knife, the woman's face registered the requisite surprise.

Through the eyepiece, he and the camera were focused on the day player's face, intrigued by the way this minor actress played the scene—startled at first, then giving in to resignation.

Interesting choice.

The blade arced down, the day player watching but not moving as its spear neared her neck. She, like the others, never even raised a hand in defense as the blade punctured, then slashed through flesh, blood spraying from the severed carotid artery.

Only then did the day player's hands move to her wound, even as his sister brought the knife back and then in from a lower angle, piercing the woman's abdomen so deep the blade might have poked out the other side.

Again and again, the blade penetrated the young woman, much as earlier he had with his dagger of flesh, his sister crying out in orgiastic fury with every thrust until, finally, the attacker moaned loudly and slumped into a ball on the floor, the day player splayed out before her, a roadmap of bloody wounds.

Now his sister, coming down from her homicidal high, lay quietly satiated. He liked that. There was a nice, artistic symmetry to it.

He had followed his sister's descent with the camera, but that would be edited out for the video. Well, later, when all the Don Juan videos came out, in uncut director's editions, the full sequence would at last be seen.

He helped her up and walked her to the bathroom. She was exhausted—it always reminded him of when James Brown had to be led offstage by his retinue, only he didn't have a red velvet robe to wrap around his sister, much as she deserved one.

While she showered, he returned to the set with that familiar melancholy for when the play was over. The woman on the bed was just another inanimate object to him. Another prop. Gradually, however, during the cleanup process, the women did transcend that status.

His supplies readied beforehand, he knelt next to the body, even as the blood still dripped. Oddly, he enjoyed this part of the experience most of all—somehow, he felt more intimate with the women, *after* the camera had stopped rolling and his sister was off showering. Only then were he and each day player truly alone together . . . soft towels and gentle soap, and a woman more than just naked, opened up so he could see inside.

The blood was still wet, so it came off easily. Barely had to scrub. This one's eyes were closed, her face peaceful despite the way her scene had ended, almost as if she were enjoying his soapy touch. As if any moment she might sit up and smile and thank him for being so careful and gentle. . . .

"Feels good, doesn't it?" he whispered to her.

Her head seemed to shift slightly on the pillow, in affirmation, as he leaned on the mattress, allowing him easier access to the wound in her neck. He cleaned the gash as best he could, and the area around it.

Her hair would be hardest to clean—no point in putting that off. Her dark tresses still felt soft and thick between his fingers as he used a wet towel to wipe them, taking care with each lock, as if fearful a rough touch might pull her hair and cause discomfort.

When finally he finished, he regarded the day player—she looked as though she had just stepped from a shower. The only remaining red spots were the open wounds, but nothing was to be done about that.

For some reason he thought of the old man.

He hated the old son of a bitch—dead or not. Their mother fleeing his abuse, the nighttime visits to brother and sister . . . then the evil bastard had to go fall over dead before they were of maturity enough to do something about him.

Daddy, in dying, had done them one big favor—with the old man gone, and when they were of legal age, they had sold the farm, the proceeds allowing them to move to LA and leave the heartless heartland behind.

Ironic—the old man had made it possible for them to come to the fame capital of the world, where he and his sister at last could be some-bodies. Where they would be rich and famous and powerful.

It had taken longer to "make it" than they hoped, and they were taking what some might consider an unconventional path . . . but they weren't helpless anymore.

Screw you, you old bastard!

Funny that the only way to be somebody in this town was to pretend to be somebody else. But that's show biz!

When their day player was ready for her final curtain call—*No small roles, only small actors!*—he went off in search of his sister. She was gone from the shower, towel hung up, mirror fogged.

He found her in his bedroom, the black womb room, already in bed, covers tight at her neck.

"You all right, Sis?"

"Yes . . ."

Her voice was tiny, childlike, as when she would ask him to comfort her after the old man was done.

". . . but I'd be better if you held me."

"Let me get my shower first," he said. "I just fin-ished with the day player. Feel kinda dirty."

"Go get clean," his sister said.

He was in and out of the shower in five minutes; he lingered to watch the blood from their victim rinse down the drain, like in *Psycho*. That Hitch-cock was good.

As he toweled off, his thoughts turned to the

only woman he ever loved. The only woman he ever really wanted, in the . . . *you know* way.

But he knew better than to put his thing in his own sister. That would be sick and dirty and no shower could wash it off. His old man never understood such a simple basic moral rule, but *he* did.

Naked, he crawled in bed next to her. She was on her side, back to him. She, too, was nude. Hairless as a grape. He spooned her, his arm draped across her. She was so warm it was like standing in front of the space heater back on the farm.

Snuggling him, she made a sound a lot like purring.

"That's better," she said. "I love you."

In the darkness, feeling her against him, he said, "I love you too, Sis."

Her hand reached back and touched him, worked him. His hand slipped around and found the warm moist place and they comforted each other.

The lovemaking was over.

When the team finally broke up Sunday night, everybody running on fumes, Harrow had been surprised to hear himself ask Anna over to his place. And astonished to hear her say yes.

It was a casual evening, delivery pizza and a Dodgers game on ESPN. They watched on the sofa, with her curled up next to him. She seemed so small, so young with her dark hair ponytailed back, almost elfin in T-shirt and jeans and bare feet.

When he fell asleep during the game, she elbowed him. Laughter had followed, and kissing and fondling and then they were in the bedroom and the lovemaking had been slow at first, amazingly so considering how long it had been for him, and then frantic at the conclusion, and now she was asleep and he was at the window, looking out into the abstraction of Los Angeles by night.

He felt empty and guilty and generally like shit.

"Are you all right?"

He jumped at her voice. Hadn't heard her get out of bed, much less come up behind him.

Looking nicely rumpled, Anna smiled. "Did I just make the heroic Harrow jump? . . . Or are you . . . hey, are *you* . . . ?"

Crying?

She didn't say it.

He just nodded.

She kissed the tears away and said, "I understand."

"I shouldn't have done this tonight. . . . I'm sorry. . . ."

"Damnit, don't you apologize. This was what you needed, and what I needed. Understand? And whether we never do it again, or if we wind up together for the next twenty years, it doesn't matter. Nothing can take tonight away from us, and it doesn't take a goddamn thing away from all your *other* nights, when you were married."

"I'm sorry."

"Quit apologizing. Damn! Come back to bed."

She led him there and he lay on his back and she cuddled him.

Her voice was soft, soothing. But there was still something cop in it.

"You had a marriage that worked," she said. "I had a marriage that went south. But what we have in common is, we don't have anybody now."

"That's true," he said.

"So quit being such a big baby."

That made him laugh, and he was kissing her when a cell phone vibrated nearby.

"Yours or mine?" she asked.

"Mine," Harrow said, reaching across her to pluck the dancing thing off the nightstand. Caller ID box read: CARMEN GARCIA. He glanced at the clock: 2:38 A.M. in blood red LED.

Warmth had filled this room seconds ago; now Harrow felt a chill.

No way this was good news.

And when Amari's phone jumped in vibration, too, he knew his suspicion had been validated.

Chapter Thirty

When the call came, and another body had turned up in Griffith Park, Detective LeRon Polk took no chances. He hit the observatory parking lot in black T-shirt, jeans, and Timberland boots.

And when Amari showed up, moments later, in typical smart work attire—charcoal gray blazer, black silk blouse, and dark gray slacks—he figured he finally put one over on teacher.

She gave him the once-over. "Going camping?"

"Call was Griffith Park," he said, cocky with confidence. "You won't see me ruinin' another new pair of Bruno Magli's."

She nodded toward the concrete parking lot and long, manicured lawn of the Griffith Park Observatory. "As a trained detective, LeRon, you may notice this is not the crest of Mount Lee."

She had a point.

A couple of patrol cars and the coroner's wagon were parked nearby, on the circular drive. No lights were flashing. A uniformed officer stood guard near the astronomer's monument maybe fifty yards from the north entrance of the wide white observatory with its three dark domes.

With the building and statue lit up against a clear sky, a nearly full moon wielding its ivory brush, the scene had a stark beauty interrupted by a single work light and two officers near the door. They stood over a body deposited atop the building's front steps.

Heading toward the crime scene, Amari said, "You *did* grow up in Los Angeles, right?"

"Rub it in, why don't you?"

A voice behind them called, "Wait up!"

They turned to see Special Agent Mark Rousch trotting up. Middle of the night or not, the agent wore a dark suit, white shirt, crisply knotted tie, and "Werewolves of London" perfect hair.

Did Rousch ever sleep, Polk wondered, or need a shave?

"Another Don Juan victim," the FBI man said.

Not a question.

As they drew closer, an answer came anyway. Uniformed cops bookended the unclad brunette sprawled at the observatory's entrance. A bouquet of Black Pearl roses draped her left arm, as if Miss America had just been crowned.

Eyes closed, dark hair fanned out, framing the pretty face. . . .

Polk had a twitch of memory.

"This is the youngest yet," Rousch said, shaking his head, his expression as pale as moonlight.

"All murder victims are old," Amari said.

Rousch looked at her.

"You can't get older than dead."

"Erica Thornton," Polk said.

The others turned.

Amari frowned. "You *know* her?"

"No."

"No?"

"I *recognize* her. She was the runner-up on the second season of *Survival Island*."

"What the hell . . . ?" Rousch said.

"Reality TV," Amari explained and sighed. To Polk, she added, "Pretty sure?"

"Real damn sure."

Amari asked the nearest uniformed officer, "Who found the body?"

The officer pointed down the building to a man in security-guard uniform, standing alone, hands fig-leafed.

"I'll be damned," Amari said.

Polk groaned. "Not our wannabe law enforcement professional. . . ."

Rousch frowned. "Who *is* that clown?"

The security guard waved to them and smiled in a goofy embarrassed manner.

Amari said, "Clown is right—he found Wendi Erskine at the Hollywood sign and screwed up the crime scene by driving through it."

"Christ," the FBI man said.

"But wait, there's more," Polk said in infomercial style. "Then our friendly park ranger opens up the gate and lets some uniforms go down and gawk at a real live dead naked female."

"He needs a new hobby," Rousch said. "Let's have a chat with the guy. Name?"

Simultaneously Amari and Polk blurted: "Jason Wyler."

The fed made a beeline, and Amari and Polk followed, hanging back a little.

"And what," Amari asked, voice low, "is the first rule of criminal investigation?"

"First on the scene," Polk said, "first suspect."

"And this sterling citizen has been first on the scene *twice?*"

"Could be a coincidence."

"LeRon—do we believe in coincidences?"

"I'm just sayin' . . . it's not Wyler's fault if some crazy-ass killer decides to dump another corpse in Griffith Park."

"We'll see."

The skinny security guard pushed his wire-frame glasses farther up his nose, smiling nervously. As the trio of detectives planted themselves before him, Wyler was bouncing foot to foot, an excited puppy blessed with three masters.

Rousch was displaying his ID, but Wyler didn't seem to notice, homing in on Amari.

"Lieutenant," Wyler said, "you'll be proud of me."

"Will I?"

"I stayed away from the body, just like you told me that other time—down at the sign?"

Like they needed prompting to remember the previous Don Juan victim Wyler discovered.

"Good for you, Jason," Amari said dryly. "Tell us what happened *this* time."

"I was making my rounds, just like always. Saw some teenagers partying over there." He pointed past the entrance. "I told them to move on."

"And?"

"And they did. I stopped back later to check up on 'em. That's when I saw . . . you know, the body. At the door?"

Prompting again. *Oh*, that *body*. . . .

Polk said, "And you didn't touch her?"

A sharp head shake. "Learned my lesson last time."

Amari said, "What time did you see the kids?"

"Just after midnight."

"Sure about the time, Mr. Wyler?"

Eager nod. "Checked my watch, in case I had to write up a report. On those kids?"

"Okay. When did you get back?"

"An hour and a half. Like usual."

Amari rubbed her forehead. "So, you didn't check back until your next round?"

"Right."

"So the killer had ninety minutes between you shooing off the party animals and coming back?"

"Sounds right."

"You see anything unusual when you were pulling up?"

"First time or second time?"

"Second time. Checking on the kids."

"Nothing unusual or suspicious, no. Except for the body."

That was *fairly suspicious*, Polk thought. *Maybe even* unusual. . . .

Rousch said, "Possible the kids saw something."

Amari asked the security guard: "Did you get any of their names?"

"The kids? No."

Polk asked, "They have a car?"

"Oh yeah—black and shiny. Looked fast."

"Make?" Amari asked. "Model?"

"Well, I think it was a convertible. Foreign, maybe. Japanese?"

Amari was studying Wyler. Maybe deciding whether to pistol whip him or not.

Polk said, "Did you get a license number?"

"No."

So they had no suspects, and thanks to their fellow professional here, they didn't even have potential witnesses to interview.

Amari and Rousch asked Wyler a few more questions, getting nowhere. Then they told him to wait, and he nodded, grateful to be needed by fellow pros.

As the trio returned to the body, Amari said, "We've got an inept if punctual security guard, and a park exhibit that's closed tomorrow."

Rousch said, "Point being?"

"Don Juan had a ninety-minute window for a body dump that required maybe three minutes."

"What about security video?"

Polk said he'd check, but added, "Knowing our buddy Don Juan, either there won't be any vid, or he found a way to circumvent it."

Amari said, "Once you've checked, LeRon, grab Security Guard Wyler and give him the pleasure of a ride to a real honest-to-goodness police station."

Polk shook his head. "What do you think we're going to get out of him? He's a dipshit."

"Is he? Or is that an act? Either way, he's the tie to two of the bodies in this investigation . . . and that earns him the right to be interviewed for real. Sweat him. Keep him there all day, if you have to. But find out whether he's an idiot or just a good actor."

"Yes, ma'am," Polk said dejectedly. "But if this guy's *acting* this stupid, he's too good for reality TV. He needs his own series."

"Don Juan *has* his own series," Amari reminded him.

Chapter Thirty-one

Carmen Garcia did not feel safe.

Doors locked, alarm system set, lights on, TV too (*some stupid infomercial*), but alone and on her couch, cell phone at her ear (*ringing, ringing, ringing*) and not feeling safe at *all.* . . .

On the coffee table before her, laptop open, the innocuous if suggestive file name with its small black letters somehow screamed at her.

Finally Harrow's voice came: "Carmen, what do you need?"

"*You,* I'm afraid. . . . Don Juan e-mailed me again."

"Another video?"

"Another video."

"Sure it's from him? You didn't—"

"I *did* look at it. Started to. It's from him."

"I can come right over."

"Could we do it at the office?" She didn't want to stay here a second longer than necessary.

Harrow said, "I don't think we should sit on this till eight, do you?"

"No. I meant go in a little early."

"Early, like . . . now?"

Quarter till three. *No one in the place except . . . me.*

"Early like now," she said.

"Okay. I think that's a good call. I'll round up everybody, and inform UBC security."

She threw on a sweatshirt, jeans, and running shoes, and prepared to go out into the night, or anyway the early-morning dark. Not that she was *afraid* of the dark—the dark didn't kill women—but the monster who knew enough about her to send a video to her personal e-mail certainly did.

The others on the *Killer TV* team, with their former cop status, were licensed to carry firearms. But Carmen was not former law enforcement, so she went into the kitchen and selected (to tuck away in her purse) the biggest kitchen knife from a cutlery set she'd purchased on another sleepless night watching infomercials.

In fact, when she switched off her TV, Billy Mays was smiling and shouting at her. That Mays was still hawking stuff on the airwaves, long after his death, creeped her out. She wondered if any of Wendi Erskine's infomercials were still airing. . . .

Her only stop on the way to the office was at a convenience mart for a cup of coffee—too early for drive-thru latte. At nearly three a.m., the freeway was weirdly user-friendly, and the streets of Los

Angeles, particularly the downtown, were all but deserted.

Even as she neared UBC, her eyes kept returning to the rearview mirror. She supposed she was just being paranoid, but *was* it paranoia considering what she'd been through? *Was* it just caution?

Like most people her age, she had never considered the fragility of her own life. That was before Kansas. Now she knew better.

She pulled her Prius up into the UBC parking ramp. If a parking garage could be naturally unsettling, being in an almost-empty one was worse—and not long ago, Don Juan had left a body on the UBC doorstep, and could certainly get in here and kidnap someone, and . . .

. . . and *that*, she thought, *was* paranoia.

Empty garage or not, she drove to her reserved parking space on the third level. She got out, saw no one else around in the concrete chamber, locked her car, and started the walk halfway across the garage to the elevators.

She strode quickly, her heels tapping on concrete echoing like machine-gun fire. Under one arm was her laptop, her purse (with butcher knife within) thrown over that same shoulder. In the other hand was a pepper-spray mini-canister, finger on the trigger.

Security lighting was minimal and most of the garage remained shrouded in darkness, a breeze whipping through to help hurry Carmen across.

Then, breathing heavily, as if she'd just run the hundred-yard dash, she found herself at the elevator, pushing the button.

The elevator doors whispered open, and a voice just behind her said, "Carmen . . ."

She whirled and saw only a blur of black leather jacket and black hair. Bringing up the pepper spray, she was about to trigger it when she realized the figure was Billy Choi.

Her coworker held up his hands in surrender and turned his head away, figuring out that he was on the pepper-spray precipice.

"Sorry, Billy."

"Talk about close calls," Choi said.

"I'm so sorry. . . ."

The elevator arrived and they stepped on, Choi pushing their floor.

"It's okay. You got another video and you're edgy. I get that. But let's work on that itchy trigger finger."

She beamed at him, relieved she hadn't hurt him, glad not to be alone.

He grinned at her. "Jeez, don't you know my voice by now?"

"I thought you were Don Juan."

"Never been mistaken for him. Been taken for John Cho a few times . . . Ken Leung, once. . . ."

"Could have been worse than pepper spray."

"Yeah?"

She opened her purse and the butcher knife winked at Choi. He did not wink back.

Soon they were in the conference room, where (predictably) Jenny had beaten them. The little computer queen—in pale blue T-shirt, jeans, and ponytail—quickly and wordlessly hooked Carmen's laptop up to the big screen.

Within five minutes, everyone had arrived, coffee distributed. No doughnuts or other goodies, though, not considering what they were about to watch.

Harrow came in last. He wore a yellow polo and jeans and looked far more alert than the rest, with the exception of Jenny. Of course.

"You'll note again that no cameras are present." He sat. "All right—let's look at this damn thing. . . ."

Chase said, "Where are the LAPD? This is evidence."

"Lieutenant Amari, Detective Polk, and Special Agent Rousch are already at the crime scene."

"Which is where?" Michael Pall asked. He was in a suit, whereas the rest were in whatever they could grab—T-shirts, sweatshirts, jeans. But at least he didn't look so bright-eyed behind the Clark Kent specs.

"Griffith Park," Harrow said.

Anderson blurted, "*Hollywood* sign again?"

"The observatory," Harrow said.

"Griffith Park Observatory," Pall said, as if tasting the words. Then: "Why there? Doesn't make sense."

When their profiler made an observation like that, everything stopped until he'd explained.

He did: "The Hollywood sign, the network doorstep, the Errol Flynn star, the Chinese Theater . . . they all have something to do with show business. What does the Griffith Park Observatory have to do with show biz?"

Chase said, "A lot of movies have been shot there."

Choi said, "Yeah, right—*Rebel Without a Cause.*"

"No," Carmen said. She'd known at once. "Griffith Park Observatory—where you go to see the stars."

Harrow was nodding. "Which is what Don Juan and Billie Shears want to be—stars. Superstars."

No one challenged the theory.

Choi said to Harrow, "Did your friend the lieutenant say whether there are any clues this time?"

"Nothing significant had turned up when I spoke to her half an hour ago. She said the observatory closed at ten last night, and isn't open on Monday. Victim was on the front doorstep."

Chase asked, "Who found the body?"

"Same security guard who found Wendi Erskine, and he's being looked at hard. The victim has been tentatively identified as Erica Thornton—she was on a reality show called *Survival Island.*"

"I remember her," Choi said.

"That's a UBC show," Carmen said. "Don Juan sticking it to us again?"

"Not just us," Chase said.

"No," Harrow said gravely. "Not just us. . . . Okay, let's get to it."

Harrow nodded to Carmen, and she made a keystroke.

And then it began . . .

. . . *the drugged nude woman on the bed, blade slashing, woman writhing, spraying blood, this attack even more brutal, more vicious than the others, over and over, again and again, knife arcing, flaying, the life literally bleeding out of the victim. . . .*

Carmen made herself watch.

She had viewed the start of it at home, before shutting the thing off and calling Harrow. Now the sheer ferocity of the attack shook her, terrified her. So incredibly savage was the slaying that even in this room full of people, she felt alone with her fear.

"You failed to grasp the inevitability of my ascension to stardom," the now-familiar, processed, metallic voice said. *"You insult me by suggesting this also-ran Shears is my equal. For this indignity, you must pay. How you will pay is my little secret—mine is a scenario with surprises yet to be revealed. Suffice to say my next lover will give you no alternative but to acknowledge that Don Juan is without question . . . the greatest lover of all."*

The video ended, the lights came up, and no one said anything for what seemed forever to Carmen. Thirty seconds.

Michael Pall said, "He's devolving."

No one disagreed.

Harrow asked, "What do we do about it?"

That the seasoned investigators around this table had no immediate response was almost as disturbing to Carmen as that video.

Choi said, "Yeah, I know the profiler lingo, too—he's devolving, he's accelerating. Well, we know he's picking up speed. But we also know he's playing us. That's bullshit about us insulting him—he and Billie Shears are in it together."

"But he doesn't know *we* know that," Harrow said.

Pall, brightening, said, "And that gives us a small advantage. He's playing out a narrative,

which would suggest an end goal—some spectacu-
lar surprise to really make him a 'star.' "

"Maybe we already know that surprise," Harrow
said. "Maybe his big finish is to reveal that he and
Billie are collaborators, or even lovers."

"Maybe," the profiler allowed. "But I would
think not—this is building to a special kill . . .
though what we *do* having going for us is, *finally*,
we are a small step ahead. We know he and Shears
are in cahoots. So do the LAPD and the FBI. We
have to keep that knowledge out of the media."

"We *are* the media," Carmen said.

"No," Harrow said. "Not anymore. We're just a
group of hard-ass investigators who are going to
find and stop this bastard."

That got a few smiles.

"You know," Choi said, "I think I could stomach
a doughnut about now. You know—like all hard-
ass investigators."

And that got a few laughs.

But Carmen neither smiled nor laughed.

She was seeing that blade arcing down. . . .

Chapter Thirty-two

For the two days following the discovery of the victim in the Griffith Park Observatory parking lot, the media had exploded with coverage of both Don Juan and Billie Shears. This pleased Billie very much. But there was an unpleasing wrinkle.

Though the link between the killers had apparently not been discovered by the LAPD and FBI (or for that matter, the *Crime Seen* clowns), an unfortunate collective moniker had been given the two killers—"The Odd Couple."

The *L.A. Times* and its satellites weren't guilty of this offense—a local radio station started it, and the national media picked up on it, with several twenty-four-hour news services using the nickname freely. This tabloid approach did have its pleasing aspects, as when one wild-eyed Fox commentator spoke of the Odd Couple being responsible for "fear gripping Hollywood."

She did not, however, follow the commentator's

logic that somehow the Don Juan and Billie Shears killings represented "the sins of show business coming home to roost," nor did she think a reference to her and her brother as "sick fame-seekers hoping to suckle at the reality-show teat" was in the least bit fair.

Still, what was the old press agent's axiom? It didn't matter what they said, as long as they were talking about you. Or what they printed, as long as they were spelling your name right. And now they were spelling it B-i-l-l-i-e, weren't they? Ha!

Her brother had the video camera set up now, with Billie Shears's latest—and very special—victim-to-be spread-eagled on the bed, hands and feet lashed to the frame with heavy, hurting cord.

Now that they'd entered Act Three, brother and sister for the first time were deviating from their established pattern—their "M.O." as *Crime Seen* would have it. This time their special guest star was not drugged, though he was indeed out cold, and naked, of course, and about to feel Billie's shearing bite . . . but he had not been so fortunate as to enjoy the ego-boosting attentions of a beautiful young woman who had picked him up in a bar.

Maybe she could make that up to him.

Their special guest had been whisked on set from right outside his hotel room door. In fact his room *became* the set! Across the way, "Sam Wild" was registered—the Lawrence Tierney character in the classic Robert Wise film *noir, Born to Kill.* After all, hadn't she and her brother been born to kill?

No, not born. Shaped. Molded. Created by the old man. . . .

She took pride in this latest scenario, devised only yesterday, in a brother/sister brainstorming session, as they searched for a way to guarantee that *Crime Seen* would have to showcase them next Friday. This diverged from their original outline, but was a worthwhile, imaginative revision.

Tracking their guest performer to this hotel, this room, had been a breeze, given her brother's computer skills. They had to forgo their usual in-depth "recon" (as her brother liked to put it). But risk carried a rush. . . .

Not long ago, she had watched from the cracked door across the way as their guest approached his room and was digging for his key card. She waited till he had opened the door and was about to step in.

Then she stepped out—a blonde vision in spiked heels, a curvy female dream in a black mini with a sheer, black silk top with spaghetti straps, ideal for her creamy complexion.

He heard her, turned, and she smiled at him.

"Looks like you're coming," she said, "and I'm going."

He gave her a goofy grin and seemed to be fishing for something clever to say in response to that loaded remark—*men . . . give them a look and the blood runs from their big head to the little one and makes them stupid.*

For all his supposed worldliness, their guest star had been no different.

Then his expression turned to a puzzled frown

as she stepped aside and her brother emerged and brought up the Taser.

And fired.

The two darts struck the victim, dropping him mostly into his room, to flop and flap like a freshly landed carp.

Her brother dragged their catch by the arms inside and closed the door. She knelt and jerked the man's handgun from its holster. When their guest began to come around and push up on his hands, she used the commandeered gun to club him.

He sagged back, unconscious.

From then on, it had been easy—strip him, get him onto the bed, tie him down. Duct-tape his mouth. Simple, straightforward, right to plan, but somehow exciting, exhilarating, since it varied from their established routine.

They had made sure the hallway was clear before moving the camera and their equipment in from across the way. While her brother set up, their guest star remained unconscious.

Or pretended to be.

Anyway, he was still breathing, with a strong, steady pulse. So if he wasn't faking, and already conscious, he soon would be.

Finally, however, she became impatient, and cracked an amyl nitrate capsule under his nose. He shuddered awake, struggling with an invisible foe, then seemed to get a least a vague fix on the situation, trying to pull free.

Eventually he stopped struggling, apparently figuring out he had nowhere to go. Maybe the blood had moved back to the big head.

She smiled sweetly down at the naked man spread-eagled before her. He blinked rapidly, as if trying to wake from this bad dream, wild eyes swiftly scanning the room. Now and then he would struggle against his bonds—apparently more in anger and frustration than out of any sense of really escaping.

Leaning forward, putting a gentle fingertip on his hairy bare chest, she said, "Welcome to *our* world, Special Agent Rousch."

Beneath the duct-tape gag, he roared with rage, so pitiful a sound she might have laughed, if she'd been truly heartless.

She ran fingers through the FBI agent's chest hair. She found hair on a man's body strangely compelling if somewhat gross; she had come to prefer her own hairless body. And her brother's.

She said, "You've been looking for us—well, here we are."

Now he was silent beneath the duct-tape strip. His eyes were wide—unblinking now.

"My brother and I—we're brother and sister, you know . . . but you *didn't* know, did you? My brother and I are a team—like Fred Astaire and Ginger Rogers? Or more, Fred and Adele. Anyway, my brother and I have been very disappointed in you. You've been in town for *weeks* now and haven't done any better than the LAPD or those TV fools. Or have you been keeping secrets?"

She clutched his chest hair and yanked out a clump. He bucked on the bed and yelled under the tape. When he came to rest, a bald patch in the jungle of curlies was pink and pearled with blood droplets.

"Perhaps we should torture you, my brother and I—and find out what you people really know. How close you *really* are? You figured out I was B-i-l-l-i-e, not l-y. But you don't seem to've known Don Juan and Billie Shears are partners. The media almost guessed it, with their stupid, insulting 'Odd Couple' thing. That pisses me off!"

He lay very still. His expression had changed. Not angry now. Scared, but . . . something else, something she'd never seen in a victim, because both Billie and Don Juan had in the past struck mercifully quick, and this was a new stage to her: pleading.

Eyes begging for mercy.

It was somewhat unsettling.

She patted his nest of chest hair, and moved a few steps from the bed.

"You're probably wondering about the camera," she said. "That's usually a Don Juan specialty, and Billie isn't known for making performance-art videos. But you're a special case. A special catch. A special *guest* star. . . ."

Rousch lay limp now. She'd seen him go through a lot of changes, a lot of stages, in a short time. What *were* the stages of the grieving process, anyway? He was grieving his own death, after all.

She'd studied them in an acting class—shock and guilt and anger and denial and depression were in there. Was this acceptance? And what was the other one? Hope?

Not tonight, Josephine.

She dropped her pose. She didn't feel like acting.

"I could tell you our whole story, about what our father did to us and so on, but it's very unpleasant. It's not the kind of thing somebody in your position would want to hear."

The FBI agent came alive, suddenly—he was trying to get something across. *What?* He wanted to talk! He wanted to exchange views and ideas and try to talk them into freeing him, because he understood they couldn't *help* themselves, and he could help *them*, and . . .

That was it! *Bargaining!* The other stage. . . .

Ironic, because she had just been about to bargain with him.

"I will give you a chance, Agent Rousch. To save yourself. All you have to do is love me. Just love me."

His eyes tensed, his forehead beaded with sweat, bulging with veins.

"If you love me . . . your love will set you free. If you love me. But you have to love me. Understand?"

She slipped the spaghetti straps off, let the silky top fall to her waist, revealing firm milky white breasts with bright pink tips (a little lip rouge had made them even pinker).

Rousch was wide-eyed, and against all odds—naked, tied spread-eagled, facing two serial killers—he proved her point about the big and little head: that flaccid thing of his twitched.

Stirred.

"Do you love me, Agent Rousch? But that's so impersonal . . . your name is Mark. Mark—do you love me? If I *believe* you love me, I will let you go."

She did not look at the camera or over where her brother stood behind it; she was too professional, but she felt him with her, his presence, his love for her.

"Love is important, Mark. Do you *love* me?"

She pulled down the skirt, taking the blouse with it; she stepped from the puddle of clothes, wearing nothing beneath—just her sleekly naked, hairless form. A blonde vision. She would leave the wig on. He might not like her *really* naked. . . .

She said, "You wouldn't want me to feel *unwanted*, would you?"

She cupped her breasts, stepped near the bed, and watched as his thing slowly rose. Like when the Frankenstein monster roused himself from that slab.

She got on the bed and knelt between his spread legs and began to stroke his half-hard member.

Even not fully erect, it was bigger than the old man's. She watched, impressed, as it grew and grew the more she touched it.

It was very hard now. Throbbing in her hand.

She let it go, slapped it away, and stormed off the bed.

"*That's* not love," she said.

She watched as the thing wilted, almost comically; she could hear the slide-whistle sound effect in her head: *WHEEEE-ooooop.*

He was begging with his eyes again. Before, it

had touched her somewhere deep, distant within. Now she felt merely disgust.

"Agent Rousch, just as a courtesy, since you must have *many* questions, I will brief you on the rest of our method of operation. Why not? It's not like you're going to share it with anybody."

Now he strained manfully at his bindings and his chest filled as he screamed behind the duct tape, yelled bloody murder, but for all that effort, the result was more annoying than likely to attract attention or help. Kind of like when a guest in the hotel room adjacent is playing the TV too loud, and you're trying to sleep.

"When they get as excited as you were? Up to a minute or so ago? I tell them I'm going into the bathroom . . . to get *ready* for them. You *do* know we drug them? Roofies? Sure. Anyway, a couple of minutes alone in the dark and the guy is so stoned and horny, he doesn't even know whether the person who comes back, in the dark, is me or not. . . . Allow us to demonstrate."

She rose and walked over to her brother at the camera, the FBI man's bugged eyes following. She pulled off the blond wig and covered her brother's bald head with it. Arranged it, getting it just right.

Don Juan stepped forward, arcs of the woman's wig swinging like scythes. He was naked, too, which their special guest had not realized before, the camera and its position making that tough.

When her brother approached a victim's bed, he had his naughty bits tucked back between his legs, as if he didn't have any.

He would say, "In the dark, it makes me look like a girl. I can't fool them that I'm you, if I'm swinging my meat."

That always made her laugh. Always just *killed* her. . . .

Billie Shears stepped behind the camera and assumed its operation. Her brother stooped, then rose—re-entering the FBI agent's range of vision—with the garden shears gripped in two hands.

What a pleasure to finally be able to do a little camera movement, she thought, as she zoomed in on Rousch's face.

His eyes were wide with terror. She panned down to his thing—little now, shriveled, limp as a morning glory at nightfall. She swish-panned to her brother as he stepped forward, oddly pretty as a sexless blonde, opening and closing the shears, their grating metal music sending the FBI man into a twisting, yanking frenzy.

She was in a wide shot, and glad she was, because it was very cool the way Rousch tried to look brave, his eyes glued to the blades as her brother closed them one last time and raised them over his head for the Aztec sacrifice.

When the closed shears came down, swift, hard, a diving bird, Rousch screamed into the duct tape. It was as though someone had died in a faraway place.

His body lurched with the impact as his flesh and organs were disrupted. The sound was like boots moving through mud.

Then Rousch gurgled under the gag and was gone.

She had caught the whole thing on video, though this production would probably not be sent to Harrow's team—it would be saved for the special-edition boxed set. Bonus features.

For once they didn't wait for lividity to settle in and make the collection of the trophy less messy. She rather wanted this to be a horror show for the agent's colleagues. A splashy mess would be good stagecraft, in this instance.

And when they had finished with their production, and she had taken her trophy (her brother did the killing, but she collected the terrible toll), they packed up. One suitcase held everything, even the collapsible tripod.

Across the hall, they showered and—in wigs and nice clothes—exited the room, just another upper-middle-class couple out for the evening.

In the lobby, she found a quiet corner and used Rousch's cell phone, which she'd taken, but not as a souvenir exactly. She thumbed through screens until she found what she wanted.

When she had the number, she dialed.

"Rousch," Harrow's voice said, "what's up?"

"Sorry," she said pleasantly, "wrong number," and clicked off.

With a hanky, she wiped the phone free of prints, dropped it in a trash receptacle, took her brother's arm, and they strolled out into a pleasantly warm California night.

You could see the Hollywood sign from here.

Chapter Thirty-three

In a comfy plump leather booth at Willie D's, Harrow and Choi were kicking back after a long day of, frankly, getting nowhere. The sports bar, a haunt of the *Killer TV* team, was off the lobby of the Deluxe Sunset Hotel just a few blocks from the UBC complex.

Both men were having after-burger beers when Harrow's cell vibrated. Caller ID read ROUSCH, but the FBI man wasn't on the line—it was a wrong number, a female voice.

What was a woman doing using Rousch's cell phone? The agent was single, so it might have been a date who borrowed the cell and misdialed or something. But Rousch had been spending so much time on the case—much of it with Harrow and his team—when exactly had he had time to meet a woman?

Harrow was tempted to run upstairs and knock

on the agent's door—the FBI had booked their man into the Deluxe Sunset Hotel, for convenience.

Choi asked, "Rousch want something?"

"Wrong number."

"Rousch dialed a wrong number?"

"Wasn't him—some woman."

"Maybe he got lucky." Then Choi frowned. "But I don't think so. Call him back."

Harrow did.

"Rang once," Harrow said. "Went to voice mail."

"I don't get it."

"So he's out with some gal, and she borrows the phone, hits redial or something and gets me, and now she's made the right call, and she's gabbing."

"Gal. Gabbing. What are you, eighty years old? Listen, J.C., let's just go upstairs. Knock on his goddamn door."

"And if he's in bed with her?"

"Then we embarrass his ass, and maybe get a glimpse of skin, hopefully not his."

"And if he's not in the room?"

"Then he's not in the room. But at least we tried."

". . . You want to wait here?"

"Hell no. She might be cute. And the more effort I make to help you, the better chance you'll buy the next round."

Harrow grinned. "You win, Billy. It's probably a fool's errand, but . . ."

"But you got that cop tingle, right? On the back of your neck?"

Harrow nodded.

"Then let's go. You packing?"

Harrow nodded. "You?"

"Always."

Both had California concealed-carry licenses.

Soon they were at Rousch's room—832—but Harrow noticed the safety catch wasn't shut, the door slightly ajar, as if Rousch had stepped away to go for ice or something.

Only they had passed this floor's ice and vending machines, and no Rousch.

"Hold up, Billy."

Choi noticed the ajar door, too. He slipped a hand under his black leather jacket and came back with a .38 snubby.

Harrow approached the door but did not touch the knob. "*Mark!* Mark, it's *Harrow!*"

Nothing.

Harrow, frowning, got out his cell. "I'm going to check in with Anna."

"What for? We're big boys."

Harrow didn't answer Choi, getting Anna right away.

"We may have a problem," he told her.

"What?"

He laid it all out for her.

"Do not," she said sternly, "go through that door."

Choi was already angling to peer in the crack.

"Gimme a break," Harrow said. "We *do* know how to handle crime scenes."

"I know, but—"

"But Agent Rousch may need our help, other side of this door. We're going in."

"*No!*" Anna said. "Don Juan has bomb-making skills—remember the box he rigged at the Hollywood sign. This could be a—"

Choi shouldered the door open, and Harrow hit the deck, with Anna's voice in his ear: "... *trap!*"

No explosion.

Choi, .38 pointing upward, gazed curiously down at Harrow. "What's *your* problem?"

Harrow gathered himself, and his dignity, told Anna that Billy had already kicked the door open, that nothing and nobody had been blown to pieces, and that they were going in to check on the FBI man.

"Don't hang up!" she ordered, and Harrow hung up.

He slipped the cell in his pocket, trading it for his own .38, not a snubby.

Choi led the way. The bedroom area was around to the right, past the bathroom, blocked from view in the short hallway.

Then Choi stopped dead.

Almost bumping into the younger man, Harrow said, "What the hell?"

Then he *saw* "what the hell"—or maybe he just saw *hell*. . . .

Special Agent Mark Rousch lay bound and gagged on the bed, blood-spattered and naked. Blood was everywhere, the bed, the floor, even the ceiling. The grotesque signature—the deep fatal wound, the butcher-shop emasculation—said Billie Shears, though the amount of blood indicated the killer had not waited for lividity to set in, rather had taken her trophy shortly after the killing blow.

The blood was so fresh, it still gleamed red, and a coppery scent lingered.

"Christ," Choi said. "They did this with *us* in the *building*—we were eating our damn burgers when . . ."

The cocky ex-cop suddenly looked ill.

Harrow said, "They probably walked right by us in the lobby."

He turned his back on the charnel house and got Anna on the cell. "Rousch is dead. Looks like Billie Shears. M.O.'s a little different, but . . . it's unmistakable.

"On our way," she said.

He clicked off. Turned to Choi. "Let's wait in the hall. This is a messy enough crime scene. Let's not contaminate it."

Choi nodded.

In the hall, the two men milled restlessly. Frustration and anger had them by the collars, shaking them. Both knew that Don Juan and Billie Shears might well have been in an elevator going down when they were going up.

"Screwing with us," Choi said. "*Screwing* with us."

"I know. But they're getting bold, which means they're getting sloppy."

"Oh yeah," Choi said with a sneer. "We got 'em right where we want 'em. . . ."

Chapter Thirty-four

The feds descended.

The *Killer TV* team and even the LAPD were relegated to *don't-call-us-we'll-call-you* status, the big boys taking over. Anna and Polk got assigned to other cases; when Anna balked, her captain generously granted her a week's vacation she hadn't requested.

A media-fueled panic burned through the city. Gun sales were up, sales of pepper spray and guard dogs, too, and the mayor and city council were exploring a curfew—an idea Harrow pronounced doomed to failure.

Although Billie Shears might pick her victims somewhat randomly, Don Juan's prey were chosen with care, and no telling how many victims were already in his queue. Even with a curfew—really, a laughable concept in LA—Don Juan still had access to any victims already scouted.

Of course, Harrow and his team still kept digging, FBI be damned. Chase was looking for connections with acting classes, producers, press agents, or any group Don Juan might troll. With all the evidence in federal hands, Pall and Anderson were left without lab work, and instead helped Chase scale her mountain of possibilities.

Choi, who had identified Billie's shears as hedge clippers, now sought a specific item—model, brand name, anything. Back at the LAPD, Polk had ruled out Jason Wyler—alibis on several of the murders.

The reluctantly vacationing Anna was helping Harrow scrutinize Jenny-fabricated copies of the Deluxe Sunset security tapes, the originals having been seized by the FBI. They started with the attack on Rousch in the corridor, but the camera was far away and details were sketchy.

Only Carmen had no work to do on the investigation. She alone was taking care of business, i.e., supervising pre-taped *Crime Seen* segments for their next show. Unlike everybody else, her hours were merely horrible, not horrific, and she was even managing something of a social life.

When Vince had suggested sushi for dinner, she leapt at the chance. Post-Kansas, she mostly ate at home, and she loved Japanese food. The restaurant Vince selected was kind of a high-profile place, which had its risks.

Vince walked her through a gauntlet of paparazzi as they approached the entrance, camera flashes strobing them.

"Sorry," he said, with a concerned frown, as they

stepped inside. "I forget you're a TV star. That stuff must be a pain."

"I've avoided it lately," she admitted. "But it's about time I crawled out of my shell."

"I don't know how you can stand it. I'm happy to be a nobody and have some privacy in my life."

Vince looked his usual hawkishly handsome self, sharp in a gray pinstripe suit, white shirt, and navy-blue tie with geometric pattern.

At their table, he said, "I don't blame them for wanting your picture, though—you look especially lovely tonight."

He didn't look so bad himself—his short brown perfect hair, his pale blue eyes leaping out of the dark tan.

But he wasn't lying—she looked good, and knew it. She'd worn a little black dress withheld for special occasions, and this was one—their three-month anniversary. The dress was almost mini-short and its neckline wasn't designed for a shy girl. They had been together all this time, and kissed and petted, like kids . . . but nothing more.

Tonight would be the night. He would not escape. He was in her crosshairs, and he didn't have a chance. . . .

When their drinks arrived—gin and tonic for him, Diet Sprite for her—Vince asked, "Still hectic at the show?"

"Oh yes. And my workload is, well, it's getting out of hand."

"Why?"

"Everybody else is still working on those . . . those *cases.* You know."

"You said the FBI swooped in and—"

"You think that's going to stop J.C. Harrow?" She laughed, sipped her soft drink.

"So you're working on other stories."

"Right. I mean, right now we don't even know whether we can even *mention* those two."

"Don Juan? Billie Shears? Why not? Everybody's talking about them."

"Even you and me, right now. Well, there are legal battles going on. I'm operating on the assumption that we need to put together a full week's worth of show *without* those two maniacs to lean on."

He half smiled, swirled his drink. "Ignoring them won't work. It'll only drive them harder."

"That's what J.C. says. You know, I appreciate your interest in my career, but we *can* talk about other, more interesting, more *pleasant*, things."

The corner of his eyes crinkled with his smile. "Oh, yeah, right. The insurance business. Everybody's favorite cocktail-hour conversation. . . . I'm ordering another drink. Another Sprite? Maybe something stronger?"

"Just another Sprite," she said.

They had talked about going to the movies tonight, and went over the possibilities waiting for them at a nearby multiplex. Nothing sounded very good, but it was fun hearing why Vince dismissed this possibility or that one. He was very knowledgeable about movies, which wasn't surprising, since his insurance agency catered to the industry.

She excused herself to go to the ladies' room,

and when she returned, a little jug of sake was waiting.

"I shouldn't," she said.

"Oh, why not? You work hard. *Relax* a little."

He'd already poured her a cup.

She sipped it—it was warm, a little vinegary, but smooth.

She touched his hand. "If you're trying to get me drunk, to take advantage of me . . . it's going to work."

"Ha. You're naughty tonight."

"We're *both* going to be naughty tonight, Vince. That I promise you."

He sipped his own sake. "I'll follow your lead," he said. "Like this place?"

"Oh yes. Kyuui's one of my favorites. But this doesn't exactly make me a cheap date. . . ."

"That's okay. You're worth it."

In Harrow's office, he and Anna sat at his desk watching the Deluxe Sunset security video on a thirty-two inch flat-screen monitor.

They had watched Rousch walk down the hall probably fifty times now. *Stop at his door, put in the keycard, turn as a woman stepped up behind him. Seconds later, he starts bouncing like a marionette, then falls out of frame, into his room, while two figures, little more than silhouettes, follow him in and shut the door.*

All they could tell for sure about the man and woman was that one wore a black dress and the other dark male attire, and that was it. Everything else was little more than a blur.

Jenny Blake popped in. "Think we found something, Boss."

"What?"

"Don Juan's female victims had no common e-mail addresses in their address books."

"Well, that's not good news."

"No, but *this* is—the IP address of one computer popped up in *all* the women's records."

"Pretend I don't know what an IP address is."

"It's the Internet service provider's way of recognizing your computer—like your house number."

Harrow frowned. "So—what you're saying is, the same computer contacted all of these women?"

"Yep."

"Do we know who that computer belongs to?"

"Various e-mail accounts all come back to a Louis St. James."

Anna said, "Sounds like two towns scrambled together."

Harrow asked Jenny, "What do we know about him?"

"His website says he's a movie producer with an office in Westwood."

He grinned. "Jenny, you're the best."

She smiled in a *thanks-but-I-knew-that* manner.

He said to her, "Step outside for a moment, would you?"

"Sure."

Jenny did, and Harrow faced Anna, both still seated.

"There are several ways we can play this," he said. "One, we could call the FBI with this new information. Two, we could call somebody you trust at the LAPD, your partner Polk maybe, who would run with it, bring us in, and not call the feds."

"Tell me about the third way."

"The third way is, we've been working hard for hours now, and it's about time to take a break. Maybe go for a nice ride on a cool evening."

"A ride sounds good."

On the way out of his office, Harrow said to Anna, "Odds of four women having only one common e-mailer, and have it *not* be the killer, seem slim."

Jenny, standing there, said, "Not just slim. Crazy impossible."

The computer goddess fell in with Harrow and Anna as they walked briskly down a corridor lined with big framed portraits of stars that included both himself and Jenny.

"Remember," Anna said, in a devil's advocate way, "all the victims were connected to the movie business, and it could be coincidental—Louis St. James is a producer, after all."

"Is he?" Harrow said.

Jenny said, "There may be a way to nail this down—we can try matching the IP address from Louis St. James to Carmen's private e-mail account."

"That's right," Anna said. "Don Juan e-mailed her two videos."

Harrow asked Jenny, "Where *is* Carmen?"

"Out with her boyfriend."

Nice to hear Carmen was getting back in the swing, finally. "Well, try her on her cell and ask her permission. If you don't get her, go ahead and do it, anyway."

"Roger that. Should I call the feds and let them know what we've found?"

"We don't know if we *have* anything to tell them. Wait for my go-ahead."

"Always."

"You have a home address for Louis St. James?"

"Working on it."

"ASAP, Jen."

"ASAP."

She went off toward her office.

In the elevator, Anna asked, "If Jenny matches Louis St. James's computer address to Carmen's computer, we have our killer, don't we?"

"The Don Juan half, anyway."

"Well, wouldn't that be a nice start."

They had barely begun the journey to Westwood in his Equinox when Jenny Blake called.

"What?"

"Louis St. James's computer sent the Don Juan e-mails to Carmen, all right."

"Home address yet?"

"Working on it."

"But we have an *office* address."

"We do. In Westwood."

"Okay, round up Laurene and Billy, fill them in, and send them over there. Toot sweet."

"You got it. And I'll get you a home address or you can dock my pay."

"Deal."

They clicked off.

Harrow pulled over into the parking lot of a strip mall.

Anna frowned at him. "What?"

"It's after seven. St. James might be at the office, or he might be at home. Which is our better shot, you think?"

"He's probably headed home."

"Right. So we wait here while Billy and Laurene hit his office." Harrow indicated a fast-food joint nearby, a Subway. "Want anything?

"J.C., you sure know how to show a girl a good time."

He got them coffee.

Before long Jenny called to report in.

"Nothing yet," she said. "Laurene and Billy say the office is closed, which is to be expected at this hour, but they didn't see anyone around, either."

"Okay. I know you have more."

"Louis St. James isn't registered with the DMV. I got a picture of him from his website and loaded it into the DMV's facial recognition program, but nothing's come back yet."

"Louis St. James doesn't really exist, does he?"

"I don't think so, boss—his website's bio is all stuff that's either impossible to trace or just links to other websites."

"What about IMDb?"

"Internet Movie Database thinks he's real, and that's a very reputable website, but it's also hu-mongous, and someone with, say, my kind of skills? Could hack in and add bogus entries without raising suspicion."

"So what makes *you* suspicious?"

"All of it. For example, the films listed in his credits all have websites of their own."

Harrow frowned. "Well, that means they're real, right?"

"Not necessarily. They're bare-bones sites, descriptions of film plots, cast lists of unknowns, a few generic pics."

"Isn't that true for a lot of little films?"

"It is, but most films, even little indie ones, you can *buy* somewhere. They've been in *some* film festival. St. James' productions, you can't buy 'em at Amazon or Barnes and Noble or any other website."

"Google?"

"Google search brings up websites but nothing else. There's no buzz about these films. No blogs, no reviews, no chats, no nothing. If these epics exist, no one has ever seen them yet. I mean *no one.*"

Harrow thought for a moment. "But there's enough online to convince a hungry, aspiring young actress that he's real."

"On the nose, boss."

"Any idea who this guy really is?"

"Facial recognition software's drawing a blank . . . wait. Here we go. Louis St. James is listed in the county recorder's office. He has a bungalow in Chatsworth, near the reservoir."

She gave him the address.

"Okay," he said. "Anna and I are on our way there. Tell Laurene and Billy what you've found and keep at it."

He clicked off, filled Anna in.

She got on her cell to call her captain and have

him order a SWAT team to the St. James bungalow in Chatsworth.

In the bathroom at Kyuui, Carmen heard her cell phone chirp in her purse. She took it out, saw it was Jenny, and almost answered.

But tonight was her night, a special night, and work could wait. It wasn't like she was one of the superstar forensics investigators—she was just "talent." She shut the phone off, tucked it in her purse, checked herself in the mirror, then headed back to the table.

Vince had another cup of sake poured, but she was giddy already. Soon their dinner came—she had a nigiri assortment, Vince a spider roll—and they sampled each other's food.

They decided not to take in a movie, though what they'd do instead remained up in the air.

As they exited the restaurant, Carmen felt a little wobbly.

"You okay?" he asked. "Too much sake?"

Actually, she'd held it to one cup.

"Too much work, too little sleep."

"Do we need to call it a night? I was kind of hoping you might come over to my place. You've never seen it, after all."

The valet was bringing Vince's car around.

She twitched a smile his way. "How can I pass it up?"

He slipped an arm around her, kissed her cheek.

"Once in a lifetime," he said.

Chapter Thirty-five

When Carmen and Vince got to his house, the place was dark. He turned a single table lamp on and they sat on the sofa. His digs—at least the living room—were furnished in a surprisingly spare fashion, more appropriate for an apartment than a bungalow.

The sofa was white with black-and-white striped pillows, the floor waxed wood with throw rugs, the eggshell-white walls hung with a handful of movie-star prints, Errol Flynn as Robin Hood, James Dean in *Rebel Without a Cause* mode, Cary Grant in a tuxedo, Marlene Dietrich in a tuxedo.

She was still feeling a trifle out of sorts from dinner. Something hadn't settled right—whenever she had an upset tummy after sushi, all she could think of was that deadly blowfish from Japan.

Right now she was both queasy and a little drowsy.

This did not dissuade her in her mission, however—she would take this relationship to the next level, or know the reason why not. . . .

Behind living room curtains, a yellow glow burned; a red Mitsubishi Eclipse perched in the carport. Harrow turned his car around, and he and Anna parked on the other side of this quiet residential cul-de-sac, a short distance from Louis St. James's house.

No sign of the SWAT team, but Harrow wasn't surprised. SWAT might be fabled for fast response, but they weren't just sitting around poised for action. A team had to be rounded up, piled into the van, then make the long drive to Chatsworth.

And only about forty minutes had elapsed since Anna had called her boss, Captain Womack.

Harrow asked, "So, you figure Womack called the FBI?"

"About fifty-fifty," she said. "He's under orders to, but he also doesn't love the bum's rush the Fibbies gave us."

Harrow nodded.

Anna fidgeted. "I don't know *where* the hell that search warrant is."

"We have promising information," he said with a shrug, "but it's no smoking gun. It could take time."

She sighed.

"His car is there. He's not going anywhere."

The windows were down and a cool breeze whispered through. They didn't speak. Just another stakeout, if they hadn't been holding hands.

Ten minutes later, Anna answered her vibrating cell.

"Good," she told it, clicked off, and said to Harrow, "Polk. On his way with the warrant. Maybe fifteen minutes."

Ten more minutes passed before the unmarked SWAT van appeared, coming their way, not hauling ass, attracting no attention.

Anna said, "Flash your lights."

He did so.

The van rolled to a stop opposite.

A tall, blonde officer in the black fatigues of the SWAT unit climbed out on the driver's side. He had a craggy, pockmarked face but wasn't old—maybe mid-thirties. Name tag read LT. MCCLELLAN.

He came over and leaned in like a carhop—a dangerous-looking one. He looked past Harrow. "Good evening, Lieutenant Amari."

"Hello, Mac. That's the house—on your side. Two doors up."

McClellan nodded.

"You know whose place that is?"

"Yes, ma'am."

"And why you're here?"

"Yes, ma'am."

"Make it 'Anna.' I'm not your mother."

He found a grin. His teeth were better than his complexion. "Okay, Anna. Warrant here?"

"On its way. Any time now."

"Suspect in the house?"

"Unconfirmed," Harrow said. "I'm J.C. Harrow."

"I recognize you, sir. I can see lights on."

"Yeah. And his car's there. I think he's home. I just hope he isn't entertaining a guest while we sit here on our asses."

"Glad to kick that door in, if you can give me probable cause."

Anna answered: "Can't cut that, Mac. We'll wait for the warrant."

As if on cue, Polk drove up in their Crown Vic, and hustled the warrant over.

"Time to saddle up," McClellan said, and crossed the street.

More black-fatigued SWAT officers piled out.

They made out on the couch. As always, there was something youthful about it, like teenagers in a drive-in as they kissed and kissed, and finally, *finally*, Vince's fingers risked unzipping her dress, and then he was kissing her breasts. So expert. So gentle.

After all the hesitation, and so much restraint over these months, at last Vince was revealing a passionate side—or anyway an experienced one. Still, he seemed to be holding back part of himself—even with his mouth at her breast, she felt he was withholding emotion.

But if Vince's technique was mechanical, it did the trick, and as his hands made a perp out of her, with a full-body search, she felt better, more into it, the queasiness gone, the fuzziness still there but lending a nice soft-focus feel. . . .

She'd never dreamed shy Vince Clay could be like this.

Such a great lover.

She kicked off her shoes as he buried his face in her neck, like a shy vampire, and with the top of her dress bunched around her waist, Carmen felt warm and ready. Should she slip out of the dress entirely, and just let him take her there, on the sofa?

He read her mind, coming up for a breath to say, "Maybe it's time to take this to the bedroom. . . ."

She stood, stepped out of her dress, in nothing but sheer panties, with her hand outstretched to her host.

The SWAT team neared the house, staying low and quiet, half going to the front, the rest circling around the back.

Anna brought up the rear, with Harrow trailing at McClellan's request. A TV star getting shot on a raid would not be a career-booster for the SWAT leader.

They crept closer to the door; then one of the officers lost his balance, his gun barrel scraping aluminum siding.

Everybody froze.

They were walking hand in hand across the cool living room floor, school kids again despite the hot-and-heavy on the sofa, Vince with his shirt off and in his socks, Anna in her panties.

A noise outside the house spooked them both.

Vince released her hand and went to the picture window, and peeked behind the curtains.

"Nothing," he said, and shrugged. "Kids."

"Whatever it was, sounded close."

"Don't worry about it."

He undid his trousers, stepped out of them, leaving them behind as he returned to guide the slightly wobbly woman to the bedroom.

The assault force waited.

Long, terrible, heartbeat-pounding moments passed, a living but not breathing freeze frame.

Then McClellan used hand signals, counting down, *Three . . . two . . . one . . .*

. . . and two team members with a battering ram crushed the front door in.

As if an echo, the sound of another ram breaching the door in back told Harrow these men knew what the hell they were doing.

When the team stormed in, Anna and Harrow were right behind them, and both the LAPD detective and the UBC host had handguns ready.

They met the other half of the team where the dining and living rooms met. Nothing in those rooms.

SWAT officers moved room to room, shouts of "Clear!" ringing through the bungalow.

McClellan shook his head. "Nobody home."

"Damn it," Harrow said. "Damn *car's* here!"

Anna said, "Well, *he* isn't."

Nonetheless, Anna brought Polk in and they took advantage of the warrant to search the place.

McClellan rounded his people up outside. They would not go till Anna released them.

Harrow bummed a smoke off McClellan and got his cell out, to bring Jenny up to speed.

But before he hit speed dial, the phone vibrated, Jenny beating him to the punch.

"Boss," she said, and her voice had a new brittle energy, "are you at St. James's?"

"Yes. Nobody home."

"*Goddamnit!*"

Coming from Jenny, that outburst hit him like a board.

"I think Carmen is in trouble."

Was she crying?

"Settle down, Jen. *What?*"

"I was fooling with Photoshop, changing hair and eye color on the Louis St. James website— there was something *familiar* about him, those prominent cheekbones. I'm pretty sure Louis St. James is Vince Clay."

"Who is Vince Clay?"

"Carmen's boyfriend. She's out with him right now."

"Shit."

"And she's not answering her cell."

"Shit!"

"What do we do?"

"You keep digging—find out anything you can. Did you leave Carmen a voice mail?"

"Yes."

"What did you say?"

"Just 'Call Jenny. It's urgent.' I didn't know if somebody might be listening."

"Good. Now get me something."

He clicked off, then hit Carmen's number, got voice mail, left a message that there'd been a break in the Don Juan case and she was needed back ASAP.

His cell vibrated in his hand again—JENNY.

"I have Vince Clay's address," she said. No emotion now. All business.

She gave it to him. It was way across the city.

Anna emerged from the house to see what Harrow was up to.

He filled her in.

"I know that part of town," she said. "Damn—take us over an hour to get there, if there's any traffic at all. We'll bring in the locals."

"I want to be there."

"So do I. Any ideas?"

He frowned. "Maybe one. . . . Let's take your car."

"Where to?"

"Toward that address."

Soon they were in the Crown Vic, leaving Polk behind. Anna put the rollers on but no siren. Harrow was on his cell.

"Dennis, I need the local affiliate's traffic helicopter."

The executive didn't fool around—Harrow's tone said not to. "All right. Want to tell me why?"

Harrow quickly filled him in.

"I'm on it," Byrnes said. "But you're coming back next season."

That actually got a smile out of Harrow. "You drive a hard bargain."

Harrow clicked off, and Anna said, "Helicopter, huh? Where you gonna have it land?"

"You tell me."

She thought. "Fallbrook Mall. We passed it on the way."

Harrow got Byrnes back, and gave him the address. The exec said the copter would be in the parking lot by the time they got there.

It was.

They left the unmarked car in the lot and ran into the wind of the chopper blades. Harrow and Amari climbed in, and the pilot, a seasoned vet with the confidence and smile of a retired astronaut, said, "J.C. Harrow! Welcome aboard—where to?"

"Whittwood Mall in Whittier," Anna said.

As the chopper rose and swung southeast, Harrow called Jenny.

"Laurene and Billy are on their way back from Westwood," she said. "They can meet you."

"Good," he said, yelling over the noise, and told her where.

The pilot was pushing the helicopter, the city a glittery blur below. No question they were moving fast.

But fast enough?

Chapter Thirty-six

When the helicopter descended into the parking lot of the Whittwood Mall, Harrow could see Choi's BMW M6 convertible, top down, tearing through the lot. The copter touched pavement as Choi and Chase screeched to a stop. Harrow and Anna climbed from the chopper, its churning blades whipping up wind and a deafening din.

The pilot yelled, "Happy hunting," as the craft lifted while Harrow and Anna ran to the convertible, and piled over the sides in the back.

The copter was still close enough that Anna had to scream the address, but Choi merely nodded.

As they approached the mall stoplight, the copter noise already distant, Choi said, "You're gonna have to guide me."

Anna said, "No problem. Run the light and take a left."

Choi did, then said, "I'm not a cop anymore. No siren or rollers."

"I got a badge," Anna said. "Break all the laws you want."

"Came to the right guy."

The convertible tore down the street toward Vince Clay's neighborhood, weaving in and around startled traffic.

In the back, Harrow thought, *Hang on, Carmen, hang on,* even as he hung on himself, Choi swerving around a car whose occupants didn't have time to swear at them before the BMW rocketed round the next corner.

Vince Clay led Carmen Garcia into a dimly lit room with a big brass bed, a mirror on the wall to its left, and a nightstand with a vase of a dozen roses.

Her first thought was: *How romantic.*

Her second thought was: *Black Pearl roses!*

Even in the vague light of a shaded table lamp, Carmen recognized the distinctive flowers, and all wooziness drained away as the pieces fell in place and she only hoped the sirens screaming in her brain didn't show in her expression.

"What's the matter?" Vince asked.

What's the matter? I'm standing here in my panties with a serial killer at my side!

"Nothing," she said, and in that moment she had a choice—going into full-on panic or survival mode.

She kissed him. She put all the acting skills she'd developed over the last year as an on-air personality and forced passion and love into it, though she knew she was kissing a monster, knew she had been a fool but also that she couldn't afford to be a fool any longer. . . .

He walked her gently to the brass bed, gestured for her to recline, and she did.

She'd seen this bed. In the Don Juan videos. How many women had died on this goddamn bed?

He stripped to his silk briefs, letting the clothes drop, then positioned himself on the bed next to her and stroked her breasts, kissed her neck, her cheeks, her mouth.

She moaned as if with pleasure and kissed him back like her life depended on it. Which of course it did, as until she could see an opportunity to make a break for it, or somehow put this bastard out of commission, she had to play along, kissing a killer. The adrenalin rush had passed and a certain grogginess tried to crawl back, her muscles aching, as if a bad case of the flu had just set in.

"You are so lovely," he said.

"We waited a long time," she said. "I'm glad we waited. This has to be *just* right."

"I know. I know, my darling. . . ."

He seemed about to mount her when she touched his chest gently and said, "I hate to spoil the moment, but . . . I need to use the restroom before we go on."

"Oh. Well, sure. It's right there. . . ."

He pointed to a door that might have been a closet but wasn't.

She slipped off the bed, trotted over without seeming too hurried about it, and shut herself in.

The bathroom was small and white and hospital

clean. The pebble-glass window looked just big enough for her to climb out, but when she unlocked it and tried to slide it open it, the thing wouldn't budge—maybe painted or nailed shut. . . .

She quickly searched the cubicle for anything she might use as a weapon—maybe a safety razor, so she'd have a nice sharp blade to slash this bastard. . . .

No—no razor at all! *What the hell?*

She tried the medicine cabinet—seeking a glass bottle, of medicine or aftershave maybe, that she could smash into shards or give a jagged neck to, while she ran water to cover the sound . . .

. . . only all the bottles—aspirin, aftershave, tubes of theatrical makeup, contact lens solution—were plastic.

Choi parked a hundred yards short of Clay's house. There were few neighbors, the nearest a good fifty yards. Woods rose behind and came around one side of Clay's place.

As they approached, guns drawn, using the trees for cover, the house was mostly dark.

Harrow said, "Anna and I'll take the front, you two take the back."

Chase and Choi nodded.

Carmen turned back to that bathroom window—she would have to break it.

She lifted the porcelain lid off the toilet tank and swung it into the glass.

It shattered first try.

On the other side of the bathroom door, a muffled voice, female, yelled, "Son of a bitch!"

Don Juan's partner, Billie Shears! Behind that mirror by the bed? Two-way glass?

No time to waste wondering.

She didn't know what was outside; she didn't care. Two killers were inside.

Nicked a dozen times by the window's teeth, she dropped into a shallow backyard, bleeding and nearly nude, her feet crunching on glass. In a moment her eyes adjusted to the darkness, trees surrounding, thick and tall—if she bothered screaming, no one would hear her.

But *she* heard a scream, and reflexively swung around to see a bald naked woman framed in the window, a wild-eyed figure baying like a wounded animal. . . .

Carmen *knew* she'd been roofied—was she hallucinating?

Then the woman was gone.

Not coming out the window through that jagged glass after her, the naked harpy must be heading for a door . . . giving Carmen time, a little time. . . .

Her bare feet (soles already nicked landing on shards) weren't on grass, rather hard dirt covered with spiny weeds and God knew what else. Carmen had to run, but barefoot through the woods? Not if she could avoid it.

To her left, up a gentle slope, nestled among the trees, loomed a greenhouse—a place to hide.

She sprinted the short distance, found the door unlocked, slipped in and quietly closed the door behind her.

When Harrow had heard that glass break, followed by

the sound of someone wailing in agony, it initially fright-
ened him. . . . Then he thought it through and a tight
smile came.

Something had gone wrong, and that meant Carmen
was likely still alive.

He fired a round into the front door's dead bolt, shat-
tering it.

He shouldered his way into the living room, Anna
right behind him.

Empty—a dim table lamp let them see as much—and
as he swept the barrel of his .38 around, he saw a purse
on the floor.

"Carmen's here," he said.

Moonlight fingered in through all that glass as
Carmen crept down a central aisle. Wooden
benches were arrayed with flower pots, Black Pearl
roses all around, their rich red looking black by
night, highlighted ivory by filtered moon glow.

She was in the midst of a mammoth bouquet of
death.

Outside, she heard someone running.

A woman screaming, "You *bitch!* You ruined
everything!"

She was coming, the bald naked woman was
coming, and Carmen, in her weakened state, with
no clothes on but her panties, not even frigging
shoes, knew she had to find a way out of the trap
she'd run herself into. . . .

Harrow moved through the living room—the dining
room looking empty, as did what he could see of the
kitchen beyond, no light on in there. Anna was checking
the rest of the house.

He remembered moving through another house in the darkness, only to find his son and his wife murdered.

Not this time. Not this time.

Breathing hard, ignoring her screaming feet and burning bloody cuts, Carmen ran down the aisle to the greenhouse back door.

Padlocked.

Shit!

Trapped. . . .

Choi and Chase entered at the rear into the kitchen and Harrow moved to meet them, his hand finding a wall switch and flooding the white room to expose a bald man in only silk boxers, waving a butcher knife.

Vincent Clay looked like a big, upright, dangerous fetus.

Chase moved toward the hairless figure, her gun in hand lowered, her steps tentative. "Vince . . . put that down, Vince. It's over."

Vince said nothing.

This man who had so craved attention was now frozen at the center of it.

"Vince," Chase said gently. "Where's Carmen?"

Vince's eyes popped and he shrieked like a scared child as he ran right toward that back door where Choi and Chase had just come in.

But there was nothing childlike about that raised butcher knife, and Chase ducked out of the way, while Choi shot him in the head.

Vince didn't go down at once—he took the shot with a shudder and then teetered there. Behind him, red splashed white cabinets. The knife clattered to the floor, and Clay dropped to his knees, as if praying, but he was already dead.

When Don Juan finally flopped in a heap in front of the man who'd shot him, Choi said, "Prick would get off easy."

"There are two of them, remember!" Chase said.

Anna was at Harrow's side. She saw the dead Vince Clay, said nothing about him, just, "No Carmen. Broken bathroom window."

"Clear the house," Harrow told Choi and Chase. "Anna, let's take the yard!"

The greenhouse door slammed open.

Carmen ducked down.

The bald naked woman had a knife, a very big knife whose point caught moonlight and winked at Carmen, though its bearer hadn't spotted her hunkered next to a bench.

As the naked woman started down the aisle, all those roses her silent cheering section, her prey scrambled under the bottom shelf of that bench, just high enough to accommodate her.

But plenty of room to hide, though hiding wouldn't be enough. Carmen would have to take advantage of surprise to take that bald bitch down.

What *then?*

Her pursuer had that knife, and what did Carmen have?

Frantically, but noiselessly, her hands felt around in the darkness. A cardboard box next to her had bulbs in it, useless. Another held bags of something, seed or fertilizer maybe.

Carmen couldn't see her, but her pursuer must have been stalking down the aisle, looking under the benches, which meant inevitably . . .

Her hands found a small wooden box containing gardening tools, a blunt trowel, *no*, a scoop, *no*, a claw, *better*, pruning clippers . . . *perfect!*

Cowering there on the dirt floor, staying as far back as possible to let the darkness shield her, Carmen watched. Waited. Watched. . . .

Suddenly, the creature was right there, her bare legs coming to a stop, and Carmen held her breath. As the bald woman began to bend down, Carmen shot her hand out, grabbed an ankle, and jerked the woman to the aisle's hard dirt floor, onto her side, with a hard *whump!*

The stalker lay motionless for a moment, her bare head making her look like a naked toppled mannequin. Then maniacal eyes popped open, seeking Carmen in the darkness.

Low and lurching forward, the woman wildly poked the knife under the bench, and the blade came within an inch of Carmen's nose. The next time the knife violated her space, Carmen slashed back with the clippers, gouging the woman's wrist.

"Ow!" the attacker said, pulling back, trying to get to her feet, but Carmen scrambled out and tackled her, the woman's knife shocked from her grasp, spinning down the aisle a few feet away.

On top now, Carmen scratched long nails across the woman's face, drawing blood and an angry scream. The woman grabbed a handful of Carmen's hair and pulled, yanking so hard it threw Carmen off into the opposite bench, knocking the wind out, the clippers popping from her grasp.

The bald naked woman went after her knife.

Harrow could hear the struggle in the nearby green-

house, ran to it and threw the door open, Anna just be-hind.

Carmen found the shears.

She was on her knees when the bald woman turned and ran at her, naked, washed in ivory, surrounded by black roses, beautiful and horrible with the knife raised high, the point aimed down.

Inside the greenhouse now, Harrow saw the bald woman with the knife raised, and drew a bead on her; but he also saw Carmen, on her knees before the woman—at this distance in near darkness, with the two women in such close proximity, did he dare take his shot?

Carmen thrust forward with the pruning clippers tight in her hand, but not in a way that parted the blades, keeping them a single pointed, knife-like double-blade and plunged it into the woman's belly, aided by the woman running into the thrust, and as she was penetrated, a bizarrely orgasmic expression blossomed on Vince Clay's sister's countenance.

But when Carmen released her grasp, the clipper blades stayed behind, to snap open into their V deep within the woman's flesh, tearing everything in their path. The resulting gurgling scream held no hint of pleasure.

Blood splashed in terrible warmth onto Carmen's bare skin. Jana Clay fell to one side, knocking hard into a bench but not feeling it. Like the roses around them, the blood on both naked women looked more black than red.

Still on her knees, Carmen slumped and began to cry. Her tears began small, whimpering, but by the time Harrow's arms were around her, her chest was heaving, sobs wracking her.

Then he was holding her, like a gentle parent, not worried about getting blood on him, just a caring daddy who whispered, "It's all right, Carmen. It's all right. They're both dead, and you're alive, and it's over. It's finally over."

Chapter Thirty-seven

Three days since they'd taken down the Clays, and Harrow still couldn't believe the amount of attention getting heaped on *Crime Seen*. And this time there hadn't even been a camera along, unless you counted the hidden one behind the two-way mirror in Vincent Clay's bedroom, adjacent to the make-up niche with its wigs, spirit gum, contact lenses, and other theatrical applications.

Entertainment Weekly and *TV Guide* wanted cover stories; and *Rolling Stone* had assigned an award-winning journalist to write about the hunt for Don Juan and Billie Shears.

Harrow found it repellent, while Dennis Byrnes was giddy, delighted to have Don Juan move from a nebulous "maybe a debit" column to the sheer asset one.

At a staff meeting in the conference room, Billy Choi—surprisingly—took a stand they all could get behind.

"I'm fine with these guys doing a story on us," he said. "Cool with them covering the show. But only with the understanding that the Don Juan/Billie Shears thing is something to touch on, not the focus. I do *not* want those sickos getting the attention in death that they craved in life. Period."

And this got Choi a round of applause from his coworkers, and a smile and nod from his boss.

Anna and Captain Womack had expressed their gratitude for what the *Killer TV* team accomplished, though the FBI sent both Harrow and Byrnes a strongly worded (if not public) statement that the network and its employees had "endangered the welfare of the community by inserting themselves into an active federal investigation."

Any future dealings with the FBI would likely be chilly.

The more inflammatory cable news networks decried the actions of "that vigilante cop show"— even right-leaning Fox—and op-ed columns from several papers wondered if Harrow and his team had overstepped.

The host of *Crime Seen* was going over the script for this week's show, which was tricky, dealing as it did with the Clays, when somebody knocked on the jamb of his open door.

He glanced up to see Carmen Garcia framed there in jeans and a plain black T-shirt contrasting the array of small white bandages on her hands and face. She managed a sideways smile.

"You're back," he said.

"Aren't *you* the detective." She came over and sat opposite her boss.

He asked, "Didn't you just get out of the hospital yesterday?"

"Day before, actually. Figured maybe I might be needed here. Not really crazy about spending time alone right now."

He tossed the script pages aside. "You want to talk?"

". . . One thing's bothering me."

"Just one?"

She laughed a little. "Well, I'm fixated on one. But it embarrasses me to say it out loud."

"Why?"

"Because it's what all victims say, and it's stupid."

"Oh . . . *Why me?* "

"You *are* a detective. Yes—why me? I'd already been through this once. Isn't that enough for one lifetime? I mean, it would be like that one nurse, who survived the night Richard Speck killed every other nurse in the house? To suddenly wake up next to Gacy or Bundy or something."

He shrugged. "You're a TV star, Carmen. You wanted the spotlight. You got it. There's baggage. Some of it pretty ugly."

"Okay. I get that. That does make sense."

"Don Juan and his sister craved the spotlight you were already in. Standing next to you gave them more light."

Another knock at the jamb.

Harrow didn't recognize the short, thin, fiftysomething sort—but the guy wasn't just anybody, not in that tailored gray suit, not with that briefcase.

"Help you?" Harrow asked.

"I'm James Watkins," he said. "Attorney for the Clay estate. May I come in?

Harrow and Carmen exchanged wary frowns, but then the host said, "Certainly," and gestured to the remaining visitor's chair.

Before Watkins sat, he offered a hand to Harrow, who shook it; then the attorney nodded to Carmen, his vague embarrassment saying he recognized her.

Settling, Watkins said, "I have a package for you, Mr. Harrow. It's not a summons or anything that involves a legal obligation on your part. If it has a value, I don't know what it is."

Harrow said, "The more you try to reassure me, Mr. Watkins, the less reassured I am."

"I'm sorry. It's an unusual situation. My clients instructed me to deliver a package to you."

Harrow sat forward. "Mr. Watkins, if you have a package for me, you need to set it down carefully and walk away. Your clients left booby-trapped 'packages' before, and I'll be calling the bomb squad. . . ."

The attorney raised a hand. "It's not like that. They have been sending me, over the last month or so, occasional sealed envelopes. My instructions were to hang on to these envelopes, and—in the event of *both* their deaths—the envelopes were to be delivered to *you*, Mr. Harrow."

"The instructions were explicit?"

"Very. Each envelope went into my office safe. My partners and I have been discussing, over the last several days, what we should do with this material. Our late clients were, after all . . . allegedly murderers."

"Right," Harrow said. "Allegedly."

"We discussed with our own counsel whether these envelopes should go to the police, rather than yourself. Ultimately, the decision was made for me to deliver them, to you, as per our clients' instructions. Passing them along directly to the police, or keeping them . . . that will be your decision. Your signature is not required. And our firm's responsibility ends here and now."

He reached down for the briefcase, then hesitated. "May I?"

Harrow nodded.

Carmen was frowning, her arms folded protectively.

Watkins placed the briefcase on his lap, removed a big clear plastic envelope containing six six inch by nine inch manila envelopes, set it on Harrow's desk, shut the briefcase, stood, nodded to them both, and started out.

At the door, he turned to say, "The one without postage—that's the first one. Postmarks will, obviously, indicate the order in which the rest were sent. That first envelope was hand-delivered to me, and I was to tell you to 'watch it first.' . . . If I may be of further service, you'll find my card attached to the outer envelope."

And he was gone.

Carmen said, "I suppose that *could* have been creepier."

Harrow emptied the plastic package onto his desk, then selected and opened the first envelope.

A small clear DVD case held a disc with a pink stick-on label featuring a border of roses and an intertwined gothic DJ. In black letters under the center hole were the words **Start Here**.

He opened each envelope in order of their mailing and found similar contents—clear DVD case, disc with the DJ / roses label; but the label lettering differed:

> **Erskine**
> **Hannan**
> **Chavez**
> **Thornton**
> **Rousch**

Four Don Juan victims and the final Billie Shears collaboration.

"Jesus," Carmen said. She had come around the desk and was looking over his shoulder. "Are those . . . what I *think* they are?"

"Probably."

". . . You're going to watch them?"

"Not with you here."

"We've already seen what Don Juan sent us."

"Right."

"But these could be . . . longer versions. Maybe more cameras. And the FBI agent's death, J.C. That's new."

"Yes."

"Should you call Lieutenant Amari? Or the FBI?"

"I should."

"Are you going to?"

"What do you *want* me to do, Carmen?"

"I . . . I want to see the first disc."

He drew in a deep breath. Let it out.

"Okay," he said. "Go close my office door, then pull a chair around."

She did.

Sitting right beside him.

He put the **Start Here** DVD in his computer, and soon a smiling Vince and Jana Clay came onto the screen, both bald as the day they were born—balder. They wore matching light blue shirts and jeans. The effect was weirdly unisex, though Vince remained a handsome man and Jana a beautiful woman.

"They're . . . they're like *aliens*," Carmen whispered.

From a bad fifties sci-fi B movie, he thought.

"*So finally we meet, J.C.,*" Vince said. "*I call you 'J.C.' because I take the liberty of considering you a colleague, and an equal.*"

Carmen's hand squeezed his shoulder.

"*If you're watching this, J.C., my sister and I are very likely both dead. There should be no other way this material could reach your hands, but you never know—lawyers can be so morally ambiguous.*"

Pointing at the screen, Carmen said, "*That's* the bedroom. They're in that *bedroom. . . .*"

This was a two-shot, and the focus was tight on brother and sister, soft-focus on the background, but Carmen was right: the siblings were apparently seated on the bed where Don Juan's "conquests" had been made, and in an eerie piece of stagecraft, a table with a vase of Black Pearl roses was visible behind and to the right of Jana, who sat with hands primly folded in her lap.

Her brother, however, gesticulated confidently as he continued in his role as their appointed spokesperson.

"You may even be naive enough to think, J.C., that this means you've won. It does not. I admit our deaths are not our preferred course of action, and our script calls for us both to survive. Still, because we are playing out our drama on the real-life stage, there are contingencies we cannot predict. So dying is our 'Plan B.' "

"He was so *nice*," Carmen said. "So *normal . . .*"

"Jana and I inherited enough money to come out here and follow our dream. To make it in LA, to be stars. We went down more conventional paths for several years without success—and our funds were running out. We needed a new course of action, and we developed one. How odd to think that you are watching this, knowing more about what we accomplished than we do! So far, we've been involved strictly in pre-production."

Jana reached over and squeezed her brother's hand—perhaps he was getting off script. . . .

"In any event, if our work has progressed as we intended, by the time you're viewing this, we'll have surely joined the pantheon of famous serial killers. Whether or not we're the most *famous, well . . . that's not for us to say. We'll leave that to the history books."*

"They look *odd*," Carmen said. "But they don't look *dangerous. . . .*"

"We are confident that you and UBC will fall in line with our script—'dueling' serial killers should be a great ratings boon for you. . . . You're welcome! *But I can take no credit for the concept, that was strictly Jana. . . ."*

"She's blushing," Carmen said. "Oh my God, she's *blushing. . . .*"

"Jana felt that one killer might get lost in the shuffle . . . TV is a hungry medium . . . but two killers? And two competing for attention? Well, that's sweeps week stuff if we ever heard of it!"

"Jesus," Harrow muttered.

"Now," Vince said, *"I'd like to throw it over to Jana, who has a few final words for you."*

"Thank you, Vince. . . ."

"She sounds so sweet," Carmen said.

The grotesque collection of mason jars discovered by Choi and Chase in the pantry, containing Jana's trophies, challenged that notion.

"My only regret," Jana was saying, *"should this creative endeavor result in our deaths, is that our ultimate goal will not be achieved. We intend to go to new heights—who are the most famous of our kind? Jack the Ripper, in real life? Maybe. Hannibal Lecter, in the movies? Perhaps. Well, we intend to outdo them both. If you are viewing this, we likely failed. But just think . . . just think what our success would mean—we would be stars . . . not reality TV, Mr. Harrow, nothing so minor . . . but the movies. The big screen."*

"Wow," Harrow said. "She's even crazier than I thought. . . ."

"I'm sure you're thinking, J.C., that these two freaks are nuttier than a fruitcake. Well, you're right and wrong—think about it. We will never stand trial. The whole world will not understand us as performance artists—we will be declared insane . . . and one day a forward-thinking psychiatrist will set us free. Free, and available to star as ourselves in a movie of our life."

Harrow and Carmen exchanged astonished glances. *Just when you think you've heard everything. . . .*

On screen, Jana was saying, *"That's enough, Vince. No one's ever to see this, anyway. Not unless we release it someday, ourselves."*

He was grinning, nodding. *"Bonus features! . . . Just one thing more."*

Jana nodded her permission.

"I want you to know, J.C. . . . and any family members and friends of the actresses I have already cast or will be casting in the days ahead . . . that there is nothing personal about it. As my own casting director, my costars are actresses who have found fame elusive themselves. And thanks to me, they will finally have their fifteen minutes. Of course, the costar I've cast for our climax has already *made it, hasn't she? She deserves special 'guest star' billing. I realize I indulged in typecasting, since she's previously appeared in a serial killer episode of* Crime Seen. *But I had to do it, J.C.—to give you a strong finish and because, well . . . Carmen Garcia is just* perfect *for the part."*

Carmen rose and staggered to her chair, slumping there.

Vince's voice continued: *"Andrew Cunanan had Gianni Versace, Manson had Sharon Tate, we have Carmen Garcia. . . ."*

The monitor went black.

Carmen said, "I would have been the next DVD."

"But you aren't. You fought back. You won."

"I . . . I don't feel anything about it—about killing her."

"You will. She was a monster, but she was a person once. It's going to hit you, Carmen. No way you can prepare for it, but just . . . don't be surprised."

She laughed bitterly, nodded toward the pile of DVDs. "Won't Dennis just *love* airing this crap."

"Why, are you going to tell him about them?"

She blinked at him. "Aren't . . . aren't *you*? You know he'll make copies before you give them to Lieutenant Amari."

"I don't think Anna needs these."

"But . . . they're *evidence*."

"Are they? That case is closed."

"You mean . . . ?"

"Vince and Jana's show just got cancelled."

And Harrow dumped the discs in his waste-basket.

Crime Seen Tips

The LAPD Sex Crimes Division herein is imaginary; that caseload is taken on by individual sex crimes units throughout Los Angeles.

Thanks to crime scene analyst Chris Kauffman CLPE, Van Buren (IA) County Sheriff's Office; computer forensics investigator Paul Van Steenhuyse, CFCE, CEECS, Data Analysis & Recovery Consultants; Matthew Schwarz, CLPE, Schwarz Forensics Enterprises; Dennis Kern, CLPE, Department of Criminal Investigation, State of Iowa; Vince Murillo, toolmarks and firearms examiner, Department of Criminal Investigation, State of Iowa; and independent filmmaker Elaine Holliman (for Santa Monica background).

Among books consulted were: *Practical Homicide Investigation* (1996), Vernon J. Geberth; *The Encyclopedia of Serial Killers* (2000), Michael Newton; *Mindhunter* (1995), John Douglas and Mark Olshaker; *In the Minds of Murderers* (2007), Paul Roland; and *Profile of a Criminal Mind* (2003), Brian Innes.

Special thanks to our editor, Michaela Hamilton, who in a brainstorming session at Boucheron 2009 in Indianapolis helped shape this novel. Also, thank-yous go to our agent, Dominick Abel, and our wives, Barb and Pam—in-house editors, and support systems.

MAX ALLAN COLLINS, a five-time Mystery Writers of America "Edgar" nominee in both fiction and non-fiction categories, has been hailed as "the Renaissance man of mystery fiction." He has also been a frequent Private Eye Writers of America "Shamus" nominee, winning twice for his Nathan Heller novels, *True Detective* (1983) and *Stolen Away* (1991), and receiving their Lifetime Achievement Award, the Eye. A new Heller, *Bye Bye, Baby*, will appear in 2011.

His graphic novel *Road to Perdition* is the basis of the Academy Award–winning DreamWorks feature film starring Tom Hanks. Max has many comics credits, including the "Dick Tracy" syndicated strip; his own "Ms. Tree"; and "Batman."

His other credits include film criticism, short fiction, songwriting, trading-card sets, and movie / TV tie-in novels, including the *New York Times* bestsellers *Saving Private Ryan* and *American Gangster*, which won the Best Novel "Scribe" award from the International Association of Media Tie-in Writers. Working with the Mickey Spillane estate, following the wishes of the late author, he is completing a number of manuscripts, including the current *Kiss Her Goodbye*, a Mike Hammer novel begun in the mid-1970s.

An acclaimed and award-winning independent filmmaker in the Midwest, he wrote and directed the Lifetime movie *Mommy* (1996) and three other features, including *Eliot Ness: An Untouchable Life* (2005). His produced screenplays include the 1995 HBO World Premiere *The Expert* and *The Last Lullaby* (2008) from his novel *The Last Quarry*. He lives in Muscatine, Iowa, with his wife Barbara, collaborating with her as "Barbara Allan" on the award-winning "Trash 'n' Treasures" cozy mystery series.

MATTHEW CLEMENS has authored or co-authored numerous short stories that appear in such anthologies as *Private Eyes, Murder Most Confederate,* the *Hot Blood* series, the *Flesh & Blood* series, and *Buffy the Vampire Slayer.* With Pat Gipple, he co-authored *Dead Water: The Klindt Affair,* a regionally bestselling true crime book, and has written for such magazines as *Fangoria, Femme Fatales,* and *TV Guide.* He has worked as a book doctor on over fifty novels, and assisted the late Karl Largent on several bestselling techno-thrillers.

Clemens is also co-plotter and researcher for Max Allan Collins on books based on the television series *CSI: Crime Scene Investigation, CSI: Miami, Dark Angel, Bones,* and *Criminal Minds.* Collins and Clemens have also written comic books, graphic novels, a computer game, and jigsaw puzzles based on the successful *CSI* franchise. Many of their collaborative short stories were gathered in *My Lolita Complex and Other Tales of Sex and Violence* (2006), and their short story, "Murderlized," featuring Moe Howard (of Three Stooges fame) as an amateur detective, appears in the anthology *Hollywood & Crime.* Clemens lives in Davenport, Iowa, with his wife Pam, a teacher.